TALES of
TWO CIT

TALES of TWO CITIES

THE BEST & WORST OF TIMES IN TODAY'S NEW YORK

EDITED BY JOHN FREEMAN

PENGUIN BOOKS

PENGUIN BOOKS

An imprint of Penguin Random House LLC
375 Hudson Street
New York, New York 10014
penguin.com

First published in the United States of America by OR Books 2014
Published in Penguin Books 2015

Illustrations by Molly Crabapple

Page 271 constitutes an extension of this copyright page.

ISBN 978-0-14-312830-4

Printed in the United States of America
10 9 8 7 6 5 4 3 2 1

Set in Janson Text

Contents

This book is for my brother Tim, who lives in both cities.

Introduction

JOHN FREEMAN

SEVERAL YEARS AGO, I bought an apartment in Manhattan with an inheritance passed to me from my grandmother, who was the daughter of a former attorney for Standard Oil. She outlived three husbands and managed her money well, and in one fell swoop from beyond the grave hoisted me out of one social class and into another.

Meanwhile, on the other side of town, my younger brother was living in a homeless shelter.

He was not far away—less than a mile. It was the second or third shelter he'd been in after moving to the city. It's awkward enough, in most instances, to talk about money, but doubly so when it involves family. So let me just briefly say that my brother had not been left out of his inheritance; he just had no immediate access to it due to the fact that he has a mental illness. He has dealt with this illness bravely and takes precautions to manage his condition. One of the first things he did after moving to New York was check in at a hospital and use his Medicaid card to get his prescriptions.

Still, it was a very bad idea for him to move to the city. From afar, the decision felt like a car crash you watch in slow motion. We'd warned and pleaded, even begged him not to move to New York, my brother, father, and I did. My father told horror stories from when we lived here in the 1970s. I talked about how hard it could be just to sleep on some nights, with the heat, the noise, the city's constant pulsing. My older brother talked to him about how difficult it was to find work, something my younger brother knew because he had been applying for jobs for over a year. Counselor, technological writer, librarian's assistant, anything to do with words that paid better than minimum wage. He held a BA and had been published in newspapers.

None of that mattered in the end. He couldn't get a job, and felt he couldn't stay where he was—Utica—so he got on a train to New York and checked himself into a shelter. He had almost no belongings. He'd given them away or sold them. He brought a suitcase, a laptop he slept with so it wouldn't be stolen, and a pay-as-you-go cell phone. These are luxuries in many parts of the world, but I assure you they were the thin string holding my brother's life together by giving him a tenuous connection to the outside world, not to the one right around him. He kept us abreast of his movements by Facebook: which shelter he'd been kicked out of for fighting or calling people names, where he'd slept—the Staten Island Ferry, a bathroom at a bus station in Albany. Eventually, he wound up at this final shelter, and it was, to some degree, a last resort, where he lived for a while and joined their job-training program.

All the time that my brother was homeless, I never invited him over to where I lived or let him into my apartment. I love my brother. He can be sweet and very funny; he is gentle and kind to older people. Even when he made less than $10,000 a year, he spent hours each week tutoring and teaching people English. He is one of the most intelligent people I know, and every time I see him I am reminded how lucky I am to have him as a brother. I am also reminded how lucky I am that I was born, for reasons I cannot fathom, with a slightly different gene structure, one that means that I thrive under the same stress that makes his life impossible. It is not fair, but long ago I decided I would not spend my time trying to ameliorate the difference in our fortunes by fighting battles I knew are not winnable, among them trying to sort out his accommodation. I have had the experience of sharing a home with my brother and have arrived at the conclusion that it is better for us to live apart. During this time my girlfriend and I were contemplating conjoining our two adjacent apartments, and my feelings of guilt did not trump my resolve to avoid putting the relationship with my partner at risk from the strain of taking him in. I had seen the stress it had caused my parents. I knew my brother would be aware of the problems he was creating, and that it would be bad for him, too. At least that's what I told myself.

So we communicated by Facebook and traded e-mails and once or twice met for lunch at a diner, where he arrived looking hollow and yet more alive than I had seen him in years. I almost didn't recognize him.

He had been walking everywhere and the food in the shelter was so bad, he'd lost forty pounds. He didn't look sad anymore, but more like the brother I grew up with in California who was handsome and had girlfriends, a golden boy. He had much more energy now, too, as a result of being more fit, and deployed it wrangling the city's social services bureaucracy. He had applied for a low-income housing program, and sent out resumes to jobs at the library. In the meantime, he was working up in Harlem, handing out free newspapers at the entrance to a subway. I realized in talking to him that to give him a lifeline to my house would have been a mistake; as hard as it was, he wanted to prove to us, and most important, to himself, that he could do this on his own. Still, I felt compelled to give him a few hundred dollars and he walked back into his life.

I couldn't have predicted it then, but he succeeded. My brother got out of the shelter. He was accepted into the housing program, found an apartment, and, for a while, achieved his dream. He was living in New York, on his own. At first, he loved his new life. But as time went by, with his benefits package constantly under threat, he became increasingly tired of the strain of the city—the way it makes everything difficult, doubly so if you need help from it. Eventually he moved back to Utica and then on to Dallas, where he seems truly happy now. It's warm, he has a car and things to do. He can live with a degree of peace and a lack of stress, and even if he has become a Republican, I still love him. I often like his photographs on Facebook.

I haven't resolved how I feel about his time in New York. I don't think I ever will, because the juxtaposition of our fates and fortunes is simply too much to assimilate. Too unequal. During the time he was here I rarely woke up later than 6:00 a.m. I was working for a British magazine and often had to travel to London for long periods. I was living there half-time, on and off airplanes on a monthly, sometimes weekly, basis and it messed up my internal clock. Meanwhile, he was living four blocks away in a shelter. On some mornings when I was in the city, I stood by the window of my apartment, drinking my first coffee while watching the dawn light up the walls surrounding the car park across the street. On some of those mornings he must have passed my building on his way from the shelter to the 1 train uptown to hand out newspapers, but he didn't ring our doorbell. Did he even look up to see if I was there, worrying about him, wondering if he'd been kicked out his shelter after another fight? I asked him once why he never stopped by after he left the shelter and had an apartment of his own. He said, "It was cold, and I didn't want to be late for work."

• • •

I TELL this story now because we need to change the way we talk about inequality. The reasons it exists are as complex as the reasons why my brother wound up in a shelter. Inequality is not an issue of *us* and *them*, the rich and the poor. You often see these same so-called divisions within one family, like mine. I have an instinct here to apologize for making this point, to add a caveat that my experience of witnessing my brother's homelessness was not nearly as hard as it was for him to live it, while I'm sure there are people who have suffered far more than both of us. All this is true, I suppose, but it leads us into a cul-de-sac. To rank suffering creates a false hierarchy of pain, as if there were a way to compare and weigh grief with, say, physical discomfort, or career frustrations, or hopelessness. It allows us, to some degree, to say that some forms of suffering are OK while others are not.

City life is defined by proximity, and when people around city dwellers suffer, it creates stresses on everyone. Mayor Bill de Blasio was elected in part because his narrative of New York as a "Tale of Two Cities" struck a chord with people living in the city. He has called it "the central issue of our time." New Yorkers related to his frustration and passion, his dream that the city could do much better. They were also, it's fair to say, galvanized by the sense he conveyed in his campaign that the gap between the rich and poor, the haves and have-nots, has grown so wide as to make New York City untenable. The city's narrative—of it being a special place, a city of dreams—shreds in the face of reality: the city's income disparity is as big as it has ever been.

Some figures are necessary here in case you have not been following the news. Nearly half of New York is living near poverty, and in the last two decades the income disparity in the city has returned to what it was just before the Great Depression. The top 1 percent of New York earners saw their median income grow from $452,000 to $717,000 between 1990 and 2010. Meanwhile, the lowest 10 percent of New Yorkers saw a much smaller percentage growth, from just $8,500 in 1990 to $9,500 in 2010. The concentration of wealth in that period has also been remarkably skewed toward the very rich. In 1990, the top 10 percent of households earned 31 percent of the income made in New York; by 2010 that number had increased to 37 percent. And the very rich make up a large proportion of that group: in 2009, the top 1 percent earned more than a third of the city's income. It is very clear. The rich are getting richer and the poor are getting poorer.

And the middle class, as it has been in the U.S. for some time, is progressively vanishing. Just prior to de Blasio's election, James Surowiecki wrote a prescient column for the *New Yorker* outlining why this has happened. The city is highly dependent on the finance industry to create revenue—the top 1 percent pay a staggering 43 percent of the income tax—and yet that same industry is driving income inequality. Meantime, the kinds of jobs that bolster the middle class—manufacturing, for example—have vanished. Between 2001 and 2011 the city lost 51 percent of its manufacturing jobs. The cost of doing business in New York City, Surowiecki pointed out, is simply too expensive, and factories, workshops, and shipyards have gone elsewhere.

These numbers reflect an extreme version of what is happening in many U.S. cities, as people move back to urban areas from the suburbs, driving up urban home prices and rents. New York City has experienced that trend in an exaggerated way. New Yorkers who are not in the top 10 percent have seen just modest growth in their income, but they have faced catastrophic rent increases. Between 2002 and 2012, the median rent has risen 75 percent. Rent in New York City is now three times the national average. As a result, nearly one-third of New Yorkers pay more than 50 percent of their annual income in rent. Forget about not being able to afford to own; many New Yorkers cannot afford to rent. The New York City borough that spends the highest percentage on rent—the Bronx, where the typical household spends 66 percent of its income to rent a three-bedroom home—is also its poorest. Incidentally, this is where my brother lived once he got an apartment.

♦ ♦ ♦

These conditions are not sustainable. Moreover, the gap between what New York says it is—in its myths and pop culture, the images we retain of it when we visit, its literature—and its reality is not sustainable either. I would like it if this anthology could help to close the gap between the haves and have-nots in the city. It can perhaps do so by addressing this second gap, by thinking and dreaming and describing what it is like in New York City today. How does it feel, what does one see, what stories do we tell about ourselves, and how, if at all, has inequality changed the city?

In January 2014 I contacted a number of writers who live or have lived in New York City, who feel it is their home. Thirty of them responded. The anthology you have here is the result of their engagement with this issue, and their responses take many forms. There are memoirs and short stories, a collage, reported pieces, an essay on bartending, an urban travelogue, dispatches from housing court fights, an oral history, a poem, and even a Twitter series that turns headlines from 1912 into a kind of tone poem about violence and the city's propensity to mulch its own.

Here is the city as it feels today, full of vanished bodegas and ghosts of a more mixed and various past. In Zadie Smith's short story, an aging drag queen who has managed to hold on to a Chelsea apartment wanders her neighborhood, tripping over shadows of what used to be there. The era of more affordable rents is gone, for now, and some writers show what—besides disposable income—has been lost with it. Hannah Tinti lovingly remembers her first rent-controlled apartment on the Lower East Side, and the gay, mohawked, gun-toting man who was its protector and conscience. Would she have met him without rent control?

Gentrification, often labeled as the scourge of New York when it is merely a symptom of its economic condition, cuts both ways; everyone dreams of moving up, even if it means leaving things behind. Fifteen-year-old Chaasadahyah Jackson, a student at the 826NYC drop-in tutoring center in Brooklyn, chronicles her family's move from Crown Heights to Park Slope, and describes the assumptions on the part of her friends about her life at the family's new address. Dave Eggers introduces her essay and sets out why his organization is committed to providing a platform for stories like hers. Sarah Jaffe, meanwhile, travels in the opposite direction, from Park Slope to Crown Heights, where the struggles of tenants to get basic services in their apartments drives her to attend the city's housing committee hearings about proposed rent hikes in rent-stabilized apartments.

Again and again, pieces in *Tales of Two Cities* return to themes that cut to the heart of New York City's problems today, pinpointing where the stress is felt. Housing is a perpetual concern. I showed my brother the draft of this introduction and he responded with an essay of his own, included here, describing his seven agonizing months of being homeless. The threat of nearly losing a home can be nearly as stressful. Jeanne Thornton, in a hilarious and moving memoir, describes clinging to a punishing, over-worked job so she can afford an apartment that a homeless friend has also made his squat. In a heartbreaking oral history, DW Gibson brings to life the voice of a housing defendant, whose job it is to stand up for tenants whose rights are being violated. One of his clients is a woman fighting a landlord who, under the guise of renovation, destroys his tenants' bathrooms, making their apartments unlivable in order to drive them out. "Who does this to other people?" she asks. "Other human beings?"

Reading these pieces, it's hard not to feel that what defines the modern city—perhaps any city now—are the challenges it places in front of those struggling to achieve basic rights and dignity. As Dinaw Mengestu points out in his essay about moving to New York in order to find the best level of care for his autistic child, these barriers are more easily surmounted by some than others. The point is reinforced by Maria Venegas in her memoir of working at an after-school program for kids in Brooklyn during an epidemic of suicides by stressed-out schoolchildren. The sacrifices that parents are forced to make, and the difficulty that others find in even imagining them, is brought to life in Taiye Selasi's story about a Russian man, his daughter, a taxi driver from Asia, and a prostitute.

Still, the city has continued to hold promise, to serve as a beacon to all comers. It depends, as David Byrne points out, on that influx to rejuvenate its creativity. In an essay on one of Mozart's librettists, who came to New York in the early 1800s, Edmund White reminds us that it was always difficult to immigrate here, especially if the person coming to America wanted to instruct it on a foreign culture. Akhil Sharma's family moved to the United States from India in the 1970s. In a short essay he writes about how the standard of poverty he grew up with in India meant he would never feel poor in New York City. That barbed gift is what allowed him, decades later, to leave a lucrative job in finance and turn to writing full time, even if it didn't protect him entirely from the loss of prestige the forfeiture of a large salary entailed.

The tension of moving up, down, sideways, or across—of placing oneself among competing lives and narratives—lends encounters in New York City their peculiar charge, which can sometimes feel like danger.

In Lydia Davis's story, a woman's train ride into Manhattan is disrupted by an incident in the car behind her. During a snowstorm from the endless winter of 2013, a wealthy couple at the heart of Jonathan Dee's story comes face to face with the 99 percent in the form of a man who is prepared to capitalize on the guilt and greed of the 1 percent. Colum McCann recalls going down into the tunnels beneath Manhattan to research a novel he was writing. He cautiously befriended a woman who lived down there and discovered, when he tried to help her, the fine line between a gift that requires gratitude and one that takes away dignity.

Such encounters do not need to happen across a large class divide. In Téa Obreht's story, an Eastern European man lets down his guard during a traffic incident when he meets a man with his own background, and regrets it. Mapping her neighborhood in Harlem, Valeria Luiselli meets migrants who are like her, but different. Michael Salu travels to New York City from London for the first time and finds a place strangely mediated by his exposure to pop culture. Going to house parties, museums, and nightclubs, he realizes that the music he loved and that helped him learn how to be black comes from a place where his blackness means something else entirely.

It is natural in all human life to search for community, but the peculiar mix of New York—of so many people, so many backgrounds, such divergent wealth—means people search even harder, and find themselves looking for it in unexpected places. Rosie Schaap describes how a good bar becomes a community, leveling the economic playing field so long as people there respect service workers. Patrick Ryan remembers his New York job on the graveyard shift at a corporate law firm with misfits, actors, and a would-be survivalist. In his essay, Victor LaValle traces his arc away from church as a boy and then back to it as a man, when he wanted both fellowship and homage to something more.

These communities, however strong, are unstable, and shift as neighborhoods change, people's fortunes alter, or the pressures of paying bills simply get to be too much. Junot Diaz recalls growing up working-class with friends whose parents struggled to pay the bills. They shared a solidarity in this fate, even when those friends stole from his family. Need can make us do abject things. Bill Cheng remembers the self-loathing and loneliness his own financial struggles provoked. He ended up feeling less like a person, an attitude he sees written on the faces of others now that his own circumstances have changed.

It can feel especially cruel living in New York when broke, since the evidence of wealth is everywhere, as Lawrence Joseph reminds us in his poem about the city a decade after the attacks of 9/11. There's violence to that wealth, and it has global consequences. It has always been so, as Teju Cole's series of "little death" tweets exposes, bringing back headlines from the year 1912. It is enough to make one wish that there could be, as Jonathan Safran Foer imagines it, a sixth borough off the coast of Manhattan to house some of us, to give the city room to breathe.

◆ ◆ ◆

It's a startling proposition—the idea of imagining a city bigger than what exists in reality, so that it can properly be itself. What would it take to do this? While politicians fight over the scale and carving-up of taxes, minimum wages, affordable housing, and better social provision, writers can join the fray, using their imaginations and experiences to provide a wider take that reinforces the nitty-gritty struggle for fairness in the city. As Garnette Cadogan reveals in his piece, the distance between here and there is not so far, and we're all impoverished when fairness recedes.

The greatest beacon in this regard was Walt Whitman, who, as Mark Doty notes in his essay, was against riches without being against the rich. Whitman walked the city, cruised its men, surveyed its abject citizens, and honored them all in his poems. He felt that every living soul deserved to be regarded equally. It's an obvious idea, but so often forgotten.

This book is meant to be a home for that task of imagining a larger city. If all books are temples of a sort, my hope is that this one has a broad arching roof under which we can find shelter and comfort. As galvanizing as thinking of New York as a tale of two cities has been, the fact of the matter, made clear in this anthology, is that New York *is* many cities. Inequality makes it harder for them to live side by side with a shared purpose.

It felt fitting, then, that the book should be a benefit for an organization that embodies just that creed. Many of the writers herein have appeared at Housing Works Bookstore Cafe, a downtown arts space and bookstore that is one hub among a larger network of thrift stores and bookshops that raise money to provide housing, job training, and advocacy to homeless New Yorkers, especially those with HIV and AIDS.

They have been among the hardest hit populations in the city during the period of spectacular wealth creation that has led us to where we are now, and Housing Works has fought ferociously on their behalf.

Any time you want to see proof that the solutions to New York as a tale of two cities are not ones of practicality, but imagination, just visit the Housing Works store at 126 Crosby Street. It is a huge, open loft space with spiral staircases, catwalks, a bustling café, and forty thousand books for sale, all of which were donated—many, certainly, by people very much on the "other side" of the divide from those who receive Housing Works benefits. That doesn't matter. The books are given to the store with an optimistic idea of what a city represents: the idea that we can all live together. The task of doing this requires watching out for everyone's well-being: it requires imagination, observation, and generosity, something we all struggle with—I know I have in my own life, with my brother, let alone walking down the block to buy a coffee while someone is sleeping on the street. It is that struggle, I would like to think, that defines us—that its outcome is not predetermined, that we can do better, and that the city can, too. Here in these pages are thirty writers showing what that struggle feels like now.

—John Freeman
NYC, July 2014

Due North

GARNETTE CADOGAN

"Walkers are 'practitioners of the city,' for the city is made to be walked, [Michel de Certeau] wrote. A city is a language, a repository of possibilities, and walking is the act of speaking that language, of selecting from those possibilities."
—Rebecca Solnit

I'm an island boy and wear that designation with pride, and so I decided that, despite New Yorkers' cautions to the contrary, I would not live in their city as some worker bee too busy to make contact with passersby. Strangers might stamp me as crazy, but I planned to talk to them. They would be my skeleton key to the city.

I came to the city—which, for me, meant all five boroughs (yes, even Staten Island)—after Hurricane Katrina flicked me north. And I intended to immerse myself in its rich, colorful cultural life by spending a lot of time walking; after all, that's how I got to know the vibrant streets of Kingston, where I grew up, and New Orleans, where I spent almost a decade. "You can tour the world at the cost of a monthly subway pass," I once heard a New Yorker boast. Indeed, tour I would, but this meant getting off at stations almost at random and walking, lots of walking and talking, to observe, to absorb, to understand.

For the myth of the place, the promise of New York, was that, with a dose of sparkling luck, you could join its throngs and have their fascinating lives broaden and deepen yours. "If you're bored it's because you're on the wrong block," said my indefatigable friend Maxine, who lived a few blocks from the never-dim (though often-dull) Times Square. I could hop on a train to Jackson Heights in Queens and walk along sidewalks made resplendent by Indians, Bangladeshis, Tibetans, and Nepalis who shop and sell side by side; and, night owl that I am, I could return at 2:00 a.m. for Nepalese food, eating yak while chatting away. This was the city of high social and cultural aspirations and achievements—the "city of opportunity"—where, I was led to believe, cosmopolitanism won the day. I had every intention, then, to join its pageant of walkers.

I arrived in New York in October 2005 and immediately began walking all over the city, exploring for hours at a time. As I traversed its landscape, I discovered a topography of social conditions. Some days, I would linger on 34th Street among the glamorous workers of Midtown Manhattan rushing to and from their high-rise buildings—in swift pursuit of their ambitions, I'd assumed. I'd watch them zigzag around and dart past the enthusiastic tourists filing into the Empire State Building, that colossus rising majestically above as a beacon of hope and symbol of American derring-do.

Then I'd stride northward, eager to explore Whitman's "Numberless crowded streets, high growths of iron, slender, strong, light, splendidly uprising toward clear skies." A little over two hours later, I would end up in Harlem at the courtyard of a housing project on 125th Street, where residents lounged on benches and welcomed each other with cheerful banter. They also welcomed me, and I sat beside them, took one of the kiddie's box drinks they offered, and enjoyed their jovial talk in that relaxed, open space far removed from the hurried dynamism of Midtown.

But as I've circulated through New York's streets, nothing reveals the city's opposites in stark juxtaposition like going from the Upper East Side to the South Bronx, two neighborhoods separated by a brisk ninety-minute walk, or a quick twelve-minute subway ride. I'd call them neighbors were it not so clear that they occupy such distinctly different worlds. To walk the streets from one to the other, as I often do, is to bear witness to a landscape of asymmetry. The city that comes into view is one of uneven terrain, vistas of opportunity alongside pockets of deep poverty too often lost in the periphery.

◆ ◆ ◆

In early 2006, almost six months after moving to the city, I was hobbled from roaming around because of a botched surgery on my right knee. A few months later, I switched hospitals to the Hospital for Special Surgery, located on the Upper East Side, where I eventually underwent two more surgeries to get back to walking the streets without chronic pain. As a result of the operations and follow-up physical therapy, the Upper East Side became a regular destination. I spent a lot of time watching people go about their lives, many of whom were middle- and working-class people employed in hospitals, museums, universities, hotels, and elsewhere on the Upper East Side. Plentiful as these workers were, they didn't define the neighborhood—at least, not in a way that forcefully impresses itself upon the mind when you think of the Upper East Side. No, the population that embosses its mark on the neighborhood is the wealthy—the extraordinarily wealthy, to be precise.

The Upper East Side houses one of the richest zip codes in the U.S. This wealth touches almost everything in its vicinity. Many of the less-flush people I met going about their day worked at institutions that were among the world's finest—The Metropolitan Museum of Art, Memorial Sloan Kettering Cancer Center, Hospital for Special Surgery—and that were easily accessible by their upper-class neighbors. In addition to stellar medical care and world-class museums, I'd walk past some of the city's best private schools, public libraries abuzz with parents and nannies—many of whom were foreigners—playing with children, and music schools with eager and not-so-eager kids developing their skills. Here was a neighborhood stocked with the resources for worldly success.

Walking through that part of the Upper East Side was not unlike a jaunt in a museum. On Park or Fifth Avenue, for example, one could walk for hours and admire magnificent buildings fronted by well-manicured gardens and quiet, clean sidewalks. Serenity suffuses the atmosphere. Nothing seemed out of place; and, to my untrained eye, it all looked unspoiled.

There are stunning apartment buildings that look like cathedrals in high heels. Über-chic boutiques—throne rooms of specialization meant to cater to people with the most rarefied, and demanding, of tastes—abound. You can pick up scented shoelaces for your teen daughter from a store filled with accessories for tweens, buy a bra for a few hundred dollars from an Italian lingerie store, and then drop off your puppy for a spa day, all in under a half hour. And, shhh, the stores were very quiet, I'll-glare-if-you-speak-loudly quiet. I was often hushed, too, since sticker-shock often dumfounds me. Though, I should confess, something perverse in me wanted me to scream upon entering those hush-up stores.

All around are luxe restaurants with patrons to match, and sophisticated bistros with fresh-looking, pleasant-smelling—oh, those lovely scents!—upscale clientele. And for outdoor relaxation and play, Central Park is a quick stroll away, across the road, even. It's as if the neighborhood was curated to cater to the needs and pleasures of its wealthy residents. Dig through the historical record and you'll find that, indeed, starting with Fifth Avenue in the late nineteenth century, later joined in the early twentieth century by Park (formerly Fourth) Avenue, elegance and convenience have characterized the Upper East Side's moneyed class and their tony residences.

Yet, for all its beauty, the neighborhood today feels like a welcome mat with spikes, or, more aptly, like a museum after closing time. You could stand nearby and look in, but that's as far as you could go: admiration from a distance. My feet met their limit.

So much of the lives of the very wealthy were a mystery to me, not least because I couldn't hope to stand and chat with them. The city was this enticing language I was learning but they were a cipher. They lived, as my friend and walking companion Suketu once put it to me, in vertical gated communities—fortresses within layers of insulation. I'd see them shuttle from cabs or chauffeur-driven cars into their elegant buildings fronted by attentive doormen. Or I'd see them interacting with each other as I strolled past a posh establishment. They were sharply dressed ghosts; I would see them for a brief moment, only for them to quickly disappear into vehicles or buildings as mysteriously as they came.

There was a come-hither-stay-away quality to it all. Apartment lobbies looked inviting, but dapper doormen in their white shirts and black ties stood between you and them. Brownstones were beguiling, but you dared not sit on their steps. And I couldn't shake the feeling that someone my shade, the color of the neighborhood's nannies and gardeners and janitors but not their neighbors (at least, none that I saw), was more unwelcome on a stranger's stoop.

Nor would I ever see people hanging out on their own steps. The beauty of the Upper East Side, the visual allure, had a placidity I felt detached from. There was something disquieting about all that silence. Certainly, one of the joys of living in the city is the wonderful solitude it affords, the option to, as E. B. White memorably put it, opt out and announce, "I did not attend." The city is a place of escape as much as it's one of pilgrimage, and, to someone outside of their circle passing through, the affluent inhabitants of the Upper East Side resemble a group who entered a compact to "not attend." The serenity felt fragile, and I feared that if I did anything that was perceived as a threat to it, no matter how simple—approaching that friendly face to have a chat, leaning over to inhale perfumy flowers—that I would be promptly reminded that I could inhabit those streets only so much.

◆ ◆ ◆

When I leave the Upper East Side on foot, the streets declare it to me almost immediately. I cross 96th Street—on Park Avenue, say, and the picturesque quickly recedes. Islands of gardens are supplanted by train tracks that tear out of the ground and rise alongside and above apartments, transporting streams of Metro-North trains and dispersing noise across the neighborhood. Pristine sidewalks are replaced by dusty ones, and time and again micro–dirt tornadoes, with candy wrappers within, whirl around. And luxury mansions are replaced by tenement-type buildings, row houses, and "superblocks" of housing projects.

And the population becomes increasingly darker. A lot more. And friendlier. A lot more. More Spanish is heard (significantly so), more bodegas are seen on corners, and the hum of the Upper East Side gives way to a skipping, sometimes clamoring, beat. (On weekends with good weather, there are block parties aplenty.) You almost begin to wonder—at least, I often do—if East Harlem is the town crier announcing, "Yeah, you've left the Upper East Side. The South Bronx is three miles, and an hour's walk, that-a-way."

When I enter the South Bronx my pulse becomes polyrhythmic. And how could it not? Afro-Caribbean music greets me from cars doubling as drive-by sound systems. Strangers greet me with friendly salutations—"Hola, Papi!"; "Whaagwaan, Bredrin!"; "Yes, Rudie!"; "Wassup, G!"; "A'ight. A'ight."—that have the flavor of family nicknames. Chatter intermingled with laughter is ubiquitous. The smells of Jamaican and Mexican and Puerto Rican and Ghanaian food pervade the atmosphere, and my stomach is at odds with my brain. ("OK, I plan to head in that direction, but that fragrant . . . Oh wait, is that curry?")

And, most delightful, people are open and ready to talk: in parks, on playgrounds, on street corners, on their stoops, from their bedrooms

("Hey, what song is that?" I'd think nothing to shout, and a reply would soar over the music through the bedroom window, "Juan Luis Guerra, Papi."). Perhaps, to repurpose the Psalmist's observation, "deep calls to deep" and the Caribbean in me is simpatico with the sounds and smells of the South Bronx. But, splendid as the food and music is, the real luxury of the walk is in the interactions. Life feels larger on the streets of the South Bronx. There are always people gathered on someone's steps and I can always find welcoming faces ready to talk and laugh and argue with me about my understanding of the neighborhood or my inexplicable belief that anything below sixty degrees Fahrenheit counts as cold or the ways New York City has changed over the past decade or half century.

This verve and neighborliness was everywhere I went in the South Bronx, no matter the circumstances. Most remarkable, to me, was Hunts Point, one of the South Bronx's and New York City's poorest neighborhoods—so much so it's often cited as the Upper East Side's economic polar opposite. In all the figures that economists quote to show standards of living and quality of life—median household income, percentage of population below the poverty line, life expectancy, educational-attainment levels—Hunts Point, a neighborhood of poor and working-class people, lay near the bottom when compared with other U.S. neighborhoods in dire conditions. When I walk around Hunts Point's industrial environment, with many of its residential houses four sighs away from collapsing, I'm struck by the nakedness, the vulnerability of the surroundings. Open spaces, with few trees to shade me, leave me exposed to the unrelenting tag team of the sun and heat-radiating asphalt. Recent development and revitalization efforts notwithstanding, the neighborhood has the aura of abandonment, particularly at night, where a motley gang of strip clubs, auto body shops, and prisons suggests backs turned.

Few, if any, people walk around the neighborhood just for walking's sake. With the high crime and severe poverty that are sadly familiar, it's a place that people who have no business there try to leave. Not that wayfarers are made unwelcome. Slow down a bit on its streets and you'll run into friendly small talk and laughter that rebuke the glum backdrop. (It wasn't all "happy town," though: people also spoke as if their lives were like one of the short, shabby dead-ends I sometimes encountered amid the neighborhood's industrial landscape, and the very poor weren't always in the mood for neighborliness.) One night, not long after midnight, my ready-to-hoof-anywhere pal, Suketu, drove me along with two of his friends to the Hunts Point Food Distribution Center, popularly called the Hunts Point Market. (Most New Yorkers who do know of it know it as where Manhattan's beloved Fulton Fish Market was relocated to join markets that deal with fruit and vegetables and meat and poultry.) We hopped from market to market, talking with some of the thousands of mainly male workers, employed by the various food wholesalers, distributors, and processors that are part of this fork-shaped collection of frigid warehouses and loading bays alongside the Bronx River.

Until before sunrise, we learned more than we would ever need to know about the food coming from all over the world to this node before dispersing all over again. In the brightly-lit produce market, we walked down corridors, one-third of a mile in length, past a field of colors—lettuce, peaches, strawberries, sweet onions, tomatoes, scallions, lemons, corn, potatoes, peppers, and many more than we could take in. We kept craning our necks to sniff, four bumblebees hovering around berries and bananas and plums and other sweet-smelling fruit. The employees, for the most part, seemed puzzled that four grown adults were walking around at 2:00 a.m. for fun. We moved on to the meat market, where, in warehouse-sized refrigerators (or, so I considered the cold-to-the-bone spaces in which my teeth were chattering), there was meat and poultry, enough to make a vegetarian queasy for months. Men ought to cry their way through the entire workday in these subzero temperatures, but this was where the party was. The four of us learned about butchering, distribution, union issues at the market, the red-light district nearby, and other things that I missed because my breaking point is cold temperatures. And the fish market was a stinky pleasure, its odor made bearable because of the laughter that filled the atmosphere. I suppose if you are going to work with guts and funk, you had better have a sense of humor. And smiling faces, Duchenne smiles, were in abundance wherever we migrated.

As far as I could tell, apart from the four of us, the only people around were those who had business there. We were like four kids let into a playground alone after closing hours, roaming at random and clowning around with the workers—in one instance, taking a photo with a knife in mock plunge to one of our throats—and learning a bit from them about the neighborhood right outside the guard-protected gates of the markets. There was joy, but there was mainly bustling, since the work done there results in billions of dollars in receipts.

After five hours or so, our happy quartet finished moving among the different markets. The sky took on a hue that announced morning was on its way. We decided it was time to go, but we were with Suketu, so that meant that it was not a simple departure for home. Another adventure was to be found. Nocturnal being that I am, I was ready for whatever enjoyment he had ahead. But when we jumped in his car, I felt dislocated. The comfort of the car felt stifling, like a cocoon of glass and steel, and the artificiality of my movement—machinery taking me to my adventure, rather than my own two feet following my senses—dampened my zeal. I wasn't being a sourpuss—near impossible around Suketu, with his radiating charm and humor—but I recognized the previous five hours of walking had only prepared me for more walking. In a car, I was too preoccupied with the landscape of my imagination, rather than attentive to the one before me. The music and movement of the car too easily displaced the movement and music of the streets I'd become used to. I felt I had at once lost and gained too much control; you ought to know where you're going when you're driving, and a surprise is the last thing you want. I wanted to be the "afoot and light-hearted" walker that Whitman praised. To "take the open road, healthy, free, the world before me, the long brown path before me leading wherever I choose." I wanted to be on foot. I wanted to meet other people on foot.

When we left the artery that was Hunts Point Market, the eerie silence outside felt condemning. The ailing conditions glared. No one was on the street. Prostitutes, who used to dot the neighborhood's corners and sidewalks, had retreated inside due to the convenience of doing business online. (So we were told by some of the men we spoke to earlier—apparently reliable sources based on their remarks about after-work recreations.) We drove around a bit, past sidewalks now bare, where in the day I had numerous delightful conversations, raising my voice above the sound of loud freight trucks expelling foul exhaust. Hunts Point at night might as well be another neighborhood, I thought; I hadn't recognized until then how much its residents imbued it with color.

On the way back home, Suketu drove through the Upper East Side, past glittery boutiques and sexy bistros, enticing department stores and showy high-rise apartment buildings. At that moment, I recognized that, for me, there wasn't much difference between cutting through the neighborhood on foot and in car. There was, of course. But I had left Hunts Point, where being in a car away from residents removes so much of the neighborhood's pleasure, only to arrive in the Upper East Side around fifteen minutes later. There I recognized that I felt at arm's length with a lot of the neighborhood's residents even when I walk through, and I saw all too vividly that inequality also deprived the very wealthy. In ensconcing themselves in their circles, the very wealthy had cut themselves off from a range of perspectives and temperaments and stories—stories that are a central part of their city's vibrancy and appeal. In Hunts Point, I witnessed deprivation due to an absence of resources; in the Upper East Side, I witnessed deprivation of a different, but related sort: the absence of enriching interactions.

◆ ◆ ◆

I became an obsessive walker as a matter of necessity. Too poor to take taxis when I was growing up in Jamaica, and living in a neighborhood where taxis (and, alas, friends) refused to go at night, I learned to walk wherever and whenever to get home. This meant walking through some very dangerous parts of Jamaica. Observation was more about survival—Will he rob me? Will he stab me? Will they shoot me?—rather than about exploration: What will she tell me about this city? What will I learn about my country? Myself? Eventually, by the time I was able to afford cabs, it had become natural for me to venture all over the island, because some frequencies I could only hear while on foot. My interactions with others would enlarge and fortify my identity. And there was something exhilarating about participating in the oldest of rituals: human dealings through the sharing of stories.

One pleasurable afternoon when spring was showing off and pulling everyone out of their homes, only to smirk "Gotcha!" and hit them with a heavy downpour, I took an acquaintance, Genevieve, to the South Bronx. She'd asked to explore it with me but I thought that the wet outdoors would make our walk a letdown. We walked around, wandering down streets that looked interesting because of the architecture, or, more commonly, because of liveliness on their corners and sidewalks. We stopped to talk to a young man laying mulch on his front yard garden. "Yeah, it comes in all colors these days. I like the look of the red," he obliged, as I cut into his gardening time. He was focused on packing fertilizer around the roots of flowers that had just begun to bloom, and nightfall wasn't far away; he had the urgency of a man trying to beat the clock, either to race the coming of dusk, or to be on his way out to enjoy the night. Nonetheless, he leaned back, arms akimbo, and spoke with us about gardening.

I asked directions of a woman on the sidewalk waiting for friends: "Uh-huh, take that street to go to the park. You'll see the playgrounds on the way." And so it went—moment after moment of stopping people to ask for directions (even when we knew where we were going; I discovered some time ago that New Yorkers are all too ready to play compass and map to those who ask, and a question for a location could become a conversation about the neighborhood). The dampness seemed to have had no effect on the neighborhood's exuberance. People were playing music and enjoying it with friends on their porches. Pick-up basketball games were all around. And just about everyone we passed exchanged a pleasant smile or greeting. Even when we cut into their gardening time.

After a few hours of wandering, we went to a Nigerian eatery named Patina African Restaurant, a homey spot made more so by the conviviality of the staff and fellow diners. We began talking with a waitress who said she was from Sierra Leone, and whose name, Ayomie, which means "joy," could not be more befitting. She was busy befriending us while juggling a bunch of responsibilities, and helped Genevieve with her decision-making: "Your first time here? OK, I'll give you a sample of everything so you can decide what you want." When she found out that my travel companion's name was Genevieve, she yelped excitedly and it seemed her only job after that was to inform all the women hard at work in the back cooking, cleaning, and organizing that "Her name's Genevieve." People came out and looked at Genevieve and smiled and asked if she knew. Well, now she did. It turned out that Genevieve is the name of a beloved Nigerian singer and actress, and I might as well have been sitting across from her, for there was such palpable excitement about the one I knew that I was sure I'd brought a celebrity to eat with me. A week or so later, Genevieve told me that she was speaking with someone from Africa and mentioned her name as "Genevieve, like the singer," and that simple acknowledgment led to a more amusing and pleasing exchange.

The stories people tell each other and the stories they allow themselves to encounter is part of what gives New York City its energy. And the stories I heard ignited my imagination and reshaped my ideas about the city. One afternoon during my physical therapy session, I had one such chat with a patient who was part of the neighborhood's elite. She was a college professor—of English Literature, if my memory hasn't deceived me—in her seventies, not much more than five feet tall, and overflowing with warmth and elan—more cute aunt than authoritative dispenser of knowledge. Her friendliness, conveyed with a mellifluous voice, made me stop my rehabilitation exercises and listen away. She spoke about the world with unbridled enthusiasm and genuine wonder, and her drive to explore it made me want to cut her off and rush in search of her adventures. But what stayed with me weren't the wonderful stories—I've unfortunately forgotten them all, inspiring as they were—but, rather, it was her ability to give one a greater sense of possibility. I often wish I could take this woman on my walks. A greater sense of wonder, a greater sense of the multifariousness of the world, a greater sense of possibility: these gifts she bestowed, and these were what I most wanted to dispense when I crossed the divide to where people too often were in desperate need of these traits along with resources.

Serendipity reveals a world of people holding views and undergoing experiences unlike ours. But serendipity also exposes our commonalities, showing how much our joys and frustrations and anxieties are similar: we all want happy marriages and healthy children and kind in-laws; we all want what we think is best for our children; and we all feel helpless and crumble in the face of mortality. Inequality manifests itself both as the inequality of resources and, looking in the other direction, the inequality of interaction. But, really, everyone is diminished by the absence of interaction, the lack of shared experience. The very wealthy and very poor—inequality makes equals of them all.

Options

DINAW MENGESTU

I was on a downtown C train at 5:30 a.m. on a Tuesday when I heard that Avonte Oquendo was missing. A flyer of him hung in the lobby of our seven-story apartment building on the southern edge of a rapidly gentrifying Harlem—his face encased behind glass, along with notices of repairs from the building's management company. I saw the flyer in passing the night before; I registered the face and assumed it part of a heartbreaking but also familiar story of a lost child, and as such, my obligation was to remember the face in case I happened upon it on the subway, in the grocery store, seeking shelter under an awning during a storm. The details of the missing boy were secondary, hardly relevant to the ordinary bystander, which I assumed myself to be.

After eight months, my weekly commute from New York to Washington, DC, had become familiar, although never quite routine. I had become convinced that I was more acutely aware of the city's condition during those predawn hours when I woke reluctantly, dressed, and packed my bags before kissing my wife and two children goodbye. Those were the only hours when there were no buses and few trucks idling at the light outside our bedroom window, and once outside, I thought the empty sidewalks and streets felt bereft, particularly during the winter, when it was dark, often brutally cold. That exaggerated sense of abandonment often followed me into the subway, and it was there the morning Avonte Oquendo became more than just a name and face on a flyer taped to a wall. I was thinking of my two children, three and four years old, and asleep in the same bed when I left them. So much of what I had tried to do as a father was erect walls, however permeable or even imaginary, against the obstacles my family had faced when I was a child. It wasn't poverty, but the frustrations of the working class and the battles that inevitably came with them—the endless fights over money, anger born from the stress of an overdrawn checking account—the hair graying over which bills could be paid and which ones could slip for another month or more. The limits of those ideas were obvious. There was no way to purchase the type of security I really wanted. I couldn't stand permanent guard over my children, but the desire to remain fixed in their shadows in order to box away whatever threats came near was impossible to suppress. And as was always the case, I thought specifically of my oldest son, who one year earlier had been diagnosed with autism. At that time he could say only a few words intelligibly. He walked through his life—preschool, playgrounds—with a curious gentleness that at times rendered the rest of the world around him unbearably crass, unduly harsh, especially when compared to a curly-haired, four-year-old boy who touched dogs, ants, and leaves as if all were equally fragile and capable of breaking.

When I saw Avonte Oquendo's face in the hallway, I connected it only tangentially with my own children. Since becoming a father, I've learned to turn away from stories involving the loss of a child since immediately I imagine my own children consigned to those roles. That small, self-indulgent imaginative leap, regardless of how short-lived, can make the next five minutes, or hour, suddenly harder to bear. The same aversion to suffering was true for the picture of Avonte, whose skin tone was roughly the same color as that of my own children, and whose large eyes reminded me of my youngest son. The subway conductor's announcement—the first of its kind I had ever heard—stripped away my ability, however profane, however reasoned, to discreetly choose among the heartbreaking facts I encountered. Here were the other parts of Avonte's narrative I had thought better to ignore: he was last seen at his high school in Queens; he was fourteen years old; he liked trains; he was a runner; he was autistic and nonverbal.

When our son was first diagnosed, the developmental pediatrician at the hospital in Washington, DC, gave us real estate advice: move to the Maryland suburbs, buy a house or an apartment in affluent Montgomery County, or be prepared to spend a lot of money in order to live in the capital. We had just moved to the U.S. from Paris, where I had met my wife and where both of our children were born. Instead of moving to the suburbs, or staying in DC, we moved to New York, which has one of the best early intervention programs for children under five with autism in the country. The city also has an impossible-to find-except-in-New-York list of autism services, from psychologists, clinicians, therapists, and, perhaps above all, a collection of private schools deliberately named and embroidered to echo the New England prep schools privileged parents envision sending their "normal" children to.

We arrived in New York expecting there to be costs, and we weren't disappointed. We came with multiple private evaluations from therapists and an autism clinic, and when those evaluations were deemed too old, or not valid, we paid for more. We drove to the city at the last minute hoping for our son to be admitted into one of those exalted private schools, only to be told after a five-minute meeting that maybe there was no opening after all. Above all, though, we waited. We worked slowly through the labyrinthine bureaucracy of New York City's department of education—a wait that would have been nearly unbearable in its frustration had we not had two of the most privileged assets available to a family in a city: flexible work schedules and, through the grace of a fellowship, the extra income to pay for not only a private school, but also therapists on the side. At that time our son was only three years old. A psychologist who had evaluated him told us we should be optimistic about the progress he could make if he had access to enough therapy. Those words alone were enough to inspire a type of recklessness in me when it came to looking for treatment and schools, one that my wife found difficult to comprehend. New York was years ahead of France when it came to treating or even discussing autism, but for what end, she wanted to know. "Who can spend this kind of money?" she asked after each bill arrived. Briefly I was convinced nothing was too expensive; nothing was out of bounds, and that there was even some nobility in the idea of emptying our family accounts year after year in order to find "the best" for our son.

Lists were made and unmade of private schools with six-figure annual tuition, of therapists and psychologists who did not take insurance and whose hourly fees of one to two hundred dollars an hour, at a modest three hours a week, equaled approximately a third of our monthly rent. The making of those lists and the household budget that could supposedly accommodate them was wishful thinking at its most pragmatic. At that time we were afraid to believe in some therapeutic miracle that could be purchased with the right doctor or school. We simply wanted the best and safest walls to protect our son—a subtle but profound evolution that with each new list, with each check signed, transformed our parental instincts into a search for a luxury good.

Avonte Oquendo's school was one of fifty-four District 75 schools scattered throughout New York. These schools are designed to serve students with the most severe social and cognitive deficiencies, and as such form a district unto themselves, one bound, unlike the rest of the city's school districts, not by geography but by need. District 75 schools often occupy a floor or portion of a building; Avonte's school, P.S. 222, was one of three schools in the building in Flushing, Queens. Shortly after moving to New York, I'd heard and read of District 75 schools located in the basements of larger public schools, the students confined to overcrowded, dark, windowless rooms. Avonte's school was not one of those. It was housed in a brand new building that had opened just that year and that was celebrated by city officials not only for the technology in the classroom, but also for the "limitless opportunities" that would come with having three different schools all together. And yet the school failed in the most fundamental and horrific way, in the first and most important task that we ask of our schools, and by extension our society: to keep our children safe, especially those unable to do so on their own. The school's failure can be seen through the narrow lens of bureaucratic mistakes— the side door left open, the school guard who failed to detain Avonte, the principal who waited to lock down the school, and the administration that waited an hour before notifying the police. But that would be the simplest possible narrative. The harder narrative is less precise, and is obscured by the staggering discrepancies in the cost and quality of services available to the children of New York.

There is, for all intents and purposes, a parallel economy of services, both private and public, that split the city in half. In the case of special needs, that split lies along two of the most contentious fault lines in our society: health care and education, both public services that have always operated for those who can afford it as wildly expensive private goods, from the forty-thousand-dollars-a-year preschool tuition, to the concierge medical services for those who can't bear the thought of dealing with insurance claims. When it comes to public education, we accept, however reluctantly, those divisions, fully aware that a public school in Park Slope or Tribeca shares only the letters P.S. in common with a similar school in the poorer neighborhoods of Brooklyn or Manhattan. Its private school counterpart, with its staggering tuition, stands so far beyond the ordinary that it has the oddly perverse effect of making the divisions in our public school system seem like an almost logically just conclusion. We would like to believe, however, that the parents of an affluent child cannot simply purchase quantifiably more or better quality medicine for their sick child—better antibiotics or braces or vaccines, or that they can threaten to sue to make the city pay for the care that's required, and yet that is precisely what happens in New York. The care that often may mean the difference between a child who can speak and one who cannot is meted out not according to need, or even zip code, but according to which parents have the resources—money, and perhaps just as important, time: to pay for the doctors and therapists that insurances won't cover; to log the seemingly endless hours of research into schools, both public and private, so that their children won't regress in classrooms poorly equipped to handle their needs; and when that isn't enough, when there are more and better options out there, to hire the lawyers to make certain they have done all they can, that they have done their best.

After Avonte's first day at his new school, his mother, responding to a questionnaire from his teacher, noted that Avonte needed one-to-one supervision, and that if not watched carefully, he would run from the building. Avonte's educational plan, created by the board of education and signed by his mother, did not require him to have one-to-one super-vision, and so none was ever provided. Among the many services offered by the private schools that appeared on my lists was one-to-one individ-ualized care, often with the type of highly trained therapists whose close attention can dramatically improve a child's ability to communicate and care for himself. It's impossible to know what that type of therapeutic care might have done for Avonte, but we do know it would have certainly saved his life. Recently, looking for a place for our son, we visited a class-room similar in size and structure to the one Avonte was in. We toured brightly decorated hallways and met with teachers and principals clearly dedicated to their schools. When we reached the classroom for children with special needs, we found six students, with one teacher and one as-sistant, sitting in near perfect silence, the students in front of computers, each with headphones on, isolated in their own private worlds, which is perhaps the best imaginable metaphor for what it's like to live with autism. Our son was working hard every day to make room for other worlds—louder, scarier, and fuller than the one he occupied on his own, and here was the opposite of those efforts.

A year and a half after moving to New York, our son's vocabulary has increased from a handful of intelligible words to fully formed sentences. He raises his hand in class to try and answer questions, and in July during his school's end-of-the-year celebration, he stood in a half circle with a dozen other students and clapped and danced along to Pharell's "Happy." He's had exceptional therapists working with him through the city's early-childhood intervention program, and wonderful teachers at the private preschool that he attends who kept him even when he was the sole child in the class who couldn't speak. During that time the once-imaginary lists have morphed into a tangible reality—a growing web of therapists, teachers, and now a lawyer and doctor, which my wife and I balance and rebalance each week, according, more often than not, to the demands of my work schedule, a pragmatic fact that has changed the course of her professional career just as much, if not more, than moving to a new country.

Our son's evolution hasn't been miraculous, but it has been expensive in ways that are impossible to justify. In nearly every facet of life, New York promises something more, something better for those with the means to pay—better Central Park views, better meals, and of course better schools. We may question the logic, even the ethics, but never the right of that commodification, and as a result, it's ebbed its way into the corners of our society where it least belongs. Less than one month after starting at his new school, Avonte Oquendo walked out through a side door. A uniformed guard saw him just before he left and asked him what he was doing, where he was going. The guard didn't know Avonte was autistic, much less nonverbal. Avonte, of course, did not respond to the question, and even if he could have, the guard's attention didn't last long enough to register one. A child from one of the other schools in the building was coming in for a hug. Upstairs, Avonte's teachers had noticed he was missing and had begun to seek additional help. According to the Board of Education's Special Commissioner's investigation, while teachers scoured the second floor of the building, "shortly after 12:38 p.m., Avonte headed down the bus hallway and left the building through the open bus door. An outside camera showed Avonte running out of the building, down the block, and across the street, eventually out of sight."

Every Night a Little Death

PATRICK RYAN

The law firm was corporate and one of the largest in the business, with offices all over the world. There were seven hundred attorneys in the Manhattan branch alone, and a support staff three times that number. I applied for a word-processing position a week after I arrived in the city, in January of 1999, and once I'd passed a proofreading test, the woman in charge of hiring offered me the job on the spot. "That's terrific," I said. She told me the hourly pay, which was a little higher than I'd expected, and I said that would suit me just fine. Then she told me the only openings they had were on the graveyard shift.

I'd never had a job in the corporate world before. I'd been a house-painter, a waiter, a stockroom clerk, an English teacher, a bartender. The graveyard shift seemed a fitting place for me to land, given that I'd just moved from the "sleepy" South to the city that never sleeps—an exciting change for me, though most of my friends back home had told me I was being foolish. "New York?" one of them had asked. "Really? I hope you have a lot of money, and a lot of tears."

Another, pulling up beside me at a traffic light, had rolled down his window to shake his head and holler, "That place is going to chew you up, spit you out, and piss on you."

"I'll tell you exactly what's going to happen," an older, chain-smoking neighbor had said as I was helping him sort his recycling. "You're going to fuck up your life beyond belief, and you're going to be back here in six months—probably addicted to heroin."

All of which made me more determined than ever to succeed (success meaning only my not having to move back south in six months). I took the job. I even decided *graveyard shift* had an impressive ring to it.

Responsible people worked the graveyard shift. Guys who wore matching-cap-and-jacket uniforms and carried lunchboxes worked the graveyard shift. Copyeditors in newsrooms, security guards who shone flashlights into warehouses, EMTs who stanched gunshot wounds—these were the secret heroes who kept the gears of the world turning while everyone else snoozed.

I was thirty-three and living in New York. I had an illegal sublet on the Upper West Side that was mine for another two months, and I had employment. To celebrate, I went to dinner with friends.

◆ ◆ ◆

My first night on the job, I showed up dressed in my funeral suit, the same suit I'd worn for my interview and for my week of nine-to-five orientation. The HR person who'd vetted me, the woman who'd hired me, the trainer who'd spent five days training me—none of these people were around. The faces were all new, and one of the first things I noticed was that none of them looked especially tired. It was almost midnight and we were on the forty-sixth floor of a needle-like building on Fifth Avenue, with windows showing views of the flickering lights of Midtown and Lower Manhattan, but these people were on the mid-swing of their day. They carried bagels, egg sandwiches. They poured packets of sugar into their coffees as their computers booted up.

Another thing I noticed was that no one looked very corporate. Some, in fact, looked like they'd come from yoga classes, or baseball games, or Broadway shows (they were carrying copies of *Playbill*, anyway). A couple of them looked as if they'd just rolled out of bed and pulled on yesterday's clothes, but even they seemed spritely. One woman, wearing a Mets baseball cap, was walking around carrying a vintage Zippy the Chimp doll almost half as tall as she was (she introduced me to it). A red-faced young man in the corner was staring at his computer, mumbling to himself as he squeezed a handgrip. Another man, older and sitting nearby, was wearing a short-sleeved shirt, a wide necktie, and a rainbow-striped clown wig. In muted tones—though not so muted that they weren't competing with one another—several people in the room were singing show tunes.

Wendell, the overnight supervisor whose walrus mustache hid both his lips, walked me around and introduced me. With the exception of the guy squeezing the handgrip, everyone seemed friendly. They welcomed me to the firm, to the funhouse, to the sausage mill, to the Death Star. I was given a desk next to square-jawed, gray-haired man who had a gravelly voice and looked like he could have been a private eye or a gallery owner or a junkie in any number of seventies television shows set in New York. Turns out he—like nearly everyone on the graveyard shift—was an actor. He'd been on TV and in films. His name was Howard, and he told me he was still acting, though he was also branching out and becoming a life coach. "And you're a what?" he asked.

"Just a person," I said.

Howard smirked, eyes fixed on the document next to his screen, fingers flying over his keyboard. "We don't get many of those. Most of us are something else. My guess is you're a writer. You look like one."

"Oh, yeah," I said. "I do that. Very astute of you."

"I'd kill an orphan for a ciggy," he said.

Wendell sauntered over and made a vaudevillian gesture of handing me a stack of papers across the top of one forearm. He explained that the graveyard shift in the Operations Group was all about doing these "mark-up" jobs for attorneys—unless the attorneys were here working late themselves, in which case word processors were sometimes sent "on assignment" to their offices to work alongside them. "Sort of like being their secretary," he said.

"Or their butt boy," said Howard.

"Or their bitch," said a tiny woman sitting on the other side of him. She was wearing sunglasses and was so pale, wizened, and fierce-looking, I thought for a moment she was Joan Didion.

Several desks away, the man in the clown wig tsk'd.

"Now, now," Wendell said, "it's not like that. It's smooth camping around here. Happy sailing. Say, Howard, the partner's calling from home about that job you're working on. He wants an ETA."

"Does he now?"

"Ballpark," Wendell said. *"Comme si, comme ça."*

"Tell him to staple it to his mother's tits," Howard said.

The woman in sunglasses burst out laughing, which caused me to laugh, too. But the man in the clown wig lifted his head and began to shout with what sounded like genuine fury, *"I don't come here to listen to filth! I come here to work!"*

"Me, I come for the lighting," Howard said.

"Never a dull moment, eh?" Wendell touched my shoulder and flapped his elbows. "Anyway, if you have any questions, you're surrounded by helpful people, so just ask."

As he walked away, the man in the clown wig glanced at the person sitting across from him—a slope-backed man in a sweater vest. "Why anyone would talk that way in a workplace—or anywhere—is beyond me," the man in the clown wig said. "The human mouth is not a toilet. Am I right, Mr. Abhinav?"

"I don't know what you're talking about," the slope-backed man said.

"Yes you do. Bad language. *Very* unpleasant."

"I can't understand a word you're saying," said the slope-backed man, and then glanced at me and smiled with a set of brilliantly white teeth.

♦ ♦ ♦

As I contemplated my new schedule, things I'd never considered before suddenly blossomed in my mind. Should I start having breakfast at night, before work? That would put lunch at around 4:00 a.m., and dinner at— 9:00 a.m.? I hadn't decided yet if I was going to try to go to bed right when I got home or put it off for a while. Putting it off would more closely resemble normal life (television, food, reading, and eventually sleep). But would I have a beer, then, when I got home at 8:15 in the morning? The idea seemed wrong no matter how I tried to justify it. I worried, too, that I might not be able to fall asleep the closer it got to noon, and if I couldn't fall asleep, what would that do to the rest of my day/night? Noon meant full-on sunlight, food carts, honking delivery trucks. And even if I could manage to drift off by noon, I couldn't stomach the idea of waking up after the sun had already started to set. That seemed even worse than sipping a beer in the morning.

Thinking about these things, I didn't sleep at all following my first night at work. I was too wound up, too worried about finding another place to live in just two months, too hyper-aware of doors closing in the hall, footsteps clicking in the stairwell, pigeons cooing on the windowsill. All for the best, I decided. This was like jetlag: I just needed to plow through it for a day or two until I eventually collapsed, slept twelve hours, and woke up a new man. In the meantime, why was I sitting around a stranger's apartment on a crisp winter's day when all of New York was out there waiting for me?

I took the train down to Chelsea and enrolled myself in a roommate service. They sent me to a six-bedroom apartment in Hell's Kitchen that had one room available. The five other bedrooms had padlocks on their doors. The sink in the kitchen was filled with dirty dishes, and on the stove sat the tiniest kitten I'd ever seen. I waved hi to it with one finger. It coughed.

I bought a coffee and carried it past bars filling up for happy hour. I bought the *Daily News* and sat on a stoop reading it—until a man stopped a few feet away with his back to me, bent over, dropped his pants, and began inspecting his asshole with both hands.

I moved on, thought about grocery shopping, ended up instead at a deli with a hot bar. Why buy groceries when I was only going to end up moving in eight weeks, I thought. I bought four plastic containers of food: noodles, stir-fry, chicken cutlets, slabs of meatloaf. Back at the apartment, I was deciding which container to eat for my late night breakfast and which to take to work for my early morning lunch when I saw a story in the paper about a suspect-at-large who was going around the city with a spray bottle, misting "poop water" onto hot bars in delis.

◆ ◆ ◆

I often ended up riding the elevator with Leo, the red-faced young man who'd been squeezing a handgrip the first time I'd seen him. The canvas bag Leo carried with him was big enough to hold nearly everything I'd brought with me to New York, and I began to wonder if he, too, was looking for a place to live. Night after night, he was never without the bag. Near the end of my first week on the job, I almost asked him about it, but Leo had a habit of slamming his wallet against the card reader—as if he'd just as soon knock a hole in the wall as clock in for work—so I didn't speak to him beyond saying hello.

The woman carrying around the Zippy the Chimp doll, I learned, was named Rebecca. She would make a pouty face if Wendell assigned her a particularly large proofreading job, and if she flipped through it before carrying it off to her cubicle and it was heavily marked up, she would start to cry.

"There, there," Wendell would say, leaning forward over his desk and smiling behind his mustache, "no need to get emotional."

More than once, I saw her give him the finger over her shoulder as she walked away.

The man in the clown wig was named Mr. Norwich, and he so respected formality in the workplace that he insisted on using "Mr." or "Ms." before everyone's names. Since no one in the Operations Group wanted to go by their last names, he attached the moniker to their first names.

"Mr. Patrick," he said to me one early morning in the kitchenette, "I have to say, I liked it better when you wore a suit to work."

"I only wore a suit that first night," I said.

"I know. And now look at you."

I was dressed in jeans, a t-shirt, and sneakers. Wendell had told me I could wear just about anything I wanted to work—"so long as the naughty parts stay covered up." Mr. Norwich was holding a coffee mug bearing the firm's name and blinking at me, waiting for me to respond.

"I like your wig," I said for lack of anything else.

"What wig?"

The next night, the clown wig had been replaced by a blond one—long and curling, the ends forming parentheses around Mr. Norwich's necktie. When Wendell approached him with a job and referred to him as Mr. Norwich, Mr. Norwich snapped, "I don't know why everyone keeps calling me that! I don't know who that is! My name is Ms. Lulu."

And so we all started calling him Ms. Lulu—until the clown wig reappeared.

The show tune singers sang sotto voce until they really wanted to be heard; then they just sang at conversational levels, and because so many people in the room were in the performing arts, no one ever told anyone else to shut up. Sometimes, spontaneously, they sang together. I sat one night at around 2:00 a.m. between two middle-aged women who quietly, and then not so quietly, performed a duet of "Every Day a Little Death." "Me harmony," one of them said when the time came. They performed the entire song without ever once looking up from their keyboards.

Though seven hundred attorneys clogged the building during the day, by night nearly all of them vanished. We were surrounded by evidence of their existence—they left heaps of work for us to do on their way home—and occasionally they called in to see how we were progressing, or to add additional instructions, or to bark an answer to a question one of us had left on their voicemail. But the scratchings on their documents may as well have been the cave drawings of a vanished tribe. They were the members of the Lost Colony, I sometimes thought. Or the firm was Ireland, and the attorneys were the snakes driven out of it. We word processors were archeologists. Or cockroaches left alive in a radioactive wasteland. Or vampires.

The lack of sleep was getting to me.

♦ ♦ ♦

I bolted upright in bed one afternoon because I thought I could hear my nose hairs rubbing together when I breathed. I was one month into the job and was managing, on average, three hours of sleep a day. My skin was starting to look opalescent, my eyes like those of a Hummel. If I couldn't fall asleep when I got home from work, I left the apartment. If I fell asleep only to wake up an hour or two later, I left the apartment. In my rattled state, I felt I could only justify my not-at-work existence if I was a) looking for a new place to live, or b) out enjoying the city.

I kept visiting potential roommates, only to have the interviews fall flat or turn weird. One sausagey man answered his door and sized me up like I was a prostitute he'd ordered. "You can look at the place if you want," he said, "but I've got to tell you, there was a guy here this morning who's interested in the room, and he's gorgeous." Another man answered his door holding a dachshund and dressed in a housecoat patterned with dachshunds. He invited me in, offered me fennel tea, then sat across from me in his living room and asked me to tell him all about myself. As I spoke about my recent move and my new job with the crazy hours, he bounced the dachshund and listened and watched me, his expression more delighted than the circumstances seemed to warrant. At least three times he said, "You just sound so *together*."

I felt anything but together. Bundled up and walking around the city, I felt as confused as Bruce Willis in *The Sixth Sense* and as hazy as Patty Duke in *Valley of the Dolls*. Being from the South, I found snow exotic—but as I was quickly learning, snow in New York is like those toxin-eating footpads they sell in Chinatown: clean for an hour or so, and then nasty. My hands ached and my eyes stung from the cold. I rode the subway just to be underground, and saw a woman sitting on a stool at Columbus Circle playing "Ave Maria" on a saw; a man standing on the platform in Times Square playing the James Bond theme on a violin; and a set of identical twins right out of *The Shining* tap-dancing in Penn Station. When I emerged onto Christopher Street, I was greeted by a man holding a sign that read, *SCREAM AT ME—$1.*

I had a handful of friends who'd been living in the city for years, and I accepted every evening invitation that came my way. Sometimes that meant meeting them for a drink before they went off to dinner, or meeting them for drinks and dinner, or meeting them for a drink after they'd gone to dinner. It made no difference to me because my drink was always coffee (even though in the mornings now, on my way home from work, I would block off my olfactory system with one hand as I rushed past the coffee carts). "New York really agrees with you," one friend told me in a restaurant. "You're so full of life!"

But it was caffeine and exhaustion I was full of. That night, the hours got away from me—I found myself in the Village when I needed to be at work, in Midtown, in just five minutes. I hailed a cab I couldn't afford so that I wouldn't be late and made the mistake of asking the driver if he could please hurry. As we shot like a malfunctioning rocket up Eighth Avenue, zigzagging around delivery trucks, I wondered if going faster made the meter turn more quickly. And did one have to tip more for a speedier trip? Was time money, or was money money?

◆ ◆ ◆

I was ten minutes late. So, it turned out, was Leo. His large canvas bag sat between us as we rode the elevator together to the forty-sixth floor. I had imagined a whole life for Red-Faced Leo: searching for a new apartment; living out of his bag; showering at the gym. He was humming. Not a tune but a single note, low and resonant, like an air conditioner.

"Do they care if you're late?" I asked.

He shot me a look.

"Not you. Us, I mean. Any of us. Do they care if we're late?"

"Ratbag asshole shitters," he said.

I was pretty sure he was referring to a group that included our employers, all the attorneys, and maybe everyone who was in a position of power anywhere, but not me, so I forced a little chuckle and said, "That's exactly right. Ratbag asshole shitters."

The elevator doors opened. Leo hoisted his bag onto his shoulder, stepped off, and slammed his wallet against the card reader. I clocked in behind him and reported to the front desk with an apology for being late.

"No use splitting hairs over spilt milk," Wendell said jovially. "Here's your mission, should you choose to accept it." He handed me my first-ever assignment sheet.

I got a coffee from the kitchenette and reported to the twenty-eighth floor, where a young, sleepy-eyed attorney was working in his office. He looked even more exhausted than I felt. His collar was unbuttoned, his tie was tugged down, and his shirt, when he stood to reach for a binder on the shelf over his desk, was untucked on one side. I logged in at the computer where his secretary normally sat, and reported for duty.

"I'm not ready for you," he said. "I thought I would be, but I'm not. Can you just hang out for a while?" He looked as if he might cry.

I told him of course, and to let me know if he needed anything. He got up and pushed his door closed behind me.

Between 12:30 and 3:30 a.m., surrounded by empty secretary desks, without another living soul in sight, I read *The Moon Is Down* from start to finish and played a half hour of solitaire. I thought maybe the attorney had forgotten about me. When I approached his office, I saw that his door wasn't latched but stood open an inch. I tapped on it, said his name. For maybe thirty seconds, I stood there waiting. Then I eased the door open a few inches.

It stopped at the sole of his shoe.

I tapped again and peeked into the gap just enough to see his pant leg and the untucked half of his shirt.

On his secretary's phone, I called the Operations Group and asked for Wendell.

"Paddy McGillicuddy O'Ryan," he said. "How goes it out in the world?"

"I think my attorney's asleep," I whispered.

"That's OK."

"I mean, I guess he's asleep. He's on the floor in his office. I think he's been there a while."

"Got it," Wendell said. "Tell you what. Come back up to forty-six, and we'll find something else for you to do."

And so I turned off the computer, gathered my book and my coffee cup, and left the prostrate form lying behind the semi-closed door.

I got back to the Operations Group just in time for the Four A.M. Floorshow. This was a nightly tradition, a pick-me-up of sorts wherein someone spontaneously "performed" something—always silly, usually lasting only for a moment or two, and entirely superfluous because most of the staff were performing from midnight until 8:00 a.m. "Four A.M. Floorshow! Four A.M. Floorshow!" Wendell would say, walking among the desks and stirring the air with an index finger. "Jenny's new sweater!" someone might suggest, at which point Jenny would get up and walk around the room like a fashion model, and those who felt like playing along would clap. "Howard," someone might call out from across the room, "do your impression of Jerry Lewis!" and Howard, typing all the while, would holler, "Hey, lady! Hey, you, missus lady person!" to a spattering of applause.

As I walked back to my desk, Wendell announced the floorshow and said to the room, "I think Patrick should show us what his attorney's been up to for the past few hours."

"Could be a secret," Abhinav, the slope-backed man, said.

"Maybe it was a bee-jay," the Joan Didion–esque woman muttered.

"A three-hour bee-jay?" Howard said. "That I'd like to see."

Mr. Norwich—back in his clown wig—tsk'd and slapped his hands over his ears.

All of this was potentially macabre given that we didn't know if the attorney on twenty-eight was dead or alive, but I was so happy to be included and so giddy from lack of sleep that I was ready to lie down on the floor to get a laugh. But before I could embark on my moment in the spotlight, Rebecca got up from her desk and carried her Zippy the Chimp doll over to where I was standing.

"I've been here seven years!" she said. "No one has *ever* asked me to do the floorshow!"

She was kidding, I thought, but when I glanced at her I saw that her lower lip was quivering.

"So do it," Abhinav said.

Rebecca sniffed. She lifted her doll. "This is Zippy."

The room fell silent. We were all waiting, I thought, for the actual floorshow, given that she'd been carrying this monkey around for at least the five weeks I'd been working at the firm.

"What does Zippy do?" I finally asked.

Rebecca's lip stopped quivering. She screwed her mouth into something close to grin, and her eyes twinkled with mischief. "This!" she said.

Then she moved her hands to the doll's ankles, swung him through the air, and brought his nose down on my head.

Zippy's face, it turned out, was made of hard plastic. I felt such a blinding shot of pain that I thought I might pass out, and when the focus came back to my vision, I was seeing flecks of silver. "What the fuck?" I said, clutching my scalp.

"*That's it!*" Mr. Norwich shouted, getting to his feet and reaching for his coat. "*I am not suffering this abuse a minute longer! Not the F word! No sir! I am going home right now, and I am talking to HR tomorrow! I was not hired to wallow around in a pornographic truck stop!*"

Which might have been funny because, whatever a "pornographic truck stop" was, it wasn't the forty-sixth floor of a Manhattan office building. But, for all I knew, Mr. Norwich could have me fired; he'd been with the company twenty-six years. Add to that the fact that, while gathering his things, he snatched off his clown wig and stuffed it into his briefcase, revealing a head as smooth and bald as Yul Brynner's.

I had to step out of his way as he left, and we could all see him as he stood on the other side of the glass wall waiting for the elevator. When it arrived, he got on and pushed the button for the lobby, his eyes meeting no one's, his lips pressed together and jutting forward.

I didn't have to ask if he'd ever stormed out before. It was obvious from the silence in the room that this was, at the very least, a rare occasion. If anyone was going to crack a joke, it would have been Howard, but Howard only resumed typing.

"OK," Wendell said in a subdued voice. "Show's over. Let's all just hope this whole thing—you know—" He didn't finish his sentence but sunk his hands into his pockets and walked back to his desk.

Was *fuck* that much worse than *bee-jay?* I wondered. Or *tits?* And what about *ratbag asshole shitters?* Granted, Mr. Norwich hadn't heard that, but I had. And I was the one who'd been whacked on the head with a plastic monkey, the only one in the room who had a knot rising up on his skull. Was I to be the fall guy in this late-night circus, the one who, out of all of us, was going to get sacked?

◆ ◆ ◆

As it turned out, no one was going to get sacked for a long time. I never understood the hesitation on the part of the firm to fire its employees, but apparently these things had to be handled delicately and couldn't be hung on just one incident; there needed to be multiple infractions recorded, investigated, and filed away. Warnings issued, and then second warnings, and then final warnings. Maybe the people in charge were just too busy to keep up with that end of things. Maybe HR didn't want to be bothered with the creatures of the night unless they absolutely had to.

Rebecca continued to bring a doll to work (Zippy the Chimp was eventually replaced with a creepy, head-sagging Dr. Dolittle) and continued to throw tantrums. She had a full-on breakdown one night wherein she crawled under her desk, curled into a ball, and screamed bloody murder until Wendell talked her into calming down and crawling back out. But it wasn't until later, at the firm's holiday party, that she finally went too far. She was on the "dance floor" (a corner of the cafeteria where they'd cleared away the tables and chairs to make room for drunken attorneys and support staff) when a crown fell out of her mouth. Having just paid good money to a dentist, she dropped to her hands and knees and shoved at people's legs as she searched for the crown; when she found it and saw that one of the partners was about to step on it, she bit his calf. And so her file was put into sufficient order for her to be dismissed.

Red-Faced Leo left his large, canvas bag partially unzipped one evening, and one of the other word processors glimpsed what appeared to be a hatchet. Security was called in, and the bag was revealed to contain not just a hatchet but a dagger, a machete, a gas mask, a set of nunchucks, a six-point Chinese throwing star, and enough cable to rappel down the side of the building from the forty-sixth floor, should the need ever arise. When HR explained to him that he couldn't bring a bag of weapons into the workplace, Leo produced a letter asking the firm to agree to pay all his medical bills should he ever be attacked—by anyone, for any reason—while at the firm. HR refused. Leo tried to bring his bag back to work the next night and was fired.

Howard made it to retirement and announced at the cake-and-soda gathering thrown in his honor that he was fond of us all but regretted ever having stepped foot in the place. Mr. Norwich, at his own retirement gathering, stood up bald and proud and told us he'd made it to "the end" without ever having learned Excel, PowerPoint, Word, or even e-mail.

Wendell eventually quit to make sailboats.

My personal low point on the graveyard shift came halfway through the year and was quiet—was nothing, really, when compared to the nightly theatrics. One morning just as the sun was starting to come up, I was writing a note to an attorney about the headings in his document when the pen I was using ran out of ink. I was managing four, sometimes even five hours of sleep a night by then, but because I insisted on keeping normal hours on the weekends I was still perpetually jetlagged. I sat at my desk, drawing a small, invisible circle over and over on the document, until the Joan Didion–esque woman looked over at me and said from behind her sunglasses, "What in the world is wrong?"

"Nothing," I said.

"You're weeping."

She was right. Tears were running down my cheeks. With a little shrug to convey *Don't worry about me, I'll get through this*, I said, "Oh, my pen ran out of ink."

She stared at me for several moments—concerned or bemused, I couldn't tell which. Then she handed me her pen.

I'd found another temporary sublet by then, and just as it was running out, I'd found my own apartment. I'd made it past the six-month mark without encountering heroin and without moving back to the South. I was halfway through my graveyard sentence, and if I continued to work hard and didn't make any trouble, I thought, New York might let me off for good behavior before the year was out.

Miss Adele Amidst the Corsets

ZADIE SMITH

"Well, that's that," Miss Dee Pendency said, and Miss Adele, looking back over her shoulder, saw that it was. The strip of hooks had separated entirely from the rest of the corset. Dee held up the two halves, her big red slash mouth pulling in opposite directions. "Least you can say it died in battle. Doing its duty."

"Bitch, I'm on in ten minutes."

"*When an irresistible force like your ass . . .* "

"Don't sing."

"*Meets an old immovable corset like this . . . You can bet as sure as you liiiiive!*"

"It's your fault. You pulled too hard."

"*Something's gotta give, something's gotta give, SOMETHING'S GOT-TA GIVE.*"

"You pulled too hard."

"Pulling's not your problem." Dee lifted her bony, white Midwestern leg up onto the counter, in preparation to put on a thigh-high. With a heel she indicated Miss Adele's mountainous box of chicken and rice: "Real talk, baby." Miss Adele sat down on a grubby velvet stool before a mirror edged with blown-out bulbs. She was thickening and sagging, in all the same ways, in all the same places, as her father. Plus it was midwinter: her skin was ashy. She felt like some once-valuable piece of mahogany furniture lightly dusted with cocaine. This final battle with her corset had set her wig askew. She was forty-six years old.

"Lend me yours."

"Good idea. You can wear it on your arm."

And tired to death, as the Italians say—tired to *death*. Especially sick of these kids, these "millennials," or whatever they were calling themselves. Always on. No backstage to any of them—only front of house. Wouldn't know a sincere, sisterly friendship if it kicked down the dressing-room door and sat on their faces.

Miss Adele stood up, untaped, put a furry deerstalker on her head, and switched to her comfortable shoes. She removed her cape. Maybe stop with the cape? Recently she had only to catch herself in the mirror at a bad angle, and there was Daddy, in his robes.

"The thing about undergarments," Dee said, "is they can only do so much with the cards they've been dealt. Sorta like Obama?"

"Stop talking."

Miss Adele zipped herself into a cumbersome floor-length padded coat, tested—so the label claimed—by climate scientists in the Arctic.

"Looking swell, Miss Adele."

"Am I trying to impress somebody? Tell Jake I went home."

"He's out front—tell him yourself!"

"I'm heading this way."

"You know what they say about choosing between your ass and your face?"

Miss Adele put her shoulder to the fire door and heaved it open. She caught the punch line in the ice-cold stairwell.

"You should definitely choose one of those at some point."

◆ ◆ ◆

Aside from the nights she worked, Miss Adele tried not to mess much with the East Side. She'd had the same sunny rent-controlled studio apartment on Tenth Avenue and Twenty-Third since '93, and loved the way the West Side communicated with the water and the light, loved the fancy galleries and the big anonymous condos, the High Line funded by bankers and celebrities, the sensation of clarity and wealth. She read the real estate section of the *Times* with a kind of religious humility: the reality of a thirty-four-million-dollar townhouse implied the existence of a mighty being, out there somewhere, yet beyond her imagining. But down here? Depressing. Even worse in the daylight. Crappy old buildings higgledy-piggledy on top of each other, ugly students, shitty pizza joints, delis, tattoo parlors. Nothing bored Miss Adele more than ancient queens waxing lyrical about the good old bad old days. At least the bankers never tried to rape you at knifepoint or sold you bad acid. And then once you got past the Village, everything stopped making sense. Fuck these little streets with their dumbass names! Even the logistics of googling her location—remove gloves, put on glasses, find the phone—were too much to contemplate in a polar vortex. Instead, Miss Adele stalked violently up and down Rivington, cutting her eyes at any soul who dared look up. At the curb she stepped over a frigid pool of yellow fluid, three paper plates frozen within it. What a dump! Let the city pull down everything under East Sixth, rebuild, number it, make it logical, pack in the fancy hotels—not just one or two but a whole bunch of them. Don't half gentrify—follow through. Stop preserving all this old shit. Miss Adele had a right to her opinions. Thirty years in a city gives you the right. And now that she was, at long last, no longer beautiful, her opinions were all she had. They were all she had left to give to people. Whenever her disappointing twin brother, Devin, deigned to call her from his three-kids-and-a-Labradoodle, goofy-sweater-wearing, golf-playing, liberal-Negro-wet-dream-of-a-Palm-Springs-fantasy existence, Miss Adele made a point of gathering up all her hard-won opinions and giving them to him good. "I wish he could've been mayor forever. FOR-EVAH. I wish he was my boyfriend. I wish he was my daddy." Or: "They should frack the hell out of this whole state. We'll get rich, secede from the rest of you dope-smoking, debt-ridden assholes. You the ones dragging us all down." Her brother accused Miss Adele of turning rightward in old age. It would be more accurate to say that she was done with all forms of drama—politics included. That's what she liked about gentrification, in fact: gets rid of all the drama.

And who was left, anyway, to get dramatic about? The beloved was gone, and so were all the people she had used, over the years, as substitutes for the beloved. Every kid who'd ever called her gorgeous had already moved to Brooklyn, Jersey, Fire Island, Provincetown, San Francisco, or the grave. This simplified matters. Work, paycheck, apartment, the various lifestyle sections of the *Times*, Turner Classic Movies, Nancy Grace, bed. Boom. Maybe a little *Downton*. You needn't put your face on to watch *Downton*. That was her routine, and disruptions to it—like having to haul ass across town to buy a new corset—were rare. Sweet Jesus, this cold! Unable to feel her toes, she stopped a shivering young couple in the street. British tourists, as it turned out; clueless, nudging each other, and beaming up at her Adam's apple with delight, like she was in their guidebook, right next to the Magnolia Bakery and the Naked Cowboy. They had a map, but without her glasses it was useless. They had no idea where they were. "Sorry! Stay warm!" they cried, and hurried off, giggling into their North Face jackets. Miss Adele tried to remember that her new thing was that she positively liked all the tourists and missed Bloomberg and loved Midtown and the Central Park nags and all the Prada stores and *The Lion King* and lining up for cupcakes wherever they happened to be located. She gave those British kids her most winning smile. Sashayed round the corner in her fur-cuffed Chelsea boots with the discreet heel. Once out of sight, though, it all fell apart: the smile, the straightness of her spine, everything. Even if you don't mess with it—even when it's not seven below—it's a tough city. New York just expects so much from a girl—acts like it can't stand even the *idea* of a wasted talent or opportunity. And Miss Adele had been around. Rome says: enjoy me. London: survive me. New York: gimme all you got. What a thrilling proposition! The chance to be "all that you might be." Such a thrill—until it becomes a burden. To put a face on—to put a self on—this had once been, for Miss Adele, pure delight. And part of the pleasure had been precisely this: the buying of things. She used to love buying things! Lived for it! Now it felt like effort, now if she never bought another damn thing again she wouldn't even—

Clinton Corset Emporium. No awning, just a piece of cardboard stuck in the window. As Miss Adele entered, a bell tinkled overhead—an actual bell, on a catch wire—and she found herself in a long narrow room—a hallway really—with a counter down the left-hand side and a curtained-off cubicle at the far end, for privacy. Bras and corsets were everywhere, piled on top of each other in anonymous white cardboard boxes, towering up to the ceiling. They seemed to form the very walls of the place.

"Good afternoon," said Miss Adele, daintily removing her gloves, finger by finger. "I am looking for a corset."

A radio was on; talk radio—incredibly loud. Some AM channel bringing the latest from a distant land, where the people talk from the back of their throats. One of those Eastern-y, Russian-y places. Miss Adele was no linguist, and no geographer. She unzipped her coat, made a noise in the back of her own throat, and looked pointedly at the presumed owner of the joint. He sat slumped behind the counter, listening to this radio with a tragic twist to his face, like one of those sad-sack cab drivers you see hunched over the wheel, permanently tuned in to the bad news from back home. And what the point of that was, Miss Adele would never understand. Turn that shit down! Keep your eyes on the road! Lord knows, the day Miss Adele stepped out of the state of Florida was pretty much the last day that godforsaken spot ever crossed her mind.

Could he even see her? He was angled away, his head resting in one hand. Looked to be about Miss Adele's age, but further gone: bloated face, about sixty pounds overweight, bearded, religious type, wholly absorbed by this radio of his. Meanwhile, somewhere back there, behind the curtain, Miss Adele could make out two women talking:

"Because she thinks Lycra is the answer to everything. Why you don't speak to the nice lady? She's trying to help you. She just turned fourteen."

"So she's still growing. We gotta consider that. Wendy—can you grab me a Brava 32B?"

A slip of an Asian girl appeared from behind the curtain, proceeded straight to the counter, and vanished below it. Miss Adele turned back to the owner. He had his fists stacked like one potato, two potato—upon which he rested his chin—and his head tilted in apparent appreciation of what Miss Adele would later describe as "the ranting"—for did it not penetrate every corner of that space? Was it not difficult to ignore? She felt she had not so much entered a shop as some stranger's spittle-filled mouth. RAGE AND RIGHTEOUSNESS, cried this radio—in whatever words it used—RIGHTEOUSNESS AND RAGE. Miss Adele crossed her arms in front of her chest, like a shield. Not this voice—not today. Not any day—not for Miss Adele. And though she had learned, over two decades, that there was nowhere on earth entirely safe from the voices of rage and righteousness—not even the new New York—still Miss Adele had taken great care to organize her life in such a way that her encounters with them were as few as possible. (On Sundays, she did her groceries in a cutoff T-shirt that read *thou shalt*.) As a child, of course, she had been fully immersed—dunked in the local water—with her daddy's hand on the back of her head, with his blessing in her ear. But she'd leapt out of that shallow channel the first moment she was able.

"A corset," she repeated, and raised her spectacular eyebrows. "Could somebody help me?"

"WENDY," yelled the voice behind the curtain, "could you see to our customer?"

The shopgirl sprang up, like a jack-in-the-box, clutching a stepladder to her chest.

"Looking for Brava!" shouted the girl over the radio. She turned her back on Miss Adele, opened the stepladder, and began to climb it. Meanwhile, the owner shouted something at the woman behind the curtain, and the woman, adopting his tongue, shouted something back.

"It is customary, in retail—" Miss Adele began.

"Sorry—one minute," said the girl, came down with a box under her arm, dashed right past Miss Adele, and disappeared once more behind the curtain.

Miss Adele took a deep breath. She stepped back from the counter, pulled her deerstalker off her head, and tucked a purple bang behind her ear. Sweat prickled her face for the first time in weeks. She was considering turning on her heel and making that little bell shake until it fell off its goddamn string when the curtain opened and a mousy girl emerged with her mother's arm around her. They were neither of them great beauties. The girl had a pissy look on her face and moved with an angry slouch, like a prisoner, whereas you could see the mother was at least trying to keep things civilized. The mother looked beat—and too young to have a teenager. Or maybe she was the exact right age. Devin's kids were teenagers. Miss Adele was almost as old as the president. None of this made any sense, and yet you were still expected to accept it, and carry on, as if it were the most natural process in the world.

"Because they're not like hands and feet," a warm and lively voice explained, from behind the curtain. "They grow independently."

"Thank you so much for your advice, Mrs. Alexander," said the mother, the way you talk to a priest through a screen. "The trouble is this thickness here. All the women in our family got it, unfortunately. Curved rib cage."

"But actually, you know—it's interesting—it's a totally different curve from you to her. Did you realize that?"

The curtain opened. The man looked up sharply. He was otherwise engaged, struggling with the antennae of his radio to banish the static, but he paused a moment to launch a little invective in the direction of a lanky, wasp-waisted woman in her early fifties, with a long, humane face—dimpled, self-amused—and an impressive mass of thick chestnut hair.

"Two birds, two stones," said Mrs. Alexander, ignoring her husband, "that's the way we do it here. Everybody needs something different. That's what the big stores won't do for you. Individual attention. Mrs.

Berman, can I give you a tip?" The young mother looked up at the long-necked Mrs. Alexander, a duck admiring a swan. "Keep it on all the time. Listen to me, I know of what I speak. I'm wearing mine right now, I wear it every day. In my day they gave it to you when you walked out of the hospital!"

"Well, you look amazing."

"Smoke and mirrors. Now, all you need is to make sure the straps are fixed right like I showed you." She turned to the sulky daughter and put a fingertip on each of the child's misaligned shoulders. "You're a lady now, a beautiful young lady, you—" Here again she was interrupted from behind the counter, a sharp exchange of mysterious phrases, in which—to Miss Adele's satisfaction—the wife appeared to get the final word. Mrs. Alexander took a cleansing breath and continued: "So you gotta hold yourself like a lady. Right?" She lifted the child's chin and placed her hand for a moment on her cheek. "Right?" The child straightened up despite herself. See, some people are trying to ease your passage through this world—so ran Miss Adele's opinion—while others want to block you at every turn. Think of poor Mama, taking folk round those god-awful foreclosures, helping a family to see the good life that might yet be lived there—that had just as much chance of sprouting from a swamp in the middle of nowhere as any place else. That kind of instinctive, unthinking care. If only Miss Adele had been a simple little fixer-upper, her mother might have loved her unconditionally! Now that Miss Adele had grown into the clothes of middle-aged women, she noticed a new feeling of affinity toward them, far deeper than she had ever felt for young women back when she could still fit into the hot pants of a showgirl. She walked through the city struck by middle-aged women and the men they had freely chosen, strange unions of the soft and the hard. In shops, in restaurants, in line at the CVS. She always had the same question. Why in God's name are you still married to this asshole? Lady, your children are grown. You have your own credit cards. You're the one with life force. Can't you see he's just wallpaper? It's not 1850. This is New York. Run, baby, run!

"Who's waiting? How can I help you?"

Mother and daughter duck followed the shopgirl to the counter to settle up. The radio, after a brief pause, made its way afresh up the scale of outrage. And Miss Adele? Miss Adele turned like a flower to the sun.

"Well, I need a new corset. A strong one."

Mrs. Alexander beamed: "Come right this way."

Together, they stepped into the changing area. But as Miss Adele reached to pull the curtain closed behind them both—separating the ladies from the assholes—a look passed between wife and husband and Mrs. Alexander caught the shabby red velvet swathe in her hand, a little higher up than Miss Adele had, and held it open.

"Wait—let me get Wendy in here." An invisible lasso, thought Miss Adele. He throws it and you go wherever you're yanked. "You'll be all right? The curtain's for modesty. You modest?"

Oh, she had a way about her. Her face expressed emotion in layers: elevated, ironic eyebrows, mournful violet eyes, and a sly, elastic mouth. Miss Adele could have learned a lot from a face like that. A face straight out of an old movie. But which one, in particular?

"You're a funny lady."

"A life like mine, you have to laugh—Marcus, please, one minute—" He was barking at her, still—practically insisting, perhaps, that she *stop talking to that schwarze*, which prompted Mrs. Alexander to lean out of the changing room to say something very like: *What is wrong with you? Can't you see I'm busy here?* On the radio, strange atonal music replaced the ranting; Mrs. Alexander stopped to listen to it, and frowned. She turned back to her new friend and confidante, Miss Adele. "Is it OK if I don't measure you personally? Wendy can do it in a moment. I've just got to deal with—but listen, if you're in a hurry, don't panic, our eyes, they're like hands."

"Can I just show you what I had?"

Miss Adele unzipped her handbag and pulled out the ruin.

"Oh! You're breaking my heart! From here?"

"I don't remember. Maybe ten years ago?"

"Makes sense, we don't sell these any more. Ten years is ten years. Time for a change. What's it to go under? Strapless? Short? Long?"

"Everything. I'm trying to hide some of this."

"You and the rest of the world. Well, that's my job." She leaned over and put her lips just a little shy of Miss Adele's ear: "What you got up there? You can tell me. Flesh or feathers?"

"Not the former."

"Got it. WENDY! I need a Futura and a Queen Bee, corsets, front fastening, forty-six. Bring a forty-eight, too. Marcus—please. One *minute*. And bring the Paramount in, too! The crossover! Some people," she said, turning to Miss Adele. "You ask them these questions, they get offended. Everything offends them. Personally, I don't believe in 'political correctness.'" She articulated the phrase carefully, with great sincerity, as if she had recently coined it. "My mouth's too big. I gotta say what's on my mind! Now, when Wendy comes, take off everything to here and try each corset on at its tightest setting. If you want a defined middle, frankly it's going to hurt. But I'm guessing you know that already."

"Loretta Young," called Miss Adele to Mrs. Alexander's back. "You look like Loretta Young. Know who that is?"

"Do I know who Loretta Young is? Excuse me one minute, will you?"

Mrs. Alexander lifted her arms comically, to announce something to her husband, the only parts of which Miss Adele could fully comprehend were the triple repetition of the phrase "Loretta Young." In response, the husband made a noise somewhere between a sigh and a grunt.

"Do me a favor," said Mrs. Alexander, sighing, letting her arms drop, and turning back to Miss Adele, "put it in writing, put it in the mail. He's a reader."

The curtain closed. But not entirely. An inch hung open and through it Miss Adele watched a silent movie—silent only in the sense that the gestures were everything. It was a marital drama, conducted in another language, but otherwise identical to all those she and Devin had watched as children, through a crack in the door of their parents' bedroom. God save Miss Adele from marriage! Appalled, fascinated, she watched the husband, making the eternal, noxious point in a tone Miss Adele could conjure in her sleep (*You bring shame upon this family*), and Mrs. Alexander, apparently objecting (*I've given my life to this family*); she watched as he became belligerent (*You should be ashamed*) and she grew sarcastic (*Ashamed of having a real job? You think I don't know what "pastoral care" means? Is that God's love you're giving to every woman in this town?*), their voices weaving in and out of the hellish noise on the radio, which had returned to ranting (*THOU SHALT NOT!*).

Miss Adele strained to separate the sounds into words she might google later. If only there was an app that translated the arguments of strangers! A lot of people would buy that app. Hadn't she just been reading in the *Times* about some woman who had earned eight hundred grand off such an app— just for having the idea for the app. (And Miss Adele, who had always considered herself a person of many ideas, really a very creative person—even if she was fourteen pounds overweight—a person who happened never to have quite found her medium; a person who, in more recent years, despite her difficulties finding suitable undergarments, had often wondered whether the new technologies had caught up with precisely the kind of creative talents she herself had long possessed, although they had been serially and tragically neglected, first by her parents—who had let shame blind them—and later by her teachers, who were the first to suggest, fatally, that Devin was smarter; and finally in New York, where her gifts had taken second place to her cheekbones and her ass.) You want to know what Miss Adele would do with eight hundred grand? Buy a studio down in Battery Park, and do nothing all day but watch the helicopters fly over the water. Stand at the floor-to-ceiling window, bathed in expensive light, wearing the kind of silk kimono that hides a multitude of sins.

Sweating with effort and anxiety, in her windowless East Village cubicle, Miss Adele got stuck again at her midsection, which had become, somehow, Devin's midsection. Her fingers fumbled with the heavy-duty eyes and hooks. She found she was breathing heavily. ABOMINATION, yelled the radio. *Get it out of my store!* cried the man, in all likelihood. *Have mercy!* pleaded the woman, basically. No matter how she pulled, she simply could not contain herself. So much effort! She was making odd noises, grunts almost.

"Hey, you OK in there?"

"First doesn't work. About to try the second."

"No, don't do that. Wait. Wendy, get in there."

In a second, the girl was in front of her, and as close as anybody had been to Miss Adele's bare body in a long time. Without a word, a little hand reached out for the corset, took hold of one side of it and, with surprising strength, pulled it toward the other end until both sides met. The girl nodded, and this was Miss Adele's cue to hook the thing together while the girl squatted like a weight lifter and took a series of short, fierce breaths. Outside of the curtain, the argument had resumed.

"Breathe," said the girl.

"They always talk to each other like that?" asked Miss Adele. The girl looked up, uncomprehending.

"OK now?"

"Sure. Thanks."

The girl left Miss Adele alone to examine her new silhouette. It was as good as it was going to get. She turned to the side and frowned at three days of chest stubble. She pulled her shirt over her head to see the clothed effect from the opposite angle, and in the transition got a fresh view of the husband, still berating Mrs. Alexander, though in a violent whisper. He had tried bellowing over the radio; now he would attempt to tunnel underneath it. Suddenly he looked up at Miss Adele—not as far as her eyes, but tracing, from the neck down, the contours of her body. RIGHTEOUS-NESS, cried the radio, RIGHTEOUSNESS AND RAGE! Miss Adele felt like a nail being hammered into the floor. She grabbed the curtain and yanked it shut. She heard the husband end the conversation abruptly—as had been her own father's way—not with reason or persuasion, but with sheer volume. Above the door to the emporium, the little bell rang.

"Molly! So good to see you! How're the kids? I'm just with a customer!" Mrs. Alexander's long pale fingers curled round the hem of the velvet. "May I?"

Miss Adele opened the curtain.

"Oh, it's good! See, you got shape now."

Miss Adele shrugged, dangerously close to tears: "It works."

"Marcus said it would. He can spot a corset size at forty paces, believe me. He's good for that at least. So, if that works, the other will work. Why not take both? Then you don't have to come back for another twenty years! It's a bargain." She turned to shout over her shoulder, "Molly, I'm right with you," and threw open the curtain.

In the store there had appeared a gaggle of children, small and large, and two motherly looking women, who were greeting the husband and being greeted warmly in turn, smiled at, truly welcomed. Miss Adele picked up her enormous coat and began the process of re-weatherizing herself. She observed Mrs. Alexander's husband as he reached over the counter to joke with two young children, ruffling their hair, teasing them, while his wife—whom she watched even more intently—stood smiling over the whole phony operation, as if all that had passed between him and her were nothing at all, some silly wrangle about the accounts or whatnot. Oh, Loretta Young. Whatever you need to tell yourself, honey. Family first! A phrase that sounded, to Miss Adele, so broad, so empty; one of those convenient pits into which folk will throw any and everything they can't deal with alone. A hole for cowards to hide in. Under its cover you could even have your hands round your wife's throat, you could have your terrified little boys cowering in a corner—yet when the bell rings, it's time for iced tea and "Family First!" with all those nice church-going ladies as your audience, and Mama's cakes, and smiles all round. *These are my sons, Devin and Darren.* Two shows a day for seventeen years.

"I'll be with you in one minute, Sarah! It's been so long! And look at these girls! They're really tall now!"

On the radio, music again replaced the voice—strange, rigid, unpleasant music, which seemed to Miss Adele to be entirely constructed from straight lines and corners. Between its boundaries, the vicious game restarted, husband and wife firing quick volleys back and forth, at the end of which he took the radio's old-fashioned dial between his fingers and turned it up. Finally Mrs. Alexander turned from him completely, smiled tightly at Miss Adele, and began packing her corsets back into their boxes.

"Sorry, but am I causing you some kind of issue?" asked Miss Adele, in her most discreet tone of voice. "I mean, between you and your . . . "

"You?" said Mrs. Alexander, and with so innocent a face Miss Adele was tempted to award her the Oscar right then and there, though it was only February. "How do you mean, issue?"

Miss Adele smiled.

"You should be on the stage. You could be my warm-up act."

"Oh, I doubt you need much warming. No, you don't pay me, you pay him." A small child ran by Mrs. Alexander with a pink bra on his head. Without a word she lifted it, folded it in half, and tucked the straps neatly within the cups. "Kids. But you gotta have life. Otherwise the whole thing moves in one direction. You got kids?"

Miss Adele was so surprised, so utterly wrong-footed by this question, she found herself speaking the truth.

"My twin—he has kids. We're identical. I guess I feel like his kids are mine, too."

Mrs. Alexander put her hands on her tiny waist and shook her head. "Now, that is *fascinating*. You know, I never thought of that before. Genetics is an amazing thing—amazing! If I wasn't in the corset business, I'm telling you, that would have been my line. Better luck next time, right?" She laughed sadly, and looked over at the counter. "He listens to his lectures all day; he's educated. I missed out on all that." She picked up two corsets packed back into their boxes. "OK, so—are we happy?"

Are you happy? Are you really happy, Loretta Young? Would you tell me if you weren't, Loretta Young, the Bishop's Wife? Oh, Loretta Young, Loretta Young! Would you tell anybody?

"Molly, don't say another word—I know exactly what you need. Nice meeting you," said Mrs. Alexander to Miss Adele, over her shoulder, as she took her new customer behind the curtain. "If you go over to my husband, he'll settle up. Have a good day."

Miss Adele approached the counter and placed her corsets upon it. She stared down a teenage girl leaning on the counter to her left, who now, remembering her manners, looked away and closed her mouth. Miss Adele returned her attention to the side of Mrs. Alexander's husband's head. He picked up the first box. He looked at it as if he'd never seen a corset box before. Slowly he wrote something down in a notepad in front of him. He picked up the second and repeated the procedure, but with even less haste. Then, without looking up, he pushed both boxes to his left, until they reached the hands of the shopgirl, Wendy.

"Forty-six fifty," said Wendy, though she didn't sound very sure. "Um . . . Mr. Alexander—is there discount on Paramount?"

He was in his own world. Wendy let a finger brush the boss's sleeve, and it was hard to tell if it was this—or something else—that caused him to now sit tall in his stool and thump a fist upon the counter, just like Daddy casting out the devil over breakfast, and start right back up shouting at his wife—some form of stinging question—repeated over and over, in that relentless way men have. Miss Adele strained to understand it. Something like: *You happy now?* Or: *Is this what you want?* And underneath, the unmistakable: *Can't you see he's unclean?*

"Hey, you," said Miss Adele, "Yes, you, sir. If I'm so disgusting to you? If I'm so beneath your contempt? Why're you taking my money? Huh? You're going to take my money? *My* money? Then, please: look me in the eye. Do me that favor, OK? Look me in the eye."

Very slowly a pair of profoundly blue eyes rose to meet Miss Adele's own green contacts. The blue was unexpected, like the inner markings of some otherwise unremarkable butterfly, and the black lashes were wet and long and trembling. His voice, too, was the opposite of his wife's, slow and deliberate, as if each word had been weighed against eternity before being chosen for use.

"You are speaking to me?"

"Yes, I'm speaking to you. I'm talking about customer service. Customer service. Ever hear of it? I am your customer. And I don't appreciate being treated like something you picked up on your shoe!"

The husband sighed and rubbed at his left eye.

"I don't understand—I say something to you? My wife, she says something to you?"

Miss Adele shifted her weight to her other hip and very briefly considered a retreat. It did sometimes happen, after all—she knew from experience—that is, when you spent a good amount of time alone—it did sometimes come to pass—when trying to decipher the signals of others—that sometimes you mistook—

"Listen, your wife is friendly—she's civilized, I ain't talking about your wife. I'm talking about *you*. Listening to your . . . whatever the hell that is—your *sermon*—blasting through this store. You may not think I'm godly, brother, and maybe I'm not, but I am in your store with good old-fashioned American money and I ask that you respect that and you respect me."

He began on his other eye, same routine.

"I see," he said, eventually.

"Excuse me?"

"You understand what is being said, on this radio?"

"*What?*"

"You speak this language that you hear on the radio?"

"I don't *need* to speak it to understand it. And why you got it turned up to eleven? I'm a customer—whatever's being said, I don't want to listen to that shit. I don't need a translation—I can hear the *tone*. And don't think I don't see the way you're looking at me. You want to tell your wife about that? When you were peeping at me through that curtain?"

"Now I'm looking at you?"

"Is there a problem?" said Mrs. Alexander. Her head came out from behind the curtain.

"I'm not an idiot, OK?" said Miss Adele.

The husband brought his hands together, somewhere between prayer and exasperation, and shook them at his wife as he spoke to her, over Miss Adele's head, and around her comprehension.

"Hey—talk in English. English! Don't disrespect me! Speak in English!"

"Let me translate for you: I am asking my wife what she did to upset you." Miss Adele turned and saw Mrs. Alexander, clinging to herself and swaying, less like Loretta now, more like Vivien Leigh swearing on the red earth of Tara.

"I'm not talking about her!"

"Sir, was I not polite and friendly to you? Sir?"

"First up, I ain't no sir—you live in this city, use the right words for the right shit, OK?"

There was Miss Adele's temper, bad as ever. She'd always had it. Even before she was Miss Adele, when she was still little Darren Bailey, it had been a problem. Had a tendency to go off whenever she felt herself on uncertain ground, like a cheap rocket—the kind you could buy back home in the same store you bought a doughnut and a gun. Short-fused and likely to explode in odd, unpredictable directions, hurting innocent bystanders—often women, for some reason. How many women had stood opposite Miss Adele with the exact same look on their faces as Mrs. Alexander wore right now? Starting with her mother and stretching way out to kingdom come. The only Judgment Day that had ever made sense to Miss Adele was the one where all the hurt and disappointed ladies form a line—a chorus line of hurt feelings—and one by one give you your pedigree, over and over, for all eternity.

"Was I rude to you?" asked Mrs. Alexander, the color rising in her face. "No, I was not. I live, I let live."

Miss Adele looked around at her audience. Everybody in the store had stopped what they were doing and fallen silent.

"I'm not talking to you. I'm trying to talk to this gentleman here. Could you turn off that radio so I can talk to you, please?"

"OK," he said, "so maybe you leave now."

"Second of all," said Miss Adele, counting it out on her hand, though there was nothing to follow in the list, "contrary to appearances, and just as a point of information, I am not an Islamic person? I mean, I get it. Pale, long nose. But no. So you can hate me, fine—but you should know who you're hating and hate me for the right reasons. Because right now? You're hating in the wrong direction—you and your radio are wasting your hate. If you want to hate me, file it under N-word. As in African American. Yeah."

The husband frowned and held his beard in his hand.

"You are a very confused person. I don't care what you are. All such conversations are very boring to me, in fact."

"Oh, I'm *boring* you?"

"Honestly, yes. And you are also being rude. So now I ask politely: leave, please."

"Baby, I am out that door, believe me. But I am not leaving without my motherfucking corset."

The husband slipped off his stool, finally, and stood up. "You leave now, please."

"Now, who's gonna make me? 'Cause you can't touch me, right? That's one of your laws, right? I'm unclean, right? So who's gonna touch me? Miss Tiny Exploited Migrant Worker over here?"

"Hey, I'm international student! NYU!"

Et tu, Wendy? Miss Adele looked sadly at her would-be ally. Wendy was a whole foot taller now, thanks to the stepladder, and she was using the opportunity to point a finger in Miss Adele's face. Miss Adele was tired to death.

"Just give me my damn corset."

"Sir, I'm sorry but you really have to leave now," said Mrs. Alexander, walking toward Miss Adele, her elegant arms wrapped around her itty-bitty waist. "There are minors in here, and your language is not appropriate."

"Y'all call me 'sir' one more time," said Adele, speaking to Mrs. Alexander, but still looking at the husband, "I'm gonna throw that radio right out that fucking window. And don't you be thinking I'm an anti-Semite or some shit . . . " Miss Adele faded. She had the out-of-body sense that she was watching herself on the big screen, at one of those screenings she used to attend, with the beloved boy, long dead, who'd adored shouting at the screen, back when young people still went to see old movies in a cinema. Oh, if that boy were alive! If he could see Miss Adele up on that screen right now! Wouldn't he be shouting at her performance—wouldn't he groan and cover his eyes! The way he had at Joan and Bette and Barbara, as they made their terrible life choices, all of them unalterable, no matter how loudly you shouted.

"It's a question," stated Miss Adele, "of simple politeness. Po-lite-ness."

The husband shook his shagg y head and laughed, softly.

"See, you're trying to act like I'm crazy, but from the moment I stepped up in here, you been trying to make me feel like you don't want someone like me up in here—why you even denying it? You can't even look at me now! I know you hate black people. I know you hate homosexual people. You think I don't know that? I can look at you and know that."

"But you're wrong!" cried the wife.

"No, Eleanor, maybe she's a divinity," said the husband, putting out a hand to stop the wife continuing, "maybe she sees into the hearts of men."

"You know what? It's obvious this lady can't speak for herself when you're around. I don't even want to talk about this another second. My money's on the counter. This is twenty-first-century New York. This is America. And I've paid for my goods. Give me my goods."

"Take your money and leave. I ask you politely. Before I call the police."

"I'm sure he'll go peacefully," predicted Mrs. Alexander, tearing the nail of her index finger between her teeth, but, instead, one more thing went wrong in Miss Adele's mind, and she grabbed that corset right out of Mrs. Alexander's husband's hands, kicked the door of Clinton Corset Emporium wide open, and high-tailed it down the freezing street, slipped on some ice and went down pretty much face first. After which, well, she had some regrets, sure, but there wasn't much else to do at that point but pick herself up and run, with a big, bleeding dramatic graze all along her left cheek, wig askew, surely looking to everyone she passed exactly like some Bellevue psychotic, a hot crazy mess, an old-school deviant from the fabled city of the past—except, every soul on these streets was a stranger to Miss Adele. They didn't have the context, didn't know a damn thing about where she was coming from, nor that she'd paid for her goods in full, in dirty green American dollars, and was only taking what was rightfully hers.

Near The Edge Of Darkness

COLUM MCCANN

In the early 1990s I was researching a novel, part of which entailed getting to know some of the homeless people in the tunnels of New York. At that stage—before physics was applied to the World Trade Center, and the Guiliani administration locked off most access to the underground—there were a couple thousand people living beneath the city.

A crack tunnel down in the Broadway-Lafayette station. A heroin tunnel not far away on Second Avenue. Organized prostitution in subways in Chinatown. Immigrant families in the railway tunnels under Riverside Park. Specious rumors of a community under Grand Central Station, fueled by journalists who wanted to apply a name to the idea: the mole people.

The idea of living underground, in the dark, feeds the most febrile part of our beings. The tunnels operate as the subconscious minds of our city: all that is dark and all that is feared, pulsing along in the arteries beneath us. There are seven hundred miles of tunnels in the city. The capacity for shadowplay is infinite. There are hundreds of nooks and crannies, escape hatches, ladders, electrical rails, control rooms, cubbyholes. An overwhelming sense of darkness, made darker still by small pinpoints of light from the grates of topside. And then there are the rats, in singles, pairs, dozens, sometimes hundreds at your feet. If anything can happen, the worst probably will.

I visited the various tunnels, on and off, for the best part of eighteen months. Sometimes I went with the transit cops and the Metro North Police; other times I went alone. I didn't try to disguise myself as a homeless person. There is nothing more obvious than a middle-class white man trying to pass himself as authentic. I didn't carry a weapon, or a phone (were there even phones at that time?), and I kept money to a minimum. Cigarettes were a currency: I kept packs in hidden pockets. Most of the time I hung around outside the tunnels, waiting for someone to chat to, a sort of cigarette firefly, pulsing red at the end of the tunnel. When I lit their smoke, I would have a chance to look in their eyes and make a split-second decision about who they were and if I could trust them to take me into the darkness. There was something Promethean about it. Here I was, at the edge of the dark, giving fire.

The tunnel under Riverside Park was one of the most fascinating of all since it seemed to embody the character and texture of most of the other tunnels. At the mouth, by 72nd Street, there was a good deal of light under the railwork fretwork. It was possible to believe that it was a scene from the Great Depression—immigrants leaning against their shacks, looking out over the Hudson, warming their hands over barrel fires. The deeper you went into the tunnel, the darker it became, down by 79th, 96th, all the way to 125th where it blazed out into daylight once more.

A consequence of darkness is mystery. The farther underground I went, the more mysterious the people became. A pair of runaways. A Vietnam vet. A man rumored to have once worked for CBS. A former University of Alabama football player who now looked at his life through the telescope of a crack pipe. Bernard Issacs, a man with long dreadlocks who called himself Lord of the Tunnel. Another man, Marco, a flute player, who lived in a cubbyhole in the rafters and wanted to be known as Glaucon. And Tony, a pedophile who pushed his shopping cart full of tiny teddy bears along the edge of the tracks.

The Amtrak train thundered through their lives. There were murals and tags on the wall: Martin Luther King, Cost Revs 2000, Salvador Dali's melting clocks, and even a replica of *Guernica*. The light slanting in from the grates up above formed a sort of natural spotlight. You could tell the time of day from the angle of the sunlight streaming down from above. Once, in spring, I watched the cherry blossom leaves fall down through the grates in the ceiling while the light caught the leaves in their peculiar acrobatic spin. The rats tramped through the cherry blossom leaves: the moisture rose where their paws pressed.

You could take ten paces and you were in an almost complete darkness. The distant light became hallucinogenic. Metal dust from the trains hung in the air. It was otherwordly . . . until it wasn't.

• • •

Each time I went to Riverside Park I saw a woman, Denise, who lived just inside the mouth of the tunnel, around about 74th or 75th: in other words, she lived near the edge of darkness, in a shack slung together from wood and metal.

Denise saw me one day cleaning my hands with a paper towel from an airplane sachet. "Can I've one of those?" she asked. I was traveling extensively, and so I had pockets full of them. Delta. United. Aer Lingus. I reached into my vest pocket and handed her a couple of sachets. She went to her toes and kissed me on the cheek. Denise was probably in her early thirties but the world had pushed an extra decade onto her. She cleaned her hands meticulously and then tucked the extra sachets away. "Thank you, Irish," she said.

The next time I visited I brought her a couple more sachets. British Airways. Virgin. Lufthansa. Denise was delighted and tucked them away in a fake fur coat that she wore, sometimes even in summertime. There was something so private and personal about the transaction: it was ours. She went to the tips of her toes and kissed my forehead.

One morning I decided to make Denise's day. I went to a supermarket and searched the aisles for an extra-large packet of wet wipes. This would last her the whole winter, I thought. Hundreds of wet wipes in one convenient plastic container. She would be so pleased. No more furtive cleaning of her hands. She could do it whenever she liked.

I entered the tunnel at 98th Street and slid down an embankment, jumped down into the tunnel, walked down toward the Seventies where Denise was living. I knocked on the aluminum sheet that went for a door. I was already patting myself on the back. She invited me in, but I remained in the doorway. I didn't like going into the shacks alone. I handed over the bag of Handi Wipes. Denise took the bag and peered inside. "What the fuck?"

She ripped it open and pulled one after the other out like a magician pulling a cloth from a dark plastic hat. The wipes fluttered to the dirt floor.

"The fuck?" she said again. A shine in her eyes. A grief.

I thought of her for a moment as bitter, tired, ungrateful, but then it struck me: What had I been thinking? Denise could not carry a huge box of tissues in her imitation fur coat. She liked the anonymity of the small sachets. They were so neat and tidy. She didn't want the humiliation of removing a wipe out of a plastic box. Maybe she did not want to carry around a single thing that might remind her of diapers. Perhaps, I panicked, she might once have had a child? Or maybe there was something about the airplane insignias? Could she have had another life? Why was I freezing her in her moment of homelessness? What did I know? What could I know? Who was she, anyway? Was she just a woman with tunnel dust on her hands? Or was there something far more complete behind her that I had refused to see?

I stepped away, along through the tunnel and out along the Hudson.

In those days, food was seldom a problem for the homeless in New York. There was always a restaurant where a friendly sous-chef could be found, or a doorman on Riverside Drive who might share his sandwich, or at least a dumpster at the back of a fast-food joint where more than enough food could be salvaged. Nor was there ever really a problem with clothing—in the nineties, there were more than enough charity organizations in the city to give out coats and boots and hats. Nor was even the prospect of breaking the law such a huge dilemma for the homeless—the cops more or less turned a blind eye. The homeless were largely unseen, unheard, left alone.

No, these things weren't a problem. Dignity was a problem. Dignity was the biggest problem of all. I had taken Denise's, or sidestepped it at least, and she had let me know.

Nothing ends really. A few weeks later I was in Denise's shack and noticed the plastic bin again. All the handywipes were gone. Perhaps they had been used, I don't know, I'll never know. She was using the plastic bin for odds and ends: a Giants keyring, a crack pipe, a swirling plastic straw, and a very small empty picture frame. The world we get is sometimes more than enough. It's the picture I carry with me somehow now, an empty space where the imagination dwells.

The Children Suicides

MARIA VENEGAS

Layla comes through the glass door, her thick black hair pulled back in a ponytail, the silver frame of her glasses resting on her nose. On her face is the same expression that settled there a few weeks ago, around the same time she started having chronic stomach pains. She slings her coat and backpack onto the back of a chair. "H" is written across the front of her oversized crimson sweatshirt. She hopes to go to Harvard someday. The weight of her backpack pulls the chair backward and sends it crashing to the ground.

"Hi, Laylers," I say, looking up from helping Joshua with a word problem.

"Hi, Laylers," Cynthia repeats.

"Hi, Laylers," says Miguel.

"Hi, Laylers," says Christina, so that "Laylers" goes echoing through the room before vanishing.

Layla turns and glares at Christina.

"Don't. Call. Me. That," she forces through her teeth, and the room falls silent. This is so out of her character. I have always called her Laylers as a term of endearment and she has never reacted like this, but for the past few weeks she's been on edge. They all have. Though nothing has been reported on the suicides, it's as though they can already feel the tension in the air. Layla's face puckers, she bursts into tears, turns and runs to the back of the room. I follow.

"I'm sorry," I say, giving her a hug. She is one of about twenty-five students that attend Still Waters in a Storm. Still Waters was founded in 2008 by Stephen Haff, a Yale graduate who taught at a high school in Bushwick for several years. It started as a writing sanctuary, but evolved into an after-school program where children from the local public and charter schools come for homework help during the week. They arrive toting brown paper bags with snacks from home, or black plastic bags with snacks from the local bodega. Tutoring wraps up at 5:30 and depending on the day of the week, they either have a violin or Latin lesson, or meet with their mentor for their creative writing group.

Layla is part of a writing group that I mentor, and though she's a very talented writer, in the past few weeks she has been unable to write a single sentence. On Saturdays, we still have the writing sanctuary, and usually have an author visit and lead the kids in a writing workshop. Zadie Smith was our visiting author recently, and in the days leading up to her visit we read one of her short stories, "Accidental Hero." The story is sort of an homage to her father, who had fought in the Second World War. Though he had stormed Normandy, he had always felt more like a traitor than a hero because on the night he was supposed to be keeping watch while his platoon slept, he decided he wanted a cup of tea. He lit a fire. While the flames roared and the water boiled, the enemy saw the glow and attacked, killing several of his comrades. The guilt would never let him feel like a hero, but to his daughter he would always be one. Had he died on that night, she would have never been.

After reading the story, we gave the kids a few prompts and then let them write for thirty minutes. We always encourage them to let their imaginations wander, to not be afraid of going to difficult places, to write from their hearts, trust their instincts, and follow their thoughts wherever they may lead.

On the day we read Zadie Smith's story, Layla wrote her own version of an accidental hero. It was about her father, a Mexican immigrant who was there on the day the planes hit the towers. He was selling coffee and bagels from a cart outside the World Trade Center, and though his initial instinct had been to run, he stayed and helped the people that were pouring from the buildings. Soon he'd given away everything in his cart and the space around him filled with the sound of sirens wailing, and the occasional thud, followed by the cascading shower each time a body hit the concrete. They were jumping from the buildings. Their life had been reduced to two choices: face the flames, or take that final leap. He grew frightened, and before he knew it he was walking, fast. He joined the throngs crossing over the bridge back to Brooklyn on foot, to meet up with his young wife. Not long after he vacated, the first building crumbled, and he would forever feel like a coward for having left. To Layla, he would always be a hero. She was born three years later.

Christina comes over and apologizes, offers Layla a box of tissues. Layla takes one and wipes her tears away. Layla is ten years old. She's in fifth grade and attends one of the local charter schools. After being in classes for nine hours she always has at least two hours' worth of homework. She's a dedicated student, but in the past few weeks she's been struggling. They all have. Their homework load has been steadily increasing, the pressure rising, as the April Fool's deadline looms.

Now in addition to her regular homework, there's the endless monotony of Common Core practice questions. The Common Core has spilled into our writing sessions, and Layla sits at the table only half listening to the Neruda poem we are discussing while she continues to solve word problems before moving on to the multiple-choice. It's as though she's plugged into an assembly line. She seems to be holding her breath. But there's no room to breathe. No time to decompress. The state exams are right around the corner. Her parents have probably noticed the change in their daughter. The chronic stomachaches, the way she no longer smiles. Perhaps they're afraid to speak up, call attention to themselves, end up getting deported. Where would that leave Layla and her younger sister?

"Did you know that most inner-city kids don't go to college?" she asks, taking another tissue, though it's not so much a question as a statement. Like she has begun to see the cracks through which she might slip. Or perhaps it's her way of asking, what's it all for? All the homework and the stress, if in the end I'm not going to go to college anyway? At her charter school, each hallway has a name: Harvard Row. Yale Square. Dartmouth Path. Princeton Crossway. The Ivy Leagues dangle before her every day like an increasingly illusory target. "Where did you go to college?" she asks.

"The University of Illinois in Champaign-Urbana," I say. She blows her nose. Her glasses are crooked, her face is wet and flushed, red blotches here and there. She's not an emotional kid. None of the students that come here are, but in the last few weeks this has become a daily occurrence. They are breaking down, have begun to snap. Yesterday alone eight kids burst into sobs.

"I wish I could just kill myself," said Ava, staring at the endless practice questions before her, and soon the tears were streaming down her face. Ava is eight years old and attends a local charter school.

"I wish there was a robot that looked like me and could take the test for me," said Natalie, another eight-year-old who attends the public school. I can understand why she feels that a robot could take the test for her. The math questions are all pretty much the same, mostly word problems with different numbers. Once you have the formula down, it's just about plugging in the numbers—any robot can plug in numbers—though it's the reading section that is particularly frustrating for the kids. The questions are, for the most part, written in a way that's misleading. I recently read through a short story with a boy named Marcus. When we got to the multiple-choice questions, we were equally perplexed.

"It can be either A or B," he said, staring at me wild-eyed. I agreed. We re-read the passage, even called Stephen over and asked for his opinion.

"Either A or B seems correct," he said, after reading the passage. We finally all agreed on B. When Marcus returned the next day, it was marked incorrect. He was devastated. If this was any indication of how the exam was going to go, how could he possibly hope to pass?

"I hate reading," he scoffed, and I thought, I don't blame you. I'd hate reading too if it was this confusing.

All of this memorizing and cramming is having adverse effects. Instead of igniting a love for learning, it's snuffing it out. But what choice do they have? Unless their parents opted them out of taking the exams, they must conform, they must complete the equations, even if it's making them feel like robots. Even if it's making them sick. There is something about the standardization of the system, about the ranking and sorting, that feels akin to factory farming. Cattle were born to wander and graze in open, green pastures. They were not meant to be confined to compact spaces and force-fed a diet of corn until their systems start shutting down, so that no matter how many antibiotics they are pumped with, some won't survive. There will be casualties.

What we don't know yet is that we are in Week Seven. That in the seven weeks leading up to this one in 2014, ten New York City public school students have committed suicide. Ten students in seven weeks. An epidemic, as the chancellor called it in a meeting she held with 250 principals, urging them to identify potentially lonely or troubled kids. This advice in itself implies that the individuals who took their lives were suffering from some chronic or pre-existing condition, rather than a situational one. Though there could be any number of factors at play, it's difficult to know what the circumstances were as the media all but ignored the suicides, and the only thing the mayor had to say on the topic was that his pre-K program would curtail student suicides. Other than those of a fifteen-year-old girl, none of the names or ages of the students were released, though they were most likely all underage. Ten suicides in seven weeks. In the past three years there have been thirty-five suicides among public school students in New York City—that's roughly ten suicides per year. Ten suicides in seven weeks is a cluster. What is setting it off? What is pushing these kids over the edge? What is making them turn their backs not only on learning, but on life itself?

I hand Layla another tissue, just so that she'll stop staring at me with that look that seems to say, *I can't take this anymore*. During our last Saturday writing session, she was unable to write a single word. One of the volunteers, a public high school teacher, tried to help her along, but Layla wrote nothing. I worry about Layla. It's as though some vital part of her has already begun to shut down.

Partially Vacated

DW GIBSON

The filing cabinet is broken in Brent Meltzer's downtown Brooklyn office: stacks of folders and pieces of disassembled drawers are strewn across the small room; miscellaneous hardware and tools have been dropped in frustration onto every surface unclaimed by the folders and busted metal parts. There is barely room for Brent, let alone visitors, so we convene in the conference room down the hall. Everyone has left and all the lights are out. The last traces of sun are coming through the windows. Brent, forty, has a knee that won't stop bouncing. He leans back in his chair and tries to wipe the exhaustion from his face.

I saw one building where on the main floor the landlord punched a hole through to the basement. You go down there and there's rooms down there. No certificate of occupancy. So someone's not supposed to live there because there's no windows, and it's a fire hazard. Two young guys rented it. Got it for 2,300 bucks and thought it was a steal, and they don't know it's a firetrap.

Brent has worked for South Brooklyn Legal Services since 2002. His office, which is a UAW union shop that provides free legal advocacy for low-income people living in Brooklyn, is part of a consortium of legal service offices throughout the city, which began in the 1960s using federal funds provided by President Johnson's War on Poverty. Brent has been the manager of the housing unit since 2008.

I come from Canada so with that alone we have different cultural backgrounds. There's some mistrust at times and you want to try and get past some biases. I'm not super judgey. I tell my clients this all the time: "You need to tell me everything because I'm your lawyer, I'm not your parents. Whatever you tell me is pretty much fine." They can tell me they've killed someone and I can't disclose it. The only thing I can disclose is if they're *going* to kill someone. Clients love that one.

He laughs.

It's just a good way of breaking down barriers.

We do have stronger tenant laws here compared to other cities but the pressures are also much, much more here than other cities. The vacancy rates in New York are under five percent. If you get evicted you can't just go down the street. A lot of people are precariously housed in New York at the moment.

I moved to New York in 1999. So I've only known Giuliani and Bloomberg. And I wouldn't say Bloomberg was hostile to us but he wasn't necessarily friendly.

He laughs.

And Giuliani was definitely hostile.

He laughs again.

Bloomberg made the government work. But the question is, for who? For instance, lots of tenants that live in public housing, they're on public assistance. And there's just not communication between those two agencies. It's shocking when you think that's what Bloomberg was all about, getting government to be more efficient and there was no efficiency for poor people. It was all for the Upper East Side and can they call 311 and, you know, get the snow removed. But meanwhile we're paying so much money for people in shelters because these agencies just weren't talking together. You know, lately that's what's been on my mind a lot—how can we make this government reactive for my clients and not just helping, but also thinking about how these agencies can coordinate together and have a better, broader approach.

To me it's just so striking because when I think of the Bloomberg administration, that's what I think of: they're modernizing, computerizing, and doing some really great work. You can go online and check stuff and it's great. But it didn't happen in any of the agencies I work with, the poor people's agencies.

No doubt there's going to be changes with de Blasio. Even the access that we're getting. But what's shocking to me, talking to people I know who are connected to this de Blasio administration, it takes time to get up and running. Yesterday I met with Vicki Been, the head of the Housing Preservation Department. And Vicki is my old law school professor. She is really smart, but we're having this meeting and there was a lot of stuff she just doesn't know. This is a bright professor. It's not her fault, she doesn't know about everything. But she needs to get briefed on it. The Human Resources Commissioner is Steven Banks, who was the head of Legal Aid, but even then he doesn't know everything—and he's one of us. So it's going to take some time.

And I won't lie, we're taking some different tactics with this administration. We'll reach out to them and say we're about to do this, and give them the benefit of the doubt, and say, "Will you work with us on this?" And if they don't, so be it. We'll shame you all to death.

I'm not trying to stop gentrification, I'm just trying to stop my client from being evicted. I'm not opposed to change. And yet there are some that say, "Well yeah, if we allow the neighborhood to start changing it's going to remove long-term housing and that might be something we should be concerned about."

And I'm like, "Well, yes, but if there's more affordable housing and it's real affordable housing, I'm all right with that."

Neighborhoods are going to change. Even people who say, "Oh, gentrification is horrible," it's sometimes rooted in that, "Oh we like these black neighborhoods, these Latino neighborhoods, and now these white people are coming in and ruining it all." And it's not necessarily the case. There are definitely neighborhoods where black middle class professionals move in—is that gentrification? I don't think if you ask most people in Harlem or somewhere else they'd consider that gentrification.

Then it gets complicated. You start talking about class, you start talking about race. Take Crown Heights for a moment. This is predominantly an African American neighborhood and it's becoming white. Really, really white. So what does that mean?

I think in the U.S. it's just hard to disentangle class and race. I live downtown, two blocks from here. I moved to this neighborhood in 2003 and every year they'd have a big Puerto Rican block party and they're all old school rent-stabilized tenants. But since I've been here, they slowly shifted out. This was a strong Latino community around here but it's just gone. I don't know what to think about that. It's problematic that we're losing affordable housing. But if it's just a shifting of ethnic groups, the romantic in me has no problem with it, you know, that's what New York's been about. I mean Carroll Gardens was an Italian neighborhood and there's still some vestiges of that, but it's changing.

When you're talking about gentrification are you talking about class? Are you talking about race? Are you talking about ethnicity, language? There are all these different things. Atlantic Avenue used to be a big Arab population, now they're all out in Bay Ridge and have started up a new community out there. And that's interesting to think about—is that gentrification? I don't know.

For instance, the Fulton Street Mall was the second or third highest grossing commercial strip, after 125th Street and the Hub up in the Bronx. But the language has always been that we need to clean this up. It used to be a Jewish strip but there's not actually a Jewish community living there so people would come in and the talk around the city, we have to clean it up. Which was code to get rid of the Jews.

And then it became an African American strip and if you went down there on the weekend it was a very black shopping commercial district. You know, Big Daddy Kane used to go down there—that's gone. I know an activist, and she had a shop down there, and they basically said you're not good enough for us. Now there's an Armani there because that was a good commercial space. And she's out of business. She couldn't set it up somewhere else because this was where people knew to come. So that, to me, looks like gentrification because it's getting rid of local businesses and putting in big box, corporate businesses. Which I'm happy to have as well, but what has that done and who is that helping?

Often desire to shift a population from its neighborhood is expressed openly. In 1929, a consortium of boosters in lower Manhattan wrote a proposal called the "New York Regional Plan," articulating the removal of the existing population, the reconstruction of high-class residencies, new shops, and physical redevelopment of the Lower East Side highway system so that it would be more directly connected to Wall Street: "The moment an operation of this magnitude and character was started in a district, no matter how squalid it was, an improvement in quality would immediately begin in adjacent property and would spread in all directions. . . . The streets thereabouts would be made cleaner."

Another question is, who's actually getting into new buildings getting developed? Who are they building these for? It's not my client who's on public assistance because the landlords are not going to take them in.

There are definitely some people in my field who think that we should only be working with people at 30 percent of area income and below, and we shouldn't do anything else. But then you're going to squeeze out the middle class. What are going to do with the teachers? Where are the police officers going to live? They're all going to live out on Long Island because they can't afford the city.

It's funny that when I first started and I was in law school I was like, "I'm never going to turn anyone down, that's the worst thing you can do." And honestly that's part of my job now; we have limited resources. I'm one of the biggest housing units in the country and we only have ten or eleven full-time attorneys for all of Brooklyn—2.3 million people. That's not a lot. If we tried to help everyone that came in, gave everyone advice, that's all we'd do. We'd never represent anyone, we'd just be doing intake and nothing else. So it's these hard choices that we have to make and, yeah, it sucks. I always say we should have a therapist on staff for us because I spend half my day going out into the hallway and being very cold and saying, "No, you have to call our hotline; no, I'm not going to give you any advice; I'm not going to help you." So there's that.

And they say, "But I really need an attorney."

And I say, "I know you need an attorney; it's just not going to be our office. We're too understaffed."

You know, I just did a training recently on unconscious bias, and it's been really interesting for me to think when I walk out into the hallway here and I'm helping someone: who do I talk to, who do I not talk to, why do I talk to them? Also making sure that I'm not being—I mean, I'm a gatekeeper, we're an institutional player as well. We spend the day railing against other institutions and it'd be pretty hypocritical for us not to look inward and make sure that we're not keeping people out too. It's trying to catch yourself in all this stuff, being equal to everybody.

I struggle: we turn away a lot of hard cases at times. Those are the ones that, theoretically, we should be doing. Hard cases. But if we just did those we'd never meet our numbers because we also have grants with requirements. So it's finding that balance, and I think we pride ourselves in thinking about ways that we can impact our clients' lives beyond the individual case. The person that really, really needs our help, but who's a long shot, can we justify putting resources into that? I was just talking to someone today, who was just completely railroaded in court. The judge was just wrong. The whole case was just wrong. But they can't afford their rent. So do we go into that case, because there's a right involved? Absolutely there's a right violated. But we'd go in, vindicate that right, and then the person is going to be evicted in two or three months because they can't afford the rent? What do you do with that? I don't know.

I always ask, "What's the exit strategy?" It's horrible to say, like it's the Iraq War. But seriously, if we're going into this, how are we going to get ourselves out, because if we're just going to go in and fight for rights, that's great, but we need to get out because otherwise what's the point?

So we really try to focus on cases where landlords are clearly violating the law. We have at least four or five cases right now where landlords go in and demolish properties. It used to be that they just wouldn't do repairs and through neglect the tenants would just move out. Or they would bring bogus cases. There's one landlord attorney in court and he has kind of a big mouth and he was saying, "I tell my clients bring ten bogus cases, it's only $45 to file. And nine of them get dismissed but you win one and you get your money back plus so much more." And that's the reality.

Housing court is definitely an experience. Go to federal court first and then come to housing court—just to see what a money court is versus a poor person's court. Family court, housing court, criminal court—those are all poor people's courts. There's no justice. And I think a lot of people don't understand that.

Have you gone to housing court before?

You need to go to housing court.

◆ ◆ ◆

The civil courthouse in Downtown Brooklyn sits amid a cluster of bureaucratic towers, adjacent to a mix of 99-cent stores and restaurants where bartenders prefer to be called mixologists. The Quaker-affiliated Brooklyn Friends School, $28,000 a year for pre-school, is just up the block.

Inside the rectangular building of steel and glass leased by the civil courthouse, the elevators break down year-round, the air-conditioner only in summer. Before he was mayor, Bill de Blasio, acting as Public Advocate, put the building's landlord on his "Worst Landlord" watch list. The city's lease for the property expired last week, but, unable to find new housing, housing court—ironically, or perhaps not—will stay in the ailing building.

The line to get in the door— to shuffle through security and wait in a second line for the persnickety elevators—usually runs out the door and all the way down the block well before eight in the morning.

On the tenth floor, the elevator doors open onto a crowded hall, filled with the strident din of heated conversations in every direction. Clumps of three or four people stand together: *always a landlord, always a tenant, usually a landlord's lawyer, occasionally a tenant's lawyer, too.* They are all haggling, trying to reach a settlement; when and if they do, the details are immediately written on a piece of paper and taken into one of the court rooms to receive a judge's approval. There are dozens of courtrooms—some for hearings, some for trial—and all guarantee long waits.

In Room 505, Brent Meltzer is grinding his way through the trial of a tenant client named Noelia Calero. He is cross-examining an engineer, and Noelia's landlord's lawyer, with the landlord at his side, interrupts every question Brent asks—*every question.* He is relentless with his objections and words them for the judge with a sarcastic tone. The judge, unexpectedly, tolerates the behavior, and what's more, upholds the majority of the lawyer's objections. Brent does not mask his disappointment in these instances but at the same time he proves impossible to rile, which, more and more, seems to be the objective of the other lawyer's comportment. Noelia sits at Brent's side, quelling a complex of emotions beneath a stoic expression. After the hearing I tell her I'd like to see her home for myself, and she agrees to meet me there the following morning.

Her apartment is on Linden Avenue in Bushwick. The closest subway stop is nearly a mile up the street. Most of the blocks between her apartment and the L train are filled with three story apartment buildings, some private developments, some public. American and Puerto Rican flags hang from several windows; in a couple of spots, banners of small flags are draped across the street from one lamppost to another. There are laundromats and barbershops and delis. Sea Town Supermarket occupies two separate buildings across the street from each other, and so the smell of fish hits you from both sides. Two live poultry shops, Kikiriki and Pio Pio, operate right next to each other. Three men are standing in front of Pio Pio; each holds a briefcase and wears a dark suit on a hot sidewalk. They point at the building, discussing its facade, trying to hear each other over the clucking chickens.

When I arrive at 98 Linden, Noelia, thirty-two, greets me at the front door and escorts me down the hall to her apartment. The first room we enter is mostly filled by a bed where her mother rests, watching television. Noelia's husband is at work, repairing potholes across the city. Noelia is currently unemployed. She has several years of clerical work experience, mostly with a construction company, where she became versed in building permits and city agencies.

Originally from Nicaragua, Noelia has a calm, sober demeanor. Her hair is brown with honey-colored highlights and pulled back into a tight bun. She takes me through her narrow railroad apartment, requiring passage through

one room to get to the next. We sit at the dining table in her living room. It is a
small trunk of a room, packed with boxes stacked to the ceiling along every wall.

Since I was six I've lived in Bushwick. Before it was a lot of Mexicans, and Puerto Ricans and Dominicans. Now there's a lot of Ecuadorians and Colombians. We lived here for twenty-three years in this apartment.

All the owners that I've known, four or five, haven't been good owners. They don't want to repair, they don't want to fix up. The previous landlord, when he bought this, he tried to kick us out, too. At that point the entire building was rent stabilized. He tried to kick all of us out. We had to go to court. We've always gone to court. We've never had a good landlord here. We've always had problems in this building—always. We've always paid our rent on time for twenty-three years. But every time we have to paint or fix something we've done it out of our pockets.

But these owners have been the worst. They bought the building last year, January of 2013. The previous owner sent a letter in January saying that he sold the building. And we didn't hear from these new people until March when they sent a letter saying they wanted to fix up the building. After the letter we were like, "I'm not going to say no to fixing up the building."

They didn't show up to introduce themselves until a few weeks after. They were actually very polite. They were like, "We just bought the building and we want to make it look nicer." They told us they want to change the floor tiles and paint and fix the bathroom. Basically he said, "Happy tenants, happy landlords."

And I was like, "OK, that's different."

So we moved all our things from the kitchen and the bathroom to this room and the backyard. He said it was going to take a couple weeks.

And we believed him.

And we're going to have a year now with no bathroom, no kitchen. Completely demolished.

Both owners came—two brothers, apparently. They brought one worker with a sledgehammer and electric saw. They took out the walls that divided my bathroom from the neighbor's kitchen. You could just walk right next door and it's completely destroyed. They ripped the walls open and the floors. They completely destroyed the sink that was in the kitchen. In the bathroom, too, they removed the toilet and the sink. There's no tub. You can't even tell where the bathroom was. It's completely destroyed.

It took them less than two hours and they left. It was very chaotic. I didn't realize they were gone already. I opened the door and saw that it was completely destroyed. I could walk over from my bathroom to the neighbor's kitchen. It's my uncle next door. From there it's even worse because you can see straight into the basement.

And I was like, "What in the world is going on here?"

The landlord came two or three days later and I asked him what's going on and he said, "The work, it's bigger than we expected."

And I was like, "You didn't say you were going to break the floors or the walls."

He said, "We want to fix the whole thing, we just want to get work permits."

A few weeks went past and I called him several times to follow up and he didn't get back to me. So one day he shows up with a work permit. And my husband said, "The landlord's here and he says that we have to move out."

I said, "That's not what we agreed upon."

So I looked at the work permit and it's an old work permit—and it was for the third floor. I was upset. So I ripped it off the door and I told him that this is not for my apartment. That's when he got rude and he said, "Well, I just need you guys to leave."

What they want is to get us out of here and fix the apartment and raise the rent. The minute you leave your apartment you don't have your rights anymore.

So I said, "That's not what we agreed on."

And he was basically like, "You're just going to have to go."

"No. We're not moving. And you'll be speaking with my lawyer from now on."

At that point we'd already seen his intentions. It had been a month and he didn't respond, and he didn't come see us, so we'd lawyered up at that time.

We've met other tenants from other buildings that are going through the same things. So we've come together a couple times to help each other out. We know a few of this landlord's tenants that actually were evicted. His workers destroyed the electric meters and the piping so the Department of Buildings actually evicted those people. Right here on Central Avenue, one of the ladies there, she went out one day and when she returned her apartment had been destroyed. From what I know of other buildings, that's his tactic. Destroy the kitchen and the bathroom and people just give up and leave. You know that's been his way of operating in this neighborhood. But too bad for him—he met with the wrong people. Now he has to deal with us. We're not giving up. We're just not.

In the living room where we sit, Noelia has set up a hot plate and a refrigerator. There is no running water in the apartment.

My aunt lives upstairs with my uncle. And that's where we use the bathroom. We started using the kitchen there but as you can see we have a little electric burner. I try to avoid going upstairs as much as possible because I wouldn't want someone invading my space all day long. We're very grateful to her for letting us use her stuff. Even though she's family, she didn't have to do that for a year.

The entrance to the back half of the apartment, with the erstwhile bathroom and kitchen, has been closed off by a hodge-podge barricade of scrap and plywood. Noelia is not allowed to enter that half of her apartment, much less show it to me.

Before, we could go through to the other side of the apartment. We were able to walk in and show whoever came in. One of the channels, 47, Telemundo, they have a Nicaraguan one, and through another foundation that I belong to I actually met him once. So we called and that's how we got the media to come here. And they've been wonderful. They were horrified to see how we were. So they took it on themselves to help us. At first I was like, no, I don't want to be on camera, but then I think about other people and other Hispanics, a lot of them don't speak English, or maybe some of them are illegal and they get scared and they leave. But I'm not illegal, I'm a citizen, and I do speak English, and you're not treating me like this so I'm not leaving.

The landlord wasn't happy we were showing the media like, "Look what you did." He got a partial vacate order so nobody's allowed to go back there because it's unsafe. Of course he destroyed it while we were here so he wasn't concerned about our safety in the beginning. But it's not convenient to him for us to show people. So we can't go back there. Sometimes we hear rats and we hear cats fighting back there—it's crazy.

One of the last times the landlord came he brought a guy to live on the second floor and basically harass us. He basically said he's the security guard. He was hired to be here. So we're like OK, as long as he doesn't touch me, I don't care. But when he first moved here, he used to walk around with bats, with a sledgehammer. He's always screaming. He puts loud music on and it's annoying but I don't let it show that it bothers me. I just sing along to whatever he's playing and I just walk around like it doesn't bother me. His friends come over and they're yelling at two or three in the morning. We call the cops and they don't show up. We've lived here for twenty-three years, we've paid our rent on time, and, you know, you're not going to kick me out of my apartment. Not in that way.

The other day I was thinking: my cousin lives next door with my uncle and we're like sisters, we have such a great relationship. But I think this has put so much stress on all of us that we're all moody and sometimes I don't even want to talk to her.

My husband and I were planning to have a baby and things haven't worked the way we planned. It just hasn't happened. And I think I've just been stressed out. Sometimes I cook here and this is my little pot where I have to put my dirty dishes so I can go upstairs to wash them and sometimes I have to go up there three times a day and I just want to grab it and throw it and, "UGGGHHHHH!"

There are days when I think we should just leave. We visit family in Pennsylvania and they're so comfortable there. And I'm like, "God, I want this." But I grew up in New York. This is home. This is where my heart is. When I look at the New York skyline: "Ah, beautiful!" There isn't any place like New York. As much as I hate the situation and I used to hate Brooklyn because it was so ugly and there was a lot of drugs—this is home. When I walk down the street I know where everything is. This is where my friends are. My family is here. My neighbor, Anna from the third floor, I've known her for twenty-three years. She's seen me grow up. In this building I know everyone. So I can walk up and down the stairs and I feel safe. You don't get that in many buildings.

When we first moved here I was eight years old but I remember it was ugly.

She laughs.

It was ugly. Down the block there are those new houses. But they were empty lots. There were a lot of drugs and people yelling. I used to know the code for "police coming"—it was just ugly. I used to want to move. I hated this place. Before they didn't care about cleaning up Brooklyn. Then they started to build things and it started becoming nicer. There's less drugs. There's still crime but not on this block. I feel safe walking around my neighborhood. And I thought, finally, they're fixing Brooklyn. But I didn't know it was at the expense of the people who were already here. Before it was a lot of Hispanics and a lot of blacks. Now you don't see a lot of them. You see a lot of white people. It's not for us to live in. It's for other people. But I'm like, "Ooh, I want to try that restaurant. It looks nice." I like organic stuff too!

She laughs.

My cousin and I, we love Starbucks, so I say, "I can't wait to have a Starbucks right by!" Everything that's in Manhattan is coming in here—I like that.

But I don't like that it's so expensive. I think change is good when it's for the better. I just wish it were in the way that we could all live here. There are some people and they don't have enough money, and the nicer it gets the more expensive it gets. So where do they go? Until this happened to us I didn't realize that people were getting kicked out of their homes to bring in new ones. Even though I'm still here, it's happening to me too.

There are days when I want to throw in the towel but when we leave this building or have to leave Brooklyn it has to be when I want. Not when someone wants to kick me out like an animal. We have to stick together to be forceful. So I say no. I say we're going to do this. We're going to be treated with respect until this is fixed. And then I can decide whether we stay here or move—on my terms. I'm not going to be kicked out of my neighborhood because it's not just the apartment. It's the neighborhood too. Rent is very expensive. Where would I go? It would mean I move out of New York and that's not something that I'm willing to do.

Who can I complain to? It's just frustrating. We used to have a back-yard and right now the door would have been open. And I would have been cooking or cleaning and my dog would have been in the back yard. Sometimes I don't even know what the weather looks like because the only window we have is in my mother's room. And I have to be in my room or this room—the living room, slash kitchen, slash storage. So it's very frustrating.

Housing court is horrible. Slow. Helpless.

Housing court, to me, is all about landlords and whoever has money and forget everybody else. I feel like they prefer to help people who have money rather than people that don't. There are a lot of laws to help and protect tenants but the courts aren't doing much to enforce them. That is the problem. When people go into court they come out without getting the help that they deserve. We just feel like we're helpless. What's the point of even going?

Brent has been incredible. He's been so good to us. We used to have the Department of Buildings coming in here and telling us that they were going to evict us. And any time that we call him, Brent is there to be like, "Hold on, let me see what's going on." We've been very lucky and so grateful that we met him. I'm sure he doesn't sleep—just like us!

We first went to court late July of last year, early August. At first they're like, the landlord can't do this. They have to fix this. It's an emergency. Blah blah. Emergency? Almost a year! Look, somebody step up! If I could fix it I would have already fixed it. But then I would get in trouble because I'm not allowed to fix it. But then they didn't force the landlord to fix it. So it was like they did it bad, but we get treated like, "Wait until they fix it."

The trial finished last week. We're waiting for the judge to make her decision; it could take two or three months. They're trying to settle with us, giving us some offers to consider. No monetary value. They've never offered a buy out. I think they thought that once we do that—

—*she points at the makeshift barricade blocking her from half of the apartment*—

—they have no choice but to leave so what's the point of giving them money? But they were wrong with us.

They tried to settle before but it's always been to delay the process. It feels like déjà vu. I don't really believe them. Why don't you just start doing the process of getting the permits so we can tell that you're serious? We aren't stopping you from getting the work permits. You should have been on that months ago.

Eventually something has to happen. I try not to make myself think, yeah they're going to fix it. Because I've been there already where we think that they're finally going to fix it and then it doesn't happen.

That's why we feel like we never win. I mean, yes, once we get the rest of our apartment back—thank God—but then we still have to deal with him. Go away already! Why did you buy a building that was like this if you don't want to deal with it? Who does this to other people, other human beings? You're a horrible person.

It always seems like regardless of whether we go to court or not we're always losing. We contacted the media. We contacted the government. And it always feels like we're the bad people. But we've lived here for twenty-three years. We work. We don't mess with nobody. We've paid our rent on time. And who's helping us? Who's there to help us?

Four More Years

JONATHAN DEE

The vast white tent had mullioned vinyl windows cut into it as a design feature, so the guests at the outer, less expensive tables could see the snow coming down heavily through the spotlights outside. But no one could hear anything, not even during the speeches—it was silent, it made silence, the way all major snowfalls do—so they were slow to take it seriously. As the waitstaff stared up nervously at the shifting depressions in the tent's ceiling, the head of the party-supply rental company got off a phone call and took the evening's MC aside to whisper in his ear.

"Folks, we are going to have to wrap it up here a bit earlier than scheduled," the MC said into the microphone on the dais. Sounds of confusion and irritation. He realized he was scowling and forced a smile. "Some of you may have noticed that it's snowing out there. We need to get off the island while the roads are still clear. Order of the Parks Department."

Victoria turned upon her husband, Chris, a look of skepticism. "Randall's Island is technically a park," he said.

That everyone was suddenly in a hurry meant they all wound up waiting an extra twenty minutes for their cars to be brought around. Inefficiencies, Chris thought. He was hoping to avoid an argument with Victoria about the storm; he'd warned her it was supposed to be bad, but she'd said the forecasters always had a stake in predicting the worst, and in any case the notion of having to reschedule on short notice an event that involved gathering four hundred very busy people under a tent on Randall's Island was one that she, as a member of the benefit committee, was not even going to entertain. If he failed to resist the urge to remind her of that now, she might counter by citing his insistence on driving rather than calling a car service, as almost every other guest had done. He hated being driven anywhere, he thought it was unmanly. So it would be a good fight not to start. But his mood was darkening, and they were liable to be alone in the car, in trying conditions, for a while.

She pulled her dress inside the door of the Expedition and they took their place in the long, slow, single file of black vehicles on the ramp that led from the island to the toll plaza on the Triboro Bridge. Only two lanes of the plaza were open. Snow jumped in the headlights, and fell into the ambient glow over either side of the bridge before disappearing in the darkness of the water.

"They should have a priority toll lane," Victoria said. "Like at the airport. This is ridiculous."

The bridge beyond the tollbooths looked like it had been plowed fairly recently, but snow was already encroaching on the center lanes as they watched.

"You think all my ideas are stupid," Victoria said.

Actually, he'd been thinking that it wasn't a bad idea at all: pay a higher toll, move through faster. More revenue, and value added for those willing to pay a premium not to waste time. Win-win. He was a little surprised no one had thought of it before. But you'd never get something like that passed in New York now, no matter how much sense it made. Not in this climate. God forbid we interrupt the great race to the mean.

The benefit had been for a charter-school foundation, the pet project of an acquaintance who ran a monster hedge fund called Erewhon Partners, named after his old summer camp. Why were all these hedge-fund guys so obsessed with public education? Chris was all for charitable endeavors if they actually improved anything, but this was like throwing your money into a wishing well. Yet over the last decade the school system had become like Moby Dick to a certain brand of macho guy: the ultimate inefficiency, its very existence taunting men who loathed inefficiency too deeply to leave it alone. The man from Erewhon had probably poured upward of a hundred million dollars of his own money into the situation by now, and nothing about it was any better, or any worse, for that matter, as a result. Not that he couldn't afford it. But the hard truth, which they all knew but which no one was willing to express, was that a problem created by democracy could not be solved by democracy. If you couldn't make people accept that as a first principle—and you couldn't—then however much money you threw at the problem would just disappear into its maw.

Still, you couldn't judge the guy too harshly. He could have spent the money on hookers and yachts. And it had been a fun evening, until the city had kicked them all out into the snow.

"Finally," said Victoria. They rolled across the bridge—frustratingly slowly, because it was down to one clear lane, the other drivers in which were, in Chris's estimation, timid pussies who didn't understand the simple calculation that driving a little faster now meant getting off the road before conditions got even worse—and had only to take the FDR four exits before they were as good as home.

But there were cop cars and sanitation vehicles parked sideways across the southbound FDR just a few feet past 96th Street, forcing them to take the exit there.

He inched west on 96th and eventually took a left on Second Avenue. It was getting hard to see, even with the height advantage the Expedition gave him. The problem, though, wasn't visibility; it was that you would turn down this or that street and suddenly find yourself not moving at all. Past 94th he came to a stop, and then watched the smudge of light on his soaked windshield go from green to red to green again without anybody in front of him moving a foot.

"This is outrageous," Victoria said. "Do you see a plow anywhere? Because I don't."

He said nothing. He realized, not for the first time, that he really only felt like talking to her when he thought she was wrong about something. The smudge went green again, and they did not advance. Some idiot ahead of them took a right turn to try to get up the hill at 93rd Street, and a few seconds later his car slid backward into view again, all the way through the intersection and into a parked car, which let fly with one of those grating alarms that everyone had learned not to pay attention to.

"I'll tell you what it is," Victoria said. "It's a message."

"A message from whom?" Chris said.

She turned to face him, and even in the darkness of the car he could see her roll her eyes. "How many hours ago did this storm start?" she said. "How many days have they been predicting it? Plenty of time to prepare."

"We didn't prepare."

"But their job is to prepare. What do you want to bet the streets are clear in, I don't know, Flatbush? Or East Harlem or Bed-Stuy, or any of the other places that voted for him. You know it's true."

In front of them was a yellow cab with its Off Duty sign lit. Chris couldn't see or hear inside it or any of the other cars surrounding his, but he began to feel incensed at them anyway for doing nothing, for feeling fine about doing nothing, resigning themselves to it. Inside the Expedition it was dry and quiet and seventy-two degrees but he felt the need to get out of there in the worst way.

"It's a slap in the face, is what it is," his wife said. "I don't know why you refuse to see it. It's just the leading edge. He really thinks all neighborhoods are the same, that some of them aren't more vital to the economy of this city, this whole city, than others? You bet your ass his predecessor knew better than that."

Up ahead of him, on the left, there was a break in the line of slowly disappearing parked cars: an active driveway. He could feel something stir in him. If you drove enough, and well enough, your sense of what the car could and couldn't do became a matter not of calculation but of physical instinct.

"Look at tonight. What were we doing tonight, and for whom? You know how much money we raised? For whom? The ingratitude is stunning. They want to teach us a lesson about how we're not just no better than the people we try to help, we're somehow worse than them. There's no logic to it. I understand he had to play a certain fashionable card in order to get elected. But there is a reality, a social reality, that you can't pander away. I don't know why you don't see what's coming as clearly as I do, as clearly as a lot of people do by the way. It's not the symbolism that's upsetting to me. It's what's being symbolized. He is intentionally putting us in harm's way. You think it's a world gone mad now?"

He spun the wheel all the way to the left and made for the driveway. Having cleared the front of the parked car, as he knew he would, he kept going, stayed with the turn, until he'd done a 180 and the Expedition was facing north on the empty sidewalk, patches of which were salted and clear; he drove back to the intersection and nosed his way into the astonished westbound traffic toward Park Avenue, away from home, but where he thought the roads might be clearer.

"My hero," Victoria said.

Two hours later, they had made their way, as through a maze, up and down whatever plowed streets they could find, to 50th Street and First Avenue, less than a block from their townhouse just off Beekman Place. They could see it, in fact. But the dead-end street was not only unplowed: the parade of plows clearing First Avenue had raised a wall of snow, ice, rock, and other street detritus that was now higher than the Expedition itself, at what should have been the entrance to their block. It was impassable.

Victoria, after a brief and ominous lapse into silence, had begun to panic. Their children were in the house. It was well past their bedtime, and they had been told Mommy and Daddy would be home to tuck them in. The sitter was with them—she could not have left for her own home even if she had wanted to—but safety was no longer Victoria's concern. She had moved into a realm of emotion. The artificially raised wall of snow between her and her children had undone her.

"Call them," Chris said placatingly. "FaceTime them."

She did, and when their two faces appeared cheerfully on the bright screen of her phone, she went to pieces. They were in pajamas and their cheeks were touching. They were excited by the storm and its laying waste to the conventions of bedtime, and they would probably be awake for hours. Chris saw the flashing lights of a plow in his rearview again, coming up First, and he put the car in gear to drive around the block rather than get caught in its path. Victoria continued declaring her love for the children as if she were speaking to them from a hijacked airplane rather than the family SUV a few hundred yards away. She hung up, and rested her head in her hand. Chris completed his circle and observed that the barricade of snow was now marginally higher than it had been a few minutes ago.

"I don't want to sound like my dad," he said. "But in my day, there would have been some enterprising local youth out here with shovels, looking to earn a few bucks."

"In your day," she repeated witheringly. "This is your day, genius. Nobody wants to earn anything."

He put the car in park again. The solution on one level was simple: get out and walk. It wouldn't be pleasant but it was probably less than a hundred and fifty yards. Still, she was unlikely to agree to it. And even if she did, it meant leaving the car on the street, to find it tomorrow buried or rammed into by some overtime-weary sanitation driver with an invincible plow-blade on the front of his truck. Or, worse, just gone. Disasters like this were prime time for thieves and looters and others who knew—as Chris knew, in a very different context—how to profit from chaos.

He could send her on her own and stay with the car. It wouldn't take all night. Every house on the block was occupied by millionaires; somebody still had to have a friend somewhere who could call in a favor as simple as re-directing one snowplow.

But she'd never make it on her own. Short as the trip was, she wasn't outfitted for it. He'd wind up going after her anyway.

He turned off the car. "Come on," he said. "I'll carry you."

She lifted her head and regarded him, letting herself grow amused. "You'll carry me? Over that cliff or whatever?"

"You don't think I can do it?" he said.

"Okay, well, this is all getting weirdly hot, but no, Galahad, I don't think you can do it. You're wearing pumps, for Christ's sake. You'll slip and drop me and then we'll both be dead in the street." She laughed, not unkindly, and wrapped her coat more tightly around her. "You come on," she said. "I can walk. We'll just do it. The first step is the hardest."

"That dress will be ruined," he said.

"I don't care about the dress. I do care a little bit about the shoes. But mostly I care about the import of this whole evening, which you absolutely refuse to see."

There was no wind now, but the air was still a shock, as was the cold that immediately penetrated their flimsy shoes. Snow continued to fall heavily. He let her go ahead of him, resisting the instinct to put his hands on her ass and push her up the barricade. By the time they were both on the other side, he couldn't feel his feet. Their block was utterly silent. Lights blazed in every townhouse. Victoria, after just a few tottering steps, reached down, took off her heels, and threw them back over the snowbank. She lifted her dress—the snow was nearly up to her waist in places—and struggled forward. For Chris, who had about seven inches on her, the going was somewhat easier. Still, it came as a surprise to him to consider that the physical risk to them both was, though temporary and contained, not unreal.

He'd bought this townhouse in large part because it had that rarest of Manhattan amenities, its own garage. Paying someone else to park your car was borderline effeminate, to say nothing of the inconvenience of having to call ahead, to walk a few blocks, every time you wanted access to it. Someone—the babysitter presumably, unless he or Victoria had done it by accident—had switched on the light over the garage door; he could see it. In front of the garage was an electronic gate; the snow had drifted too high against it for the car to drive through, even if the gate itself could still go up. It would have to be cleared. And that's if he could magically get the car itself over or around or through the snowbank that now hid it from his view. In a hurry suddenly, he took Victoria's arm. She shook it away from him, but not before he felt how violently she was shivering.

"I can't believe this," she said. Her breathing struck him as too fast, as if she were in some sort of shock. "I can't believe it's come to this. And you won't do anything." He didn't know what she was talking about. "What's that?" she said, more urgently. "Christopher, what's that?"

His feet were so numb they felt huge. He looked up from them and saw what she saw: a figure walking across the street at the dead end of their block, a soaked hood around its head, dressed in what looked like a hundred thin layers, dragging something behind it on the snow.

"It's nothing," he said, "let's just hurry." When they were almost at their door—when they could see, but not hear, the children at the front-parlor window, jumping up and down in excitement—he turned again and saw the figure, a man, gaining on them. Lifting his knees high, he made straight for their house, and Chris could now see that what he was pulling along behind his back was a snow shovel.

"Go on inside," Chris said. "I'll be right there. I think we may have lucked out."

Victoria looked at him oddly but went through the front door without hesitation and let it shut behind her.

"Good evening, sir. Shovel your walk?"

"Could have used you a few minutes ago," Chris said. "But now we're here."

The man smiled. "Your driveway, then? Have a hard time getting the car out of there tomorrow, especially after the plow comes through."

"Car's not in there," Chris said. But he was feeling charitable and tired, enough so to let go of his instinct for negotiation. "How much, though?" he said. "To clear the driveway."

The man cast an eye over it. The distance from garage door to curb, Chris had reason to know, was a scant six feet. "First driveway I've seen," the man said. "Don't really have a set price for it." Then he looked back at Chris, in his sodden tuxedo and ruined shoes, for at least as long as he'd looked at the driveway.

"One hundred dollars," he said.

Chris laughed. "Good one," he said. "Seriously."

The man took another moment and then nodded soberly, as if he had just re-calculated and come to the same sum.

"A hundred dollars?" Chris said. Just like that, all the outrage his wife had been asking him to feel was right there in his chest, in his fingertips. He laughed again. "Fuck off, a hundred dollars! It would take you five minutes max. You really think your labor is worth twelve hundred dollars an hour? *That's* your price?"

"Ain't about that," the man said.

"No? What's it about, then?"

"It's about I got the shovel," the man said.

Chris smiled and shook his head. He could feel that his anger was about to take him someplace unproductive, so he made one last attempt to head it off. "You're clever," he said. "I should give you a job. I mean like a real job."

"Already got a job," the man said patiently. "Got two jobs."

Even at this close range, little about his face, deep inside the hood, could be gauged. He had a dark beard, and the streetlight, itself under an eight-inch cap of wet snow, caught points in his eyes. Chris had stopped shivering. The greatest compliment you could pay another man, he felt, was to get interested in defeating him.

"This is like first-year b-school," he said. "Like a word problem. I love it. The thing is, though, your whole model falls apart if I have a shovel too. Right? Inside that garage, let's say. In that case, I really am offering to pay for your labor, and you overcharged and blew it."

"But you don't own no shovel."

"How do you know that?"

"Look at you," the man said.

With that, the civility of negotiation was pretty well shot. The possibility, even, of a more physical resolution seemed to Chris to have been suddenly introduced. And, shovel or no shovel, he had reason to feel confident should things take that turn. But he knew he couldn't let it play out that way. Not only couldn't he instigate it, he couldn't even defend himself, couldn't pop this lowlife in the jaw no matter how legitimately threatened he might feel, on his own doorstep no less. Because he knew how that could all be made to look. Poor people lived for the opportunity to sue you. It was just one more way they tied your hands.

"So it's fucking larceny, then, is what this is," he said. "Let's just call it by its name. You're a fucking thief. No different than the rest of them."

"It's called the marketplace, bitch," the man said. "It's called knowing what your customer will bear."

"You know what's the really galling part? The only reason we were out tonight at all was because we were doing something for charity. For you, basically. And it's not even like I'm asking for charity in return. I'm willing to make a fair transaction. But to you it's just an opportunity to steal whatever I haven't already given away. She's right. You do hate us."

They stood in their deep footprints for what seemed like a long time. They could see each other's breath. At the end of the block they heard another plow pass by.

"Two hundred dollars," the man said.

He looked like the reaper, with his loose dark clothes, his hood, the long-handled tool of his trade. Chris no longer had any idea what time it was. Most of the lights on the block had gone off. It felt like the night might never end unless he took some step to end it. He reached into his vest pocket—the man took a half step back—and pulled out his wallet; he took every bill out of it, and counted, leaning toward his garage to get into its light.

"Nine hundred and thirty-seven dollars," he said. He held it folded between his fingers in the light, closer to him than to his adversary. When the man finally reached toward it, he pulled it away.

"For the shovel," he said. "Nine thirty-seven for your shovel."

The man cocked his head, but he had no great interest in the metaphorical qualities of whatever was going on; he held out the shovel handle with one hand, an open palm with the other, and the transaction was completed. Chris weighed the shovel in his hands, looked back at the hooded man, then stuck it blade-first upright into the deep snow. He reached into his pocket again, took out his phone, dialed 911, and waited.

"Yes," he said, "there is a very suspicious-looking black man going from house to house on the block of East 50th between First and Beekman. I know the weather is crazy, but could you please send a patrolman right away? He is acting erratically. I live here and I definitely do not recognize him. Thank you."

He put the phone back in his pocket. "Better move along," he said. "Unless you have a legit excuse for being here."

The man shook his head and exhaled a great cloud; then he began plucking at his sleeves and his pant legs, brushing the snow off of them, preparing to go, making a display of how little hurry he was in. He pulled down his hood, flicked water off of his hair with his fingertips, then straightened and looked squarely into Chris's eyes. After a few breaths he pulled his hood back up and started down the center of the street toward First Avenue.

"Bad move, dipshit," Chris called after him. "Now I've seen your face."

His footprints already filling in behind him, he clambered over the frozen wall of snow and was gone.

Chris's initial plan, once in possession of the shovel, had been to break it over his leg, but the moment he'd weighed it in his hands he knew that his femur probably would have snapped before that handle did. It was a quality shovel; he was glad to own it. He looked up and saw his wife staring at him without expression from the parlor window, wearing a bathrobe. He waved to her. Then he put his head down and cleared the driveway; as he'd estimated, it took him five minutes tops. His feet were so cold he felt like he was walking on the stumps of his legs. He shouldered his new purchase, turned away from his house, and headed down the street, in the direction of First Avenue, to liberate his car.

So Where Are We?

LAWRENCE JOSEPH

So where were we? The fiery
avalanche headed right at us—falling,

flailing bodies in midair—
the neighborhood under thick gray powder—

on every screen. I don't know
where you are, I don't know what

I'm going to do, I heard a man say;
the man who had spoken was myself.

What year? Which Southwest Asian war?
Smoke from infants' brains

on fire from the phosphorus hours
after they're killed, killers

reveling in the horror. The more obscene
the better it works. The point

at which a hundred thousand massacred
is only a detail. Asset and credit bubbles

about to burst. Too much consciousness
of too much at once, a tangle of tenses

and parallel thoughts, a series of feelings
overlapping a sudden sensation

felt and known, those chains of small facts
repeated endlessly, in the depths

of silent time. So where are we?
My ear turns, like an animal's. I listen.

Like it or not, a digital you is out there.
Half of that city's buildings aren't there.

Who was there when something was, and a witness
to it? The rich boy general conducts the Pakistani

heroin trade on a satellite phone from his cave.
On the top floor of the Federal Reserve

in an office looking out onto Liberty
at the South Tower's onetime space,

the Secretary of the Treasury concedes
they got killed in terms of perceptions.

Ten blocks away is the Church of the Transfiguration,
in the back is a Byzantine Madonna—

there is a God, a God who fits the drama
in a very particular sense. What you said—

the memory of a memory of a remembered
memory, the color of a memory, violet and black.

The lunar eclipse on the winter solstice,
the moon a red and black and copper hue.

The streets, the harbor, the light, the sky.
The blue and cloudless intense and blue morning sky.

Round Trip

AKHIL SHARMA

I have never felt poor. I have believed that other people might be better than I am because they had more money—that they were smarter, more interesting, more worth listening to, and even more virtuous than I was because they had more money—but I have never seen myself as poor. This is because for me poverty has to do with certain absolutes. I have always had a place to live. I have never been in a situation where day after day I opened the refrigerator and was able to see all the way to the back. The fact that I think of poverty in this way has allowed me certain choices. I have been able to take risks that might not have been possible if my baseline for what is an acceptable life had been different.

My family immigrated to America in 1979. We had been middle class in India and were technically poor in America. My father earned nine thousand dollars a year and my brother and I received free breakfast and lunch at school. (I was eight then and to me there was no embarrassment in receiving free meals. In fact, I actually felt luckier than the boys who did not get free meals because, to me, getting something for nothing was wonderful; it was like my family had tricked somebody.)

When we arrived in America, I found the country astonishing. My family lived in Queens, New York, and I was constantly aware of the wealth around me: the wide roads, the traffic lights, the tall apartment buildings with elevators. All these things showed a lifestyle that was better and more glamorous than even that of rich people in the Hindi movies I watched. Though I was a child, I understood that it was better to be poor in America than to be middle class in India. Partially I think this is obvious economic logic. To have a tiny piece of a vast pie is better than to have a large piece of a speck.

Another reason I think I never felt poor was because my family had so much hope. We were in America and my brother and I were smart and we knew that we would work very hard and good things would come to us. For us there was never the hopelessness that can come to people who are trapped.

All this does not mean that I was not aware of money and did not feel the pressure of limited resources. Once I asked my father for twenty-five cents to play a pinball machine and after I had played the game, my father said that he only earned about three dollars an hour and that the quarter had been five minutes of his life. Another time, my mother, as was usual for us, bought a slice of pizza and had it cut into three pieces so that she and my brother and I could share it. The slice turned out to be burnt and when my mother showed this to the cashier, the cashier threw away the slice and wouldn't give us our money back. I remember walking home from the pizza shop and crying with frustration and helplessness.

The anxiety of money was near me all the time when I was a child. Along with the anxiety, though, like solid ground that I could walk on, was the awareness that I was OK. This awareness was so clear that it was almost like what I imagine rich people feel, that they can always retreat to a place where they are safe.

Growing up I never spent money. I was always willing to tell people that I couldn't afford something rather than spend more than I could afford. I went to college at Princeton and while I was there, a friend invited me to his parents' ski chalet. I told him that with the cost of the Greyhound bus and renting skis, I would end up spending more than a hundred dollars and my family couldn't afford it. I was embarrassed telling him this, but I was more scared of spending the money.

And by not spending money I learned how little I could live on. In graduate school I had a fellowship that gave me eleven thousand dollars a year. I typically saved three thousand of this. I shared a small house with two other students for nine hundred dollars a month; I never ate out; the beer bottles that my housemates drank, I would collect and recycle for the nickels. To me living so frugally was a sort of freedom.

I went to Harvard Law School and became an investment banker working in Midtown Manhattan. I made a great deal of money, but I still acted with extreme frugality. One winter I needed a pair of gloves. At this point I had three hundred thousand dollars in my checking account.

I couldn't make myself spend the money and instead just kept my hands stuffed in my pockets.

One way that I was willing to spend money easily and even cavalierly was on other people. I paid off sixty thousand dollars of my girlfriend's student loans. I was happy to pick up the tab when I went out for dinner with friends. I would even pay for people whom I did not know especially well. I think I was trying to buy love. I also think I didn't know how to behave with a lot of money. I was perfectly fine having very little, but I found it very difficult to have a great deal. Having money made me want to return to what it was like when I had very little.

Other than buying things for others, I did not gain much pleasure from spending. The vanity that comes from money never infected me in a serious way. I remember going to a wine store and I think I was radiating money the winter day that I did this because when I asked for a bottle of sparkling wine, the woman showed me vintage Dom Perignon. I picked a thirteen dollar wine from Arizona instead.

I think it was because money seemed to matter very little that I was able to quit my job as an investment banker and decide to be a novelist. (I had already written one novel and so this was not as crazy a decision as it sounds.)

As soon as I quit my job, though, I began to feel that I had made a terrible decision. When I was a banker I was so busy, so many people wanted my time, that I felt important. Now, nobody cared what I was doing and it was like I might as well not exist.

But part of my regret was the awareness that for the rest of my life I would never again make as much money as I had as a banker. Until then I had always felt myself on an upward trajectory; now I saw myself as sliding down. It was then that I realized that while it is not that hard to go from very little money to a lot, it is absolutely devastating to make the return journey.

My first response to not having a paycheck was to live as frugally as I used to when I had very little money. I stopped taking the subway and started walking to places. When my allergies kicked up I would just sneeze and sneeze instead of buying Claritin. Each of these decisions, however, made me feel stupid. I used to think: I am intelligent. How could I decide that money did not matter?

I stopped being a banker thirteen years ago. For the first five or six of these, I thought every day of what it was like to be a banker and never worry about money. Now, in the way that one can adjust to almost anything, I rarely think of my old life. Instead I am appreciative of how much time and flexibility I have as a college professor.

I have been changed, though, by no longer seeing myself on an upward path. Recently at Whole Foods I saw a friend whom I hadn't talked to in a long time. My friend works for a hedge fund and is very successful and probably makes around a million dollars a year. I saw him and I began to walk away because it embarrassed me to not be as well off as he was despite having gone to better schools and my first jobs having put me on the path to much greater success.

I took a few steps away from him and then turned back. I feel that one of my strong points is that I am able to walk toward the things that scare me.

My friend and I began speaking. Immediately our conversation was as warm and intimate as it had ever been. I told my friend that I had nearly avoided him because of my insecurities. He said that he was glad I had not.

Aliens of Extraordinary Ability

TAIYE SELASI

1

The white man enters, closes his door, announces his destination, then turns his attention to tapping his thumbs on the screen of a rubber-bound phone.

The Indian man doesn't like this behavior. He prefers that his passengers start with hello. And sir. Or chief. The black men say chief. Or boss. The point is acknowledgment. "Hi." Nothing extravagant. "How are you doing?" No need to pretend to await a response. "Hello how's it going sir good Sixty-Seventh and Central Park West at the corner please thanks." At least, like this, the partition is trespassed, the terms re-established: a man greets a man. Demander, supplier in human relation. The Indian man prefers this.

Then, he can lower the volume of his radio, which is permanently tuned to WQXR (no shāstriya sangīt for cab 6-J-1-7), in order to make polite queries. "Do you come from the city?" "Do you think it will rain?" "Do you want to try Park or take Lexington down?" which the well-mannered fare will invert and return, "Is there rain in the forecast then?" "Where are you from?" The Indian man will glance back at this juncture to see if the fare holds a four-year degree. He can tell by the way that they'll look for his eyes and his humanity in the rearview mirror. The educated passengers enjoy showing off. "Let me guess. Bangladeshi? No. Indian. South." The educated white women sometimes exhale, "I've been to Benares. I practice at Pure."

The Indian man enjoys showing off also. "Symphony No. 5. Shostakovich. Did you know that he died in 1975? Much later than one might imagine." The passenger, startled, will ask how he knows—meaning: how does a cab driver come to know—about classical music and Russian composers, and why does he speak such good English? Then the Indian man will start to chuckle, a low and warm and knowing chuckle that means, to those who do yoga at Pure, that nothing is as it appears in this world. "I came to your country on an O-1 visa, the visa for aliens of extraordinary ability. That's what we're called. What I was, when I came." The monologue lasts for some minutes. Main points: born to a farmer in Puducherry (formerly Pondicherry), excels in school; wins scholarship to study at the Indian Institute of Science in Bengaluru (formerly Bangalore); gets recruited to work for IBM in Armonk, New York; changes name to Al (formerly Allaiyamuthan); the tech bubble bursts; loses wife; is made redundant. "My life B.C., before cabbing," he'll chuckle, a high chuckle, baffled and cold.

The white man receives a telephone call. The Indian man watches, scowling. He turns up the radio to little avail. Satie can play only so loudly. For a display of aggression Carl Orff is required—nothing spells trouble like "Carmina Burana"—but WQXR almost never plays Orff, despite his denazification. He thinks of the things he might say in this vein—of the formerly-ness of all places and things, of the changing of names and the nature of change—but the white man has given no audience. "In a cab," he is saying in lieu of hello. *So it isn't just me*, thinks the Indian man. The white man lacks tact, to say nothing at all of his powers of observation. *A cab*. The Indian man scoffs. As if his were *a cab*, just your regular, run-of-the-mill TLC cab and not spotlessly clean with Gymnopedie No. 1 growing louder with each passing second. Were the white man to ask he would speak of Satie, who had called himself a phonometrograph rather than a musician. "One who measures and writes down sounds." The Indian man finds this lovely. He is not a cabbie, but the ferryman Charon. One who delivers. Attends to transitions. Bears witness, gives refuge with sound, scent, and story to travelers trapped between points A and B.

But the man doesn't ask. He says, "How is this urgent?" then listens, then snaps, "To a meeting, dear daughter. Yes, *someone* has got to put food on the table and diamonds and pearls on your gluttonous mother and coming home early to offer my comfort is not a request I can honor," then laughs. "Excuse me? I'm sorry? Fuck *me*? Did I hear that? Is that how you speak to your own fucking father? When I was in Russia—" He tries again, louder. "WHEN I WAS IN RUSSIA, MY FATHER—you what? You don't give a shit about Russia? I see. Very well, then this chit-chat is over."

The Indian man watches through the rearview mirror as the white man, enraged, throws his phone to the seat. *This is what's wrong with American parents*, he thinks with some pleasure. *The children are feral.* He thinks of his daughter, the third of his children (the other two boys with their mother's mild manners), a bullheaded girl with a penchant for drama, but still *nalla peṇ*, still respectful. Jaishanmugapriya, her mother had named her, despite his best efforts to make her see reason. What could he do? They had waited so long for a girl that his wife was deranged by the joy. Jaishanmugapriya. Arriving in springtime a cool thirteen years after Ravi, their first. They'd married so young, become parents at twenty; their sons were at Fieldston when Priya was born. How could he know that they'd run out of money? That both of his boys would turn out me-diocre? That cancer would burn through his savings, then prayers, then Thali his wife, dead at fifty years old? That Jaishanmugapriya, the star of the family, the one of his children who shares his own interests—a gifted pianist, hardworking, good-looking, all moon-wide brown eyes and black rivers of hair—would be working two jobs to help pay back the hospital? *And still*, he thinks smugly, *the girl doesn't swear*. Was raised with good manners, demure with her elders, has missed two semesters and never complains. *This is what's wrong with American parents. They show too much weakness. The children smell fear.*

Behind him the white man is saying "God *damn* it!" and running a palm down his reddening face. He looks out the window and says to the traffic, "And this is the thanks that I get, for fuck's sake."

The Indian man hears the trace of an accent, the shape of the vow-els and the struggle with "th," and he peers at the man with a trace of compassion. Satie never sounded this sad, or this loud. He turns off the music then wishes he hadn't. The silence is worse. He can hear the man breathing: that soft rhythmic choking of dry, kept-in sobbing. He tries not to look but his eyes don't obey. He watches the Russian man sobbing in silence. The man is attractive, he sees, if not young. Maybe fifty, fif-ty-five, a bit older than he is. A full head of hair, wildly curly and gray. Most certainly a "formerly." Formerly a soldier or athlete or lover of con-siderable talents. A few pounds past plump with the look of a man in a Tod's catalog, calmly wealthy. But dressed like those middle-aged men in

Manhattan who haven't accepted that time has moved on: beaded necklace, jeans, T-shirt (and fashionable sneakers, the Indian man knows, though he can't see the shoes).

The sobbing ends quickly. The Russian man straightens. He wipes off his eyes, which are more or less dry. Still, the Indian man opens his glove compartment and pulls out a fresh box of Kleenex. "Here." He hands back the box. The Russian man takes one. "Take the whole box. Adolescence is long."

The Russian man laughs, as surprised as delighted. "I'm sorry you heard that," he says. "You got kids?"

"Two sons and a daughter," the Indian man answers.

"Two girls," says the Russian man. "Counting the wife." He looks out the window. "I can't understand it. To swear at your father. I would have been . . ."

"Murdered."

The men laugh together.

"I would have been murdered and no one in Moscow would call it a crime."

The Indian man nods. "You're from Russia."

"I was. Once. Thirty years here. Even more. Thirty-five."

The Indian man smiles. "I was born in Puducherry—"

But the Russian man stops him. "This corner is fine." The Indian man stops at the corner abruptly. The Russian man hurriedly opens his door. He passes a ten through the open partition and says, climbing out, "Keep the change."

2

The Russian man enters the well-maintained lobby and nods to the doorman, who touches his cap. He watches his sneakers flash white on the carpet, a stately dark red, past the palm trees in pots. He always moves quickly when coming to meet them, though knows that it's silly; there's nothing to fear. These meetings are always in bland Midtown buildings of glass-box apartments that look like hotels: stainless steel, Bauhaus windows, white walls, parquet flooring of yellowish wood, cheap and waxy. Beige blinds. Wednesdays' appointments are always at this one on West 58th between Broadway and Eighth. He used to object to not changing locations, afraid that he'd see or be seen by a friend, but in over six weeks hasn't seen the same face more than once in this lobby, much less any friends. Even the doormen change weekly—all stocky, Latino, good-natured—and choose whom they greet; they will speak to the kids and West Indian nannies but rarely to white men in sports coats and Chucks.

So the Russian man crosses the lobby unnoticed, or observed but dismissed as unworthy of note: both relieving and irksome, this novel sensation. He likes, it turns out, to be recognized. He likes being led to his Balthazar booth hearing watching girls whisper, "Is that who I think . . . ?" He likes that the Sant Ambroeus waiters all know that he likes his boiled eggs extra runny. He likes that he enters a dinner or party and feels the air move as it will, in this city, for rare forms of beauty and great sums of money. He likes that he trades in the dazzle of both. The charm of his business, he knows, is the contact of beauty with money, not canvas with brush. Painting is manual labor. The thrill for the buyer is public opinion. In thirty-five years he has mastered the magic of dealing the drug of applauded good taste, has established a gallery small but respected by those whom he wants to extol his good eye. But he isn't ungrateful. No matter how often he narrates his journey for magazine profiles, he still feels some manner of awe at the distance from state school in Moscow to loft space on Mott.

This is what his daughter doesn't realize, the ingrate. That wealth comes from *working*, from effort, from sweat. She thinks that his job is all auctions and openings. She thinks that it's hers, being pretty and rich. And depressed. Her new hobby. Inspired by her mother. He never should have married American. Twice. The first one was passion: Rosella from Brooklyn, Italian, mad as a March hare but happy. They'd both been assistants to Sussman the sculptor. Their firstborn was stillborn. She never bounced back. The present and second is where things went pear-shaped. Amanda. Latin for "worthy to be loved." Or, as he later learned, "needs to be loved." Not an option. "She must be, demands to be, loved." She came to the gallery directly from college, a breed standard intern of Conyers Farm stock: frequent nosebleeds, blond highlights, neurotic, anorexic, obsessed with Cy Twombly, compulsively tidy. But wildly devoted. To art, to the artists, the making of money, the making of him. The fact of the matter is now he can't leave her. She knows every peso he has to his name and their daughter would hate him. The girl may dislike him but desperately needs and so loves him somehow.

He hurries across the lobby and gets in the elevator. A heavyset black woman gets in as well, with a double-wide stroller. Blond babies, both sleeping. He smiles at the woman. "Which floor?"

"Twenty-eight."

He presses the buttons. 28, 37. No one else comes. The doors close. They go up. The silence unnerves him. "What beautiful babies."

"Sank you." Haitian accent.

The Russian man smiles. But thinks in the yet louder silence that follows, *Who compliments nannies?* The children aren't hers. They belong, very likely, to some joyous couple that paid a good sum for these gold-en-haired twins and now pays a good sum for this francophone nanny to keep said twins out of said joy.

3

The Senegalese woman is vacuuming the carpet—"not a carpet, a *kilim*," the white woman badgers—and, lost to her thoughts of intaglio printing, doesn't at first hear the racket. The vacuuming and dusting are of critical importance as the white woman is violently allergic to dust (and to gluten, bees, shellfish, all manner of melon, mold, pollen, cats, dogs, and her husband's cologne) so the Senegalese woman works slowly and daily, enjoying the view from the thirty-fourth floor. She's heard from the women who work in the building that vacuuming needn't be done every day, that it's better to sweep certain carpets (like kilims) than risk doing harm to the delicate wools, and she knows she should listen, take notes from these women, her sistren in arms, but she can't stand their scorn. They've tallied her failings—poor walking of "puggle," warm chitchat with doormen, cold chitchat with them—and have deemed her unworthy of joining their circle, which suits her just fine. They have nothing in common. *They* are short, chubby, mid-thirties to fifties, with loss-hardened faces and lye-hardened fingers. The cleaners speak Spanish, the nannies bad English. Few do both duties and none hold degrees. *She* is tall, slender, was raised in Little Senegal, speaks flawless Noon, Wolof, French, English, and Arabic, turns twenty next weekend, and just took this job to raise money to pay for tuition.

She attempted to model but hated the go-sees. She felt like a slave on an auctioning block. Waitressing tired her, office work bored her, hair-braiding felt like the longest way out. Through one of her cousins—a restaurant hostess—she learned that a gallerist was looking for help, namely, someone to cook, clean, and help his spoiled daughter learn French for her summer in Paris. She had zero experience either teaching or cleaning but won the man over in two minutes flat with a short, heartfelt speech about Iba Ndiaye, the preeminent Senegalese Modernist. Also, she is beautiful. This is why he hired her. This is why they hate her. The same thing at home. She is doe-eyed and small-boned and baldly ambitious; abhorrent, in short, to most women. No mind. As soon as she can she is going to art school. She refuses to braid for the rest of her life (although braiding is a form of fine art in itself, she insists) with her aunts in their Harlem salon. She is going to learn etching. She knew from that day in the after-school workshop that this was her calling; the creativity and dexterity required for braiding prepare her uniquely for printmaking's tools. It was entirely by chance that she went to that workshop at Columbia University, for Harlem adolescents, one in a series of creative arts workshops directed at low-income youth. "Outreach." She finds the whole notion misguided at best, as if printmaking classes on Ivy League campuses might dull the effects of economic inequality as heightened by gentrification. *Quand même*. One day they'll call her the Rembrandt of Senegal. She just needs to raise enough money for Pratt. She couldn't care less about carpets or kilims or envious bitches, her colleagues or aunts.

Still. She likes to be close to these windows, pretending to vacuum with rapturous care while she stares at the view from the Broad Street apartment, imagining how she would etch it. The skyline is a print itself, the frantic marks in blacks and grays against the flat impassive sky hatched through with Vs of bird wing. Back and forth and back she walks, pushing the high-suction vacuum along. When she steps on the button to turn the thing off she starts at the sound of the music. Nirvana. "Smells Like Teen Spirit," at maximum volume from Dariya's room at the end of the hall. How is she meant to work, she'd like to know, with all this racket?

She stands there considering. The sound is assaulting. What to do? She can't barge in. Can't reprimand as other nannies do their younger charges. And, anyway, she likes the girl. Despite the horrid manners, moods, and wretched French, she pities her. The parents are impossible. The white man comes and goes at whim, is almost always drunk when home, keeps condoms in his jacket pockets, can't control his temper. The woman spends her afternoons in clothing stores and medical spas, has all but gone off solid food in favor of raw juices. They'll ship the girl to France in June to study Braque despite the facts that she hates French (it hates her back) and shows no gift for form. The Senegalese woman used to laugh, imagining the family who stayed in Dakar and how they'd weep with joy to eat the food the white girl vomits. She used to mock the so-called depression, wondering what in all this wealth could possibly warrant all those clearly lazy stabs at suicide? Mostly it was swallowed pills, enough to get one's stomach pumped but not enough to knock one out, much less to end one's life. But the fifteen-year-old has grown on her. They are, after all, only four years apart, and something in the girl's inchoate rage suggests real vision. Beneath the bleached blond bangs, Goth black, and brittle limbs, she sees *herself*: a girl who sees, and knows how sad it is to see, the truth.

"DARIYA," she shouts, though she knows that it's pointless; she can't hear herself. She tries knocking instead. "CAN YOU TURN DOWN THE MUSIC, PLEASE?" Kurt Cobain answers. She tries the door. It opens. Later she will wonder if the volume of the music somehow compromised her eyesight when she looked into the room. She sees the white girl lying there across the bed, one arm splayed out with rivulets of bright red blood advancing to her fingers, but she doesn't immediately process what she's looking at or what it means. The only thought she has at first is, "What is this man saying?" *A mulatto, an albino, a mosquito, my libido.* What? Seconds on clear thought returns and panic mutes the music.

4

The Russian man stops at the same door as always (3727) and knocks, lightly, twice. It amazes him how organized, how civil, is this process. He doesn't like to use the word, which sounds to him like "destitution" (human traffic, STDs), but isn't self-deluded. He'd very calmly faced the facts—was fifty years old when his wife went off sex—and considered the options available to him: misery, mistresses, or madams. Misery was too tiring. The gallery suffered. He gained too much weight. Mistresses were complicated. They always wanted more. He is still amazed that he found this service, that such a thing exists at all: a dignified solution for a man with certain standards.

An Italian dealer tipped him off when visiting the city for the Whitney Biennial months ago. "Geisha," said the business card. The service works through referrals only. Appointments are made by telephone. All of the so-called "reservationists" have British accents or fake them. Most of the "geishas" are college students (Yale, Columbia, NYU). The "madam" worked in recruitment for an investment bank for years. She noticed, explains the recorded message, a glaring unmet consumer need: bankers wished to pay for sex but not with vapid women. The transactional quality appealed to them—cash for control, no confusion of roles—but not the suggestion of tawdriness, the whiff of exploitation. What her colleagues were after was something akin to the twenty-first-century courtesan: well-spoken, well-presented, consenting girls paid goodly sums of cash. Working through undergraduate sorority connections, the madam recruits on campuses mostly, promising men and women both a rigorous vetting process. The rules are: 1) conversation first; 2) sex is not compulsory; 3) repeat visits can only be requested by the woman. The man selects the day and hour, is directed to an apartment, then waits to see who will answer the door. The Russian man enjoys this. None of his geishas has ever said no but the fact that one *could* excites him. He likes that the woman has a choice. He likes, it turns out, to be chosen.

Today he waits with bated breath. He usually isn't so nervous. He hears the footsteps approaching the door and feels his heartbeat quicken. A woman's voice asks, "Who is it?" The code. The Russian man says, "A friend." The most beautiful woman he has ever seen unlocks and opens the door.

5

The Indian man has paused for lunch at the Veronica's Kitchen food truck where the roti is as good as what his mother used to make. He is sitting in the driver's seat enjoying Liszt and eating when his cell phone rings. He heaves a sigh and turns down "Liebestraum." He finds the phone, which isn't ringing, frowns, and listens closely. The ringing continues shrilly from the back seat of the cab. He swallows, wipes his mouth, gets out. The rain has started, thinly. He opens the back door, looks around. The phone is on the seat. He picks it up and looks at it. The screen reads "Mariétou." Another phone for the Lost and Found. He returns to the front to keep eating. The phone continues ringing.

Mariétou. He wonders how to turn it off. He stares at the thing, at the name on the screen. He can't say why he answers. He's recovered countless phones before and never thought to pick them up. Perhaps because the caller's name seems foreign somehow? Familiarly. *Someone far from home*, he thinks. *Another person far from home*. He must alert this comrade that some friend has lost a phone.

"Hello?" he answers.

"It's Dariya!"

"Dariya," repeats the Indian man. "Somebody left this phone in my cab—"

But the woman isn't listening. Sobbing, she continues speaking in a frantic stream of words and sounds as crying women often do, ignoring interjections. "It's Dariya, Sasha! She cut her wrist! She told me not to call her mom or 911, just you—"

"I'm not—"

"*Ya Allah ehfadna*! What do I do?"

"If someone with you slit her wrist, call 911—"

"She took the phone! I was talking to them and she grabbed the phone. She said I had to call *you*."

"I'm not the man who owns this phone."

"Then give the phone to Sasha, please! Tell him that his daughter's hurt."

"I can't," says the Indian man.

"You don't understand," the woman sobs. "He has to come. It's worse this time. She cut the wrist with a razor blade."

The Indian man nods. Remembers. Thali, near the end, had tried. To spare them all the trouble, said. He thinks of it and wipes his face. "I can try to help," he says.

A different voice shouts, "ARE YOU HAPPY NOW?"

"She's still awake," says the Indian man.

"Yes," the crying woman says.

"Can you put me on speakerphone?"

The second voice shouts, "WHO THE FUCK IS THAT?"

"Allaiyamuthan," says the Indian man. "Whichever of you cut the wrist, I ask you to lie down. Lift your wrist above your head and prop your feet, you hear? The other put pressure on the wound itself until the bleeding stops. It will. Use clothing, bed sheets, anything clean. Are you there?"

"We're here," sniffs the crier.

"If your friend does not intend to die she will let you now call 911. If she intends to die she should have cut both wrists instead of one. I will drop off this phone if you give me an address. There is not much more I can do, I'm afraid."

"Fifteen Broad Street. Thank you."

"You're welcome. I am five minutes away."

6

Massive eyes, smooth, pale-brown skin, a shock of curly jet-black hair, thick brows, a plaintive shadow on her face: his own Scheherazade. "Come in, friend," she says to him as all of them are trained to say, but softly, even anxiously. At first he doesn't speak. He tries to, tracing her face with his eyes—then the long, slender neck, then the small, slender feet—but the sentence dissolves into indistinct sound, first an "mmm," then an "oh," then, "OK." He crosses the threshold. She closes the door. He steps aside to let her pass. She walks, barefoot, to the living room, a generic arrangement of couches. His drink (two fingers of Pappy Van Winkle) waits on the bent glass coffee table, a golden-amber beacon in the sullen white-gray light. The drink is another subtle touch to put the so-called guest at ease, the echo of the cocktail function, something light (and legal). The geishas tend to down their chosen poison before their guests arrive, and often sit and watch him drink with bright, unfocused eyes. Some wear lovely dressing gowns, dark silks, from Kiki Montparnasse; others white ribbed tank tops, hair in studied disarray. This one—and he thinks again, Scheherazade—is different: clearly sober, freshly showered, smelling faintly of sweet almond. She wears the soft white bathrobe that one finds in finer chain hotels, her hair left loose but guilelessly, a waist-length mass of spirals.

She goes to a couch, pulls her feet by her side. He stays by the door, frozen, silent. The windows mute the sound of rain now coming down with vigor. She is watching him with wary eyes, a shrouded gaze of expectation, nothing of the cheerful sort of gamesmanship he's used to. *First time*, it occurs to him. He notes a surge of tenderness, a feeling so unsettling that it almost feels like grief. Presently, he clears his throat and takes a step, then two, then three, enough to bring him stiffly to the armchair by her loveseat.

"I'm—" he begins, then catches himself. "I'm Martin. Nice to meet you."

"Nice to meet you, Martin," she says. "I'm Jay. Like the bird."

"Eurasian."

"I'm sorry?"

"The Eurasian jay. The original jay, after which all jaybirds get their name." He pauses, flustered. "I'm assuming that you're . . . Turkish? Persian? No?"

"My parents came from India. I grew up in Westchester County. You?"

"Russian. American. Ish." He smiles. "We're Volga German originally. Invited to Russia by Catherine the Great. A bust as invites go. Forced labor, dispossession, ethnic persecution. You name it, we survived it. I was born in Kazakhstan. My family all speaks German. But I grew up in Russ—" He laughs. "Who gives a shit about Russia?"

"Me. Say something. In Russian," she says. "Anything. First thing that comes to your mind."

"*Ty samaya krasivaya zhenshchina kotoruyu ya kogda-libo videl.*"

She laughs. "*Spasiba*, Martin."

He falters. " . . . You speak Russian, then."

"*Nyet*. Just *spasiba*, *da*, and *nyet*. My piano teacher's Russian—." She stops. "Say the same in German."

"*Sie sind die schönste Frau die ich je gesehen habe,*" he says to her. "Would you like to know what I said?"

"No need. Was it true?"

"It was. . .It is."

"How do you know about birds?" she asks. She cups one foot in the palm of her hand. She tucks a curl behind one ear. "Is that what you do?"

He chuckles. "For a man over fifty it's one of two hobbies. Birding or geology."

"Three." She nods to the bedroom door. "And this."

"And this. Touché." He smiles. "Do you do 'this' often?"

"No." She frowns. "This is my first reservation."

"Oh." The fact of it. The smell of her. "Are you nervous?"

"Me? Look at *you*."

His laughter in the sterile space, a pure thing in the pretense, brings to mind the set of keys he once let fall in a silent museum. "You're not like the other girls, Jay like the bird."

"How are the other girls?"

"White."

"Not all."

"Most. So far."

"And you?"

"Me what?"

"Are you white?" She is laughing also. "Dispossession of land? Forced labor? What? Ethnic persecution? Aren't such things reserved for those disqualified from whiteness?"

He says, before he knows he's thought it, "You're too bright for this."

She shrugs. "I'm a girl who needs the money. You're a man who needs the sex."

He laughs again, with shock at this, a jolt from throat to chest to gut. He reaches for his drink and sips, then sets it down, then laughs again. In many years he hasn't felt this crushing mix of gentleness and grief and lust, which long ago had made him turn to art. He is reminded of a painter whom he used to show before he died, a Frenchman fond of "paid help" as he called it, dead at ninety. The last they spoke the painter told a story of some years before, of finally booking a particular hooker, infamous at fifty. "Best lover on earth," the painter mused. "All men should know such paradise." He'd offered the woman's Parisian number. The Russian man refused it. He knew that the woman would bring him boundless pleasure as the painter claimed, but feared—perhaps for the first time since boyhood—that he would disappoint her. The painter, then, was seventy-something, hunched and gaunt with trembling hands but famous still for bedding women half his children's age. When the Russian man would visit he would rarely see the old man's work but humor him by listening to his lively, lurid stories. This story, though, had moved him to a very certain kind of hurt: a caving in, as he feels now, the present threat of heartbreak.

The aging hooker, the painter said, had served post-coitus peppermint tea, then turned her attention to dressing for a theatre date that evening. As he sipped his tea undressed in bed, she sat to do her makeup. "The eyebrows were too strong, you see. They made her face look garish." The painter asked the hooker for her makeup bag and picked his palette. Perching nude on the edge of her bed, he painted her face to perfection. "More pleasure than the sex itself, and the sex itself was heavenly." The Russian man had thought of it. The careful strokes in failing light, a moment of affection in two swiftly ending lives. He had wanted to weep. He wants to weep now. Such artistry has left his life. The gentle touch, the act of grace. What can he offer a woman?

"I don't *need* the sex" is all he says.

"You want it, then," she counters. "I *need* the money."

"For what?"

"My dad." Abruptly, she softens. Embarrassed. "That's what they all say, isn't it? The hooker with a heart of gold."

"What parent would allow this?"

"None. She's dead. He doesn't know."

The Russian man starts at the thing in her voice, at the thing in his chest. "I'm sorry." Silence. Spray of lashes, downturned eyes, fierce longing to embrace her. "Please. I'll give you the money."

The woman laughs. "This isn't *Pretty Woman*. Shit."

"I'll give you the money. I don't want sex."

"What do you want?"

He thinks, *beauty*. "For you to stop this job," he says. "How much?" She doesn't answer. He pats his blazer pocket for his wallet. Thinks, *Where is my phone?*

7

The Indian man arrives at the building. He hesitates at the entrance. The lobby's dazzling chandelier throws glitter in his path. He proceeds apace to the doorman's station, gives the name Dariya, holds out the phone. The doorman is cheerful. "That's good of you, captain. I'll be sure that she gets it." EMTs wheel in a stretcher behind them. The doorman leaps up to attend to their needs. The Indian man steps backward, distracted, observing the fray with a sense of remove. He is thinking of Orff, of Satie, of Shostakovich, of the white man he left on the corner of Broadway, of Jaishanmugapriya at work teaching music, determined to help him repay what he owes. He waits in the lobby until the rain lightens, unnoticed, absorbed, staring out through the door, then hurries back out to his taxi deciding to end his shift early today, to go home.

The Baffled Courtier: Lorenzo Da Ponte in America

EDMUND WHITE

Mozart's librettist, Lorenzo Da Ponte, had a hectic life even before he came to the United States in 1807 at the age of fifty-eight. While there he tried unsuccessfully to champion Italian culture, especially the opera.

He had been born in 1749, named Emmanuele Conegliano—a Jew in Ceneda, a small town in the Veneto—and had lived in its ghetto of just fifty people, where his father was a leather worker making belts and bridles. Jews were rigidly controlled. A gentile who had recently converted from Judaism, for instance, was not allowed to work for a Jew in the ghetto. Jews were obliged at all times to wear something red (a man wore a red beret). But when Emmanuele was just fourteen, his father, a widower, wanted to marry a Christian woman; the laws of the day insisted the father must convert. The whole family converted, and his son Emmanuele took the name of the local bishop, Lorenzo Da Ponte, as custom dictated. The conversion was celebrated joyfully by the entire town and the bishop; cannons were fired for four days. At the time little Lorenzo wrote a letter to his religious instructor, lamenting "the blindness of the poor Jews." Lorenzo's conversion and his sudden removal out of the local ghetto, as well as his being forced to give up his old Jewish playmates and make new gentile friends, must have hardened his heart and prepared him for a life of play-acting.

Because of this conversion, little Lorenzo and his brother were enrolled in the local seminary school, where he prepared to become a priest while studying Latin and Greek and even modern Italian, as well as geometry and rhetoric. He excelled in languages and soon was an instructor in a nearby school. He memorized all of Dante and much of Petrarch and wrote hundreds of verses (which he burned, because he judged them inferior).

Before long, however, he surrendered in a very non-ecclesiastical way to the temptations of nearby Venice. He fell in love with a tiny Venetian named Angela Tiepolo—who was married. Her aged husband divorced her (and became a priest), whereas Lorenzo (at age twenty-four) resigned from his teaching position and moved to Venice at the moment Angela bore him a child. Still wearing ecclesiastical garb and styling himself an *abbé*, he was soon seized by the rhythms of a city that never slept—in which the Carnival lasted half a year, during which everyone was masked, servant and aristocrat alike, and much addicted to gambling. Da Ponte succumbed to the mania for gambling and fell into the clutches of Angela's scheming brother, who bilked him of whatever money he had. Throughout his life Da Ponte could be quite credulous, quick to befriend dubious people and even quicker to hold grudges against them. His memoirs are tiresome because they try to settle so many scores.

Lorenzo was temporarily saved from his vices by his brother, who whisked him off to a teaching job in the more sober town of Treviso. But there Lorenzo ran afoul of the Venetian Inquisition when he wrote two Latin elegies with advanced liberal views—holding, among other things, that laws increase crime and reduce the chances for general happiness. One of these elegies, oddly enough, was named "The American in Europe," perhaps in honor of the recent American Revolution and its egalitarian ideals. He was eventually accused of converting to Christianity only to debase the religion, and his questionable dalliance with Angela while still styling himself an abbé was brought to light. Because of his seditious poems, immoral behavior, and bad company, as well as his mockery toward the authorities, he was banished from Venice for the next fifteen years; if he ignored the banishment he was warned he would be confined to a cell without light for seven years. By the time the verdict was declared he was safely over the border in the little town of Gorizia, which counted seven or eight thousand citizens.

At this time of his life, when he was about thirty, he had many amorous adventures, somewhat like his friend Casanova. There was one important difference, however: whereas Da Ponte was ambitious (for money and prestige), Casanova was indifferent to everything but amorous conquest and perhaps literary renown and flashy clothes. He preferred "brilliant" court costumes to plain, ordinary nudity. Whereas Da Ponte all his life was constantly working, at everything from grocer to bookseller to librettist and professor of Italian, Casanova never worked at all except for a moment playing the violin in an orchestra in Venice. Da Ponte's memoirs are full of complaint and indignation, almost as if he were the virtuous woman deceived, whereas Casanova's are spirited and joyful—and far more affectionate toward all his women than is generally admitted. Of course Da Ponte was writing (if in Italian) for his virtuous American students (he made his memoirs required reading).

Da Ponte soon made his way to Vienna, where in 1782 he was quick to devise a new career for himself as a librettist, though he had no previous theater or musical experience. Later he would claim he'd been the "imperial poet," though more exactly he'd been the poet to the theater. While still in Italy, Da Ponte had made a name for himself as an *improvisatore*, the then-fashionable vocation of improvising rhymed verses on a given theme. Drawing on this gift for invention as well as on already-existing stageworthy texts, he wrote three of Mozart's great operas (*The Marriage of Figaro, Cosi fan Tutte*, and *Don Giovanni*) as well as many others for several composers—some twenty-two premieres between 1783 (when the Emperor established an Italian opera company in Vienna) and 1791. His gift for inspired chatter is particularly evident in the recitatives, the continual quick-witted repartee of impertinent servants or lovelorn young women or strife-weary aristocrats. Mozart himself disliked the constant rhyming, which came as naturally as breathing to his librettist.

Like freelancers everywhere, Da Ponte either had no work or too much. At one point he was writing three libretti for three different composers, morning, noon, and night, and he hired a pretty girl to come in and embrace him every half hour to keep him going. Oddly enough, he was proudest of his association with the Spanish composer Martin y Soler, whose *Una Cosa Rara* was a total triumph that eclipsed *The Marriage of Figaro*, and he ranks Salieri quite as high as "Mozzart," as he spells the name phonetically. At the end of his life he still ranked his libretto for Salieri's *Axur* as one of his "immortal" works, comparable to what he'd written for *Don Giovanni*. Da Ponte devotes only a few uninteresting pages to his collaboration with Mozart, though he does suggest they had different concepts of the opera. Mozart thought it should all be of a piece (an ideal that Wagner later achieved), whereas Da Ponte felt there should be a maximum contrast between succeeding solo arias and duets, between the gay and the serious, between fast and slow (Da Ponte got his way). Mozart also favored orchestrations that were fuller, more symphonic than ordinary and that the musicians found hard to play. *Don Giovanni* was dismissed as "learned" by the frivolous public, but Haydn modestly (and truthfully) commented, "One thing I know and that is that Mozart is the greatest composer the world now has."

Da Ponte was a successful courtier. He was able to convince the enlightened despot Emperor Joseph II to let him and Mozart write an opera based on Beaumarchais's *The Marriage of Figaro*, even though the Emperor had just banned the politically controversial play from the Viennese stage. Da Ponte had promised the ruler he would excise the objectionable passages while reducing the text to the necessarily shorter length (for an opera), which he did, mainly by cutting out characters and subplots.

To be sure, Joseph was an unusual monarch, one who loved music (more than literature), had seemingly democratic manners, and liked to mix with the populace disguised as an ordinary citizen. He abolished the death penalty but replaced it with excruciating tortures. Nevertheless the French Revolution (and the beheading of the Emperor's sister, Marie-Antoinette) made the ruler nervous. He was also challenged by the military advances of the Ottomans. When Joseph canceled his subvention of the Italian opera because his budget was stretched, Da Ponte arranged for various aristocrats to make up the difference, as long as the Emperor would provide the theater free, which the monarch did.

And yet, Da Ponte wasn't universally liked. The singer Michael Kelley based a ridiculous character on him, with his Venetian lisp, his impressionistic German, his arrogance, and especially his womanizing and his way of placing his cane behind him and leaning on it insolently. Everyone recognized who was being parodied and laughed heartily, turning to look at him in the opera house. Even the Emperor laughed. If Da Ponte was extraordinarily loyal to his many siblings, supporting them for the most part through the Viennese years though he seldom saw them, he could be treacherous to friends in his effort to ingratiate himself to the authorities.

Later in life, when he was questioned on why he left Vienna, he had an elegant response. He said that he left because of two deaths—of the Emperor, who was such a friend to the arts, and of Mozart, the "emperor" of culture. In fact, he was exiled by the new emperor, Leopold, who was deeply suspicious of artistic and intellectual foreigners living in Vienna; he was afraid the French Revolution might spread. Joseph II had himself buried under the epitaph he had written: "Here lies Joseph II, who failed in all he undertook."

Da Ponte, ever resourceful, went to London, where he dabbled with the opera and with selling books. He always imagined English speakers should be more interested in Italian literature than they were, not just in Dante and Petrarch and Ariosto but also in lesser known figures from the eighteenth and beginning of the nineteenth centuries. As he writes in his memoirs, he was always consulting "the great Parini's *Giorno*, Cesorotti's *Ossian*, Foscolo's *Sepolchri*, Monti's *Bassvilliana*, or the *Canzone* of Pindemonte"—not exactly household names in my humble home.

In the meantime, Da Ponte had gotten married to a Jewish woman converted like him to Christianity named Nancy Grahl, who had a level head and some money. Her father was a rich merchant from Dresden who'd moved to London. Da Ponte was forty-three, prematurely aged, and twenty years her senior. She preceded him with their children to New York. Da Ponte joined them later as he fled his creditors after a terrible, squalid crossing in which he gambled away his pocket money.

It would be tedious to trace out all the ups and down of his American years, but certain characteristics emerge: he was sentimental and credulous, easily fleeced and exploited by merciless new "friends"; he was a passionate and unwavering champion of the Italian language and literature, to which most Americans were indifferent; he shows in his memoirs a complete inability to scrutinize his own behavior, a total lack of interest in members of his family (his wife and children), and a disposition to suspect everyone else of wrongdoing; and, finally, a misplaced conviction that he could succeed if he could only win over the favor of the elite. The America of his day was fiercely egalitarian and no one wanted to serve another person; when Fanny Trollope, for instance, asked a maid in a Memphis boarding house to bring her tea to her room, the landlord himself angrily came up and told her she could damn well take her tea with the others downstairs. Even the wealthy worked hard and scrupulously respected their fellow citizens, or at least pretended to. Da Ponte, an avid promoter of Italian culture, was especially indignant that the American newspapers, filled with trivialities, never bothered to praise him in print: "There is a three-page article in praise of the wrinkled throat of a eunuch; and another announcing the arrival of an elephant and two monkeys in such and such a place—and a hundred other things of no account. And yet for more than twenty years there never appeared a writer charitable enough to deign to color a scrap of paper black to let the literary world, and Italians especially, know the work I was doing in America! 'Is it possible,' I said, that no one of them in all these years has heard from the many travelers who go from America to visit Italy, or read in the many periodicals that are sent thither, of the sacrifices I have been making, the losses I have sustained, the obstacles I have overcome, the intrigues, rivalries, and vexations I have disregarded, and the fatigues which I have exposed myself to in my declining years, in the miraculous enterprise of introducing the Italian language into the vastest and most remote portion of the globe, and of making known, diffusing and establishing there our divine literature, which before my arrival was either unknown to all or despised of all—to such an extent had those who had learned everything they know from Italians, slandered and degraded us!" He noted that New Yorkers were no more interested in learning Italian or Latin than in Turkish or Chinese.

Characteristic of Da Ponte, unlike Toqueville or Talleyrand or Chateaubriand or so many other cultured European émigrés of roughly the same period, it never occurs to him to *learn* anything in America about its wildlife or plants or many inventions or novel forms of political life or the habits of Native Americans; Da Ponte assumes he can only *teach* Italian literature and opera to an ungrateful nation. To be sure, even Toqueville thought that America was the country where contrary opinions were the least easily tolerated.

But Da Ponte was plucky. His wife, Nancy, had put aside several thousand dollars, which he invested in a grocery store in Elizabeth, New Jersey. He sold it and moved to Sunbury, Pennsylvania, where he built the largest house in town and traded in distilled liqueurs, medicines, and spices, crossing the hills between Philadelphia and Sunbury some seventy-two times—until his wagon was overturned, not once but twice, and he injured his back and broke a collarbone. When his wife's rich relatives, wary of his bad business sense, put strings on their will, not allowing him to touch the capital, he went into major dudgeon and returned to New York, plagued with his own debts and promissory notes he'd foolishly signed for other people's debts (although his pal Casanova had specifically warned him years before against ever signing anything).

The New York of his day must have seemed hopelessly provincial to him. Everyone had unlimited self-esteem, and no one was deferential to anyone else. The War of 1812 consolidated American identity and patriotism. Children became important in a way they'd never been in Europe; the middle-class family's efforts were devoted to molding their offspring into upstanding citizens. Although Da Ponte claimed to like the freedom and egalitarianism of the New World, one wonders. Perhaps he felt like Talleyrand; when Napoleon asked him what America was like, he said, "Thirty-two religions, Sire, and just one recipe." Da Ponte said he thought it was strange he'd ended up selling snuff with the same hands that had written *Don Giovanni*. Most foreigners commented on how money, where all other distinctions had been eliminated, ruled supreme.

Da Ponte, in his memoirs (and presumably in his behavior), was careful not to offend puritan sensibilities. He died in 1838, well after the Great Awakening, a new surge in evangelical Christianity. Temperance movements were equally strong, as Evangelicals attempted to banish the working man's curse. Sabbatarians tried to make Sundays free of all enterprise and consecrated to devotion. Women enjoyed an unusual degree of freedom (as workers and active members of society) but they were obliged to protect their moral reputations. Nothing unseemly must be permitted to occur—which affected Da Ponte directly when the old libertine and his wife opened a boarding house for young ladies. Especially when a fellow Italian circulated a pamphlet accusing him of crimes back in Venice and various improprieties—and even claimed his Italian accent was substandard.

Da Ponte did find a powerful and rich young patron, Clement Clarke Moore, the man to whom the most famous American poem, "'Twas the Night Before Christmas," is attributed, the son of an Episcopalian bishop, and the developer of the Manhattan neighborhood known as Chelsea. The two men met by chance in a New York bookstore, where Da Ponte butted in to correct some misinformation about Italian literature, and the friendship eventually led to Da Ponte in 1825 being named the first professor of Italian at Columbia (though without a salary—the students paid him directly). He was also the first Jewish-born member of the faculty, though that wasn't generally known. Moore was a professor of Hebrew at Columbia.

There were so few truly cultured people in New York in the early republic; Moore was impressed that Da Ponte could speak Latin and Italian and invited him around. People marveled at his erudition and memory (he could recite reams of Dante by heart). Though he'd lost his teeth early on when a rival for a lady's favors had convinced him to apply nitric acid to his gums for toothache (which caused his teeth to fall out), the old gentleman made a striking appearance with his flowing white locks and strong profile. And yet a German novelist (Ferdinand Kuernberger) wrote in 1855 that he recalled meeting a vagrant, hungry and cold, dressed in frayed clothes. When he discovered the old man was Da Ponte, he exclaimed, "I beg you to accept the tribute of my fervent esteem. Wherever culture is to be found on earth, there each man is in your debt."

Once again Da Ponte shot himself in the foot. He decided in 1833 to build an opera house, which was already a wildly impractical idea. But he also insisted on constructing six tiers of box seats, perhaps inspired by the Teatro San Carlo in Naples, considered the most famous opera house in the world. But whereas the San Carlo was designed for the members of the court (who were all visible to the king, since none of the boxes was allowed to be curtained), the Americans weren't seduced by the idea of listening to long operas in an incomprehensible language, and the house was converted into an ordinary theater three years later. A critic of the day said that the boxes had been a bad idea since they suggested "a sort of aristocratical distinction," inimical to the new democracy. Perhaps no symbol better typifies Da Ponte's inability to adapt to his new culture than those horseshoe-shaped box seats. Only a half century later, New York was ready for the Metropolitan Opera. Whereas an opera house in Europe's capitals was a place where diplomats could conduct business, where courtiers could display themselves to their sovereign, where illicit romances could spring to life, in puritanical America few people were rich enough for such extravagances. It wasn't until 1830 that John Jacob Astor decided to invest in Manhattan real estate; he correctly foresaw that New York would soon grow into a great city. But when Da Ponte opened his opera house, the city was not yet ready for it. In 1829 New York had entered a serious depression, and the 1830s would see the rise of violent class conflicts; no reason to exacerbate them with the conspicuous display of opera house culture.

Nevertheless, Da Ponte did get to hear an American performance of *Don Giovanni* in 1825, nearly forty years after he wrote it. He outlived his wife, his daughter, one of his sons, and one of his grandchildren.

He died on August 17, 1838, at the age of eighty-nine, and like Mozart and Casanova, he was buried in an unmarked grave; later the bones were disinterred from 11th Street and moved to less expensive real estate in Queens. The opera house burned down a few years later. Toward the end of his life he wrote, "I dreamt of roses and laurels, but from the roses I had only thorns, and from the laurels bitterness!"

Quid Pro Quo, Just As Easy As That

JEANNE THORNTON

It was a book launch; one of the fiction authors I edited was being feted by a European government. A princess would be there and everything. I would be there as well to support my author. The question from my boss was: *What would I wear?*

This was a pretty common question my boss asked me in those latter days of my New York City publishing job. The question started when I'd elected to come out as a trans woman in the workplace. Foolishly, I'd assumed that there would be no problem with this: the press was accounted radical, had published at least one well-known trans author and a beloved gender-progressive kids' book, people generally liked me there, etc.

I have a lot of transgendered friends, my boss said to me at one point shortly after I told him. They're always talking endlessly about their identities. I don't want to hear anything like that at work.

Of course not, I told him. *Thank you for not firing me* was the implicit coda.

I felt really lucky not to be fired for being trans in the workplace. I felt really lucky about a lot of my early experiences as a trans woman in New York City. My family was generally supportive, and based on some of the truly horrible stories I heard people at the 13th Street LGBT Center tell, I'd been fortunate. Aside from a lovesick *AM New York* salesman who invited me to give him oral sex on the street at 3:00 a.m. and some miscreant teens on the subways, I didn't have any awful stories.

About the worst was the guy who played drums on the transfer between the L and 1 trains. I used to smile at him; seeing this guy with a big smile playing joyous drums against the urine-slick wall of a molding subterranean tunnel stuffed with *Metropolis*-level numbers of numbed commuters was one of the highlights of my own commute. It made work seem more okay. One day, the drummer called me over, huge smile still on his face, and passed me a note.

If you want to get fucked hard call me at this number some time.

I didn't really want to meet his eye the next day, so he screamed as loud as he could to the whole tunnel that I was a fucking bitch. But it was okay; no one even looked up or noticed.

And I guess it was okay at work for the most part, albeit awkward for me and the different authors and foreign rights agents when my boss introduced me—six months into being out on the job and wearing pinstripe skirts and tights as my everyday "comic strip character" outfit—using a male name and pronouns. The boss was sorry; it was hard for him to remember sometimes that I was not actually a male employee. I had to understand this about him.

I felt bad for making trouble for him and everyone. It was difficult to go from being considered A Good Employee to being considered 100 percent the opposite.[1] My boss once told me that prior to a plane flight, he'd quickly sketched out a will regarding the press that essentially left operations in my hands as some kind of heir apparent.

I would *never* do that now, he told me after I'd been out at work for a few months. He had reasons, specific assignments I'd failed in that I don't remember now and don't feel that I need to.

I hope it is okay for me to come to your book launch, I wrote my author, *but if it isn't I will understand. It's your launch and I don't want to mess it up. I'd understand if the princess didn't want to be seen with me.*

I would have a problem with anyone who didn't, my author wrote back to me. It shocked me because I didn't believe, fundamentally, that anyone could really believe that. Later, at the event—a consulate rooftop near the UN Building, dozens of stories up in a garden in the setting sun, European security guards smoking and bumming lights to the royal entourage—we talked about the princess, whom this author knew somewhat socially.

She's really a down-to-earth person, he told me.

It was a flush time for me in New York City. According to invoices I still have, I was making the sweet sum of $12 per hour and working

---

1. Now he treats you as badly as he treats us, one of the women in the office told me once, not without satisfaction.

enough to clear about $1600 every month. The rent at the time was $1100, which I split evenly with a roommate. My share of the bills was usually about $125 total, and the Metrocard rate $100 per month. I knew of a cheap grocery store and cooked when I could. I smoked back then too, a hideously expensive habit at $13 a pack in NYC. So I'd switched to smoking three or four "lucies" a day at $0.75 per cigarette, or $2 for three, from the grocery store just down the street from me that kept lookouts. Sometimes you could run across illicit cig pushers on the streets—especially, for some reason, on Roosevelt Island—who'd let you have a whole fat pack of Delaware-smuggled Newports for seven bucks. A devotee of *The Richest Man in Babylon*, I kept back about $100 to $200 from each paycheck to put into a savings fund, though I inevitably ran out of money every three or four months—food, doctor bills, miscellany—and had to raid it back to zero. But it all worked.

Many friends were not so lucky, and many of them ended up staying with me and my roommate for free. For a solid year we had people on the couch or on the floor of the not-really-a-bedroom second bedroom. There was the old high school friend, the depressive construction worker battling a slow slide into a nebulous drug addiction, the woman trying to get her software business back on its feet between multi-hour games of *Knights of the Old Republic* and bimonthly DJ sets. She once took a photo of the desk where I drew comics and posted it to Facebook under the caption *Mobile Studio Now Back in Operation*. I didn't draw a lot of comics that year.

And then there was my friend.

I believe that "luck" is an attribute doled out unequally, some undocumented quantum property determining that some people's probability waveforms will collapse into elegant Busby Berkeley fractals and that other people's waveforms collapse with the grace of a bag of burger meat slapping hot sidewalk. My friend the writer was one of the latter. When I first met him, he had a day job as a manager at the Long Island branch of a retail chain, but then the city decided it should send the police to shut down his illegal basement apartment in Jamaica—i.e., the exact same kind of apartment I was living in in Long Island City during the eight months of unpaid internship required for me to get my Good Publishing Job, starting salary $90 per week, my half of rent $350 per month. Because the cops came to my friend's apartment and not mine, he was thrown onto the street, losing all his possessions. He fought it; he ended up crashing at another friend's place in Bensonhurst, which, due to the way public transit works, transformed his commute from a ninety-minute bus and train ride to a four-hour multiple-transfer odyssey, all so that he could arrive fifteen minutes early for his 10:00 a.m. opening shifts (because if you're not fifteen minutes early, you're *stealing time*). Somehow he managed to make this work for a number of months before getting bounced on a three-strikes absence policy after something like nine or ten years at the job.

It is here that his troubles began. I don't know the precise set of intervening steps, but he had been in a homeless shelter before and slowly gone crazy from the stress of it (coupled with a couple of really, really unwise Facebook messages he'd sent to certain parties), landing in psychiatric treatment, rehab, and then a halfway house in our neighborhood. Sometimes during the day he would leave the halfway house and turn up in our living room, and we'd tell jokes and talk about writing. He was on food stamps. One time, in a festive spirit, he went with my roommate and me to a grocery store on 14th Street in Manhattan, where he ordered us all sandwiches on the NYC taxpayer dime. The trick is that food stamps don't cover "prepared foods," so the deli counter sold us sliced bread and different slices of cheese and meat, which we then had to assemble ourselves to our liking. We ate them in a doorway surrounded by metal shutters and we smoked seven-dollar Newports while good people passed us by.

Still, despite my roommate and me both liking our friend the writer a lot, we had at this point been sheltering guests for nine months solid and were sick of it. But my roommate was about to move to Chicago to start a job at Groupon, which meant he could happily invite our friend to move in consequence-free. Surely I could take care of the task of kicking him out eventually. Or who knew? Maybe he would find his feet.

Initially, the idea that this friend living on our couch was a temporary measure hovered in the foreground: he'd get a job, was going on interviews, etc. There is a whole acceptable Protestant work ethic narrative that people who are living in your house for free are obliged to give you, one that no one feels good about, and I personally felt relieved when we dropped it. He kept appointments at the welfare office when the food stamps cut out, and he renewed his Adderall prescription so that he had a source of income. He gained weight; he left the apartment more and more seldomly. Sometimes he talked about writing he was doing; slowly he stopped writing new things and turned to revising old ones, and then we stopped talking about writing so often.

Still, it was nice having someone to come home to. He'd met my boss on previous occasions and trusted him not at all. So when I came in, burned out from work, I liked having someone there to whom I could complain about the situation at my job.

My boss had it rough. Radical publishing is hardly a lucrative business at the best of times, and the business was at that point operating pretty close to the wire—*running on fumes* is the exact expression he used once when I was an intern and he had to explain why he couldn't afford to pay me. Royalties were in some cases fantastically overdue, and there were authors it was generally understood you could not call on the phone without being shouted at and threatened. It's a testament to my boss's raw skill and deserved reputation as a publisher that we stayed open at all: key best-selling titles came out exactly when they needed to, receivables and payables revolved about one another in a delicate balancing act, business relationships were carefully weighed and negotiated.

Some of his boldest financial initiatives had to do with payroll, of course. For example, there was the time he attempted to fire my girlfriend's boss and transfer her title and all of her duties—publicity responsibilities for eleven-plus books per season—to my girlfriend without increasing her salary.

You're a much cheaper date, he told her. It's a really great opportunity for you, he added.

She quit and got a job as a dog walker in Battery Park for substantially more money.

Many people were quitting or otherwise departing the job, and they were as a general rule not being replaced. Because of this, the amount of work I was doing steadily increased. I had been responsible for editing some titles, maintaining the website, fulfilling online orders and shipping books to author events, and running the company academic department. Now I was also collecting receivables, maintaining social networks, assembling a company newsletter every month, putting our books up on Wikipedia, helping to get all of our backlist available for purchase as e-books, designing print and web advertisements, and performing IT support in the office, among various other tasks. Everyone was doing a similar amount. All of it was an excellent opportunity, and I did ask for these assignments when they became available—if I didn't do some of it, who would? But it was plain that I was slipping up—ten books failed to be shipped to an author event; ancient backlist titles failed to be converted to epub in a timely fashion; Wikipedia pages for our books stubbornly failed to appear; the newsletter was late. The fact that my workload had tripled and my salary remained constant was surely a chimera. Here I'd come out as trans at work, and he hadn't even fired me, even though I couldn't be trusted to pick out my own clothes for important publishing events. I was letting him down.

Your boss is a real asshole, my friend told me. This was pretty good to hear.

He means well, I always said. He's doing really important work in the world.

Friends—without exception, female friends—began to tell me explicitly that they would not come over to see me when my friend was at the apartment. After the Facebook message incident, my friend was not a big fan of women, and he liked to discuss this with other women whom I was friends with. He would discuss it with me, too. In part this was because I hesitated to defend myself *as a woman* to him, and because I don't think he particularly thought of me as one anyway. (As evidence of this, the time he laughed at me and said *you're a dude*.)

More and more, I would come home and feel as if all I wanted was to sit on the couch and disappear, but *he* was on the couch, two-hundred-plus pounds, shirtless, and sweating in the lack of air conditioning. He was working his way through a science fiction series some fifty or sixty episodes long, all downloaded on a cracked laptop, smoking Black & Mild after Black & Mild. Sometimes I would join him in this. Sometimes I would have to catch up on editing work from the office or work on a freelance project to try to stash some extra money.

A lot of this period at home is a blur. I remember one time being upset with him and rearranging all the furniture in my bedroom into a kind of fortress, mattress and boxspring walls, sheets and clothes draped, cabinets as armored plates, books scattered everywhere. He knocked on the door to ask a question about something in the kitchen, and we held a conversation, a pretty outwardly civil one, me sitting within the fortress and him in the hall.

When you tore up your room and made a fortress to hide in, he told me one time after this incident, that was fucking hilarious.

Other times, we talked about *Final Fantasy 7*, or songs he liked that I still like,[2] or dumb things we could read on the internet, or things we were afraid of as writers or in our childhoods. I told him about the guy on the transfer between the L and 1 trains, and my friend was pissed off about it. He said he would always try to protect me from situations of that kind.

Once you start taking hormones and you get real hot, you're gonna have such a problem with me, he told me another time. This was a strange statement to live with, at once chilling and aspirational.

But there was a time bomb in the whole happy situation: the rent. The rent!

There was no way I could make up the entire $1,100 rent per month—$1,300 per month, the landlord informed me, after August. (Bushwick was becoming a hot neighborhood, especially along the L train.) My roommate had agreed to continue paying half for a few months while he had gotten started at Groupon, where his salary was sufficient to cover both his rent in Chicago and his half of the place in Bushwick, but once that grace period ran out, I was going to be homeless, and my friend with me.

I mentioned this to my boss at one point while we were out buying sandwiches, this fact that if I didn't receive more money—or if I couldn't somehow take additional time away from work to get a second job, do some additional freelancing, *something*—I would have to quit working at the press and move back to Texas, ending my career in New York publishing. He considered the problem and offered a solution. One of the press's authors had a luxury two-bedroom in Dumbo, he told me, that he'd asked my boss to help him find tenants for. It was only about $2,400 per month to rent, and it had good skylights.

Just get three other guys together, he told me, with each of you splitting a bedroom.

I don't think it occurred to him that I might have basic objections to this plan of sharing a place with three men, but why should it have? Why should he have to worry about my problems for me?

I *could* quit my job, I thought. I *should* quit my job. I could get another job in publishing. I had actual accomplishments: books I'd acquired that had been nominated for awards, years of experience, a literary agent who

---

2. LCD Soundsystem, "All My Friends." Lyrics = ironic, as will be seen.

knew people. That was all there was to it: go get another job. I thought about this a lot: sending out resumes to companies, with my list of publication credits and job references, almost all of whom knew me by a male name. Going to job interviews at big publishing offices—at a time in publishing history when hundreds of people with dozens of years of experience apiece were applying for jobs as editorial assistants—as a twenty-seven-year-old trans woman. I imagined sitting down with my boss to ask him his advice about these interviews. *What are you planning to wear?*[3]

But what I *could* or *should* do—beyond hang on to whatever stability I had then, even if I hated it and it harmed me—was beside the point. Here is why: I had spent six years at this point thinking of every possible reason that, despite being trans, it would be folly and disaster to transition. I would lose my friends. I would lose my job. I would lose my ability to sustain myself as some kind of independent person, a sense that I had been born with enough privilege to cultivate and expect. In deciding to come out, I had consciously prepared myself for the idea that all of this would disappear. Now I had one small, cool fact to hold on to, like a new-forged ring cooling in my hand. I had married into disadvantage. Every day, that ring got easier and easier to bear, but it took all of my strength to bear it. The strength to be a good person who was honest about what kinds of relationships I could and could not tolerate—the strength to do something productive and adult about it—was not something I had in excess at this time.

So instead, I took the bad-faith train in to Manhattan to my boss by day, back to Bushwick and my friend on the couch by night. In my sketchbook there's a drawing from this time: a skyscraper with a goat's head atop it, its distended jaw forming a kind of hellish front door. I drew my severed head attached to a tank tread, being directed into the goat jaw by remote control. I wrote in a journal too, its front page bearing the title *YUKIO MISHIMA IS BOTH INSPIRING AND A TOOL*, which I meant.

---

3. I'm writing this in 2014, and I should note for the smattering of cisgender readers who will buy this anthology that It Gets Better or whatever and that a lot of these fears seem abstract, toxic, and needless to me now. And even though I've changed in this regard since 2010–11, so has the world in fairly complicated ways, not least of which is HR sensitivity to—or even basic awareness of—the possibility of trans women in the workplace. And it bears mentioning that a close friend of mine was just told, this very summer of 2014, that she would not be receiving health insurance from her job at a well-known NYC university entirely because she's trans. All is complicity.

At one point I went to a therapist to talk about gender issues. I told him I figured I could handle the gender stuff, but that we could talk about it if the therapist wanted. Instead I talked about how I felt my job was actually killing me. (I didn't tell him about the what-are-you-going-to-wear stuff, as I didn't want to be unfair. I didn't tell him about my friend.)

It's not the job's fault, I said. I'm just not very good at dealing with it. I need to stay, though. The authors are depending on me. I can't get another job and I can't quit this one without knowing that there's some way to pay the rent. We're doing good work in the world.

The therapist said we could work on the gender issues and that it sounded as if I should quit the job immediately. I explained that if I quit the job I couldn't pay him for further therapy, that I actually technically couldn't pay him anyway. He said that he would do fine without my business.

You don't have to worry about me, he clarified.

Privilege is exponential, just like chess: you may think you understand it, but the person above you—or below you, I guess—understands more about it than you ever will, and there is always someone who understands that much more about it than *him*. My friend and I used to make fun of our neighbor, a Section 8 former military chef who didn't understand song lyrics, who only ate canned tuna and crackers, and who frequently tried to sell us shirts, socks, and children's toys in exchange for crack money. The same neighbor used to make fun of the women he knew who prostituted themselves for crack, deadbeats on the train, and us—or anyone who thought that they understood the ridiculous elements of his own life better than he did. My boss made fun of me sometimes, since I had gotten my degree from a state school and everything.

Said another way: You may have it rough, but you can't even understand the ways in which other people have it rough. You have no idea. They laugh at you for trying. You can think you are being kind and understanding, but it is impossible. Every line of this essay is deeply shitty, myopic, and hateful to someone.

The best it's possible to do, ethically, is to give to the limits of what we can without causing ourselves so much pain that we disintegrate. Those limits are always inadequate, but they're the only thing that matters, and fuck anyone forever who attempts to withhold even that bare minimum of human connection. Who dares to refuse to accept guilt about the need to remain alive and sane and to do so necessarily at others' expense—whether that's through gentrification, exploitation, or other techniques alarmingly close at hand.

The final straw at work came when I went into the publisher's office to ask a question about a contract. As soon as I came in, he told me that a lot of people had been leaving lately, claiming that they needed more money or less stressful situations. Accordingly, he let me know that if I were ever to ask him for a raise, a reduction in hours, increased benefits, or anything else that would improve my labor-to-income ratio, he would fire me and get a five-day-a-week intern to do my job for free. I told him I understood, got him to review the contract, and took the next day off. When I came back in, I gave eight weeks' notice and told my friends in Texas I was coming home.

Everyone finds their niche eventually, one of them told me.

My boss and I had lunch one last time in my final week on the job.

I feel like there's been a real erosion of the personal relationship between you and me, he said. He was sincerely concerned about it, and at the time I felt very bad for him about that.

Money flowed from radical bookstores and conferences across the world to my boss; from him to me; from me to my landlord; from my landlord to my friend and I in the form of shelter against summer heat and hurricane wind. Now the connection had been cut.

My friend began to talk seriously about what we were going to do next, what kind of place we might find together. I could get my bookstore job back maybe. He could sell Adderall maybe. His Black & Mild smoke filled the living room and I listened, knowing I was a traitor now to literally everyone.

Here is a question for the class. Why am I writing this story and not my friend? Seriously, why? Because I was luckier about my illegal money-saving apartment? Because I took a lot of shit for a long time in order to stay in an economically ruinous job that gave me Publishing Connections upon which I still rely? Is it important that I am white and my friend is black?[4] Is it important to note that he is often kind of a jerk to interact with personally? Is it important to note that I'm a gay trans woman and he's a straight cis male? What facts are salient here and why? Whose story of economic disadvantage is this, actually, and who

---

4. Yes.

determines whose story ultimately gets told? Publishers like my boss, or like the publishers of this volume? *Thank you for your confidence in me.*

Whatever the case: Reader, I threw my friend to the curb.

He'd been in the apartment since March; it was now summer. Feeling him out, I asked what he would do if I asked him to leave, what his plans were.

I'd go back to the homeless shelter, he told me without hesitation.

I took the subway to Williamsburg, where it was raining, and squatted behind a parked car in the rain, thinking about how I shouldn't go home, I didn't deserve to go home, I should stay in the rain, live in the rain forever. I called my former roommate at his office at Groupon, who told me I should go home.

You live there, he told me. You pay rent there. You do that horrible job so that you can pay rent there. *I* still pay rent there, he added.

The next day, I told my friend in the apartment that he had to leave. He said okay. Then he gave me a hug, like he was proud of me. A day or two later he gathered his things into a duffel bag and went back onto the streets in the August sun.

I haven't seen him since. He got married and I think got divorced. We like each other's Facebook statuses sometimes.

And I should say this: when I was returning to NYC for the Lambda Literary Awards ceremony in 2013 (tl;dr, longlisted, didn't win) and my housing fell through last minute, he sent me a message saying I was welcome to stay with him anytime. One of the other couchsurfers during That Final Year in NYC sent me a message saying the same thing. *To return the favor*, she wrote. As if it's quid pro quo, just as easy as that. I didn't respond to either of them.

Introduction

DAVE EGGERS

I have the honor of introducing a beautiful and richly evocative essay by a young writer named Chaasadahyah Jackson. I want to first say how important I think it is that this collection contains a young person's voice; taking the measure of a city really shouldn't be done without consulting the young people who surely absorb it on a more profound level than anyone else. Chaasadahyah is fifteen and has lived her whole life in Brooklyn, and there can be no one whose perspective on New York is more valuable than that of an exquisitely sensitive student like Chaasadahyah.

How did John Freeman, editor of this volume, find this new voice? He reached out to 826NYC, a nonprofit writing and tutoring center in Brooklyn, and asked Joshua and Mariama, the directors of the center, to point him in the direction of a gifted young writer. They introduced John to Chaasadahyah, and she produced this essay, an essay that does two things with incredible and seemingly effortless efficiency: it paints a portrait of a neighborhood that is fully realized and deeply personal, while also managing to complicate—to upend, actually—just about every contemporary misconception about her neighborhood, Park Slope.

People assume all residents of Park Slope are wealthy. Not so, Chaasadahyah explains. People assume all residents of Park Slope are white. Not so, Chaasadahyah explains. People—younger people—assume that Park Slope was always bursting with boutiques and upscale restaurants. Not so, Chaasadahyah explains, citing the memories of her father, who grew up in the neighborhood in the 1980s—with the actor Terrence Howard, no less. The accepted narrative of Park Slope now says that it's been compromised—or even ruined—by the influx of wealth and young upscale families with their strollers and nannies and taste for expensive coffee. Ruined? No, Chaasadahyah explains. "I see everything that everyone else may see," she writes, but it's clear she sees a lot more.

Chaasadahyah and her family moved from Crown Heights to Park Slope when she was eleven. "I can rewind my brain back like a tape," she writes, "and remember walking to daycare with my parents, glimpses of vacant buildings or torn down ones, that over the years got fixed up and changed." She loved Crown Heights, but, as becomes clear in her essay, Chaasadahyah throws her arms around new places and experiences, and through her eyes, and her clear-eyed optimism, the world in general, and Park Slope in particular, is remade for us. "Before we moved, I heard many great things about Park Slope from my dad who grew up here," she writes. "In our Park Slope apartment, my sister and I have a room we love. I like to sit in my room and watch the sunrise fade away into those peachy-orange and sorbet pink colors. Watch the sky drift away."

Can't you feel it? Can't you see those sorbet colors playing across a bedroom shared with a sibling? Park Slope, like any neighborhood, cannot be reduced to a cliché, an abstraction, a stereotype. It is a real place, full of people, each one of whom will contradict your preconceptions. It's also, in Chaasadahyah's words, a place of good pizza and bagels, rude people, trash overwhelming street corners, and a favorite restaurant, La Villa, where she and her family have the half-sausage, half-spinach pie, the pasta, and fried calamari.

This isn't to say that Park Slope hasn't changed. Of course it has. I lived on Ninth Street, between Sixth and Seventh Avenues, for a few years, around 1998 and 1999. Back then, Fifth Avenue was a place where you could get a check cashed, you could get an $8 haircut, you could get a beer in a place that may or may not have had a name. There were dollar stores, there was a dangerously crowded hardware store, and if you were looking for a white dress shirt, good luck finding one without a *Goodfellas*-style collar. It was wonderful. It was democratic and bustling and anything but fancy. That's why we set up 826NYC on the corner of Fifth Avenue and Fifth Street. We found an affordable building near M.S. 51, and the families poured in. They were working-class families, single-parent families, immigrant families—all of them looking for a bit of extra help for their school-age kids. They loved Park Slope, and we loved it, too. I maintain that there's no more gorgeous urban park in the world than Prospect Park, and I maintain that the brownstones of Park Slope have no equal anywhere in the city. Of course there are families there now, and there have been families there always. Families like Chaasadahyah's and her father's, too.

Over the years, the block where 826NYC sits has changed—a lot. But the families that come to 826NYC haven't. They're not fancy. Maybe they're not buying homes on the park, but they're finding a way to stay in the neighborhood, where the public schools are excellent and the feeling of community is strong. They're still in need of some help, too, some extra assistance after school. Chaasadahyah's little sister, Ahsadah, comes every day, and for four years, Chaasadahyah has come into 826NYC two or three times a week, to work on math and then to work on stories, films, and books. (Did you know she's working on a novel?)

And we get to benefit from hearing her words. When young people write, they tell a very different story about their city than we adults, jaded and saturated with received narratives, are able to. "I am an ordinary Brooklyn girl," Chaasadahyah begins her essay, and that might be true, but she's extraordinary, too. Through her lyrical prose and steady moral compass, she tells us about a neighborhood that we thought we knew, and she reminds us what makes it great, what makes it defy any easy categorization, what makes it home.

Park Slope Livin'

CHAASADAHYAH JACKSON

I am an ordinary Brooklyn girl who lives in Park Slope and goes to school in the city. I am a girl who loves the attractions, like all the fancy restaurants I encounter every day on 5th Avenue. I see everything that everyone else may see: people in Bagel World on the corner every morning at 8:00 a.m. sharp. The strong aroma of light and dark coffee, as I get my poppy seed bagel with cream cheese and head to school. Every day I walk into the dirty, smelly subway at Fourth Avenue and Ninth Street and emerge at 23rd Street in Manhattan. On both sides I see classy business people walking up and down the streets.

I didn't always live in Park Slope. When I was eleven we moved here from Crown Heights—another Brooklyn neighborhood. Park Slope is very different from Crown Heights— there are more fancy restaurants and small boutique shops. In Crown Heights there are soul food spots, ordinary apartment buildings, parks, and families. I can rewind my brain back like a tape and remember walking to daycare with my parents, glimpses of vacant buildings or torn-down ones, that over the years got fixed up and changed. When I lived in Crown Heights I would have to take the 72 bus with my mom and little sister every day to go to my elementary school in Park Slope. But now, in Park Slope, every day at the train station I hear, "Oh nooo, train! Wait, wait!" as people rush to crowd into the already packed cars—it gets kind of annoying, but you just learn to deal. I was excited to move, not because I didn't like Crown Heights, but because I like new places. Before we moved, I heard many great things about Park Slope from my dad who grew up here. In our Park Slope apartment, my sister and I have a room we love. I like to sit in my room and watch the sunrise fade away into those peachy-orange and sorbet-pink colors. Watch the sky drift away. We have a huge kitchen and my mom, who loves to cook, is happy there. My mom cooks dinner three or four nights a week, but like any other New York family we get take out and eat at restaurants a lot. Our favorite place to eat is La Villa on 5th and Bergen. It is the bomb. We eat a pie with half sausage and half spinach and order fried calamari and pasta.

My dad's Park Slope was very different from the Park Slope that I walk down today. He grew up here in the 1980s on 5th Avenue, along with his friend and now famous actor, Terrence Howard. My dad is definitely not your ordinary dad; he may be very cool and calm with you, unless you get on his bad side and push his buttons like no tomorrow, get ready for that. My dad is about 5'8", has a short beard, and has been working at Con Edison for thirteen years. He gives great advice, always gives a helping hand, and is there when you need him.

When my dad grew up in Park Slope, he used to hang out with his friends on the streets and in the subways. He was one of the kids who played music from a boombox and got into dance contests on the subways. He did it for fun, though, not for money. In the summers, he and his friends used to go all around Park Slope and Brooklyn, and go to big block parties. My dad says that back when he grew up, the block parties were huge, with many kids and parents in the street. There was music, games, food, and dancing. Nowadays it's not like how it was back then. It's quieter and everything is more separated and broken up. The last party on my block was nice, but I don't really think it was like how it used to be. My dad wants to do a big barbecue for July 4th to bring everyone together and try to make it like it was.

My dad has watched this neighborhood be wiped away like a clean slate and turned into this new, outgoing, flourishing area that my family and I admire. Many new businesses have popped up on every block like popcorn popping in the microwave. One day my dad took me for pizza and told me that he and his friends used to go to the corner of 5th Avenue and 3rd Street to play handball. The whole sidewall used to be a handball court where they would go on the weekends. When my dad walks by there now, he can't believe there used to be a court; now it is just the side of a school called M.S. 51. He used to live next to a building that is now a bar called Loki, and now it is his favorite spot on 5th. My dad also went to the same elementary school— P.S. 321—that my little sister and I both went to. He even knows the janitor, Joe, who has been there since he was little, and "the school" my dad says, "has not changed that much."

Knowing that my dad grew up in Brooklyn, and has seen many things change, and has had some of the same experiences as my sister and I, and is still here, makes me feel exceptional. I feel good that I'm in a place that most of my family grew up in, that's not a bad place, but a place that is constantly turning around.

Even though I have roots here, there are still many things that I disagree with and that frustrate me about my city. The traffic can be overwhelming—people are either on their phone or driving like it's their first time, or people are just in a rush to get to work and they get backed up on the road because of other drivers. The garbage can also be overwhelming. Restaurants like to keep their trash on the corner, with the bags piling up against one another, and they just think this is fine until someone trips out of nowhere. I would like it if there were a change concerning these piles. My hope is that people can stop littering, and put their garbage in the can like they are supposed to so there won't be this problem. Having to take the train every morning is quite crazy. It's always crowded and some people get cranky, especially since it's early in the morning.

One Monday, I was waiting for the F train to take me to school. The train came rolling down the tracks and the door stopped right in front of me—isn't that a qawink-ca-dink! So, I was standing there waiting for the doors to open and five seconds later they did. I was very kind and moved aside to let people out and then I tip-toed my way into the train. But then this lady was in such a rush to find a seat (mind you there was a person in every seat already) that she pushed me and said, "Why the f#*k didn't you move! Why do you move so slow?!" Thank God I am a nice person, because what she did was just plain rude. I just looked back at her for like five minutes and two seconds and then looked away, as if to say, "You know what you said was not right!" It wasn't right, but I let it slide. But next time I might not let it slide.

These are the small things that bother me about this city, but mostly I get really frustrated with people's assumptions about where I live and who I am.

People ask, "Where do you live?"

"I live in Park Slope," I reply with amusement, knowing people don't expect this answer.

"You do, wow, you are rich!"

When people respond this way I get mad because I'm not rich, and it makes me feel like I don't belong here, but I do. Most people think only white people may live in Park Slope, because they have a lot of money. Wrong answer. Anyone can live in Park Slope, just as anyone can live anywhere. We all go straight to judging each other, and never take the chance to talk with one another and learn about different experiences.

Don't get me wrong, I love Park Slope a lot. I sit down and think every once in a while about why it's important to me. There is a quote that I love from the movie *A Thousand Words* with Eddie Murphy that says, "Life is not worth living without family." What gives me the strength is my family, but also seeing people doing the right thing and walking straight forward toward their dreams. I want to think positively and grow as a person or else I might not go anywhere and forever be stuck in a box like a mime. After I graduate my dream is to go into the Service and also go to college. I want to join the Air Force; it's good to go after something that you truly believe in and want to accomplish in life. People react in many ways when I talk about the Service. They say, "You want to go into the Service? Wow, I don't think you should go, it's dangerous." The Service can be dangerous at times, I understand that, but the Service will prepare me to go out into the world and see new things. I would love to come back to Brooklyn to see how it looks and see what has changed. I love New York, but I want to explore and probably settle in a new state or even a new country. Even if I don't come back to live in Park Slope, I will always remember and love the bustle of the streets, my roots, and the memories that live here.

One, Maybe Two Minutes from Fire

TÉA OBREHT

Out of nowhere, the kid stopped in the middle of the crosswalk and put both hands on the hood of Marko's car.

That was what happened, Marko told himself. That would be the official story.

Marko had been drinking coffee. Did that matter? He had picked up a small house roast at the corner bodega before getting into his car. The cup was in his hand when he looked up and saw the kid. All of it came together so fast that he couldn't form what was going through his mind, whether he'd still been thinking about Kelly, whether he'd noticed the kid advancing toward the crosswalk, whether the kid's hat was blue or green. Only that the kid hadn't been smiling.

"Oh my God," the kid said, leaning toward the windshield. "Jesus, man!"

At first, even though he was sure he'd been stopped at the light for what must have been thirty seconds or more, Marko thought he'd hit the kid. That's what he would say. For an instant, he thought maybe his foot had slipped off the brake and that the car had drifted into the crosswalk and into the kid while he was tipping the last dregs of the coffee into his mouth. At least that hadn't happened. It could have. The instant the kid's fingertips touched the hood, Marko slammed down so hard on the brake that the rim of the coffee cup shredded his gums. But the car didn't budge. The brake was already stiff against the floor.

The light was still red. There was a gray hatchback behind Marko, its blinker flickering for the left turn down Amsterdam. Across the avenue, the tiny harridan from downstairs was shuffling her rag-doll dog toward the park. The kid, still standing there with his hands braced against

Marko's car, looked like he was the only thing keeping it from sliding down the street and into the colorful onslaught of children funneling out of school in a storm of sound on Amsterdam.

"Your car, man!" the kid finally said. "Your hood's smoking. Pull over right now."

Marko cut the wheel all the way to the right and the car slid in toward the curb. The front wheel lurched up onto the sidewalk and he heard a scrabbling thump from the back seat. He rolled down the window and peered along the flank of the car. He couldn't see smoke, smell anything—though he remembered that a garbage bag had siphoned onto the hot undercarriage last week, and the smell of it burning still drifted up to him sometimes during prolonged bumper-to-bumper standstills on the RFK bridge. He yelled "Thank you!" at the kid, whose form he could see weaving in and out between the neon-vested delivery drivers and halal carts on the avenue. That's right. That was what had happened.

Now this next part: how long did he just sit there, watching the street, letting the relief of not having hit the kid wash over him? Long enough to dab at some of the coffee that had lashed all over the dashboard. Long enough for the light to change and the gray hatchback to go by while the driver lanced Marko with stone-faced disgust. He was parked under a tree, two blocks from where he had started, just beside the little shop that sold Italian sandwiches and the kind of cured meats that he always regretted having to eat on the sly in this part of town.

What did he actually remember about the guy sitting on the pavement outside the shop? That the guy was about sixty—this was crucial, the guy's age. That the guy had a weather-beaten complexion that reminded Marko of orchardists back home, and that some kind of red-smeared sandwich rested on his knees. That he said "Holy shit"—seriously, too, in a way that yanked down at Marko's gut, like he'd seen the whole thing and he couldn't believe his eyes. When the guy got to his feet, Marko noticed the oil stains on the knees and sleeves of his blue utility jumpsuit. He knew he remembered this.

He knew the mechanic's uniform had a handwritten name tag, but he couldn't remember what it said. Pavle, maybe. Or Petar. Some name remotely and reassuringly tied to Marko's neck of the woods, anyway.

"Holy shit," the mechanic said again. It stood out to Marko now, the way the guy had rested his knuckles on expansive hips. "Wow, wow, wow. That's bad, boss. Start counting your stars. What a day."

Marko had probably said, "What? What is it?" a few times. He had turned off the engine, but the mechanic made him start the car back up again and pop the hood. The latch took a moment to find, but as soon as the red bonnet went up, Marko heard it: an unmistakable, frantic clattering.

Then he had gone around the front and stood staring down into the dusty, inscrutable maw of the engine compartment. He remembered the mechanic's finger—black-nailed, he could see it now—pointing at an insanely shivering tubule that had destabilized and was now thunking furiously against the spark plugs.

"Boss," the mechanic said. "This is about to blow. You better go to church tomorrow—God is with you today."

It hadn't felt that way yesterday.

The previous morning, he'd had a quarrel with Ivana, this time about—of all things—turnips. He spotted them, between shishito peppers and garlic, on the extensive write-up of delicacies he was supposed to procure for the dinner party to honor the upstairs neighbors' engagement. In her immaculate English handwriting, Ivana had put down: *baby hakurei*.

"What's this?" he asked.

"The turnips," his wife said, carefully, in English—goading him, of course. "They are Japanese. I think they will go very nicely with the lamb."

"Japanese turnips?" he said. "Potatoes go nicely with lamb, and maybe a little tomato salad on the side. Why don't I just get some of those?"

"That does not fit the flavor profile I'm working with," she said. She was trimming the fronds off a flower arrangement she had been, for the better part of an hour, shifting from one end of the hallway table to the other. The flowers were the soft yellow of lemon cream, and the light, she insisted, better complemented them on the left side—but putting them on the right, apparently, really opened the room up. "Glazed turnips will very finely bring out the ginger marinade of the lamb."

"Turnips aren't for company, they're what my father and his brothers used to dig out of the ground to eat when they were starving in winter," he said. The air conditioner—a rattling inheritance from the apartment's last legal tenant—was off-limits for the afternoon to accommodate the electrical workload of the oven, where some sort of chamomile cake was in progress, hot-boxing the apartment and making the dog insane.

Marko's sweat was running the letters of the shopping list. "This is just another one of your cooking experiments where you're trying out some exotic bullshit that nobody who's not a fag on TV actually eats, and I end up paying $15 for a pound of glorified pig-feed."

The look she leveled at him was the same one reserved for the inevitable stare-downs over the joint oil and curative pomade stockpiles he ordered whenever some relative from back home decided to visit. "There is a world beyond tomato salad. It would not harm you to give the wider horizons a chance."

"Oh turnips—turnips are going to broaden my horizons? The way to worldliness is through turnips?"

"Just get what is on the list, please, Marko."

Anyway: "You not from around here, are you?" the mechanic said.

It sounded too accusatory for a guy who had an accent himself—Bulgarian, Marko suspected, or maybe Czech. "Not here, no," Marko said quickly. "I'm just passing through the neighborhood."

"You live in the city?"

"In Astoria." He could hear Ivana already, asking him what the hell he was thinking, telling strangers where they lived. But what did she know, the guy seemed like the kind of person who might feel allied to Astoria; maybe he had some family living out there; maybe he, too, had a wife who'd been compelled to cut her working hours to just Wednesdays and weekends so she could "manage the car during the street cleaning" because it was either that or pay for garage parking. And what was he supposed to do if the guy just left him there with his hood open and the last-century Honda death-rattling its last, in this part of town, of all places?

"I see this all the time," the mechanic said. "See, potholes in the road, you go bumping all over them, they knock out pins in your motor. See all these moving parts? See how this is loose right here? And you don't know until: boom! God is with you today, my friend."

"This is just incredible," Marko said.

"And then—boom."

"It blows up?"

"All the fluids gone, there's no—look, there's no nothing! It's dry. You are one, maybe two minutes from fire here."

"Mother of God."

"I know, boss. It's bad."

They both crossed themselves. This was important.

"I can't believe that kid noticed it."

"And what luck for me to be taking my lunch just now?" the mechanic said. "God is with you today."

"Thank you."

What happened next, though? The mechanic told Marko to shut off the engine, and then got on the phone to his boss at the shop. He told the boss he'd be late, he was dealing with a roadside breakdown. Did he have permission to take care of it right here? No, he didn't think the man could safely drive it all the way to the shop. Marko knew he overheard this—he remembered a fizz of relief at the idea that, possibly, he would not have to call a towing service and then spend the next month intercepting that bill in the mail. He remembered, too, glancing up and down the street for the mechanic's vehicle—there was a white van parked nearby, its doors scrawled with the silhouette of a hammer. Marko stood by and watched the disconnected tube in the engine compartment palpitating. Two young black guys hoisted themselves up onto the railing outside the Italian sandwich shop. If he was honest with himself, he was pretty sure he saw them nudge each other. But Ivana didn't need to know that.

"I don't trust those kids," the mechanic said, closing his phone carefully. "What are they looking at?"

"Nothing better to do than stare at people's misfortune, I guess."

"You got some water and paper towels?"

"In the trunk."

Maybe if his knees hadn't been shaking—and he could really feel it then, that rush of relief hitting him in the legs first, the way liquor always did—he would have glanced into the back seat and remembered. Maybe he wouldn't have just handed the mechanic a water bottle and roll of paper towels and said: "Thank God you're here."

"You got that right, boss," the mechanic said, and went to work.

At some point in the next five minutes—while the mechanic laid out one of the floor mats from the front seat and got down on his hands and knees and reached under the car, and then got up and poured water into the tank, and tightened the pins and then went back down again—they established that they both knew people at the technical university of Novi Sad. Not the same people—but still, Novi Sad. The mechanic had grandkids in Australia: two little girls, Marko remembered, Ana and Clara, maybe. He didn't see them much, but he was saving up to visit this winter, God willing. It was hard with two jobs. Marko knew. And the best *burek* in town, they concurred, was at Zaha's in Brooklyn—even though it was technically run by Turks.

"You got a card?" the mechanic said.

"Sure." Marko sorted through his wallet and found one. He remembered thinking he really had to print a new set, update the old Newark address. He held it out to the mechanic. "That's my mobile there, but we're in Astoria now. If you're ever in the area, your dry cleaning's on the house."

"No—a card to pay for the service," the mechanic said. He was sitting up now, blinking at the card in Marko's outstretched hand. The wisps of hair dotted about his moist pink scalp looked like they were coming out of the top of a pillow. "You heard my boss on the phone," the mechanic said. "If it were up to me, I wouldn't charge, but you heard my boss. Three hundred dollars—that's what it would be at the shop, probably more, they'd push you to change your O2 filter. And that's not even with labor. That doesn't include me. But I'm on lunch—I'm not gonna count that. I was just here. God is with you today. How about $250 instead?"

It sounded reasonable. You couldn't argue with that. It sounded like not much, a lifeline for what this little adventure would cost him in real terms. And what did they have money for—Ivana's Japanese turnips, or moments like this, situations where it really mattered, where fortune interceded and sent one of their own to eat his lunch right at the corner where Marko had almost lost his life to a latent automotive explosion?

"But I can't do card," he said. It would obliterate any of the breaks he'd caught in this incident so far. "I've got to get cash."

"You go ahead," the mechanic said. "I'll just finish up here."

It had taken less than five minutes to go to the bodega and back. Of this Marko was absolutely certain. The bodega had the closest ATM—even if he hadn't known, from past experience, that the address of the withdrawal would not appear on his bank statement, he would have gone there. He could tell anyone—including himself—that much with a clear conscience. He hadn't even paused when Ahmed greeted him from behind the counter—just smiled apologetically and waved his fistful of twenties and said "Car trouble!" and flung the door open. He heard Ahmed say: "Oh—that's bad luck!"

Down the block, the street was empty. His brain was running on so many tracks, then, that he couldn't remember—really couldn't—the progression of his thoughts when he reached the sandwich shop. He re-membered the smear of oil and AC drip that was pooling, shifting, ad-vancing slowly down the slope toward the crosswalk, a sun-streaked fish that reshaped itself as it went.

The black kids were still perched on the rail. "Dude," one of them said. "For fuck's sake."

He could hear Ivana's questions now: did you leave the car with him? A total stranger, and you just left him alone with the car? *What the fuck is wrong with you?*

But I had the keys, he thought. The keys were with me. He knows people in Novi Sad. He gets his *burek* at Zaha's. God was with me today.

There were ways to smooth this out. That was the important thing.

There were ways to explain, as he had explained at the police station later on, that it had all happened so quickly, that his brain had been in a vortex of confusion and relief from the instant he'd realized he hadn't, in fact, hit the kid in the crosswalk. That it didn't actually occur to him that he had not seen any smoke with his own eyes because of the kid's frantic earnestness. That the kid had been in on it—at least according to responding officer Daley who, in Marko's version of events, had taken down the report gravely and patiently, and without the slightest hint of amusement. Officer Daley, who had reassured Marko that these things happened all the time—that he shouldn't blame himself, these people were professionals working in tandem and clearly with uniforms to en-hance the ruse—in a voice that in no way indicated that he thought Mar-ko was some sort of woeful plebe who'd just moved into the city from directly behind his plow.

Marko would say, too, that Officer Daley had said—or at least im-plied, or at the very worst allowed Marko to conclude—that many stolen cars were often retrieved within forty-eight hours of theft; that Marko's description of the mechanic fit the profile of a suspect whose case they already had on file; that he was confident his team would find the car.

And yes, Ivana was all about the questions these days. But she wouldn't ask to speak to Officer Daley herself—and even if she did, Mar-ko himself would dial the number. And even if they spoke, he very much doubted that the question of which precinct the report had been filed in would come up. And in the event that it did, Marko didn't believe for an instant that she would have the energy to track down the precinct or look it up on the map, and furthermore piece together that she had followed him into that part of Harlem last year, when she first had her suspicions, about a month before she caught him outside Kelly's apartment and he swore he would break it off.

No, she had the ginger-marinated lamb and Japanese turnips to preoccupy her. And if Marko could get her to see it all in the right light, it would be a thrill, a slice of New York life, and they would recount the unfairness and surprise of it at the neighbors' engagement party that evening.

"I never would have guessed," Marko would say, "that crooks would make such an effort over a compact car."

Of course, more questions would surface by morning. But he wasn't worried. The folks at Penelope's Pet Spa and Salon dealt primarily with him, anyway—and it wouldn't be the first time he sent a little extra their way to blur the exact hour he had brought the dog in for its weekend stay. He would tell Ivana he'd arranged an extra-long stay this time, the works, a special treat to make up for his insensitivity about the turnips. And meanwhile the absence of the car would discourage Ivana from venturing into Manhattan, at least in the coming days, while he scoured the neighborhood and put up posters:

LOST: Teacup Pomeranian. Last seen crated in rear seat of 1999 green Honda Civic. Answers to the name Nikola Tesla.

Service/Nonservice: How Bartenders See New Yorkers

ROSIE SCHAAP

BE NICE

There's a sign taped to the mirror behind the bar where I work in Brooklyn that says, "Be nice or you'll get the boot." (To animate its message, the sign is in the shape of a boot.) Some customers notice it, point it out, have a laugh. Others don't. Still, it's as good a declaration of this particular bar's ethos as any—and once in a while, when I sense intimations of aggression, if someone starts getting out of line, I point to it, smile, and repeat aloud what it says. It usually breaks the tension in the room. This is a good-natured, friendly place, this little neighborhood bar in a gentrifying but still relatively modest part of Brooklyn, in the fuzzy borderlands between Park Slope and Sunset Park near Green-Wood Cemetery. We don't want any trouble here. We want everyone—and that includes you—to make nice, to make friends, and have an easygoing, no-pressure $3 Miller High Life, $3 shot of Evan Williams good time.

And the happy truth is: Most people here *are* nice. I love my job. In my four years behind this bar, only a few incidents have given me real grief, and those have been extreme, anomalous cases. Once, a raving madman, jacked up to his eyeballs on speed, sweating through his T-shirt, came in, ordered a shot of whiskey, didn't drink it, and proceeded to pace the length of the almost-empty bar enumerating, in a loosely coherent monologue, the many conspirators arrayed against him: The Bloods. The Crips. The Hollywood establishment. Old friends who'd betrayed him. The Brooklyn Academy of Music. Then he became eerily still for a moment, as if finding the quiet center of his self-made storm, looked me right in the eye, and told me that he was the Angel of Death. "You were kind to me when I walked in," he said, "and you will come to regret that kindness." Suddenly, it felt like a siege. It took a long, tense time to get him out of the bar. But he was wrong: I don't regret whatever kindness I showed him. That's what I expect of all bartenders, and what I wish for from all customers.

Like many bartenders, I've been propositioned from time to time in uncomfortable ways. I've had to intervene more than once when male customers have bothered uninterested women customers. And, sure, sometimes I've had to cut people off and give them the boot—but nicely.

There are innumerable ways to be not nice in a bar, and mostly they're not extreme. They're about manners, assumptions, and ways of asserting power and control. It's everyday stuff: seemingly small, constant reminders that there are two kinds of New Yorkers: those who work in service, and those who do not.

SO, WHAT *ELSE* DO YOU DO?

I had a friend in college whose dad, an Italian immigrant, tended bar at a beloved old-school Italian restaurant on Manhattan's East Side for decades. Many of his regulars were character actors, some regularly seen in the films of John Cassavetes. (Maybe that's irrelevant, but I just like Falk and Gazzara and Cassavetes.) Anyway, the man, my friend's father, made a good enough living behind that bar to buy a nice house in a nice New Jersey suburb, and put two children through college.

I like to think those actors tipped well. Something makes me suspect they did. But good tips alone don't pay mortgages and tuition. It may seem as though bartending is now a more respected office than ever before, but I don't think that's true. As taste in drinks has become generally more sophisticated, tending bar may require special skills, and it may have acquired some cultural cachet, but my sense is, for all that, it used to be more professionalized, and pre-tip wages reflected that. Tending bar was once regarded as a real job, a way to make a living without having to make a living many different ways, as so many bartenders do now.

I doubt that anyone ever asked my college friend's father what else he did, or what his real job is, but I've come across very few bartenders now who haven't been interrogated in this way. Most weeks, I'm asked at least once what else it is that I do. In the years since I returned to bartending after a long absence, I've had some good luck as a writer. My memoir was published. I write a column for a newspaper. But I still bristle at the question, and hesitate before answering. Partly because I think "What do you do?" is never the most interesting question one might ask someone they've only just met. Partly because I'm as surprised as anybody that I wound up with another career that's working out OK, and that wasn't always true for me, and it hasn't been true for many other bartenders I know, irrespective of their talent and ambition, so it's a matter of solidarity. Partly because I think bartending is an excellent occupation in itself, and I'm uneasy with the assumption that it can't possibly be enough. (Sometimes I do tell them that I'm a minister, which is also true—I was ordained as an Interfaith minister in 2002, and have served as a Red Cross chaplain—even though I hardly consider it my job, because it generates pretty spectacular reactions, and because it pleases me to consider the ways in which bartending so often feels like a kind of ministry.)

My friend Susan, who was possibly the greatest bartender I've ever had the pleasure of watching, learning from, and being served by, probably handled it better than I did. She'd just make shit up, and have fun with it. "When people asked me, 'what do you really do?' I would laugh so hard." I can just hear that laughter—it was one of the many joys of drinking when she was behind the bar. "I would say things like, shshsh, but I work on the corner of 43rd and 9th. I was a sheepherder by day. I was a nun. A ditch digger—just for the exercise."

Other bartenders' responses and reactions sound more like my own. I returned to bartending at forty, after more than fifteen years away from it. I'd never really thought about getting behind a bar again. But when the owners of a then-new, cozy, unfussy bar in my neighborhood asked if I'd give it a shot, it felt like a blessing. I was recently widowed, still mourning. That loss—and the two sad and stressful years during which my husband had been sick with a very rare type of cancer—had made me retreat, close ranks, and isolate myself. I think the bar's owners knew that, and offered me a shift as a kind of mitzvah, an act of kindness, a way to get me out of my apartment and out of the worst depths of my sadness. It couldn't put an end to grieving—nothing can, save time—but it helped. At least one day a week, I had to wake up, shower, brush my hair, and talk to people. I hadn't been doing much of any of that since Frank died. Doing work that was physical and social—unlike writing, which is sedentary and solitary—turned out to be just what I needed. But that felt like more story than any customer wanted to hear when they asked what else I did. What was I going to say? Write and mourn?

◆ ◆ ◆

We all have our reasons for winding up on the working side of the bar, and a certain kind of customer always wants to know what they are. Christy left a career in advertising in Boston because she'd always dreamed of living in New York. Advertising jobs weren't easy to find after 9/11. Instead, she got a gig at a bar in Tribeca, and discovered that she liked it, a lot. (It was at my favorite place, the much missed Liquor Store bar. I remember it largely as a peaceable drinking kingdom, with a great mix and range of regulars, where fun and politesse reigned.) "I looked back only when pegged by a shitty conversationalist—a suit wandering in accidentally or some other arrogant overachiever —with the question, 'So, what else do you do?' That would send me reeling into a shift-long panic attack, or self-doubt. Over and over again."

But mostly it isn't arrogance or self-importance that compels bar patrons to ask this question. Evan, another former bartender, hated "the assumptions people made about my life—that I must be in school, or had been laid off from a real job, that I was nomadic." But he quickly adds: "The curious were well intentioned, I assume." And I believe that, too. I recently had an argument about this with a curious, well-intentioned friend. We'd just had lunch together, and agreed that our waiter was funny and charming. "I wish I'd asked him what else he did," my friend said. I told her that it's probably best she didn't. That the question, regardless of how kindly one asks it, is often unwelcome, and sometimes even makes people feel bad. Would you ask a teacher what else she did? A banker? An editor? It's a question only asked of those of whose jobs seem to many others to be transient, temporary, somehow less than substantive.

WHO'S IN CONTROL?

At their best, bars are social levelers. It doesn't matter to a bartender if a customer is rich or poor, young or old, male or female. How a person tips doesn't even matter as much as you might think. Some of my favorite customers over the years haven't been great tippers, but they contribute something valuable to the culture of the bar—by being kind, by being considerate, by being funny, by telling good stories, by being good listeners. These qualities matter more than big tips.

As of December 2013, the basic combined cash and tip minimum wage rate for non-unionized, tipped employees (this includes bartenders and food servers) was eight dollars an hour, up from $7.25 the previous year. Wages this low inevitably mean that the great bulk of a bartender's income comes from tips, creating a condition in which customers can easily feel a sense of power over those who serve them drinks.

At two bars where I've worked, one of the first things I was told when I trained was: "When you're behind the bar, you're in charge." A bartender is a master of ceremonies, the host of a party, the person running the show. But to some customers, the power is always theirs—whether they tip well or not.

"I have a little resentment of the rich arrogant folks that insist on putting me in a category of non-human by not treating me respectfully, not looking me in the eye, and not saying 'please' and 'thank you,'" Terri, a seasoned Brooklyn bartender, told me, "all while I'm expected to treat them like they're my employer."

The one group of people from whom bartenders never get this kind of treatment: other service people. It's commonplace that bartenders get the best tips, and the best attitude, from other bartenders, most of whom are neither richer nor poorer than ourselves. A sense of entitlement may come most easily to upper-middle-class, white-collar professionals, like those in Christy's and Terri's stories (they're the ones most guilty of one of my least favorite bar phenomena—I call it the "circle of power"—wherein a bunch of guys in suits make a circle in the center of the bar, even when there are plenty of barstools available, and block the path to the door, the restroom, the bar, because they can). But lines are blurry at bars. I've rarely met a bartender who hasn't told me that he's had terrific regulars who happen to be wealthy, and terrible ones who happen to be poor. Often, the division instead is between service and non-service. To some, anyone whose job is in service is a person over whom one can establish power.

Another longtime bartender, who also loves his job, told me a story from one of his first jobs in New York, at a bar on the Upper East Side, long ago. "At Ridings circa 1978, we got a certain number of rugby players, and for the most part these guys were fun, but cheap when it came to tipping," he said. "One guy, after just a couple of beers, got up to leave, and he threw a one-dollar-bill tip into the ashtray. 'Don't do that, Mark,' I told him. 'Why not?' he asked. 'Well, it's not very nice to put your tip in the ashtray, is it?' I countered, lifting the bill out of the ashtray and placing it onto the bar. 'Yeah, well, if you want it, that's where it will be,' he said, grabbing the bill and throwing it once more into the ashtray. With that he turned and walked out of the bar. Mark was neither wealthy nor poor; he just had to establish that, in this situation, he got to make up the rules."

Gary recalls this story from nearly forty years ago because it's a stunner, an extreme case, an unforgettably aggressive, demeaning exchange. Most of us, most of the time we spend behind bars, aren't subject to anything quite so mean-spirited. But the tension—who's in charge here? who has power?—always exists in bars.

Bartenders usually wind up becoming friends with at least some of our regulars. Some even start to feel like family, and we spend holidays together, or cook them dinner on a night off. These are the customers I miss if they have to skip one of my shifts. With regularhood comes responsibility, both ways: these are the patrons who ask me how I'm doing, how my shift is going, if I want anything from the bodega. I want to hear all about their day, their family, their vacation. I feed their cats when they're out of town, and they feed mine. I'm happy to spot them for a drink or two when they're between paychecks. But I never ask them what they do for a living. I wait for them to tell me—or not.

A Block Divided Against Itself

SARAH JAFFE

On one of the coldest days of the year I put on long underwear, a flannel shirt, my thickest sweater, a hat, and a scarf, and took the subway two stops down to 1059 Union Street, a block south of Eastern Parkway and on the corner of Franklin Street, to join the new Crown Heights Tenant Union's first public action.

It was so bitterly cold that I couldn't help but think about the previous winter, my first in Crown Heights and fourth in Brooklyn, when my heat would mysteriously shut off, often just in time for the weekend when my landlord didn't answer the phone. My partner likes to say that most New York landlords operate on a continuum between greed and laziness. I figured at the time that mine were hovering closer to the "lazy" end with a bit of extra cheapness thrown in; they just didn't want to pay the extra money to really fix whatever was wrong.

One of my frustrated phone calls went like this:

"I spent two days without heat! I need to have someone to call on Saturdays if there's an emergency."

"Well, we're Jewish—we don't work on Saturday."

"I'm Jewish too! That doesn't mean I don't freeze!"

I never chalked up that lack of heat to gentrification in action. But the folks standing on that freezing sidewalk on Union Street knew better. The disappearing heat wasn't just a problem in my building. All over Crown Heights, tenants were shivering through nights without heat. The *New York Times* even reported on the problem. The record cold in the winter of 2014 saw complaints of the lack of heat nearly double from the year before. As the residents exchanged stories, they began to conclude that it was more than just the usual neglect that working-class neighborhoods expect from absentee landlords, that it was a calculated effort to drive residents out so that people who looked more like me—young, white, presumably more affluent—could move in.

And so there I was in the cold, huddled with forty or fifty strangers and some acquaintances I didn't recognize at first under their hats and scarves. We stood beneath a scaffold that had been, according to tenants, thrown up that week to supposedly make needed repairs after the land-lord got wind of the upcoming rally. Many of them held handmade signs with pithy slogans ("Affordable housing is a right" and "Resident pow-er not REBNY dollars") and specific demands or call-outs ("5 year rent freeze" and "ZT Realty Rank 58 Worst Landlords in Brooklyn," that last with a small toy rat taped to the cardboard). When I arrived, the crowd was chanting "We won't leave!"

This winter's cold made my previous heatless nights seem mild by comparison. The weather phenomenon called the "polar vortex" had swept down on us with single-digit temperatures and mountains of snow for weeks on end. I couldn't imagine one night of this with no heat, but some of the people standing out there with me knew that feeling well. Resident after resident stood to tell their stories, decrying constant ha-rassment from new landlords who'd purchased the buildings they'd lived in for decades, big brick pre-war structures like the one we stood in front of, solid exteriors that often hid leaky sinks, clanking pipes, and crum-bling plaster within. One woman wanted her landlord to stop threatening to take her to court if rent was late—"You don't respond to us in a timely fashion! I waited thirty days for them to fix my ceiling that caved in."

For another, it was being charged extra for "improvements" to the building. "For months we had a truck outside our building to provide us with heat, a temporary boiler. They put in a new boiler and every day, every day we have no heat or hot water for some span of time. We are not paying for that boiler; that is not our responsibility."

A third declared, "The only way we going to stop this is if we orga-nize. In numbers there is strength."

The rally wasn't simply an opportunity for tenants to voice their grievances. Instead, through months of meetings, outreach, and debate between tenants from twenty-five buildings, they had come up with a list of demands that they'd formalized into a collective bargaining agreement that they were pushing for landlords to sign. Those demands, including a five-year rent freeze, a forty-eight-hour response time maximum for necessary repairs, tenant approval of renovations, and a limit to buyout offers, were printed on four-foot sheets of paper that the tenants pasted up inside the lobby of 1059 Union. By organizing tenants from multiple buildings into one union, they hoped to have more power to wield against landlords who might otherwise ignore them, and to be able to influence the entire rental market in the neighborhood.

Still, some of the tenants expected consequences for daring to speak up. One woman, buried somewhere in the crowd, called out, "1059 is not going to have hot water or heat over the weekend because we're doing this in front of 1059 Union Street."

"Retaliation," agreed another voice from the crowd.

◆ ◆ ◆

The formulation "a tale of two cities" has been used a lot to describe New York at the end of the Bloomberg Age, but it doesn't entirely encapsulate the way some neighborhoods have split into two within themselves.

Being part of the first wave of gentrification means that you experience the abuses along with the cheap(er) rent. It means that as soon as you've moved in they want you to move out again, so they can raise the rent still more. It means that you're a problem when you come, and a problem when you leave.

Crown Heights is the razor's edge of Brooklyn gentrification, a West Indian and Lubavitcher Hasidic Jewish neighborhood with very little crossover between the two. Its boundaries are roughly Atlantic Avenue to the north, Washington to the west, Ralph Avenue to the east, and Empire Boulevard to the south. It was a good place to be when Superstorm Sandy swept over New York, living up to the "heights" of its name, suffering only a few downed trees and busted traffic lights. Its median household income, according to WNYC's maps, is around $41,000 a year and on the rise, and it's getting whiter.

The idea that white skin automatically means more money is both a product of and a perpetuator of American racism. Before gentrification, you had disinvestment. Legally sanctioned housing discrimination both created segregated neighborhoods and kept home values and rents low; white flight sent middle-class people off to the suburbs. Landlords and cities left black and brown neighborhoods to crumble. The return, now, of white people to the cities their parents and grandparents abandoned means that prices have been on the rise, and neighborhoods once written off as "bad" and "scary" are now desirable lower-priced alternatives for mostly young people trying to make their city dreams come true. And landlords are ready for a chance to increase their profits—whether they be long-term property owners pushed out of absentee equilibrium into paying attention to their buildings and making improvements in order to raise rents, or the private equity and hedge fund hawks circling, looking for new "investments."

But these days, new young gentrifiers are less and less likely to find a full-time job that pays them enough to cover those rising rents. Instead, they move from neighborhood to neighborhood, priced out of the place they moved into just a year before, following that wave further out. They leave, and someone who can afford the slightly higher rent moves in, and the cycle speeds up.

◆ ◆ ◆

Not long after I moved into my Crown Heights place (my third Brooklyn apartment), my upstairs neighbor—who had warned me of shoddy repairs to my bathroom ceiling with a cheery "You live here now? My floor caved in through your ceiling a little while back!"—disappeared. I found out she was gone when I woke up one morning to broken furniture flying past my bedroom window to crash to the sidewalk below.

I never learned what happened to her, her constant whirl of activity, her two sons who shyly petted my dog at first, then grew bolder and came looking for us. I rescued a kitten that I guessed must have been theirs in my hallway when workmen carrying new appliances nearly tripped over it, but they never returned for it.

A new family moved in shortly thereafter.

A few months ago the folks in the apartment across from mine, a shy teenage boy whose college information packets often wound up in my mailbox by mistake and his mother, who worked nights and came home in scrubs, disappeared as well and were replaced by a crowd of those dreaded white "hipsters" who embody the worst loud-partying gentrifier clichés.

I still got those college information packets for two months.

It's almost too easy to write clichés about gentrification in New York. And yet you find contradictions everywhere—the bodega owner who tells you that it's good to have more people like you in the neighborhood and the neighbors who invite you to their backyard barbecue, not to mention the white woman who is the angriest that there are "yuppies" in the neighborhood. And then there's that feeling of rage I too get at my new white neighbors.

I met my next-door neighbor when the Cablevision guy arrived to turn on my cable and couldn't get to the wires and boxes. He couldn't access them through my backyard because my landlord had left it a jungle of weeds and trash. Never mind that a neatly kept backyard that we could access would perhaps raise the price of the apartment a few hundred bucks.

Instead, the Cablevision worker pulled a ladder off his truck and asked my neighbor if he could bring it through his house and put it up in his backyard to access the wall of my building. While he did that, I stood outside and got to know Sion.

Sion is a talker. A brief run-in with him on a nice evening will result in hours on the stoop. He has told me countless stories of the neighborhood, about how it used to be "Murder Heights" when he was growing up in the seventies, how his family bought the house next to mine and how he watched my landlord and others buy their buildings, slap some paint on crumbling walls, and jack up the rent for unsuspecting people like me. Sion looks at new residents with something more like pity—when I first told him how much I was paying per month, he laughed and told me I was getting robbed. In the first-floor window of his house there is a "Raise the Wage" sign.

It is easy, for a somewhat self-aware person living in a gentrifying city, to look for a way to blame yourself, or absolve yourself. The impulses are two sides of the same coin: heads, you're the "good gentrifier" because you like your neighbors and don't blast your music too loud; tails, you should just move out of the city because anywhere you go you are destroying something. Neither answer is productive. Neither one is political.

I moved to Brooklyn to take a job as a political reporter—really, to take an internship that I hoped, against the 2009 economy's lack of hope, would lead to real work. I was one of the lucky ones. I did get a job, for a whole $35,000 a year. My first apartment was a Ditmas Park studio; my second was a full one-bedroom in Lefferts Gardens. Both of those were rapidly gentrifying as well, but in them I felt disconnected. It was in Crown Heights, where I moved in with a roommate in order to leave a job, that I decided it was time to fight.

Because the only way for me not to be a gentrifier at this wage is to move back in with my parents in their South Carolina suburban home, a thing I did for three years post-college in order to stop accumulating debt on top of my student debt. In order to live in this city whose streets I cover, I have to be part of it.

◆ ◆ ◆

I found out about the Crown Heights Tenant Union through an e-mail from a friend I met at Occupy Wall Street, telling me about that first public action. She invited me as a reporter, and I arrived with my recorder and camera in hand, but left with a stack of flyers to deposit in the entry to my building and the intention to go to their next organizing meeting as a member.

The meeting on March 13 at the Center for Nursing and Rehabilitation on Classon Avenue featured documentary filmmakers hovering in the back, an ever-growing circle of chairs spanning the atrium, and me sitting in back trying to figure out whether to take notes or to simply be present as a participant. I can't actually separate my writer-self from my activist-self or any number of other possible ways I could split myself up. So here I am anyway writing about it, though I decided then not to make notes.

We went around the room and introduced ourselves that day and instead of doing the usual New York thing of explaining who you are and what you do for a living, we gave our names and addresses and how long we'd lived in the neighborhood. Answers ranged from a few months to nearly fifty years.

That's the thing about the Crown Heights Tenant Union—it aims to bring these two parts of the neighborhood together, the new residents and the long-time ones. Because our needs aren't actually different. We need livable apartments at reasonable rents, landlords that respond and that aren't trying to drive us out. We need repairs done and the heat to be on when it is legally required to be. We need to be seen as important enough to deserve a nice place to live. Young people, new residents, many of them radicalized by or before Occupy Wall Street shaking up the city, need this too.

"We can't be divided and conquered," Joel Feingold said.

Because the problems of Brooklyn's gentrifying neighborhoods won't be solved by a housing-market version of "ethical consumption." It's going to take collective action.

It seems to be paying off for the CHTU. They've succeeded in bringing landlords to the table to make repairs, and in growing the union by bringing in more residents from other buildings, both rent-regulated and market-rate. At the rally, march, and picnic on June 7 in Brower Park, state assembly members joined the union to call for affordable housing.

But elected officials' definition of "affordable" varies, and it's not simply construction that is needed. It was rent-stabilization laws that allowed people to stay in their rental apartments for fifty years, paying rents that went up only a small amount determined by the city's Rent Guidelines Board. That landlords could raise the rents based on a percentage of an amount they could spend on renovating a vacant apartment incentivized those landlords to only do renovations when they could profit from them, leaving longtime residents in lousy conditions that the landlords then use to help lever residents out of their homes. Policy changes can improve this, or failing that, the CHTU can try to get landlords to sign on to its contract demands.

◆ ◆ ◆

It's not just Crown Heights that has a gentrification problem; more important, slowing the process down in one part of the city will only speed it up elsewhere, as new residents search for new housing. It'll take citywide change and at least some of that will have to come from policymakers as well as organizers.

New mayor Bill de Blasio told me in an interview last year that he thought it was time for a rent freeze. On May 5, 2014, I took the subway to Manhattan's Bowling Green stop, just a short walk from the famous Wall Street bull statue, to join the CHTU at the preliminary Rent Guidelines Board meeting, where the possibility of a rent freeze was due to be discussed.

It was no longer freezing in New York but it had taken weeks this spring to get my landlord to send someone to clean black mold from my bathroom; I still have to step over crumbling plaster from the ceiling when I walk down the hall.

I rushed, worried I would be late for the 5:00 p.m. meeting, but when I arrived no one was allowed into the building. Instead, outside, a crowd formed slowly, as members of community groups from all over the city trickled in carrying signs that demanded a rent freeze or even a rent rollback. Groups like Good Old Lower East Side, the Flatbush Tenant Coalition, and more showed up and formed a loose circle outside the building, walking and chanting, a feeling not unlike a picket line. Cop cars turned up, too.

Undaunted by the large crowd of renters, one middle-aged white man carrying a sign that had something incoherent about welfare scrawled on a broken-down white cardboard box approached the demonstrators and began to shout at them about his costs increasing. At first it was hard to hear him over the steady chant of "We say roll back!" but when it became clear that he was not one of the tenants, he was backed off by several organizers. He stepped to the side with another man, also white, also middle-aged, presumably to compare notes on the hardships of being a property owner in the most expensive city in the U.S. One tenant circled the two of them, trying to take photographs, but the landlords spun away from her as she taunted them for their unwillingness to show their faces on camera. One of them finally snapped at her, "Shut up, you drug addict!"

I shouldn't have done it, I knew it even as I did it, but I stepped in to shout back. "Why do you think you're better than her?"

He snarled something at me and I snarled back "fuck you," and he said "Couldn't pay me!" and laughed with his buddy as if he was the first one to imply that a woman was ugly when she dared disagree with him, but the crowd gathering at our backs made the two white men step away from us and closer to each other.

I calmed down and circled around to snap a photo from the top of 1 Bowling Green's stairwell. "This is what NYC looks like," I told Twitter, posting the photo. "Renters on the left, two landlords on the right."

In the photo, the renters are black, brown, white, young and old, in business suits or sweats. Two of them lean on canes. There are at least forty of them. The landlords stand together, their backs to the crowd.

The process of getting inside the building stretched out for another hour. It was 6:20 when I made it through the metal detectors and security wand to the room where the rent board sat. The airport-level security meant the meeting started over an hour after the time on the agenda handed out to the audience and two hours after the time I'd been told. Board chair Rachel Godsil, a de Blasio appointee, expressed concern at the amount of time it took to fill the room when there was a long line outside, and Harvey Epstein, one of the tenant representatives on the board, asked that the board "consider the accessibility of our spaces" when future public meetings, particularly ones that would rely on public testimony, would be held.

The board was seated from left to right, or so it seemed—tenant representatives Epstein and Sheila Garcia on the far left, then public members, Godsil dead center, then on the right landlord representatives Sara Williams Willard and last of all Magda Cruz.

The crowd, as heavily dominated by tenants as is New York's population, kept breaking into chants as the meeting progressed—and burst into raucous applause and cheers when Garcia introduced the tenant reps' proposal for a six percent rent rollback. Throughout the city, she said, landlords have seen revenue increases; meanwhile, wages are stagnant and tenants have been expected to pay increases even in 2008.

Epstein seconded the motion, but it was voted down by the rest of the board.

Williams Willard then put forth, to loud boos, a proposal that rents be increased 3.6 percent to 5 percent, also voted down despite her repetition of the word "facts."

Instead, the board voted, with one "no" from Cruz, to support Godsil's proposal of a range of zero to 3 percent increase. It was the first step on the road to a historic rent freeze, and the tenants poured out of the building jubilant, cheering.

The landlords weren't so pleased—I stepped out of the restroom to find a be-suited white man waggling a finger in Williams Willard's face, accusing her of abdicating her duty to them by voting for the zero-to-three range.

I walked out with Nicole Carty, a CHTU organizer whom I met for the first time at Occupy, to head back to Crown Heights. It was just the beginning of a bigger fight—she was already preparing the testimony she wanted to give at the Brooklyn public hearing, scheduled for June 18, in which, we'd been informed, landlords and tenants would be given an equal chance to speak.

That wasn't exactly fair, she noted, as tenants outnumber landlords by quite a lot in Brooklyn, where nearly 73 percent of homes are rentals.

• • •

When the tenants got to testify, it was a ten-year-old boy who shook up the crowd in Brooklyn's Borough Hall, the tenants in T-shirts and landlords in suits and polo shirts packing the seats and standing in corners and aisles.

Ruben Rojas stood in front of the board and told them, his voice never wavering, about the rats in his apartment. "My dad is working class," he said, "Maybe I'm not going to college because my dad has to pay the rent. They're ruining our future."

As the crowd rose to its feet to give him a standing ovation, he called into the microphone, "Mayor de Blasio, it's your choice, make a rent freeze or ruin our future!"

De Blasio wasn't in the room to hear Rojas, but City Council members Jumaane Williams and Mathieu Eugene were—both spoke in favor of a rent freeze.

Going into the final vote on June 23, the tension was palpable. Last spring at Cooper Union, students had occupied the dean's office for sixty-five days to protest the long-free university's decision to charge tuition. This year, the crowd wore the orange and yellow shirts of multiple community organizations and carried giant cutout zeroes to indicate a zero percent rent increase. CASA, New York Communities for Change, Make the Road, and of course the Crown Heights Tenant Union circled around Rent Guidelines Board member Harvey Epstein and State Assemblymember Brian Kavanagh to whip up energy before settling into long lines to get through the once again heightened security. I stood behind two grandmothers with canes who had to be helped through the metal detectors so the city could be sure that they weren't a threat.

Inside Cooper Union's basement great hall, a room with excellent acoustics for chants but no cell-phone service for my frantic live tweets, the security strategy seemed to have backfired—every minute we waited, the room grew more electric. One of the grandmothers sang, "We're gonna roll, gonna roll, gonna roll those rents back!" Her hat, dingy with age, read "I'm a renter and I vote."

The votes of renters were deemed problematic by the rent board's Magda Cruz, whose voice rose in anger as she made a speech, even as the room continued to fill. "Some tenants," she acknowledged, face financial pressures, but "tens of thousands of landlords" (in a city of eight million and change) were struggling, and a rent freeze would be "confiscatory" and "politically motivated," because Bill de Blasio promised it during a campaign which led to his election by 73 percent of voters— exactly the same percentage as the city has renters.

Cruz, red-faced, reminded me of the angry man who insulted me at the first RGB meeting. These meetings were one of the few moments where landlords had to face the people who rent their apartments, whose calls for service they often casually ignore. For Cruz to hear cries of "Bullshit!" from a crowd seemed to be nearly too much for her.

In the end, though, it was Cruz and the landlords who won, even if her angry speech made it clear that she was unhappy with the proposal she was about to make. It was Cruz and Williams Willard who, instead of the written proposal for a much bigger increase they'd put forth, introduced de Blasio appointee Steven Flax's proposal for a one percent increase. Garcia pointed out that this was a calculated move, that rather than putting forth a large increase that Flax would likely have voted against, they used his proposal in order to co-opt his expected progressive vote.

Flax, who used to run affordable housing, called the landlords' use of his proposal "duplicitous," and the crowd's hope hung on his words, as the chants went from "Make history" to "Steve, do the right thing!"

"This moment is a nightmare," he said, before voting yes, despite Garcia's arguments, despite Epstein's citation of data that shows landlords' incomes are up and tenants' are down, despite Godsil, the board chair, pointing out that part of the board's mandate is to correct excesses by previous boards—which handed, in 2008, a large increase to landlords even as the economy crashed down around our ears. The increase, tiny but momentous, passed by a five to four vote.

The difference between one percent and zero won't make much of a difference in the profits of landlords. It won't even make that much difference to most renters. It was a rebuke, though, to the mayor, to the City Council members and borough presidents and Public Advocate and Comptroller, all of whom had called for zero. It was a rebuke to the people in that room who had shown up, stood in line, pulled their keys from their pockets, and laid their canes on the table to go through a metal detector.

Outside the hall as we filed out, the Rude Mechanical Orchestra played "Which Side Are You On?" and tenants gathered in a circle to speak. Cea Weaver from the Urban Homesteading Assistance Board and the CHTU had an armful of petitions with four thousand signatures on them, calling for the rent freeze, that they had not been allowed to hand to the board members before the vote.

The question of how the vote came off, whether it was a Machiavellian move by the landlord representatives or if the fix was in before anyone made it through the metal detectors, may always be a mystery. In the aftermath, the vote felt huge and weighty, but the list of next goals that fell easily from Jumaane Williams's lips as he addressed the crowd reminded me that halting gentrification was never going to be as simple as a rent freeze.

The chant you hear at the end of a lot of labor and community actions in New York is "We'll be back, we live around the corner!" Some of the tenants in the hall after the vote took it up again with new poignancy—if something is not done about the upward spike in rents, how long will those people be able to live around the corner?

There is no other answer than the one Donna Mossman of the CHTU gave, that a small win is not enough, that "We will definitely be back next year."

The system is rigged, of course. But maybe, just maybe, we can tip the balance a little.

Starting Out

JUNOT DIAZ

THE MONEY

All the Dominicans I knew in those days sent money home. My mother didn't have a regular job besides caring for us five kids, so she scrimped the loot together from whatever came her way. My father was always losing his forklift jobs, so it wasn't like she ever had a steady flow. But my grandparents were alone in Santo Domingo, and those remittances, beyond material support, were a way, I suspect, for Mami to negotiate the absence, the distance, caused by our diaspora. She chipped dollars off the cash Papi gave her for our daily expenses, forcing our already broke family to live even broker. That was how she built the nut—two, maybe three hundred dollars—that she sent home every six months or so.

We kids knew where the money was hidden, but we also knew that to touch it would have meant a violent punishment approaching death. I, who could take the change out of my mother's purse without thinking, couldn't have brought myself even to look at that forbidden stash.

So what happened? Exactly what you'd think. The summer I was twelve, my family went away on "vacation"—one of my father's half-baked get-to-know-our-country-better-by-sleeping-in-the-van extravaganzas—and when we returned to Jersey, exhausted, battered, we found our front door unlocked. My parents' room, which was where the thieves had concentrated their search, looked as if it had been tornado-tossed. The thieves had kept it simple. They'd snatched a portable radio, some of my Dungeons & Dragons hardcovers, and, of course, Mami's remittances.

It's not as if the robbery came as a huge surprise. In our neighborhood, cars and apartments were always getting jacked, and the kid stupid enough to leave a bike unattended for more than a tenth of a second was the kid who was never going to see that bike again. Everybody got hit; no matter who you were, eventually it would be your turn.

And that summer it was ours.

Still, we took the burglary pretty hard. When you're a recent immigrant, it's easy to feel targeted. Like it wasn't just a couple of assholes that had it in for you but the whole neighborhood—hell, maybe even the whole country.

No one took the robbery as hard as my mom, though. She cursed the neighborhood, she cursed the country, she cursed my father, and of course she cursed us kids, swore that we had run our gums to our idiot friends and they had done it.

And this was where the tale should end, right? Wasn't as if there was going to be any *C.S.I.*-style investigation or anything. Except that a couple of days later I was moaning about the robbery to these guys I was hanging with at that time and they were cursing sympathetically, and out of nowhere it struck me. You know when you get one of those moments of mental clarity? When the nictitating membrane obscuring the world suddenly lifts? That's what happened. I realized that these two dopes I called my friends had done it. They were shaking their heads, mouthing all the right words, but I could see the way they looked at each other, the Raskolnikov glances. I *knew*.

Now, it wasn't like I could publicly denounce these dolts or go to the police. That would have been about as useless as crying. Here's what I did: I asked the main dope to let me use his bathroom (we were in the front of his apartment) and while I pretended to piss I unlatched the window. Then we all headed to the park as usual, but I pretended that I'd forgotten something back home. Ran to the dope's apartment, slid open the bathroom window, and in broad daylight wiggled my skinny ass in.

Where the hell did I get these ideas? I have not a clue. I guess I was reading way too much Encyclopedia Brown and the Three Investigators in those days. And if mine had been a normal neighborhood this is when the cops would have been called and my ass would have been caught *burglarizing*.

The dolt and his family had been in the U.S. all their lives and they had a ton of stuff, a TV in every room, but I didn't have to do much searching. I popped up the dolt's mattress and underneath I found my

D&D books and most of my mother's money. He had thoughtfully kept it in the same envelope.

And that was how I solved the Case of the Stupid Morons. My one and only case.

The next day at the park, the dolt announced that someone had broken into *his* apartment and stolen all his savings. This place is full of thieves, he complained bitterly, and I was like, No kidding.

It took me two days to return the money to my mother. The truth was I was seriously considering keeping it. But in the end the guilt got to me. I guess I was expecting my mother to run around with joy, to crown me her favorite son, to cook me my favorite meal. Nada. I'd wanted a party or at least to see her happy, but there was nothing. Just two hundred and some dollars and fifteen hundred or so miles—that's all there was.

Engine

BILL CHENG

1

He is nineteen—the boy—when he lands his first job at the neighborhood cineplex. They issue him a uniform: short-sleeved button-up with the company logo etched into the breast, a baseball cap to tuck back his hair. The rest of the outfit—black slacks, black shoes—he has to buy on his own. They put him behind the concession stand. He works thirty-five hours a week—not enough to qualify for benefits—at just north of minimum wage.

In the mornings, it's prep work: stocking the display cases with candy bars, filling the warmers with last night's popcorn, reconciling the register. At night, he scrubs down the counters, the floors, dismantles the poppers and the hot dog machine, muscling the pieces clean with rusty off-brand Brillo in the utility sink.

Mostly it's dead hours on your feet—keeping your station tidy, waiting for the shows to start—punctuated by pure Bedlam. Burnt popcorn. Malfunctioning soda foundations. Credit card machines voiding long ribbons of blank receipt paper. And always there are the customers: impatient, irritable, outraged by the prices of the schlock that passes here for food. They want more salt. More butter. Less. They want to talk to a manager.

And it isn't any wonder that his coworkers are all lunatics. At closing, one pisses gleefully into the stairwell. Another lobs an undercooked hotdog into the recessed lighting. Fruit flies invade the soda fountains and no amount of washing and bleaching can purge them from the stand. The management refuses to call an exterminator. One day, a rat dies in the walls and for months the boy breathes in the decay.

Some nights he gets off so late that the buses stop running. So he walks home the mile and a half back to his parents' house. He doesn't mind. He needs to breathe, to think, or rather to not think. To *unthink*. To walk clear the noise and rage of the night. It is two or three in the morning and the roads are empty. He steps off the sidewalk and into the street. He follows the yellow strips in the middle of the road, and he wonders if he keeps walking, could he just walk out of this place, out of this life.

2

I don't know how to talk about money. It's one of those things we can't seem to get shook of. As much as we pretend it doesn't matter, it sets the stage for all our relationships. What I have, what you don't— all of it bound up in our identity, our careers, our ambition, our self-worth.

That was the gall of this first job, the improbability of being seen, how a stranger could just look at you and shrink you down into nothing. I was in college. I wanted to be a writer. I considered myself intelligent, ambitious, sensitive, with a full inner life. But every day wore me down to the nub until I carried in me a reservoir of abiding hate.

One summer at the theater, I spotted someone I knew from high school lining up at my register. He had gone to college upstate, and now he was back for the break. He looked good: lean, tan, handsome.

He recognized me.

Hey, Billy, how are you?

And it wasn't embarrassment but rage prickling at my face.

I pressed the bottoms of my hands to the counter.

I glared at him.

Would you like to try our super combo?

3

The boy spends his money on books and video games and underage drinking.

A joke he hears: "Working is like a turd sandwich . . . the more bread you got, the less shit you got to eat."

He tells himself he is done eating. He quits.

At night, he writes. He keeps a journal. He locks his bedroom door and writes stories that aren't very good. He joins a gym and three times a week, he races his anxiety out on the treadmill and exercise bikes.

It is at this point in time that the boy meets someone—a girl from upstate New York. They meet in the city for dinner, drinks. He talks to her about looking for work, living at home with his parents, and to his surprise this information doesn't faze her.

Being with her, he feels like the air has been let in. He feels human.

The boy finds work in Newark, writing copy for a home-based business. In the morning he gets off at Newark-Broad Street and ducks away from the gutted factories into a square of townhouses, where there are placards that read "Stop the Murders." He passes behind St. Lucy's Church and then up into the massive apartment complex overlooking the park.

His boss, Barry, is a madman and the boy loves this about him. Fifty years old with all the charm and innocence of an eight-year-old. Barry is quick to anger, quick to joy, excited by the turns of his own idealism.

During the phone interview, Barry asks the boy for his date of birth.

"I have all my employees' star charts done."

Minutes later, Barry calls the boy back.

"You're not going to believe this but that's MY birthday."

They take it as a sign of auspicious beginnings. The boy works twenty hours a week at $12 an hour as an independent contractor out of Barry's living room. For a while the boy delights in the ramshackle nature of the whole undertaking—his quixotic boss, the small business owner who'd invested everything of himself into this rickety venture.

The two become close.

Barry would fly out of his office, agitated by some new idea and the boy would follow him back, clear a space through the stacks of paper, aborted artwork, CD jewel cases, and they'd talk through what they could try, what they didn't have the resources to do.

Because everyone who works here is an independent contractor, Barry writes his checks made out to cash. Then one day, the checks keep getting post-dated later and later. Payday gets pushed back further and further until finally the pay cycles start adding up. Two pay checks. Three pay checks. Clients pull out. Angry messages are left on the main office line.

The strain seems to wear on Barry. A pipe bursts upstairs and the apartment floods. The vinyl from the flooring buckles.

The boy comes into work one day and sees a woman he doesn't recognize wrapped in a towel. She's young. Eighteen or nineteen. Her hair is wet and stringy. She lights a cigarette on the kitchen burner. It is Barry's new girlfriend. A few weeks later, money starts disappearing. Loose change, petty cash, a camera.

The boy worries about his job, the company. At the same time, his relationship with the girl has started to unravel. He becomes oppressive and jealous, wracked with insecurity. Soon they cannot talk at all without fighting. He wishes he were not jealous. He wishes he were not insecure. And yet there isn't a place to put that naked terror inside of him.

In the shower, the boy notices freckles on the underside of his arm. He convinces himself it's melanoma.

Makes sense, he thinks, *with my luck*.

He has no health insurance so in his idle hours he digs at the freckles with his nails. Tries to reduce the complicated nature of the human body to just layers of meat. But the girl convinces him to go to her doctor. She sits with him in the waiting room, reading a magazine. And even though it will be nothing—a mild fungus he picked up in the gym—something any reasonably minded person would know will be nothing—he weeps, confused, frustrated, stupid, unable to articulate why.

4

I kept writing.

Telling stories was the only thing that made my place in this world worth a goddamn thing at all.

On my desk I kept a whiteboard of all the graduate schools I'd applied to. To me, it was a foregone conclusion: I'd get my MFA, write a book, maybe teach. I'd turn this train wreck around.

In the summer, the heat was unbearable in my bedroom. I wedged a box fan into the window. Dusty air roared in through the mosquito screen as I waited for the responses to trickle in.

That year I'd applied to over a dozen schools. As the rejections came in, I crossed them out one by one.

I sat on my bed, punctured—everything I was, everything I was ever supposed to be runneling out of me.

It wasn't too long after that the girl did what I couldn't. She told me that it was over. The next day, I quit my job.

5

The boy lies in bed. He takes long walks, all day sometimes, to nothing-places. He goes to the parks, school playgrounds—places where he spent his time when he was younger. He gets lost in the trails, wanders back. He likes the mindlessness of it. By now he is well into his twenties—the Nothing boy—a time by all accounts that should be the prime of his life. Instead, he is overweight, cynical, deteriorating physically and emotionally.

He feels, as in the Tom Waits song, lost at the bottom of the world.

His parents convince him to start looking again for work and after months upon months of failure, he gets hired on as a researcher at a charitable organization in Midtown Manhattan. The job offers fifteen hours a week for $12 an hour. They tuck him into a small cubicle by the fire exit, an out-of-the-way place that's easy to forget.

The work consists of writing profiles of people who might donate to the organization—doctors, lawyers, industrialists. It's a good gig for a writer, being able to suss out the components of a person's life, chart the trajectory of their successes, their fortunes.

The boy likes the rags-to-riches stories most: a German immigrant who started with nothing and made his first million hauling scrap metal on a horse-drawn carriage; a man who turned a single apple cart into a grocery chain. He reads about people who build empires out of nothing but wit and opportunity.

All around him, he sees his coworkers: bright, ambitious, confident in their work and bearing. He doesn't know how to talk to them and except for his boss, no one stops by.

As the weeks pass, the silence vaults up around him.

He rots.

On the subway he discovers a cyst on his left buttock. After trying repeatedly to lance it in the bathtub, the area becomes swollen and painful. In the course of a week, the cyst swells to the size of a ping-pong ball. Sitting becomes unbearable. When it finally bursts, blood and pus stain the seat of his work pants.

It is a cycle that will recur every four or five weeks and instead of going to a doctor, the boy stocks his backpack with gauze.

Then in August 2008, something happens.

Here is what he writes in his journal:

Somewhere along Lexington, I noticed something wet and slick be-tween the cheeks of my ass. I tried to ignore it, thinking maybe it was just sweat. I thought about [what it would be like] dealing with this discomfort for the hour and a half [commute] back home.

I passed the Burger King twice before I decided to go in and use the restroom.

[...]

I locked the door behind me and dropped my trousers. I wadded up some toilet paper and made an exploratory swab. The blood was bright red and seemed wet and fresh. I swabbed a couple times until most of the bleeding had stopped and dropped it down the ring of the toilet.

Someone banged on the door.

I pulled my pants up and tucked my shirt in. Then I slung my bag across my shoulders and went home.

Do most people bleed out from their asses? I don't know. It's unset-tling and embarrassing and I just told you about it. But I don't care. Because I'm getting the feeling I used up all my dignity a long time ago, that there isn't much for me and there isn't much to me. I came home around six to an empty house. I chewed two sticks of gum. I thought, how am I going to get through all these goddamn hours? And I try not to think that at the end of those hours is another day, another week, another month, another year.

[...]

6

If I'm honest, I don't really know what any of this means or why I told it to you. The truth is I *like* my life. I *like* the people in it. And in spite of myself, I still love this desperate city.

It has been years since I've thought about the boy. I'm embarrassed by his self-loathing, his self-pity.

I distrust his pain.

Somewhere near the end of my twenties, my fortunes changed: I moved out of my parents' house, got married, found full-time work at a place that valued and respected what I did. I went to graduate school. I wrote my book.

And yet even here, now—in good health, financial steadiness—there are still times when I can almost glimpse the Engine in its entirety: its high walls, the gears and cogs and avenues through which wealth and power traffic, and it's easy to convince myself that if I'm honest and industrious, I can carve some small piece for myself and mine.

But I don't know how true that is.

In spite of what I've written, of what I've said, I *am* privileged: a product of the middle class: never had to worry about where I was going to live, how I was going to get my next meal. I own a computer, a cell phone. I have high-speed internet and every now and again I can go on a vacation.

The truth is I'm just a writer. I don't know how to fix these things. I don't even know if we can. All I know is that these days I'm thankful that I can do what I love and go to a doctor if I need to, make the rent, pay the utilities, and not drive myself crazy along the way. And it isn't commitment, or talent, or industriousness that brought me here.

It was stupid luck.

In 2009, we lost our shot at a national public healthcare option. We got sick.We watched our bodies betray us cell by cell. And those who could help us didn't give a good goddamn. Instead, they called us lazy, spoiled, entitled.

What do you say to something like that? How do you reckon with the extent of that indifference?

The story they tell you is work hard, build your life with your own two hands.

They tell you, "You are where you deserve to be."

But I know the way bad luck can build into streaks—a day, a week, a month, a year—all the avenues you thought were open shutting off one by one until all of a sudden you're drunk and shaking and can't see or hear for all your howling.

I think of the boy—who he was, where he might be—and there is both a relief and an anger.

A few months back I was in Oregon for a few days promoting my book. My last day there the airport shuttle picked me up to fly me back to New York. It was four in the morning. As we were pulling out of the hotel driveway, the driver slowed down and locked the doors when he saw someone rummaging through the dumpster.

"They like to come out at night and dumpster dive," the driver said.

I got a look at who he was talking about in the headlights. Young. Scruffy. Lean.

Suddenly one of the passengers behind me spoke up. "I'm sorry if this is offensive, but I don't understand that at all," he said. "I'd sooner *wash dishes* than not have a job."

And I sat there and I didn't say anything. But in my heart of hearts I wanted to. I wanted to tell him that not everyone has that choice, or is given choices. I wanted to tell him that not everyone was like him— white, male, born into means and privilege—and that there are those out there for whom the whole fucking world isn't pre-configured.

I wanted to tell him. I wanted to wring his goddamn neck.

The Sixth Borough

JONATHAN SAFRAN FOER

Once upon a time, New York City had a Sixth Borough. You won't read about it in any of the history books, because there's nothing—save for the circumstantial evidence in Central Park—to prove that it was there at all. Which makes its existence very easy to dismiss. Especially in a time like this one, when the world is so unpredictable, and it takes all of one's resources just to get by in the present tense. But even though most people will say they have no time or reason to believe in the Sixth Borough, and don't believe in the Sixth Borough, they will still use the word "believe."

The Sixth Borough was an island, separated from Manhattan by a thin body of water, whose narrowest crossing happened to equal the world's long jump record, such that exactly one person on earth could go from Manhattan to the Sixth Borough without getting wet. A huge party was made of the yearly leap. Bagels were strung from island to island on special spaghetti; samosas were bowled at baguettes; Greek salads were thrown like confetti. The children of New York captured fireflies in glass jars, which they floated between the boroughs. The bugs would slowly asphyxiate, flickering rapidly for their last few minutes of life. If it was timed right, the river shimmered as the jumper crossed it.

When the time finally came, the long jumper would run the entire width of Manhattan. New Yorkers rooted him on from opposite sides of the street, from the windows of their apartments and offices, from the branches of the trees. And when he leapt, New Yorkers cheered from the banks of both Manhattan and the Sixth Borough, cheering on the jump-er, and cheering on each other. For those few moments that the jumper was in the air, every New Yorker felt capable of flight.

Or perhaps "suspension" is a better word. Because what was so inspiring about the leap was not how the jumper got from one borough to the other, but how he stayed between them for so long.

One year—many, many years ago—the end of the jumper's big toe touched the surface of the water and caused a little ripple. People gasped, as the ripple traveled out from the Sixth Borough back toward Manhattan, knocking the jars of fireflies against one another like wind chimes.

"You must have gotten a bad start!" a Manhattan councilman hollered from across the water.

The jumper nodded no, more confused than ashamed.

"You had the wind in your face," a Sixth Borough councilman suggested, offering a towel for the jumper's foot.

The jumper shook his head.

"Perhaps he ate too much for lunch," said one onlooker to another.

"Or maybe he's past his prime," said another, who'd brought his kids to watch the leap.

"I bet his heart wasn't in it," said another. "You just can't expect to jump that far without some serious feeling."

"No," the jumper said to all of the speculation. "None of that's right. I jumped just fine."

The revelation traveled across the onlookers like the ripple caused by the toe, and when the mayor of New York City spoke it aloud, everyone sighed in agreement: "The Sixth Borough is moving."

Each year after, a few inches at a time, the Sixth Borough receded from New York. One year, the long jumper's entire foot got wet, and after a number of years, his shin, and after many, many years—so many years that no one could even remember what it was like to celebrate without anxiety—the jumper had to reach out his arms and grab at the Sixth Borough fully extended, and then, sadly, he couldn't touch it at all. The eight bridges between Manhattan and the Sixth Borough strained and finally crumbled, one at a time, into the water. The tunnels were pulled too thin to hold anything at all.

The phone and electrical lines snapped, requiring Sixth Boroughers to revert to old-fashioned technologies, most of which resembled children's toys: they used magnifying glasses to reheat their carry-out; they folded important documents into paper airplanes and threw them from one office building window into another; those fireflies in glass jars, which had once been used merely for decorative purposes during the festivals of the leap, were now found in every room of every apartment, taking the place of artificial light.

The very same engineers who dealt with the Leaning Tower of Pisa were brought over to assess the situation.

"It wants to go," they said.

"Well, what can you say about that?" the mayor of New York asked.

To which they replied, "There's nothing to say about that."

Of course they tried to save it. Although "save" might not be the right word, as it did seem to want to go. Maybe "detain" is the right word. Chains were moored to the banks of the islands, but the links soon snapped. Concrete pilings were poured around the perimeter of the Sixth Borough, but they, too, failed. Harnesses failed, magnets failed, even prayer failed.

Young friends, whose string-and-tin-can phone extended from island to island, had to pay out more and more string, as if letting kites go higher and higher.

"It's getting almost impossible to hear you," said the young girl from her bedroom in Manhattan, as she squinted through a pair of her father's binoculars, trying to find her friend's window.

"I'll holler if I have to," said her friend from his bedroom in the Sixth Borough, aiming last birthday's telescope at her apartment.

The string between them grew incredibly long, so long it had to be extended with many other strings tied together: the wind of his yo-yo, the pull from her talking doll, the twine that had fastened his father's diary, the waxy string that had kept her grandmother's pearls around her neck and off the floor, the thread that had separated his great-uncle's childhood quilt from a pile of rags. Contained within everything they shared with one another were the yo-yo, the doll, the diary, the necklace, and the quilt. They had more and more to tell each other, and less and less string.

The boy asked the girl to say "I love you" into her can, giving her no further explanation.

And she didn't ask for any, or say "That's silly" or "We're too young for love" or even suggest that she was saying "I love you" because he asked her to. Her words traveled the yo-yo, the doll, the diary, the necklace, the quilt, the clothesline, the birthday present, the harp, the tea bag, the table lamp, the tennis racket, the hem of the skirt he one day should have pulled from her body. The boy covered his can with a lid, removed it from the string, and put her love for him on a shelf in his closet. Of course, he could never open the can, because then he would lose its contents. It was enough just to know that it was there.

Some, like that boy's family, wouldn't leave the Sixth Borough. Some said: "Why should we? It's the rest of the world that's moving. Our borough is fixed. Let them leave Manhattan." How can you prove someone like that wrong? And who would want to?

For most Sixth Boroughers, though, there was no question of refusing to accept the obvious, just as there was no underlying stubbornness, or principle, or bravery. They just didn't want to go. They liked their lives and didn't want to change. So they floated away, one inch at a time.

All of which brings us to Central Park.

Central Park didn't used to be where it now is. It used to rest squarely in the center of the Sixth Borough; it was the joy of the borough, its heart. But once it was clear that the Sixth Borough was receding for good, that it couldn't be saved or detained, it was decided, by New York City referendum, to salvage the park. (The vote was unanimous. Even the most obdurate Sixth Boroughers acknowledged what must be done.) Enormous hooks were driven deep into ground, and the park was pulled, by the people of New York, like a rug across a floor, from the Sixth Borough into Manhattan.

Children were allowed to lie down on the park as it was being moved. This was considered a concession, although no one knew why a concession was necessary, or why it was to children that this concession must be made. The biggest fireworks show in history lighted the skies of New York City that night, and the Philharmonic played its heart out.

The children of New York lay on their backs, body to body, filling every inch of the park as if it had been designed for them and that moment. The fireworks sprinkled down, dissolving in the air just before they reached the ground, and the children were pulled, one inch and one second at a time, into Manhattan and adulthood. By the time the park found its current resting place, every single one of the children had fallen asleep, and the park was a mosaic of their dreams. Some hollered out, some smiled unconsciously, some were perfectly still.

Was there really a Sixth Borough?

There's no irrefutable evidence.

There's nothing that could convince someone who doesn't want to be convinced.

But there is an abundance of clues that would give the wanting believer something to hold on to: in the peculiar fossil record of Central Park, in the incongruous pH level of the reservoir, in the placement of certain tanks at the zoo (which correspond to the holes left by the gigantic hooks that pulled the park from borough to borough).

There is a tree—just twenty-four paces due east from the entrance to the merry-go-round—into whose trunk are carved two names. They don't appear in any phone book or census. They are absent from all hospital and tax and voting records. There is no evidence whatsoever of their existence, other than the proclamation on the tree.

Here's a fact: no less than 5 percent of the names carved into the trees of Central Park are of unknown origin.

As all of the Sixth Borough's documents floated away with the Sixth Borough, we will never be able to prove that those names belonged to residents of the Sixth Borough, and were carved when Central Park still resided there, instead of in Manhattan. So some believe that they are made-up names and, to take the doubt a step further, that the gestures of love were made-up gestures. Others believe other things.

But it's hard for anyone, even the most cynical of cynics, to spend more than a few minutes in Central Park without feeling that he or she is experiencing some tense in addition to just the present. Maybe it's our own nostalgia for what's past, or our own hopes for what's to come. Or maybe it's the residue of the dreams from that night the park was moved, when all of the children of New York City exercised their subconsciouses at once. Maybe we miss what they had lost, and yearn for what they wanted.

There's a gigantic hole in the middle of the Sixth Borough where Central Park used to be. As the island moves across the planet, it acts like a frame, displaying what lies beneath it.

The Sixth Borough is now in Antarctica. The sidewalks are covered in ice, the stained glass of the public library is straining under the weight of the snow. There are frozen fountains in frozen neighborhood parks, where frozen children are frozen at the peaks of their swings—the frozen ropes holding them in flight. The tzitzit of frozen little Jewish boys are frozen, as are the strands of their frozen mothers' frozen wigs. Livery horses are frozen mid-trot, flea-market vendors are frozen mid-haggle, middle-aged women are frozen in the middle of their lives. The gavels of frozen judges are frozen between guilty and innocent. On the ground are the crystals of the frozen first breaths of babies, and those of the last gasps of the dying. On a frozen shelf, in a closet frozen shut, is a can with a voice inside it.

Mixed Media, Dimensions Variable.

MICHAEL SALU

THE RITUAL OF THE HIPS

"Where you from? You ain't like the brothas around here," she told me.

It took a moment to respond to her. I needed all the strength in my neck muscles to navigate upward through Tina's mountainous cleavage to find room enough for oxygen and an utterance.

Tina was tall. Tall and very direct.

Tina was from somewhere down south.

Tina had that drawl.

I can't remember where exactly she said she was from and at that precise moment it didn't really matter. The last tequila shot had scorched my disposition, rendering me a little less, well, obsequious. I claimed the bar stool next to me coldly lit by LEDs for support.

Tina seemed to be in the mood.

Or at least in a mood.

Instinct suggested I flee, but I didn't.

I asked her why she thought I was different from the "brothas" here, but her hastily muttered response in between sips drowned in reverb.

She drank in a hurry, pausing occasionally to look around, self-consciousness thinly veiled as the manicured hair that hung over her left eye. I could see she was concentrating. Swiveling her hips, she gradually caught up with the monotonous cadence of the beat benevolently spooning our awkward conversation.

We danced a little, or tried to.

Beginning the Ritual of the Hips is a delicate and considered process. Let me explain. Typically (but not always) The Male and The Female begin by finding a sort of inaudible but mutual gesture of acknowledgment. Often just a glance. That glance may not even appear with a smile, but contains enough semantic data to encourage the eros instinct of The Male. This welcome is often indicated by a subtle opening of the hips and the dorsal spine, until The Female's rhythmically bewitched torso is positioned immediately opposite, but at a precautionary distance. The crucial precipice of this moment has now arrived; the very next gesture determines either The Male's success or failure in gaining a closer encounter with The Female. Until the next time. So what The Male requires here is spirit-level precision in combining posture and cadence (moving very crucially to the formulation of the underlying beat or, if The Male is particularly adept, the space in between *beats*).

The Female may also sometimes welcome The Male by actually turning her back to him. Only very experienced males will intuitively read this signal, as the draw often lies in the position and pace of The Female's hips; an opening usually appears, but this moment is fleeting and can easily be missed.

There is only a short moment for The Male to make his intentions known. Linger too long and The Female begins to distrust his efficacy and that opening will very quickly slam shut. Equally, The Male may also fail if his actions are too hasty, which can smack of a lack of self-possession. The Male must very quickly gather poise, rhythm, and plumage together for a decisive move just as the opening is at its apex.

Once The Male is up close, the remaining ritual procession flows smoothly, though the finale is often determined by . . .

We really did try to dance, but Gravity and Tequila had harbored their own plan, easily dismissing our clumsily choreographed attempts. Instead, rather, they coaxed us into veering precariously left at an increasingly acute angle onto, or into, what I thought at first was a dance floor. It then dawned on me that what I was actually looking at was a rather inappropriately placed swimming pool in the center of the room. The whole time I thought I had seen a night that was just young, its palette yet to be fully awash with high jinks. We peered through tequila-tinted fuzziness at a baroque fresco of fawn heels and big hair teetering two-dimensionally around a shimmering polygonal surface.

Before the ominous inevitability I could see in a christening of the pool, Tina, with a vigorous shake of her head broke stride and in that drawl said with assertion:

"Come with me."

"Where?" I asked, but thankfully she didn't seem to hear. Revelers of the night unwittingly bounced off her voluptuous figure as she led me through the crowd in the direction of what appeared to be the bathrooms. She paused outside the ladies', and without turning, she muttered something else unintelligible. She let go of my hand and entered the bathroom.

I am very British. Something I've often been reluctant to acknowledge, but I am. Quintessentially. That said, this mesh of British birth and Nigerian heritage make for an interesting idiomatic clash. There's a default British stoicism, bristling inwardly with ideas and desires, and a host of apologetic mannerisms bequeathed by the Empire's own quasi-apologies that don't necessarily travel well. This is then a cumbersome locking of horns with the gregarious, outwardly emotive, delightfully grandiloquent Yoruba culture that is also undeniably me. So this time British won out. I opted to wait, thinking maybe she was just in need of a chaperone for the eventful journey to the bathroom.

Tina's drawl. It conjured memories of those early years of musical discovery and one of my earliest introductions to "The South." This introduction was delivered via the intriguingly named Outkast. A pair of voices that overwhelmed my impressionable ears with a thick, luxurious, and intensely flavored stew of accents. Creole (and ultimately French) inflections. Rhyming couplets that grammatically shouldn't have been and a paradoxical swagger seemingly conscious of both the necessity for chest-out determination and yet an acknowledgment of its veritable absurdity amidst the grand economic and social circus of America and that particular demographic's rung on society's hierarchical ladder. I first came across Outkast's Southernplayalisticaddilacmuzik *at the age of thirteen. I was already a couple of years beyond shedding the Michael Jackson skin that liberally coated my youth and that of many other kids of my generation. Entry into teenage discovery brought with it findings of an altogether grittier, seemingly more tangible form of storytelling than Jackson's somewhat hallucinatory flights of fancy that we escaped into. I discovered hip-hop.*

The Bad *double album cassette that was my first-ever music purchase had long been jettisoned and the couple of years that followed were an exploration of mixtapes, coastal contrasts, rhymes, intoxicating beats, and most important, profanity. At the age of eleven, nestled awkwardly in a suburban England I failed to master after the nomadism of my early childhood, this was quite a discovery. The technicolored flights of my preteen imagination had seeped away, leaving a gritty residue of a much more monochrome, muffled, rusted industrial landscape. A landscape teeming with unrest and anguish. Intricate tales of conflicts I didn't really understand; of desires and opinion, of malaise and ideals.*

I struggled with my own new landscape. This is the age I arrived with my family in Birmingham, England. Just about preteen, back into Britain's post-Thatcher economic lumbering. Sprawling Ballardesque suburbia, within which identikit red brick homes kept secrets, while the streets remained silent. Birmingham is the UK's second-largest city, populous and "multicultural," but segregated into reclusive pockets of ethnicity. Acrobatics were a treacherous activity on rusted climbing frames, as the residue of corroded paint and metal formed the beginnings of calluses on my hands. I was used to climbing trees, whether in the leafy southern counties of the British Isles or tugging at a papaya from the top of the compound wall at my grandmother's home in Lagos.

We had been around as small children. Seen parts of the world. Spent a few years as oddly revered kids at school in Lagos. Our British accents a novelty. Not so much so as to avoid any disciplinary encounter with teacher and ruler, mind, but it did offer us a mild celebrity.

N.W.A.'s Straight Outta Compton *was the first hip-hop album I found in my possession. Copied from a friend's original on an old dual cassette Aiwa hi-fi. Well, not so old at the time, actually—it had a CD tray—but at that point this friend only had one CD in the collection, which actually belonged to his mother. We, on the other hand, were all masters of the cassette. We could cut! Record and manipulate sounds from wherever they were available. We would plug into the television's auxiliary input, finger hovering over a chunky red plastic record button. It made a satisfying "thunk" when pressed as we snatched a whole track from* Yo! MTV Raps *before Fab 5 Freddy routinely interrupted with his well-crafted beige-colored platitudes. Or we would*

sit attentively listening to pirate radio stations, deftly grabbing por-
tions of tracks in between voiceovers. My entry point was the woozy,
sunburnt soul samples of G-funk on the West Coast, but I very soon
after happened upon the home of Hip-Hop, New York.

So anyway, here I was amidst the voluminous hyperreality of the Big
Apple, oddly enough for the very first time, convinced I knew the city
intimately, had seen it, smelled it, hungrily lapped up its exports without
ever walking its streets.

Here I was, standing outside the ladies' toilets, in a club somewhere
in the Meatpacking District, high above the city's own conversations in
an aquarium of noise. In truth, I'd barely had time to expel some of Tequila's hold through resting on the wall opposite, when the door of the
ladies' room burst open, its hinges straining, and Tina charges out, toro-
like. Enraged. Her eyes ready to leave their sockets and take umbrage
with whichever hapless soul happened to be within their immediate
range. Like Jordan against the entire Knicks team. The tequila fog was
yet to lift and things happened more quickly than I could blink in some
comprehension. I'd had no time to process that she had just hurled herself
at a small man I hadn't noticed standing immediately to my right, her
arms leading, fingers outstretched and seemingly aiming for his throat.
The type of small man that just does innocuous.

"What the fuck did you say to him, huh? HUH? What the fuck did
you say to stop him coming in the bathroom with me?"

Mr. Innocuous coughed, reeling from the sudden violence, unable
to reply. He looked pleadingly in my direction, as those long fingers remained clasped around his reedy neck.

"I . . . I . . . I ain't do nothing."

Aghast, I intervened.

"OK, you are clearly insane! I'm leaving," I said, also apologiz-
ing sheepishly to Mr. Innocuous, whose usual color had just begun to
reappear.

"FUCK YOU!!" she screamed.

I headed for the lift.

"FUCK YOU!" I heard again, those screams very quickly drowning
in reverb as the glass doors of the lift closed.

My phone buzzed with a notification.

"So, how's it going?"

"... That doesn't shit doesn't happen back home."

"What shit?"

"The lack of colonial sexual repression was rather refreshing I must say."

"Oh ..."

"Like some alternate reality or some shit?"

"Huh."

"I heart NY"

CAN IT ALL BE SO SIMPLE?

The taxi driver had no idea where he was going, or at the very least intended to make it appear so. My attention flitted back and forth between the small screen in the foreground selling me The World on credit and the driver's disinterested voice in soft focus at the rear. Crossing water has never felt so circuitous. The night played forward and backward. The lights danced and the skyscrapers themselves swayed whenever I tilted my head. This may not be common knowledge, but GPS smartphone functionality is available even with the data roaming switched off, so any one of us may have a bird's-eye view of ourselves being ripped off in real time. Suddenly my little blue dot felt a lot lonelier than usual, as it made slow, frame-by-frame 90-degree turns intermittently around the gridiron geometry of a couple of blocks at an hour that bade me no farewell.

My friend Sasha and I crossed the river eventually, after I pointed out our precise coordinates to our grouchy African American driver and the street names we had been repeatedly covering for the last twenty minutes. By this point I thought it a good idea to mention my awareness of the city's topography and social history, alerting him to Brooklyn's historical independence as a city and even when the Brooklyn Bridge itself was built, all in a condescending bid to shame him into the right direction.

Upon arrival in New York one is left with a discordance, a disorientating visual intoxication having grown up knowing a place like New York so well, yet never actually setting foot upon its shores. What immediately bludgeoned me was scale. The scale of everything. An almost four-dimensionality of towering reflections, echoing noise, exuberant gestures, speed, stride, color, and smell cutting adroitly through my beautifully crafted but two-dimensional simulacrum of a city, or The City. The city as a concept. As an expressionist garden of dreams.

It took me a long time to see The City in color. At the age of eighteen, Paul Auster's *The New York Trilogy* built a noir-ish papier-mâché of a city for me. A city hewn meticulously in soft colorless charcoals where the shadows hung low and long, peering down menacingly from narrow, tall buildings littered with secrets and enigmatic contradictions. Lifting those shadows up like a blanket, I then found the crackling, vibrant, but often fragile worlds of Goldin and Basquiat and imagined being laconically draped across the glittered floors of Warhol's factory.

◆ ◆ ◆

There is a vignette of dialogue toward the end of Quentin Tarantino's (much underrated) *Django Unchained* during which Calvin Candle, played by Leonardo DiCaprio, puts sardonically to Jamie Foxx's Django—and I paraphrase—"Why did y'all not fight back?" A line that remained for me a constant memory of the film as the rest slipped away into a cartoony lexicon of images we store for later appropriation. I can't help but think of Calvin's words as I recall my first late-night visit to the store at the end of the tenements on my quiet, leafy, tree-lined street in Brooklyn. Ahead of me, shadowy stationary figures huddled closely in conversation and in defiance to the cold. I walked, digging through playlists on my phone, though curiously it seemed, the closer I got to those figures, the farther away I appeared to be.

> *The track I had often on repeat from the* Enter the Wu-Tang (36 Chambers) *album as a teen was "Can It Be All So Simple." Amidst an album full of the muffled din of metallic percussion, fragmented eastern philosophy, and an array of angry sounds akin to drunkenly scraping ill-fitting aluminum hubcaps on a curb, "Can It Be All So Simple" was nestled quietly in the center of the album, sending me, at the age of thirteen, peering into a frozen rabbit hole down to a ruthless Cold World, but a world presented through clearly distilled drops of lucid storytelling. It opens with the sound of a storm. Rain and thunder loom menacingly outside, kept temporarily at bay by the partition of a window pane. The Gladys Knight of "The Way We Were" gently encourages Raekwon to speak, coaxing from him an anguished ode to*

a way of life born of a splintered fallout from the twentieth century economic and racial tumult. Ghostface, in typical gladiatorial stance, interjects, touching up the paint on the walls of hallowed stairways on project blocks, stepping reverentially over the bodies that failed to make it.

As I inched closer to the store at the corner and the men huddled in its fluorescent glare, something felt different. I knew this scene well. These streets, those ignored shadows. Often the streets I knew were more winding and staccato than those I was currently traversing, the houses smaller, their retired chimneys remaining redundantly aloft. They were discordantly arranged and more densely packed back home, but the scene was the same. The kids on the corner. I knew them. I knew them growing up. I would pass then as I did now, headphones on, a (sometimes) mutual nod of acknowledgment as I continued on my way to wherever wasn't there. The politics of the corners never held any interest and neither did their hollow imported swagger masking disconsolation and boredom. Even then during those pubescent years I found such posturing incongruous with the homogenous vernacular of British suburbia, particularly as I was being carried along through most of my teenage years by stories of other worlds in my ears.

The fluorescent light of the corner store brought into focus a sharp observation. These kids were different. Their shoulders slumped and necks hung forward and low, like they wore the oppressive burdens that made me flinch as a child when I looked at pictorial depictions of John Bunyan's "Christian" in *Pilgrim's Progress*. Weekly liturgist teachings at Baptist Sunday schools and coercion into preteen devotional baptism left me with great resentment. Enough to accelerate the escape (when old enough to do so) from a lifetime under the legacy of colonial crusader flagellation.

I reached the men and peered through their branded hooded shrouds of 70 percent polyester and 30 percent cotton as I passed. They gave an upward nod in my direction which I returned in kind, all the while noticing clumps of unkempt, sporadically determined facial hair. Eyes intent on maintaining contact with my own even though their natural inclination seemed to be a more furtive glance followed by swift reacquaintance with the ground below. I saw black skin empty of the bountiful sheen that adorns faces on orderly shelved and freely colored tubs of hair products in "Afro-Carribean" beauty stores. The monochrome celluloid of my memories was rendered here, but with a real and fragile skin arid with generations of defeat.

Yet I saw they weren't kids at all, but men. Men on the corners. Men, I noticed, somewhat cowed. Hollow men. Men without spirit. Men with slumped vertebrae, men ravaged by the imbalanced annals of history, but yes, men. Black men. Our nods were historic but our mutual confusion was entirely contemporary. Our faces were the same but our masks were very different. We looked at each other's clothing, we compared each other's poise and eventually failed to recognize each other at all. As I strode away toward the light, I felt myself leaving them behind.

Museum Security Taking a Nap. 2013. Mixed Media. Dimensions Variable.

The frame is square and the hand less than steady. I continue to record and snap, the oddly satisfying digital shutter obediently framing my obtuse observations of the landscape.

Walking and scrolling, walking and scrolling, giving my iPhone a shake to refresh my audience's attention.

I walk and snap. A twisted, mangled heap of metal glistens in its abandonment. A single piece of frayed fabric caught in the tributaries of this circumstantial sculpture flapped in an autumnal breeze.

I created the story.

A narrow escape.

The disorientation of an upturned automobile.

The pace of panic.

The claustrophobia, the guttural whine of an engine floundering in the air.

The smoke and the dust.

The minuscule flecks of glass you can't see, but can feel further deepening tiny cavities on the back of your neck each time you lean back to relieve the pressure of the windscreen on the bridge of your nose.

I zoned back in as I reached the southwest corner of Franklin and Putnam in Bedford-Stuyvesant, and stopped abruptly in front of an endlessly recolored, graffiti-baiting wall. The muddy red wall held neatly in its center a mural that piqued my interest. A mural in homage to Ol' Dirty Bastard.

The album sleeve art for Ol' Dirty Bastard's Return to the 36 Chambers: The Dirty Version *has to be regarded as one of the greatest album covers of all time. Within this image lies a beautifully succinct but layered commentary of an entire perpetuated system of control, and a moment in history when the transition of hip-hop from being the sound of the real post–affirmative action, post–Black Panther disillusion to when the most lucrative commercial commodity began to take hold. This was 1996. Before sneakers made it to the couture catwalks with a 500-percent markup and were sold back to the streets as aspirational lifestyle brands. Before the difficulty in accepting the hood as an essential part of corporate America. Before Jay-Z and the Billionaires Boys Club created bulbous, linear tapestries of aspirational lifestyle brands that amplified the land-grab mentality of generations still gripped by their parents' and parents' parents' struggles. Before getting rich and/or dying trying. Long before Apple and Dr. Dre were bedfellows.*

The artwork consisted simply of a scan of a welfare identification card, with ODB's own artist information scrawled with disdain in the designated areas supplied. IDENTIFICATION CARD FOR FOOD COUPONS AND/OR PUBLIC ASSISTANCE. His "mug shot" had ODB's twisted and defiantly anti-gravity hair, a mouth full of heraldic gold, and eyes that stared right back. The face America may not have wanted to meet without the protection of a glass divide (or CD cover). It was every mug shot. It was the lines of control that defined the penitentiary system both inside and out. Even the circumstantial lack of typographic precision lent its own voice to the acerbic commentary. It wasn't pretty. This shit isn't pretty. This is where we are, who we are, and I'm still going to pick up my check after going platinum. You made this system, so here we are!

◆ ◆ ◆

Larger Galleries and museums are principally the same all over the world. One can overhear their brand and marketing strategy meetings. Audible words like:

"accessible"
"inclusive"
"deliverables"
"overarching"

"umbrella"
"tone of voice"
"atmosphere"
"brand positioning"

Crop, copy, paste, and repeat.

I stepped around these words in synesthetic discomfort as I strolled the glass-encased halls of the Museum of Modern Art, passing a seated museum security guard taking a furtive nap and passing the MoMA logo time after time. MOMA, Moma, moMa, MoMA. At every turn lines and curves of lumpen, clogged, tightly kerned letterforms greeted me clumsily.

Yet these large, corporatized museums are a favorite place for idling. The non-committal wandering of such spaces offers the solace of anonymity without the agoraphobia and a lack of need or expectation to proffer anything more than a surface-level engagement with the works, while still leaving one open to the vague, wistful possibility of moments of profundity. Corporate gallery visits often take me anywhere but the space I'm in, triggering a chain of linked visual thoughts between the redrawn outlines of history's shadows.

I thought more about that ODB mural in Bedford-Stuyvesant as I meandered around the permanent Dadaist works in the museum. Fleetingly encased like an exhibit myself within the smooth glass and concrete facades, I wondered about the lack of cultural links rarely made in these spaces, while connections between the white spaces and the hallowed streets are a short subway ride away in any direction.

Dadaism as an art movement was not acknowledged as an art movement by its own protagonists and practitioners. Dadaist art was not regarded as art at all. Dadaists were essentially fed up with the societal malaise around them at the time and decided consciously to reject it all. At the time, the public were reviled by such behavior, the scatological humor, the obscenities, the impudence. I took in the sterility of the white wall upon which these works now hung, in one of the biggest and most respected art museums in the world. The name "Dada" even supposedly derives from baby talk. I chuckled to myself as I headed to the museum with Big Baby Jesus playing in my ears.

(SH)IT HAPPENS.

Toward the end of my week in the city, the weather began to turn unfavorably. The winds swirled yellow early fall leaves like maternal folds of drapery around the tall concrete neighbors of Central Park. I continued my walks. I rode back and forth on the L train watching other passengers as we thickened the air of the carriage with our thoughts. I saw New York again and again, a layered time-lapsed collage. My eyes followed the repeated movements, picking out the traces of endless journeys left on the concourse of Grand Central Station. The real was becoming the simulation at each right turn, look up or down, at each typographic overture or the relentless hooting and staccato shuffling of gridlocked cars.

On a blustery street a man who bore a strikingly similar appearance to the Pablo Picasso of advanced years (you know the one—poor in coiffure but fond of baguettes) stared at me unflinchingly, fixing a somewhat curious gaze as we hurried past each other to our respective destinies. I didn't turn back.

First Avenue & Second Street

HANNAH TINTI

Al was hanging out on the stoop as I dumped my crates of books and records on the sidewalk, glaring at me like I was a fool. I was twenty-three and had just driven a U-Haul the wrong way up First Avenue. He was a large, dark-skinned black man, dressed in a brightly colored African shirt and a leather vest with boar's-teeth buttons. The rest of him was covered in jewelry: giant rings around each finger and at least six necklaces made of bone, chunks of amber, silver and turquoise. He wore his hair in a high fade with a short beard. In one hand, he held a cigarette; in the other, he clutched an intricately carved wooden staff with the head of a jackal on top, its teeth open and bared.

"Is that a squash blossom?" I asked.

Al glanced down at the necklace I was pointing to. His face softened a bit. Not quite a smile, but enough. "Navajo," he said. "It's supposed to protect against the evil eye."

"I have one too," I said. "My mother collects them."

"Then your *mother's* a smart woman." From the way he said this, I could tell that the decision on me was still out.

It was my first New York City apartment. My roommate had taken the place over from the previous tenant. There was no written lease, no rental agreement, only a handshake with the shady Ukrainian man who owned the building: an old brick tenement house that shook whenever a truck drove past; a six-floor walk-up with marble stairs worn with divots from thousands of climbs; a run-down bit of history that had sheltered immigrants fresh off the boat for a hundred years and now held us: the recluse on the first floor, the Colombian family on the second, the Indian family on the third, the rock musician on the fourth, Al on the fifth floor, and me on the sixth, as well as everyone in between—the cigar-smoking eighty-year-old, the drug dealers, the Australians, the painter, the woman with the feminist press and the middle-aged man who lived with his mother. As tenants we saw each other every day but kept our distance, nodding in the stairwell. We knew and did not know each other. Except for Al. Everyone knew Al and Al knew everyone, whether they liked it or not.

Al played many roles in our building: protector, gossip, friend, advisor, organizer, preacher and captain of the front stoop. Night or day, he was nearly always there, leaning against the railing and smoking. Sometimes he'd carry a staff and sometimes a shillelagh—a kind of cane/club from Ireland, made from the knot of a tree, and used to bash in people's skulls. I know this because I am half Irish, and also because Al explained to me, in great detail, how he had used his cane in different circumstances over the years to do exactly that. Al needed the cane now because he had trouble walking—one of the reasons why he rarely left our building. His health was deteriorating, a combination of diabetes and cancer that limited his mobility. So instead of getting into fights, he mostly smoked cigarettes and talked to people on the front stoop, about his life in the Navy during Vietnam, where he'd been sprayed with Agent Orange (and which he blamed for his cancer); about the neighborhood and how much it had changed since he'd moved there in the seventies from the Bronx; about his sexual exploits picking up men at the piers, full of gritty and shockingly salacious details; about guns and weapons he stockpiled for protection; about the people he was in current disagreements with; and, perhaps more than anything else, about the latest infractions and regulations that were being violated by our landlord.

Sometimes, we didn't have hot water. Sometimes, we didn't have water at all. Sometimes, there was no heat. Sometimes, there was so much heat we had to open all the windows in the middle of winter, the steam radiators clanging so loudly it was like someone whacking a baseball bat across the pipes. There were cockroaches. Mice. In the spring, ants would march in lines from the windowsill across the kitchen floor. Anything we wanted to eat, we had to keep in the refrigerator. There was no sink in the bathroom, and so we did all of our face-washing and tooth-brushing in the kitchen by the front door, over a sink of dirty dishes. When it rained, the roof leaked, and we would put out pans and buckets and move the couch we'd found on the sidewalk into the middle of the room. Once, Al told me, he had knocked a hole in the wall. "It was full of dead pigeons," he said. At night, I could hear the birds cooing, and I imagined their bones inches away from my face.

But there were good things about the building, too. In the afternoon, the rooms filled with sunlight. The bathtub was an old clawfoot, and although it flaked layer after layer of paint whenever I took a shower, it also gave a perfect view of the World Trade Center, framed in the slender glass of the bathroom window. At the top of the stairwell there was a door with a latch that opened onto the roof—a wide platform covered with tar that stuck to our shoes, but also delivered fresh air, cool breezes, and a secret million-dollar view. To the left was Houston Street, the Lower East Side, Chinatown and City Hall, where the grid broke apart into old Manhattan, numbered streets transforming into names. Behind us, the Williamsburg, Manhattan, and Brooklyn bridges hung like a triptych in lights. The sun set straight ahead, a pink and orange sky illuminating rows and rows of water towers, their shadows decorating the tops of buildings from the East Village straight across to the Hudson. And on the right: a classic movie skyline, with the glittering Chrysler Building and the majestic Empire State, its evening colors changing to reflect the holidays as they passed—blue for Hanukkah, red for Valentine's Day—and just beyond, nearly an afterthought, stood the U.N., a slender column set along the edge of the East River. On the night I moved into the building, I climbed up to the roof to get my bearings. I had no job. I had no money. But the entire city was spread out before me, a map of possibility. I'd never seen anything more thrilling, more intimidating, or more alive.

Six flights was a long way to walk up. Al taught me to use the windows that lined the stairwell as mirrors, to make sure there wasn't someone waiting to jump me around the corner. It was good advice, especially when the entry door locks were broken, as they sometimes were, or in the winter, when the homeless and the drug addicts in the neighborhood would wander in looking for shelter. A roommate of mine came home late one night to a creepy guy lingering in the hall. She did not call the police. She knocked on Al's door instead. "You did the right thing," he told her.

Then he threw the bum out. A different roommate decided to have a drunken crab-walking contest across our living room floor at 1:00 a.m. with a few friends. Convinced she was being attacked, Al ran upstairs and burst into the party waving a gun, which quickly sobered everyone up. Once, a group of guys living in the building hired a transvestite hooker and then refused to give her any money. The hooker was screaming and banging on their door. Al threatened the guys and made them pay up. Then he escorted the hooker down the stairs and out the front door, meeting every curse and insult with a louder, more colorful one of his own.

I saw Al nearly every day as I came and went from the building. I knew that he'd worked as a photographer, and I talked with him on the stoop about jewelry, and I helped him lug things up the five flights to his apartment whenever I saw him struggling, especially later when his illness progressed. But I also purposely kept myself from getting too close. Not only because I wanted to keep some distance between myself and anyone who carried a gun, but also because I was learning this was how people survived—by not knowing things, even when you knew them. The walls of New York City apartments are thin. At night you hear your neighbors crying. You hear them having sex. You hear them fighting with their husbands and wives, with their boyfriends and girlfriends. You hear them say terrible things to their children. You know when they are sick—you can hear them coughing. You know when they are out of town—or possibly dead—their mail piling up on the doormat. They are like family members that you live with but pretend not to know. There is a strange kind of intimacy. And when they are gone, you do not miss them.

I have one picture of Al. It is a photograph of him taking a photograph. We were on the roof with all of our neighbors, waiting for the U.N. to be bombed. Al was convinced it would be next, after the towers fell. "Just watch," he said. "They're going to hit everything." And so we watched the wall of dust and fire, and Al watched the Empire State Building, the Brooklyn Bridge, anyplace else that might be a target. In the photo, he is bare-chested, a tattoo on his right arm, his camera focused north. His body framed by a cloud of smoke and destruction. He is wearing purple pajama pants. It seems strange, and then I remember: we were all just waking up.

A few months later Al went away for treatment. When he came back he was diminished. I would hear him climbing the stairs, grunting and struggling with his breath. The sound of his pain echoed up the air shaft. When I asked him how he was, he never said all right. He never said OK. He listed all the things that were wrong, in excruciating detail. I did not know what to say to him—I was used to people hiding the worst parts of their lives. Any words of comfort Al rebuffed. I was younger then. I know better now, that when someone does this, they are not looking for answers.

One day I was walking down Avenue A and Al passed me on a scooter. It was more of a standing moped, really. A skateboard with a handle in front and a motor attached to the back. He was going full throttle, at least thirty miles per hour, and the grin on his face was enormous. It was like watching a giant riding on the back of a bee. I had never seen him so gloriously happy. Later, when I asked him about the scooter, he told me it was his escape plan for the next terrorist attack. He said the motor had just enough gas in it to get him home to his family in the Bronx.

Al got sicker. He went into the hospital for weeks at a time. Whenever I saw him he seemed more tired, more ashen and more alone, even when friends came to visit. He smoked weed in the hall with some of the other neighbors. I helped him carry his groceries up the stairs. He stopped hanging out on the stoop. And then one day Al went into the hospital and he did not come back.

I put on every piece of jewelry I owned, the largest, most ornate necklaces and rings and bracelets and walked over to St. Mark's Church, where Al's friends had arranged a memorial service. Sitting in the audience were all the tenants of our building, and even, surprisingly, our landlord, sweaty and intimidating in his jacket and tie. Different people from Al's life got up and spoke, and as often happens at funerals, I learned new things about him. About his family that he was estranged from. About his artwork and photography. And about how he tried to help teenagers who were homeless, who had been turned out by their parents for being bisexual or gay. A few of these teens got up and spoke of how he had supported them, and I was moved to know that Al had been quietly doing this work, without say a word about it, at least not to me. But who was I to him, anyway? Not family, not even really a friend; just the girl who lived upstairs, the one whose noisy boots he'd once threatened to saw the heels off of. As I was leaving the church, I eyed our landlord. A part of me wondered if the man had come to make peace. But another part of me, the part that had been trained to watch for muggers in the reflections of windows, was sure that our landlord was at the funeral for one reason only: to make sure that Al was really dead.

When no one came to claim Al's belongings, a bunch of tenants from the building volunteered to help clear out his apartment. I had never been inside Al's place before, even though I lived in the apartment directly over his. The layout was the same, and I had a strange feeling moving from room to room, seeing how different the same space could be, while sifting through the contents of Al's life. Boxes of junk were piled straight to the ceiling, the detritus of thirty years. He'd refused to let the landlord in for repairs, and so the fixtures were all from the 1920s or '30s, the paint peeling, the window frames rattled and broken. I looked up at the ceiling. Every evening, Al would have a cigarette before he went to sleep, the smoke drifting from his bedroom into mine through the slats in the floorboards. It was a habit. I had grown used to the smell. For the first time, I wondered what parts of my life had filtered down into Al's place. What he might have come to know about me, in the years we had lived stacked together.

The tenants got to work separating what was possible to donate, what was personal, and what should be thrown away. We found all the things you might expect: family photos, old clothes, porn, Al's photographs and negatives, printing paper and his jewelry. We also found some things you might not expect: a bullwhip and a keg of TNT. It was hidden behind a pile of boxes in the bedroom—a white plastic drum dusted with yellow powder.

"Is that what I think it is?" someone said. We looked at each other. We checked the labels.

"How the hell did he get this?"

"And what the hell do we do with it?"

"Put it out with the trash?" someone suggested.

For a moment we imagined the barrel being thrown into the back of a garbage truck, unloaded onto a barge, and then blowing sky-high at Fresh Kills. In the end, we decided to turn in Al's TNT at the police station instead. Afterward, we carried trash bags down the same five flights of stairs that Al used to struggle to go up each day. We brought his clothes to Goodwill and piled the rest of the bags on the sidewalk.

That night my fellow tenants didn't feel like strangers. Instead, we were almost friends. We swapped stories about Al and laughed. At times, each of us would turn silent, understanding that one day we would die and that everything we owned would be put on the curb like this. With each trip out to the sidewalk, I expected to find Al on the stoop, flicking the ash of his cigarette, commenting on the men and women walking by, shouting at the druggies, reigning over his small spot of earth. When the last bag was carried down and Al's apartment was empty we went our separate ways, closing and locking our separate doors. I took a shower and got into bed. Before I closed my eyes, I leaned over and looked at the floor. For the past ten years I'd been sleeping directly over a barrel of explosives. Enough to bring the whole building down.

Not long after Al died, I came home from work and there was an eviction notice taped to my door. There was a notice taped to nearly everyone's door—or at least, the people like me, who didn't have rental agreements on paper. The neighborhood had been changing for years. Bloomberg was mayor now, and boutiques had sprouted in places where people used to shoot heroin on the sidewalk. On the other side of Houston Street, high-rise luxury condominiums with doormen were being built. Our landlord had finally realized that he could charge five times what all of us were paying. And so before long my apartment, too, was cleared out and made empty. My young adulthood boxed up. I hired a bunch of Russian movers and they carried my life down six flights and over the bridge to Brooklyn. I could not help thinking that if Al was still there on the stoop, glowering and leaning on his staff, our landlord would not have had the guts to evict us.

After I locked the door to my apartment on East Second Street for the last time, I climbed the stairs and went to the roof. I looked out over the city that had once seemed so dangerous and unknowable, a place for me to strike my mark. I wasn't sleeping much those days, and before Al died, I used to cross paths with him in the gloom of the early hours, not quite day but no longer night. Al would find me sitting on the roof at four in the morning, and he would not ask why; instead he would light a cigarette and tell me the latest gossip from the building, and how he was doing with his new therapy, and then he'd show me one of his necklaces, moments of time captured in amber that glowed gold when I held them to the brightening sky. Then we'd look out over the city, at the people in the buildings on the other side of First Avenue, waking up, getting dressed, having sex, eating breakfast, each apartment window a box of brilliant light.

"I don't know why they don't use curtains," I said.

Al took a long drag off his cigarette, the ember glowing hot and red before he pitched it over the side of the building. "Curtains?" He said this as if he was disappointed in me. "Those folks know we're watching. They want us to see it all."

Zapata Boulevard

VALERIA LUISELLI

I remember that I'm invisible and walk softly so as not awake the sleeping ones.

—*Ralph Ellison*, Invisible Man

The house in front is baby yellow. From the window on the top floor, a woman used to stick out her head and yell "Motherfuckers" at the passersby. The passersby were usually students from City College, and sometimes workers, or tourists, or deliverymen. They didn't look up. The insult was never acknowledged. Perhaps because there was no nastiness in the tone of her call. Or perhaps its recurrence had rendered it innocuous or inaudible, like sirens, car alarms, or the cries of certain birds. When I was a child, living in South Africa, there was a large bird in our street that, around sundown, let out a call that sounded almost like "Por favoooor." This woman's cry reminded me of that bird.

◆ ◆ ◆

"Por favor, pase usted / Please come in" is what many of the signs outside the small businesses in the neighborhood say. These signs are usually handwritten and taped onto the storefront windows. Sometimes they are bilingual. They say: "Necesito mesera / I need a waitress" or "No tenemos ATM / We no have ATM." My favorite sign says: "Ester no está / Ester is not there." My daughter is learning to read and asks me to tell her what things say. She wants to know what everything says. I have to recite entire menus sometimes, and I'm easily caught out if I try to cheat by skipping dishes. Whenever we pass "Ester no está" she becomes

196

meditative, and speculative: where is Ester, is she coming back, why did she leave, how old is she, is she a daughter or a mother, and where is "'there'"?

• • •

Here is Convent Avenue, Hamilton Heights. It begins in a community garden at the crossing of Saint Nicholas and 152nd Street, runs parallel to Amsterdam until 135th Street, cutting through City College's Gothic schist-and-white-terra-cotta buildings, and then curves its way around the hills and cliffs to the west of Saint Nicholas Park until it reaches 126th Street, where it becomes Morningside Avenue. I think we were discreet as newcomers to the street. I think we were even invisible. Not the way Mexicans are usually invisible, but still, fairly invisible. I understood this as a good sign, a kind of silent welcome.

We had brought only the books we were reading that week. We had brought half of our clothes. The plan was to stay just for a while. At the very last moment we had packed the Bialletti coffee maker, in case, and a small framed photograph of Emiliano Zapata, which had hung for two years in our kitchen in Tacubaya, back in Mexico City. The glass and frame were still covered in a layer of grime—or is it soot?—when I hammered a nail into our new kitchen wall and carefully hung the photograph next to the refrigerator. In it, Zapata is standing upright, his double cartridge belt hanging crosswise; he holds a rifle in his right hand, and what looks more like a spade than a machete in the left. Under the picture, there is an inscription of Zapata's most famous political slogan during the Mexican Revolution: *"La tierra es de quien la trabaja"*— the land belongs to those who work it.

• • •

It's difficult to imagine that this area was once farmland and that Broadway was an Indian trail that connected these hills and valleys to Manhattan's southern tip. Only on warmer days, walking the trails along Riverside Park, or cycling along the path next to the Hudson River between the wastewater treatment plant and the lighthouse under Washington Bridge, is it possible to intuit the soundscapes and landscapes of the island's former days.

Other layers of the past are easier to disinter with a little imagination. Their ghosts still linger. It's less difficult to imagine, for example, that the area now occupied by Columbia University's Morningside campus was the lunatic asylum until the late 1800s. The city must have been full of them—colonial lunatics, maddened by their own expansionist ambitions, souls sickened by solitude and nostalgia, minds turned against themselves for having seen too much—for having *undone so many*.

There is one story whose Conradian horror has remained with me since I read about it. In 1643, the director of the West India Company, Willem Kieft, ordered a raid on the Weckquaesgeeks Indians, one of the original Wappinger groups of the eastern bank of the Hudson. The attack happened at midnight, when everyone was sleeping. They killed the men first, but did not hesitate to go on to massacre the women and children. When at sunrise his soldiers returned, carrying with them the heads of the fallen, Kieft decided to organize a soccer match—a primitive version of the game, of course, and in more than one sense. Up and down the street, in front of their husbands and children, the wives of the soldiers kicked the heads of the Indians.

◆ ◆ ◆

I often raise my head upward when I'm walking. I play a game with my daughter, which consists in making an inventory of neighborhood buildings that have lost their cornices. We have more than thirty in our collection. At other times we look down at the ground. We count dog turds and flowers, and marks left on the pavement by bubble gum "chewed in the olden days," as she explains. Along the streets there are rectangles of earth cut into the asphalt, each with a small tree in the center. Things sprout or lie about around the tree. Sometimes flowers, almost always weeds, cigarette ends, litter, debris. Coming out of school, we find a dead rat in one of those miniature rectangular gardens. She stops and fixes her eyes on the corpse of the rat. Very serious, she whispers: "Wake up, little mouse, it's wake-up time." Just that, two or three times. No reply from the rat. Then, offended by the animal's silent indifference, she takes my hand and says, "He's not waking up, Mamma, let's go find a swing."

◆ ◆ ◆

Silence, a certain form of silence, is like a slow fire. If it is not stopped, it expands and scorches everything around it. On the last day of the school year, I had a long conversation with Martina, the mother of one of my daughter's classmates at P.S. 153. They are from the Mixteca, a region in the Mexican south that spans Oaxaca, Guerrero, and Puebla. We were standing in line, waiting to vote for a parent representative for the following year, exchanging stories of our daughters' linguistic and cultural confusion. My daughter understands Spanish well, but speaks it using English syntax, so the result is far from comprehensible. It's like scaffolding embracing a vacuum instead of a building, I was about to say, but I didn't—it's an analogy full of pretensions. Instead, I asked her what language she speaks at home. Her first language is Trique. The only thing I knew about Trique was that it's one of the most complex tonal languages, with more than eight tones. My great-grandmother was Otomí and spoke Otomí, a more simple tonal language with only three tones. She passed it on to my grandmother, but my mother didn't learn it. When I asked Martina if her daughter could speak Trique, she smiled and told me no, of course not. Why would she teach her a language that others would laugh at? Better to keep it silent. She is wrong and she is right at the same time.

If her ancestors had lived here in the nineteenth century, someone might have played football with their heads. But she migrated to the United States in 2005. That was around when the decapitations began—in Mexico, this time. The Mexican government opened fire against the drug lords, the drug lords answered back with thousands of bodies, and heads, and noise—so much noise. In the U.S.A., a few years later, the massive deportations began. There have been more than two million deportations since 2008—and most have gone by in silence.

◆ ◆ ◆

To draw a map of a space is to include as much as to exclude. It's also a way to make visible what is usually unseen. A map is a silhouette, a regrouping of elements. Maps of Harlem have become more and more detailed and sophisticated in their layered articulation of history. Scholars and chroniclers of black Harlem have successfully heeded the call: "History must restore what slavery took away." I've been reading the historian and writer Sharifa Rhodes-Pitts, for example, who has written one of the most delicately crafted and intelligent maps of the neighborhood, *Harlem Is Nowhere*, where she walks "with the dead and with the living," and moves in and out of books and conversations, along streets, inside buildings and vacant lots. "We are all looking for the underground city," she writes. "Sometimes it seems the library *is* that city, and we at the library wander its unnamed streets—alone yet in a crowd—walking with our heads down to solve mysteries written on the pavement."

I'm not a historian, but I share with her and many others the compulsion for hearing stories and reading traces of the past on sidewalks and buildings. I often find myself seeking out the history, the histories, of Mexican Harlem. The taciturn, silent presence of Mexicans on this side of Harlem remains uncharted. It's a relatively recent migration, compared to many others, so its invisibility is somewhat understandable. It's also a silenced history, toned down by its own makers, who are often illegal and prefer to remain unseen and unheard. Even when summer comes and the Caribbean residents move out of their tenement apartments and into the street, where the elderly play *dominó cubano* and children flap their arms like oversized birds around the streams of water gushing out from fire hydrants, Mexicans stay indoors; they don't claim any right to use the street, to inhabit this, or any other place.

◆ ◆ ◆

I used to avoid 145th Street. I preferred 144th, where the dividing line between inside and outside, between public and private life, is more diffuse. Or even 146th, more serene and placid, despite its infestation of rats and the ominous back windows of the Upper Manhattan Mental Hospital on the corner of Amsterdam Avenue.

I started using 145th on my way to the 1 line when I heard that a new Arab deli had opened and was selling rolling tobacco. For a long time, the only building I noticed on 145th was the carcass of the old P.S. 186—an H-shaped Second Renaissance building from the early 1900s that has been abandoned for almost half a century. My daughter calls it "the school for trees," because, from its large windows—all without glass but still beautifully framed on the outside with their original stone masonry— the heads of saplings stick out like undisciplined pupils.

The school, formerly owned by the Boys & Girls Club of Harlem, shut down in 1975 after a long struggle with the board of education and a series of violent incidents. That same year, my daughter's school, P.S. 153, opened. The new school is nothing like the old one and exactly like most of the public schools in Manhattan: oppressive, dark, with barred windows. I don't pride myself on my fetish for decadence as much as I used to, but there is a quiet beauty in that old Renaissance building— its creeping overgrowth, the tall, leprous ceilings that can be seen from the street, the construction's ultimate resistance to finally crumble and collapse. Perhaps I like it because it reminds me of the future—of what the future would look like if nobody speculated with it. I like to walk on the south side of 145th, from where I can see a niche in the facade of the building's east wing that embraces a bust of the goddess Minerva. It is just visible behind the elevated platform of the sidewalk scaffolding. She looks down toward the passersby, as if she could be saying, softly and almost tenderly: "Motherfuckers."

◆ ◆ ◆

Sometimes you see them around here, speculating, looking heavenward under the cool shadow of old brownstones boarded up with slats. They look like sleepwalkers, these speculators, these men and women of the future, ignoring absolutely everything that happens around them on the streets, their eyes fixed on some sort of infinity where supply and demand are two sides of an equation that benefits only the few. Every week, a new sign appears: Town House For Sale. Every month, a new article: Up and coming.

◆ ◆ ◆

Real estate maps of Hamilton Heights draw the east–west borders of the neighborhood between the Hudson River and Edgecombe Avenue, and the north–south borders between 135th and 155th Streets. I like to think that the map of my everyday life in this neighborhood is a combination of chance and purpose. Or rather, that it's a map of little purposes intercepted by chance. That during the walk between my house and the supermarket, there is at least one new find—a store I hadn't noticed, a detail on the facade of a building, an encounter with a stranger. My map during the winter months is restricted to a few streets, a few circuits. In the summer, the invisible barriers shift and readjust; the neighborhood opens up like a foreign city, pregnant with possibilities.

♦ ♦ ♦

My daughter's favorite building in the neighborhood, one of the few constructions from the 1960s, is, objectively, the ugliest. But she doesn't see it that way. She sees in it what I see in certain old buildings or in vacant lots: a possibility, a story. She likes it for two reasons: it is crowned by a menorah of notable, Disneylandish proportions, and she knows—because I am repeatedly asked to read it out—that above its doors a sign announces "Phase Piggy Back." I can imagine the equation she has worked out in her four-year-old head. In her world of literal meanings she must think that in that building people get piggybacks, and that it's always Hanukkah.

There are another three organizations similar to Phase Piggy Back around the neighborhood, all of which treat patients with a history of drug abuse. There is also a Sisters of Mercy Prison Services, the Upper Manhattan Mental Hospital, and an AA for Spanish speakers. I once had a brief cigarette conversation with one young woman, standing outside the Hamilton Heights branch of the NYPL right next to the Piggy Back, as I waited for the library to open its doors. I asked her what the program was like. She said that it was OK, that they had at least helped keep her steady. She also told me that Phase Piggy Back is now run by the Argus Community, after a scandal in which the CEO of Piggy Back was accused of diverting funds. I tried to read up on it but found nothing substantial. I did find out that the menorah on top of the building is actually a Kwanzaa kinara. I also came across the Phase Piggy Back's mission statement, which draws on Kwanzaa's principles, and is a confusing mélange of political history of the 1960s, cultural history of the 1920s, religious references, and clinical problems of past and recent years:

In 1968, four men had a dream, a dream that saw a community, Harlem, rising up from the severe blows of inadequate sanitation services; health services; educational services, social services; and the rising dangerous levels of drug abuse. In short, they saw a need for a revolution. The dream envisioned by these men, imbued with the philosophy of "self-help" and "total community involvement" and, fortified with the power of the Principles of the Nguzo Saba, saw themselves conquering these ills and safely returning the community to the levels of civilized living that is enjoyed during the Renaissance.

Much more confusing, and in a very ominous way, is the mission statement of the new yoga space two buildings down from the Piggy Back. Their home page announces that "Brahman Yoga was opened in May 2014, shortly after a team of scientists in Antarctica discovered evidence that the universe inflated into being faster than the speed of light." I am no connoisseur of the respectable discipline of yoga. The only time I subjected myself to it I was seven months pregnant and therefore generally confused and disoriented. But I have friends who talk about yoga, and even some who talk a lot about yoga, and had never heard of that particular strand of it until recently. Classes are only $5 in Brahman Yoga, but I decided to not go, even if the experience could have made for an entire article.

◆ ◆ ◆

We arrived in Convent Avenue during the heat wave in the summer of 2011. I remember the vague disappointment when, after unpacking all our belongings, the house still looked completely empty. During the weeks and months that followed, we bought cheap furniture, some plants, many books, and, later, a framed photograph of Malcolm X that I hung next to Zapata.

It's never clear what turns a space into a home. Our apartment remained soulless for a long time—until one day it wasn't. I think that day was the same day I bought the Malcolm X photograph. All at once, the new books ceased to fit in the bookshelf, so we had to buy a second, and the marks we had made on the wall in the hallway to register our daughter's height suddenly summed up to a vertical timeline. I knew then that somehow time had passed, and we'd stopped building a life—furnishing its vast empty spaces—and had just started living there. But where is there?

◆ ◆ ◆

"There are a lot of mangoes . . . but not a lot of berries." I read this line in an article in the *NYT*, where new, affluent residents of Hamilton Heights were asked to comment on their new, perhaps up-and-coming, but still not-so-affluent neighborhood. The line could easily translate to "There are a lot of Latinos, but not a lot of whites." Hamilton Heights is the most unequal neighborhood in Manhattan in terms of its residents' annual income (the top fifth of the population here earns more than thirty times that of the lowest fifth). Most of its eighty thousand residents live either in rent-stabilized tenements or in single family–owned brownstones built in the nineteenth and early twentieth centuries. The neighborhood is undoubtedly gentrifying. Compared to when we arrived here, there are many more new coffee shops and fewer *fondas*, more sports bars and more yoga spaces, and next to Margaret's Beauty Parlor, which has been offering cheap cuts and braids for over forty years, there is a new luxury pet spa.

Farther down in that *NYT* article, I also read that one new neighbor believes that if the neighborhood gentrifies, "there will be a lot less chicanery and hustling going around." Chicanery does not have an etymological relationship to Chicano, but the word takes me there immediately. That comment could translate to "fewer Mexicans." And perhaps, also, "fewer Dominicans, poor blacks, immigrants, and people in need of Piggy Backs in general." Ester is not there and perhaps she should not come back.

◆ ◆ ◆

The story is always more complex than it seems. The more you dig, the more dust you stir up. The more closely you observe, the less you understand. I go back to the notes I keep in a journal and reread a week of discouraging conversations with a relatively happy ending:

Monday. Conversation with a Dominican gypsy-cab driver:
 —To 125th Street, please.
 —Where are you from, mami?
 —Mexico.
 —Really?
 —Yes.
 —You are the first Mexican I meet who's not a midget.
 —Really?
 —Yes.

I don't really know what to respond after that so I keep silent. I don't tip him.

Tuesday. Conversation with a Ghanaian gypsy-cab driver:
  —Where are you from?
  —Me, from Mexico. And you?
  —Ghana.
  —Good soccer match the other day.
  —Good Mexican match too. I like you Mexicans.
  —Thank you.
  —Not the Caribbeans.
  —Why?
  —They are all racists.
  —Yes?
  —Yes.

Wednesday. Conversation with the owner of La Fortaleza, a Mexican deli:
  —How are you today, señora?
  —Not so good. My bike was stolen.
  —Really? I'm sure it was one of those *morenos*.
  By any standard, both of us are *morenas*, so I'm not quite sure which group she is accusing of being thieves.
  —What do you mean?
  —*Los dominicanos*. They're all thieves.

Thursday. I take my daughter to a ballet audition on 152nd Street. As we sit in a waiting room packed with equally overdressed little girls—the tutus, the bandanas, the pink tights, the sparkles everywhere—I fill out the routine questionnaire. The second question demands a racial description of my child. I mark, as I often do, "Other," because I don't think that "Hispanic" is a race.

Friday. I walk up to Saint Nicholas and 152nd to buy a tea. The owner of the deli, a Yemeni, is standing behind the counter singing a beautiful, repetitive song in Arabic. His assistant, a Mexican man in his forties, prepares the tea. He watches me watching his boss. I'm quietly smiling to myself, thinking that the song and the sound of his voice are beautiful. As he hands me the tea he asks me, in Spanish:

—You like his voice?

—Well, yes, I do. It's angelical.

—Angelical? This man is Satan.

—Why do you say that?

I prepare for the next comment, as an insecure goalkeeper might morally prepare to not stop a ball as he sees it approaching at high speed.

—You know how many kids this man has? He has twenty-five kids.

I nod in return, trying to gauge the moral weight of his remark. Then, in recently acquired but good Spanish, his boss corrects him:

—Twenty-seven, not twenty-five. You're just saying that because you're envious of me, Ivan, because you're short and I'm tall and handsome.

They look at each other and laugh, with full-hearted complicity. I pay and leave, quickly and silently.

◆ ◆ ◆

A line from an essay by Richard Selzer comes to my mind whenever I ask for a sandwich in the deli on 145th and Saint Nicholas, and watch the young man, whom I call Primo and who calls me Prima—which means "cousin"—as he carefully layers ingredients on a bun. This line is: "the quietude of resolve layered over fear." Selzer is describing the instant before a surgeon cuts into the body of the person lying beneath his scalpel. But he could be describing the way that illegals cross the border, and the way they wake up every morning to face another day of work: the quietude of resolve layered over fear. He could be describing the way they carve out the small space they inhabit in this map.

◆ ◆ ◆

Malcolm X shared with Zapata the idea that land was the basis of independence. In his 1963 speech, "Message to Grassroots," Malcolm X demanded land for a nation, an independent nation. Zapata, in 1911, had proclaimed the "Plan de Ayala," which demanded that land be seized from landowners and redistributed among Mexican peasants. It has always been about land; it always will be.

◆ ◆ ◆

The small rectangular space behind the salad and sandwich counters; the underground storage rooms under the metal trap doors; the corners within street corners where flowers are sold for five, ten, and fifteen dollars; the street carts that sell pastry and coffee; homes shared with ten, twelve relatives; detention centers where hard labor is paid at the rate of thirteen cents an hour; deportation limbos; the narrow strip on the right of roads along which bicycle deliverymen speed, wearing their bike chains crossed around their chests like modern Zapatas—that is the map most Mexicans occupy.

• • •

Almost on the corner of Convent Avenue and 145th, right in front of the Sisters of Mercy Prison Services, there is a small street cart that sells pastry and coffee. It rolls up the hill at dawn and back down toward the Bronx at sundown. Alfredo, its owner, arrived in New York ten years ago. When I asked him once how he got here, to this country, he just smiled and said, "With these two legs."

I know that he's from the Mixteca, in Oaxaca, and he knows I'm from Mexico City, a *chilanga*. This information sets us apart as much as it brings us together. We are somehow foreigners to each other, brought closer by a deeper sense of foreignness. We have to zigzag our way through the conversation, swiftly but carefully, dodging prejudices and possible misunderstandings, always looking for the most comfortable ground on which to stand. It is a very narrow ground, the one we find, somewhere between mutual respect and mutual teasing.

"Here comes the *chilanga* writer, watch your wallets," he'll say when I arrive. "Give me a cup of your horrible petroleum," I'll respond.

Sometimes, I stick around while I sip on my coffee. Most of his clients are students from City College, hurrying to class. They order, pay, and leave. Other frequent customers are taxi drivers, deliverymen, and, of course, the unemployed. Those always stay to talk, sometimes for hours. One of them once told me that since he got his legal work permit, no one hires him. "For the boss, legal is more expensive than illegal," he explained.

If I strike up a conversation with any of his regulars, Alfredo warns them: "If you give her your stories, you have to charge her for it, because she's probably going to write about them." I'm not sure why, instead of becoming suspicious, instead of shying away, they talk. A Peruvian man who Alfredo calls Perú, and who in turn calls Alfredo "Cara de Nopal"— cactus face—once told me, after he'd heard I was a writer, a minutely detailed story of when he used to deliver dolls to New Jersey. He explained how he'd pick up the dolls' hair in Queens, the bodies in Brooklyn, and the clothes somewhere in Lower Manhattan, because these were good dolls, the kind you don't get anymore, all of whose parts were carefully manufactured in different places, by skilled people, not by machines, and then, once all these pieces were put together in the factory, they were packed inside boxes, little boxes, and then he'd drive a van full of them to New Jersey. The factory manager was a Spaniard, and was a good man, a generous man, but possibly too flirtatious with the ladies. He used to buy them all perfumes, boxes and boxes of perfumes. Alfredo interrupted him at a point where the story was becoming rather confusing:

"So what, Perú?"

"So what what, Cara de Nopal?"

"So what's the point of your story?"

"The moral of the story is that now the factory moved to China."

"And?"

"And nothing, but maybe she could write about the dolls."

◆ ◆ ◆

I should write about Ester, and find out where she is. I should write about P.S. 186, and Martina, and Alfredo, and his street cart. I should also say, for example, that one day the police came and knocked on the door of the yellow house opposite ours. I was smoking out of the window of the attic where I work, and the trees were swollen with new summer leaves, so I could not make out who it was that opened the door for them. A few minutes later, they came out with a woman and led her to their car. She offered no resistance; she did not say a word. I would have liked to scream "Motherfuckers." I should have, but instead I just stood there, another silent, petrified Minerva.

◆ ◆ ◆

Perhaps one day there will be a Zapata Boulevard, invisible, like there is an almost invisible Martin Luther King Boulevard. It would start on

Convent Avenue, inside a house, in a kitchen, above a refrigerator, on a wall where the pictures of Malcolm X and Emiliano Zapata hang next to each other. Then, it would meander gently at the foot of Sugar Hill toward 145th Street, where it would run down past Edgecombe Avenue and Jackie Robinson Park, past Adam Clayton Powell Jr. Boulevard, across the rather sad empty straights before the Harlem River wetlands, and finally intersect with Malcolm X Boulevard, exactly where the bridge that connects Manhattan to the Bronx begins.

Home

TIM FREEMAN

Ever since I can remember, I loved New York and wanted to live there. I was born in New York—at North Shore hospital in Manhasset, just outside of Queens. My parents lived in the middle class suburb of Westbury on Long Island for a few years before moving to Pennsylvania in 1979. My father worked for the welfare department.

I remember taking trips to the city as a young boy. One of my earliest memories is piling onto a bus in Allentown with my parents and brothers and a hundred other people to attend a peace march in New York protesting the escalation of nuclear weapons. This was around 1981 or 1982. I held up a sign that my brother drew of a giant hand blocking two missiles being fired simultaneously from the USA and Russia with the word "stop" written beneath it. I remember walking down the wide avenues of Manhattan and looking up at the brick apartment buildings. I recall hearing a man on a balcony looking down at all the marchers saying, "They look like ants."

On another trip, we went to the top of the Empire State Building and rode the Staten Island Ferry. Our family Christmas card photo from 1983 shows me and my brothers posing on the ferry with the Twin Towers looming in the background.

I still remember that trip well. I remember right before that picture was taken, walking to the ferry terminal holding my mother's hand. It was a beautiful day. As my mother and I walked, the cavernous alleys of Lower Manhattan giving way to the waterfront with its invigorating sea air, we encountered several homeless men and women. I was seven years old, but up until that time had never seen a homeless person in real life. I stared in half-wonderment at these individuals. They weren't the sort of people I was used to seeing. They were bedraggled and raw, not unlike the pigeons that pecked at the ground around them.

I tugged at my mother's hand and pointed at the people. "There's a bum," I said. "There's another bum." My mom leaned over and informed me that it was not polite to say that. "There's a bum...There's a bum... There's a bum," I chimed. A homeless lady sitting on a bench looked up at me with a hurt and offended look. My seven-year-old mind didn't know how to make sense of the situation. I didn't understand what a homeless person was at that age. Yes, I had heard about being homeless on TV or from my friends, but I didn't fully grasp what it meant.

My mother began to tell me why it was impolite to point at homeless people. "They are poor and have nowhere to live," she said. I continued to stare, now trying to understand them rather than identify with them.

Looking back, I always associated this incident with the tactlessness that is childhood innocence. I never knew it would provide a context for something that would happen to me many years later.

Almost three decades after, in July 2010, I vacated the apartment I was renting in Upstate NY and bought a one-way train ticket to New York City. I had a few hundred dollars, a suitcase with a couple changes of clothes in it, a laptop computer and a cell phone. The first night I stayed at a hotel in Midtown Manhattan. The next afternoon I went to the Bellevue Men's Shelter on First Avenue in Midtown and declared myself homeless.

It is less easy to remember the circumstances that led up to me being homeless than it is to remember the experience of actually being homeless. I was angry about a family inheritance, I was angry at my dad, I was unhappy with my life—and, more than anything, I had wanted to live in New York for as long as I can remember. Also, since the age of sixteen, I have been seeing a psychiatrist and taking medicine for a mental illness and depression. Mental health issues have a way of exacerbating life's stresses and problems.

The Bellevue Men's shelter is a foreboding nine-story pre-war red brick building surrounded by a high wall and wrought iron fencing. The building used to be a psychiatric hospital until it was converted into a shelter. When I arrived there, I was fingerprinted and photographed before being assigned a bed on the seventh floor. The room where I found my bed was large and empty. The walls were painted a yellowish-white color and a large heavy door with a small square window provided a modicum of privacy. In one corner of the room, there were brown water stains and a gaping hole in the ceiling that leaked drips of water. Dirty puddles collected on the floor below the dripping. In another corner next to a metal locker there was a cot with white sheets and a scratchy wool blanket that smelled of banana peel. The pillow was like a half-inflated beach ball. On the night that I arrived, somebody else's possessions were still in the locker.

I spent the next seven months as a homeless person. For much of that time I was at Bellevue, but sometimes I stayed at other shelters in the city. I also stayed at a couple of shelters in Albany for a few weeks before returning to New York City. On some nights, if I had enough money, I would get a hotel room. If I was too weary to follow the rules of whatever shelter I happened to be staying at, I slept on the street.

I had many different roommates at the various shelters. I had one roommate who smoked crack. Another smelled so bad that the other people in the room would spray him with air freshener. I shared a room with a group of guys who smoked marijuana like it was tobacco. I had a roommate with a degree in sociology from the University of Chicago. There was even a guy at one of the shelters who dressed like a businessman.

All types of people become homeless for all kinds of reasons. Financial problems, alcoholism, drug addiction, family and relationship issues, depression, mental illness, laziness and problems with the law tend to be the most frequent causes. Some young adults in New York end up in shelters after aging out of the foster care system. There are also a lot of veterans living in shelters. I met several men who had served in Vietnam or who were recent veterans of the Iraq and Afghanistan conflicts. According to shelter census figures on the Coalition for the Homeless website, during the time that I was homeless, there were approximately 38,500 people in shelters each night in New York City. Today, that figure is closer to 55,000. A large number of these homeless people are children. According to the Coalition's figures for April 2014, there were 13,000 homeless families residing in New York City shelters consisting of 20,000 adults and 23,000 kids. A major reason for the rise in the city's homelessness over the last few years is cuts the Bloomberg administration made to vital programs that were designed to move people out of shelters and into housing. The city terminated a rental subsidy program that helped me get an apartment in the Bronx for a year. If it hadn't been for this, I might still be living in New York today.

Regardless of the reasons why people become homeless, everyone in the shelters is treated like an equal. And when I say equal, I mean it in the way that livestock are treated as equals. Life in the shelters is very regimented. You wake up. You wait to take a shower. You shower. You get dressed. You wait in a long line to eat breakfast. You bolt your breakfast. You shuffle out of the shelter and try to find something to do to keep you busy until lunch. You come back to the shelter and wait for lunch. And so on.

The days go by like this. Days turn into weeks and weeks turn into months.

I was homeless on my birthday and on Christmas. That year for Christmas, my dad and my brothers were in England. They had invited me and the family could pay, but I couldn't get a passport in time. They called my cell phone on Christmas Day but I didn't answer. What do you say to your family on Christmas when they are surrounded by warmth and happiness and you are alone in a homeless shelter? I wanted to say fuck you, but I thought I would spare them that grief.

Family issues become awkward when you are homeless. Nobody knows how to talk about the homeless family member. When I was homeless, some relatives invited me to their house in New Haven, CT for Thanksgiving. We had a good time visiting. There was good food and good vibes. I got to play with their dog and sleep in a real bed for a change. We even went to the Peabody Museum of Natural History and looked at all the dioramas. For a couple of days everything was normal. Never once was the subject of homelessness broached. Certainly they must have heard that I was homeless from my dad or another relative, but the subject never came up. I wonder what they were thinking when they drove me to the train station the day after Thanksgiving, knowing that I didn't have a home to return to?

I did not want anybody's help when I was homeless. If a family member had offered to take me in, I most likely would have declined the offer. When I was staying at Bellevue, my brother John lived less than a mile away on the other side of town. I only saw him twice during the whole time that I was homeless. Again, I think this is because of the awkwardness. I also didn't want to be a burden on anybody. I know this probably sounds like an old homeless cliché, but it is how I felt.

Looking back, if given the choice, I do not think I would be homeless again. However, I believe I benefited in some ways from my homeless experience. I learned important lessons about personal discipline and self-reliance. I learned how to follow rules, I learned how to be patient, I learned how to get along with others, and I learned how to endure (or make the best of) difficult hardship. But mostly when I think about being homeless, the bad experiences come back to haunt me. I was evicted from several shelters more than once for breaking petty rules. I spent a night wandering around the streets of downtown Albany, and ended up sprawled out on a restroom floor. During an altercation at Bellevue, I was slammed to the ground repeatedly by a young man who had recently been released from prison. I was nearly maimed for life when a shelter window slammed down on my hand, practically amputating the tip of my right index finger. I also suffered a severe panic attack that landed me in the emergency room.

Sadly, for many people, homelessness is not a choice. And for the nearly 55,000 homeless New Yorkers, the shelters are a kind of indefinite home. With programs like the rental subsidy program that helped me get an apartment gone, they now have nowhere else to go. The homeless people in New York are the city's refugees, and the shelters are their refugee camps.

I learned from my year and a half of living in New York that it is a privilege to live in New York City. It is not a right, but a privilege. Everybody wants to live in New York, but the availability of space and resources place a limit on how many people the city can accommodate. The economic laws of supply and demand favor those who have money over those that don't. Everywhere in New York there are gleaming condos going up, and gentrification is transforming former working class neighborhoods into enclaves for the rich. Displaced New Yorkers can no longer afford to live in the neighborhoods that they grew up in. Those at the bottom of the economic ladder are affected the worst.

This competitiveness is one of the reasons why I left New York when my rental subsidy was terminated. I now live in Texas, a place that is friendly and welcoming and where the cost of living is much cheaper.

For most of my life, I loved New York and wanted to live there. Now, I am not so sure that I want to live in New York anymore.

I think the city that I was always attracted to was the unattainable New York. New York is a large exporter of its culture—from movies to music to fashion and literature. The average American consumer is exposed to hundreds of New York references each week, and they generally portray the positive, fun, rich, glitzy neon side of the city. They show us the young bohemian artsy hipster, the chic model and the sophisticated socialite. What the references don't usually portray are the long lines at the welfare office, the children living in homeless shelters, the single mother on welfare receiving an eviction letter and the tenement housing residents who had their gas shut off because their landlord failed to send a check to Con Edison.

I did not move to New York to be poor and get welfare, but unfortunately that is what ended up happening. I did not fully understand New York before I moved there, but now I feel I do. New York is a tale of two cities—there is the Rich New York and the Poor New York—but it is the tale of the Rich New York that we most often see and hear about.

Introduction to Small Fates 1912

TEJU COLE

Every day, there are items in the news deemed too minor to report at length. For these tiny stories, French newspapers of old had a solution: a section called *fait divers*, with stories of a paragraph or a few lines. These radically brief stories were typically of some tragedy or odd occurrence. There were many train accidents, lovers' quarrels, drownings, suicides—the choice of material in some way indexical of the modern predicament. The *fait divers* remained a practical form, intended to convey a story without taking up too much space, but it also developed into an art. In Francophone literature, it crossed the line from low to high culture and influenced the writing of figures as varied as Stendhal, Flaubert, Gide, Camus, Le Clézio, and Barthes, sometimes as the initial spark for what later became a novel. But though a version of it was present in American newspapers, it never quite caught on in the Anglophone press as a literary form.

Perhaps the finest flowering of *fait divers* was in the reports anonymously filed by the anarchist and art critic Félix Fénéon for *Le Matin* in 1906. He gave the form more wit and bite, more emotional unease and formal perfection, than it had had before. In his hands, it became ironic, dark, and very funny. His collected *fait divers*, published in English as *Novels in Three Lines* (beautifully translated by Luc Sante), was a revelation to me. It inspired me to undertake a pair of projects. One was a sequence of *fait divers* set in contemporary Nigeria and drawn from the newspapers there. The other, from which a selection is published below, was based on stories from New York City's newspapers in 1912: the *New-York Tribune*, the *New York Herald*, the *New York Times*. I called my projects "small fates," a punning nod to the original form, but also as acknowledgment that so many of these stories are ultimately about the strange workings of chance.

One can go days in New York without really thinking about how populated these streets once were by crowds of people all of whom are now dead. I found in writing the small fates that these long-gone New Yorkers suddenly came back to the present tense. The fine details made their lives vivid and believable. They were no longer ghostly, and at times seemed even more real to me than the latter-day crowds outside my window.

—*Teju Cole*
July 2014

Small Fates 1912

TEJU COLE

"I hope you will be satisfied with the next one you get," wrote Beaver, of Yonkers, to his wife, before he drew a knife across his throat.

While waiting for the Coney Island train, Brady, 22, of Brooklyn, suddenly lost his mind and became convinced he was St. Bartholomew.

Envious of the White Star Line's *Titanic*, which is on its maiden voyage, Cunard announced plans for *Aquitania*, which shall be even larger.

Deaf-mute Max Katz crossed Canal Street. Peddler Selig Katz (no relation) hurried down the Bowery. "Look where you're going!" Blows ensued.

With an elegant dive in Atlantic City, McCartney broke his neck. Jumping in to help, Haley fractured both legs. Shallow water.

At East 43rd Street, Funk, toy maker, gassed himself. No note.

Relieved of $45 on 96th Street last week, McNally, playing detective, returned to the crime scene and was robbed again.

It's true, R. C. Foote heads the National Iron Bank. But the thieves who invaded his Morristown home took only silver.

Strike! The Furriers Union of Greater New York hired prizefighters to beat scabs.

The comedian Carr's car crushed Frieda, 4, on Fifth Street.

Nobody's perfect. The artiste on East 22nd Street who shoots at high heels from a distance got Rebecca Sussman in the foot.

In addition to heading a 4th Avenue firm, Rosa Zindel also wrote fiction: $5,795 in fake checks, to be exact. She was arrested for forgery.

The White Star liner *Titanic* collided with an iceberg off Newfoundland last night. All passengers were safely taken off at 3:30 a.m.

Where: Horatio Street. Who: Coles. Whom: Scarangello. What: baseball bat. Why: "self-defense."

Brooklyn dentist Dr. Brown was exploring his assistant's oral hygiene when Mrs. Brown walked in.

As he made his way up to the fourth floor window during a nighttime visit to a lady on Manhattan Avenue, McDonald lost his footing.

Because his love for an older cousin was unrequited, James, 12, of Hoboken, hanged himself.

Dr. Butterfield, in Greenwich to answer a traffic charge, was told Judge Burnes was himself in New York answering a speeding charge.

On 9th Avenue, Patrolman McKelver arrested Miss Cosgrove for drunkenness, not long after he made her drink three whiskeys.

Swimming in the East River, Whitestone found a message in a bottle from the State Hospital on Ward's Island. It read: "Some of us are sane."

Seeing someone move about his Prospect Place home, O'Callaghan took aim and opened fire. He was drunk, and it was his wife.

Penniless Miss Berger tossed herself into the East River. Mr. Mora, unable to mind his own business, dived in and saved her.

In Yonkers, Nagle, 70, anxious he might live forever, got into bed and shot himself.

On Pike Street, Rubin, 4, who fell six stories from a roof while flying a kite, was saved by the clotheslines below.

Intrigued by the ambulance sent for Rubin on Pike Street, Abraham, 9, leaned too far over the edge of another roof and fell, but was unhurt.

Rand, 56, a busybody, running after the ambulance that came for Abraham who had fallen on Pike Street, slipped and broke his leg.

With the death of John Lyle, 94, in Tenafly, Julia, 32, lost a dear husband. It is true she also gained a $20,000,000 fortune.

Andrew Carnegie complained that he and other American millionaires are insufficiently taxed, an injustice, in his view.

After a four-hour cab ride around Manhattan and Brooklyn, Robrich tried to pay with a quarter. He's now in the psychiatric ward at Bellevue.

Sullivan, plying the squirrels of Central Park with nuts, was forced to stop by Dr. Simms, an insane retired physician, at gunpoint.

"Good night, dear," wrote Colonel Cornwell on a train leaving New York, just before he shot himself in the head. Accounting troubles.

At West 36th Street Station yesterday, police overestimated the cranial resilience of Insane Fox, a clown, and he died of a fractured skull.

"I would rather be dead here than alive in London," said Oscar Hammerstein yesterday, arriving on the *Lusitania*.

They are ever returning. At latitude 49.06 N and longitude 42.51 W, the sea gave up the body of W. F. Chiverton, chief steward of the *Titanic*.

The snug row of slats on which J. B. Danbury lay down to sleep last night in Princeton was, unfortunately, a railway track.

A bomb went off near Guerrier's fish shop on 12th Street, a gentle reminder from the Black Hand that he pay them their $2000.

As he stepped outside to watch last night's storm in the Bronx, Myer was struck by lightning and left speechless.

"Two sailors murdered a girl at 2205 Neptune Avenue," Lillian O'Neil told police by phone. They hurried over. "In a dream I had," she added.

As he sped to a Manhattan court to answer a previous charge of speeding, James Waters was killed in a car crash.

John Bowes, 3, tumbled from the roof of a four-story house on West 40th Street, and was caught by the clotheslines below.

Albert, 13, making a swing for his mates in a cellar on Hoyt Street, accidentally hanged himself.

Rouquette, a large Briton, is no more. He was heroic in the Boer War, but lost a fight at the Café des Beaux Arts on 40th Street.

But what is Fate up to? Alice Breman, 65, sitting on the subway at 116th and Broadway, breathing one minute, the next gone.

Patrolman Chaffee, beating his wife because dinner wasn't ready, was shot in the head by Patrolman Collins, their guest. In Brooklyn.

While at dinner with his wife and children in Hoboken last night, Max Kunow suddenly jumped up and fired two bullets into his head.

Death did not part Mr. and Mrs. Wagner, who were found in each other's arms in Sodus Bay, drowned.

After a fender bender on 45th Street, Miller, an architect, and Granville, an actor, leaped out and reorganized each other's faces.

While disentangling Mrs. Donelly's clotheslines high above West 127th Street, Peter McCarthy (1879–1912) slipped.

"Are you Rocco?" the stranger asked. "Yes." And with two bullets, Rocco's game of checkers, and his life, ended on East 10th Street.

Immekus, a painter, dropped his wallet into the Erie Canal. He quickly dived in after it, and didn't come back up.

Yesterday a cycling accident on Riverside Drive left Wozny, 35, noseless. Dr. Brown at St. John's renosed him.

Perfection or nothing. A gray cat, its hind foot mangled by a Williamsburg trolley car, committed suicide by jumping into an open sewer.

During an electrical storm in Oswego, the engineer F. B. Lewis picked up the telephone, which was ringing, for the last time.

In Gloversville, terribly worried about Reverend Hogan's appendicitis operation, Mrs. Hogan swallowed a fatal dose of arsenic.

Some husbands have platonic friends? Good for them. Mrs. Weber's may not, and Mrs. Farrell, in Williamsburg, has been violently warned.

Leo Gano, 15, caught on the L train with a bag full of women's hair, isn't talking.

"Kid" Schuffer, our leading specialist in the picking of politicians' pockets during speeches, was caught on 8th Avenue.

On the Lower East Side, Josephine laughingly said she could only marry a fellow Italian. Paul, who was Greek, shot her and himself.

Crossing 5th Avenue, the actor William Beach, star of *Deep Purple*, was knocked black and blue by an automobile.

Shackled, locked in a box, and thrown into the East River. Two-and-a-half minutes passed. Then he surfaced, unshackled. He who? Houdini!

It was hot. It got hotter. It got hotter still. Returning from Coney Island in the evening, Clarence Schorb, 24, collapsed and died.

Last Thursday, $800 went missing in Harlem, as did William Murphy, in whose pocket the money was.

On Crimmins Avenue in the Bronx, while playing "Indian Ghost Dance" with his friends around a bonfire, Morris, 5, fell in.

The frame of the Woolworth Building, the world's tallest building, was completed yesterday. People down below look like ants.

The engineer John Griffiths is a family man. He has one in Queens, with Sadie, and another in Long Island, with Rose.

On West Street, Miss Tucker, elegant, clad in black, horsewhipped her neighbor Mr. Armstrong, who will think twice before insulting her again.

Lorenzo Corello and Annie Pollilcolski, in Jersey City: love was his question, no her answer, a razor his riposte, critical her condition.

On 152nd Street, M. de Rougelaine, scholar of the Sorbonne and Cambridge, forged a $37 check, and will study our prisons for a year.

At St. Agnes' Catholic Church in Midtown, Reverend Hawley, 70, drank too much of something, and was arrested for disorderly conduct.

Get rich quick! William Mason, of Norfolk, just born yesterday, was relieved of $20,000 by New York City scam artists.

Love is blind, and so is Israel Levine, after Anna Paris, marriage to whom he had postponed, poured acid on him at Grand Street.

Many have died for love through the ages. Garito, perforated by a rival's bullet at a Brooklyn coffee shop, is the latest.

Dr. F. F. Budd, of 329 Grand Avenue, seeks a new housekeeper, as his last, Amelia Jaynes, was both a pyromaniac and a poisoner.

During Edward Tobin's wedding in Brooklyn, Annie Collins, whose favors he had enjoyed, entered the church and had him arrested.

As the cyclist Slavik was crossing the Queensboro Bridge, an automobile crossed him.

Because of the great love between our nations, Rear Admiral von Rebeur-Paschwitz and the German fleet were wildly feted at City Hall.

The fate of burlesque actress May Yohé is not known, but her coat, her bag, and a note were found near the Central Park lakes.

The turkey trot is a strenuous dance. In an effort to master it, Agnes Day of Atlantic City died of aneurysm.

Full of red wine and cheered on by a crowd, Frankhauser, an otherwise sane Swiss father of four, ran naked through Harlem.

On West 85th Street, the maid Mrs. Bernheimer hired last month knocked her out with a potato masher and walked off with $10,000.

Gordon Elliott teaches Sunday school on the East Side, leaving him six days of the week free for stealing women's underwear.

In Brooklyn, with a carving knife, garden shears, and gas, F. Tuero failed to kill his mother, his three sisters, and himself, respectively.

There is no law against beating a dead horse. But Henry Frank, of East Orange, who beat a living one to death, was fined $100.

The petty thief Haas, 16, was just about to be lynched by passersby in Brooklyn when Officer Lynch interfered.

Hit by a 2nd Avenue car on Tuesday, Helma, 2, lived. Falling from the third floor on Thursday, she was bruised. It's true she wears an amulet.

During the funeral vigil for his wife and child at West 49th Street, Warner's house caught fire. He escaped. They were cremated.

Dr. Palmer, a dentist, caused pain, but not in the usual way: Miss Müller, whose love he failed to requite, shot herself at West 57th Street.

Shortly after boarding the *St. Paul*, bound for Spain, Señorita Puertolo, obsessed with the *Titanic* for weeks, lost her mind.

Martin, whose mother is sickly, whose father was stabbed, whose sister has heart disease, was run over by a car on 60th Street.

Broadway and 5th Avenue is a zoo during the morning rush. Arthur Mason was bitten by a fugitive baboon whom police later detained.

Having downed a few drinks too many, Nixon, of Long Island, wrote a suicide note, took aim, fired, and only removed a bit of scalp.

So far, 140 people have died in plane crashes. But yesterday in Dayton, Wilbur Wright, the first pilot, died in his bed.

Ludato, 21, a student at City College, was twirling a loaded revolver on his fingers. Bang! He's in bad shape.

In the morning, on the Hudson near 149th Street, Jessel saved a drowning man. In the afternoon, Jessel's canoe capsized, and he drowned.

In Ocean City, Mary Holzman, a white woman, befriended a negro. Her strict neighbors dragged her out, beat her up, and covered her in tar.

Laura Ping, of Brooklyn, left her husband Loo Ping for Lee Loy. The Ping divorce is the first filed by Chinese in New York.

Nice spring day in Central Park. Caras found a man near the reservoir, a suicide by bullet. Holmworth found another on West Drive, cyanide.

In Williamsburg, gas inspector George Hill, suffering maddening insomnia, gassed himself and finally slept.

A fine lady, found on Broadway and 35th Street, knows neither her name nor where she lives. She giggles. Doctors are perplexed.

Because fair's fair, the avid fisherman Hutton, who died Saturday, bequeathed his ashes to the fish of the Hackensack River.

While performing in Williamsburg, Edward Morris, 50, comedian with the Reeves burlesque company, became mentally unbalanced.

On purpose or not, Mrs. Heickemrath, 38, of 201 West 105th Street, ingested something fatal.

The books of Harry Elkins Widener, 27, a zealous bibliophile who sank with the *Titanic*, were donated to Harvard University.

At play on Pearl Street, James Fleming, 10, caught a foul ball with his skull, and is insensible.

During Giuseppe Monoco's funeral at Green-Wood Cemetery, forty of the jostling mourners tumbled into open graves. Fractures.

On Allen Street, Francis, 6, who fell from a fourth floor fire escape, landed on the clotheslines in the yard, and only bruised his cheek.

On the campaign trail in Ohio, an owl tried to bite Colonel Roosevelt.

After a visit to her husband's grave at Holy Cross Cemetery, Mrs. Corcoran spent days looking for the way out, and nearly died of exposure.

With two bullets, Mrs. Teitelbaum, of Coney Island, ended Mr. Skemene's interest in her niece.

To prevent him from giving chase, the three masked men who robbed Tony Tropana on Coney Island confiscated his trousers.

The body on the 149th Street tracks was, in life, either "G. W." (as engraved on his signet ring) or "O. R." (as stitched on his derby hat).

The sisters Finn fought on East 78th Street yesterday, neither of them wearing much.

To her father's astonishment, Miss Frances Petry, of East 16th Street, eloped with an Indian intern, Dr. Ram Pal, to Amritsar.

In Secaucus, Minnie K. awoke from a nightmare in which her aunt had been murdered, to find that her aunt had been murdered.

In a fit of melancholia, Mrs. Burroughs, 40, wandered around New Jersey for three days.

The clerk Doyle, who had danced elegantly all night in Hoboken, tripped as he descended the ferry, and fell to his death.

In Stockholm, August Strindberg, a playwright, died of cancer.

Since his wife kept dodging each time he shot her, Robert Schuman, a candy dealer in the Bronx, stood perfectly still and shot himself.

At Centre Street Court, Mr. Hecker and Miss Sullivan insulted each other viciously but silently, as both are deaf-mute.

Yesterday on 4th Avenue, H. A. Johnson's car hit an engraver. On 5th Avenue, O. J. Johnson's car knocked down a stenographer.

From the roof of her home, Mrs. Katz, whom insomnia had been driving mad, flung herself into Grand Street.

Eighty chickens died when a bomb exploded on Snediker Avenue in Brooklyn.

At East 116th Street, Mary Ritter, 13, who frightened her mother with a pretend suicide, received an actual beating.

As Mrs. Allender returned home from a *Titanic* memorial service on Sterling Place, an automobile knocked her down.

Drowsy while awaiting the late train at the Van Cortlandt Park platform, Baggett, a clerk, dropped off.

Funny how? Alto, on hearing Max's little joke at his expense, shot him four times, in Union Springs.

Perfectly sane except for persistent paranoia about being sent to an asylum, Miron, 20, of Elizabeth, NJ, was sent to an asylum.

The architect, contractor, secretary, and two presidents of the Maple Avenue School in Morristown have died of various ailments. Hoodoo.

In need of quiet, Knowles, of Flatbush, hurled a cup at his proselytizing wife, but silenced the baby instead.

Snyder, 19, does not remember chasing his mother and grandmother through the streets of Paterson at night with a loaded pistol.

In White Plains, Thaw shot White.

Overjoyed at getting a nickel, eager to buy a paper crown, Willie, 6, dashed across Westchester Avenue without looking both ways.

Remarrying, Mrs. Orange, a widow in the Bronx, sidestepped the hassle of a name change. The new Mr. Orange is her stepson.

Having caught Tony, 4, littering, J. Martin, an unsentimental grocer on West 29th Street, tied him to a pole and gave him ten lashes.

On East 223rd Street, Nellie Flemming, 16, who had a passion for matches, set herself alight and could not be saved.

Bronx coroner Schwanneke confirmed just one person died in the Ashokan water supply shaft. Then he lost his footing. Two.

Who is the red-haired man, 5 feet 7 inches, 150 pounds, found at 439 East 107th Street a few days after he fell down the stairs?

"She's gone away," sighed violinist Albert de Brahms, of West 35th Street, after strangling his wife, and with a bullet he went away too.

Yes, the soothsayer at Coney Island predicted Giuseppe would marry Josephine. But not that two weeks later he would gas himself.

On East 62nd Street, using her age (85) as an excuse, Colburn's mother was slow bringing his dinner. She got a good kicking.

On the Bowery, toward a rug held by firemen, Jacob Schlectneck jumped from the fifth floor, and missed.

G. Shock, a drunk baker of East 135th Street, axed his wife and, having failed to kill her, cut his own throat, and failed to die.

John "Happy Jack" Mulraney, declared guilty of the murder of Paddy "The Priest" McBreen on 52nd Street, couldn't stop laughing.

Years after his love for Mrs. Lunn went unrequited, Leary, 60, of Nichols, NY, eloped with Miss Lunn, 16.

Children are a blessing, but a dissenting mother abandoned her 2-month-old at East 115th Street.

The lovebirds Anna S. and Barney B. were shot dead on Wooster Street by Samuel M., who did not approve.

The largest steamer in the world, the *Olympic*, sails from New York on May 4.

Fong Lee, dead in his laundry, was thought a suicide until the official report of Coney Island police: "The Chink was shot."

Forty pounds of butter, held in evidence, were replaced with bricks in Jersey City. Higgins and Sniffin, cops, have been suspended.

On Long Island, Mrs. Heinz (wife of the condiment man) was thrown from her car and bruised.

Joyriding between cars on the New Jersey Rail, Murphy, 16, lost his legs.

Lipson jumped in front of the downtown train at 145th Street. Dead. An hour later, Feinback proved the uptown train just as effective.

With a noxious gas, J. Massern exterminated every insect at 454 Fort Washington Avenue, on purpose, and himself, by accident.

After the Negro Ball in Jamaica Bay, Mr. Jones bashed in Mr. Green's skull with a baseball bat. The beaux had in common a belle.

J. Walters, of Albany, Georgia, who married an octoroon woman in New York thinking she was white, shot himself when the truth came out.

Mr. Roberts, of Lawrence Street, Brooklyn, who was fond of examining his revolver, did so for the last time yesterday.

Traffic on 34th Street was halted while a crowd looked, in vain, for Mrs. Cornely's nose, torn off when she fell down the station steps.

All Chinatown is proud of Miss Mabel Lee. She is prepared to enter Barnard College, and is of the view that women should have the vote.

Worried that his persistent cold might be fatal, Rauschenberg, 82, drowned himself in the East River.

Mrs. Remsen, of East 62nd Street, who died rich, bequeathed $5 to her beloved husband, to be paid in weekly installments of 5¢.

Annie Boyarski, 17, rather liked the idea of having a baby. So she went to Mount Sinai Hospital and took one.

The number of independently wealthy Dicks in Long Island increased after sugar magnate William Dick left $20 million to his children.

Descending the stairs at 237 West 136th Street at night, Benjamin Raynor reached for a nonexistent railing.

With a leap in front of the northbound local, Philip Joseph, of Henry Street, canceled his wedding plans.

Abdul Baha Abbas, teacher of the Bahai faith, arrived on the steamship *Cedric*. One of his peculiar beliefs is that women are equal to men.

Elly laughed hith teeth out at a movie on Park Row. Unable to perthuade the theater owner to return them, he thubthithth on thoup and milk.

Harvey had an eventful trip on the *Olympic*. Swindled on the first day, he quarreled on the second, and drank himself to death on the third.

Andrew Saks died, on Fifth Avenue.

An eleven-word message arrived at East 60th Street: "Dear Augusta: Money lost. Wedding off. Very sorry. Good bye. William."

The New York broker Frederick Beach, charged with the aggravated assault of his wife, insists a mysterious negro did it.

Mr. Wanger, a physical education instructor at West 180th Street, has been exercising with another woman; Mrs. Wanger seeks a divorce.

The baby born to Mrs. Flora, a watchmaker's wife in Schenectady, is normal in all respects, save his four teeth.

At Freeman Street, Page was flattened by the Lenox Avenue train, in front of which he had placed himself. No note.

Miss Eberly heard a muffled yelp from a mailbox on East 125th Street and Lexington. Someone (small boys, probably) had posted a puppy.

Prosper, of Houston Street, didn't. His wife is dead and he cannot afford to bury her.

The journalist Dayton, of West 21st Street, unable to find his glasses, took what looked to him like his medicine, and is no more.

Alma Howard wrote letters to the president and governor predicting war with Germany. Lunacy! She is under observation at Bellevue.

Joseph Fiber, a laborer at the American Linseed Company in Staten Island, toppled into a mixing machine.

In Central Park, Joe Ursus, a black bear, strangled his mate Jennie, who had been flirting with the bachelor polar bears next door.

"Kathleen, you'd better put on your heavy coat," Mr. Lorillard said, at Holland House. His wife said yes, went upstairs, and hanged herself.

In spite of a truce in Chinatown, Chin Hun Gun was pumped full of bullets at 22 Pell Street. Mock Duck was arrested.

T. White and wife stayed at the Hotel Washington, Hoboken. "Wife" was Miss Delaney, and "T. White," Mr O'Connell, who died during the night.

Mrs. Amos, of Hawthorne Street, Brooklyn, hid her diamonds in her shoes, as it's the last place a thief would look. Well, a thief looked.

As his Flushing home burned, the eccentric millionaire Ewbanks wandered inside it reciting Bible verses. A policeman saved him.

A flour sack on the corner of Chauncey Street and Hopkinson Avenue in Brooklyn moved strangely. Inside it: a healthy day-old boy.

Charles Goodrich, of Oswego, sorry his uncle died but sorrier he was left nothing in the will, killed himself by drinking laudanum.

Rudolph Hanneseck died when a fire broke out at 178 West Houston Street. (Run over by the fire truck.)

Yesterday, weighted down with thirty pounds of handcuffs and chains, Houdini jumped into the Harlem River, and lived, as usual.

Dreyer, an inspector, was strolling southward on the track at Columbus Avenue and 65th Street when the northbound express arrived.

Robert Thompson, 40, an undertaker on Court Street, Brooklyn, filled out a death certificate for "Robert Thompson," and gassed himself.

Arrested for speeding on the Nassau Boulevard, George Beatty said he forgot he was on land and thought he was in his Wright biplane.

Cardinali, a rich man from Palermo, Italy, entered a drug store on 1st Avenue and 11th Street, keeled over, and died. Bullet in the heart.

Harold Callahan, class of 1912, won the Curtis Medal for Oratory at Columbia University, for a speech on war's great benefit to humanity.

Seeking

VICTOR LAVALLE

1

My mother used to send me to church alone in a cab. Every Sunday she dressed me in a blue suit and called a car. Minutes later it showed up out front of our building, always an old white sedan, though the drivers were never the same. My mother walked me down and gave the driver the address for St. John's Episcopal Church on Sanford Avenue. She gave me ten dollars for the fare there and back and another ten for the collection plate. She helped me into the car and shut the door and waved goodbye. This practice began when I was ten years old. Before that we went to church only on the High Holy Days. I looked forward to going it alone every week. As soon as the car turned the corner I'd give the driver a new address. We were headed to Adventurer's Inn, a game arcade that lay in the shadow of the Whitestone Expressway. No cabbie ever protested. Not once. When we arrived I paid him five and kept the other fifteen for me. I was the best-dressed kid in the place but no one noticed; kids were all too busy making offerings to Zaxxon, Missile Command, and Galaga. When I got home—a bit of a walk—my mother asked how I'd liked church. I told her I loved it, of course.

But it didn't take too long for her to hear back from the priest, Father John, and an older neighbor, the one who'd convinced her I needed to attend regular service. They asked why I wasn't coming and blew up my spot entirely. My mom gave me the appropriate amounts of shit about it, but here's the funny part: it never occurred to her that she should come with me to ensure that I arrived. Instead, she said she'd be checking with Father John and our neighbor to make sure I'd been there. No doubt the priest and our neighbor expected my mother to start attending too—I can't remember another kid who came to church solo—but when I brought this up to my mother—really I meant it as a kind of dare—she told me she'd "done her time." That's verbatim. If that makes church attendance sound like a prison sentence, then you're hearing it right. My mother had been forced to go to church until she turned eighteen; thus, she felt it only right—proper—to do the same to me. She would have described herself as a believer, but her belief came with a very particular interpretation. She believed in God, but doubted His interest in our daily affairs. Was he really checking attendance? Such a thing seemed impossible to my mother when so much of the world's hardships seemed to slip his notice. He was real but he wasn't around. My mother described God like a distant dad.

Really, I don't think my mother would've had a problem with me skipping church—I'd been baptized so me and God had met already—but she was not going to be embarrassed. *What kind of son are you raising?* I imagine Father John and our neighbor asking something like this of my mother. And they say peer pressure is just for kids. Nevertheless, it had been decided. My job, over the next few years, was to attend church *enough*. I showed up about twice a month. The congregation was large so it's not like Father John and this older neighbor were scoping for me constantly. Twice a month I made it to church, and each service I listened to about half of what was said. I figure that made me, at best, about one-quarter Christian by the time I turned eighteen.

By the time I turned thirty-five I'd lost even that much faith. I didn't attend Easter or Christmas services, the Christian bare minimum, after I left for college. My grandmother might make us say a little prayer in the living room, but that hardly seemed to count. I shut my eyes and bowed my head out of respect for my grandmother. The only spirit that moved me was hers. And yet some behaviors, if started early, are ingrained. Impossible to forget no matter how long it's been since you've practiced. In this way faith is like falling in love.

◆ ◆ ◆

In 2007 I lived in Greenpoint, Brooklyn, and found myself missing a feeling I couldn't quite describe. Let's call it longing. I had a pretty good life, writing and dating and teaching, but none of that was the satisfaction

I missed. It's obvious now—since I'm writing this damn essay—but it wasn't clear to me then. So I found myself, generally speaking, seeking. One evening I went to visit two friends who lived in an apartment on Kent Street and passed two churches on that block. The first, St. Elias Church—a Greek Rite Catholic Church—sat enormous and empty, a beautiful, hulking red building that had been bought up by developers since it was no longer in use. I guess the Greek Rite Catholics had gone away. When I passed that building, with a For Sale sign out front, I day-dreamed about turning that space into the baddest bachelor pad since Jay Gatsby built his mansion on West Egg.

Then halfway down the block I found the Church of the Ascension, a much smaller sanctuary. Episcopalian. The red front doors were open. This meant an evening service was going on. Even though I was late to see my friends I stopped short and stood outside feeling a kind of pull, nearly a riptide, leading from the sidewalk right inside. I laughed at myself, remembering that ten-year-old boy in his starchy blue suit. I didn't go in. Instead I visited my friends. The week after that, though, I showed up for evening service on a Wednesday. I stepped inside the church to find just three congregants—an old woman, a man in his fifties, another in his forties—and the priest, Father Rob, who was only twenty-eight. All four welcomed me and I'd like to say I fell into the old rituals perfectly, but I only embarrassed myself again and again. I got the Lord's Prayer right, mostly. When had they modernized "forgive us our trespasses" into "forgive us our sins"? If this was falling in love then I sure did it poorly. When service was over, Father Rob and the old woman, Rose, both invited me back. I left feeling unsure if I'd ever return.

It wasn't until my third evening service that I realized what exactly I'd been seeking. When it happened, my legs nearly gave out. It came about three-quarters of the way through the service. It was a hot evening and the church's fans blew loudly, not cooling but only spreading heat evenly. Father Rob stood at the table with the cup of wine and a plate with a handful of communion wafers. There were only four of us in the pews. I still wasn't entirely used to the service so, unlike the others, I read along with every step in the Book of Common Prayer. When I looked up from the book Father Rob held the cup of wine toward the ceiling, and suddenly I felt *transported*. Not just emotionally moved, but as if I'd traveled to another time and place.

But before I can explain what I mean by that, I need to tell you what came later.

2

Holyrood Church, in Washington Heights, sits in the shadow of the George Washington Bridge Bus Terminal, on the corner of Fort Washington Avenue and 179th Street. It was founded in 1893 by Reverend William Oliver Embury. Before founding the church he was the chaplain of the House of Refuge for Problem Girls, operated by the Sisters of Saint Mary in Inwood Hill Park. There have been two Holyrood churches in Washington Heights. The first was a country-style church with a tower built on Broadway and 181st Street in 1895. By 1910 that area had become too crowded, so they built a second version of the church, in a Gothic style this time, where it still stands on 179th.

I moved to Washington Heights in 2010 along with my girlfriend, Emily. We bought a place one block away from Holyrood. Before we moved in together I'd brought Emily with me to some of the evening services at the Church of Ascension. Emily had been raised a Catholic and while she, too, had spent her adult life away from the church, she found our little Episcopal services familiar—close enough to Catholic rites— and so they were pleasing. It helped that at Ascension's weekday service there were only ever four or five of us in the pews. And that each of us, in his or her way, was an oddball. We only attended the Sunday service at Ascension once. The rows of pews had been full, the people were all quite nice, but the service felt much more formal, like going to a concert instead of an intimate show.

Soon after we'd moved into the place in Washington Heights, I noticed Holyrood on the corner, where homeless guys regularly camped out on the front steps at night and the police were never called on them. I asked Emily if she'd like to try an evening service there. She was enthusiastic about keeping up the practice, but we learned that while the church remained open in the evenings, it was only to fulfill more practical needs. There were evenings of English lessons for Spanish speakers and evenings when they ran a soup kitchen. One evening set aside for the kids' choir practice, another for church administrators to meet. But if we wanted to worship we'd have to show up on a Sunday. This fact acted like a repellent; besides, we had a lot of work to do on our little apartment. We'd bought it in bad shape and our Sundays could be better spent painting and sweeping and taking garbage down to the basement. For about three months Holyrood threatened to remain just another building on a nearby block, no more important to us than the podiatrist's across the street. Then, on a trip in Argentina, I asked Emily to marry me, and dammit if we didn't need to find a church to hold the ceremony.

We arrived at Holyrood to the drone of organ music and that special dimness of Gothic churches and their stained glass windows. Holyrood had to be twice the size of Ascension. The ceilings stood sixty feet high instead of thirty. There were twice as many rows of pews, enough to accommodate four hundred people. All this might've sent us running, except that there were only twice as many congregants as Ascension ever had. We didn't make a dozen even when Emily and I entered the room. A big church with a small crowd—I wouldn't be surprised if both Emily and I smiled when we saw this. The last ten rows of pews were roped off so a visitor had to sit closer to the front. This was a smart play. The congregation seemed tiny even with all of them gathered in the first two rows; it would have been much more diffuse if people were allowed to spread out like they tend to do at readings or in classrooms.

Since an Episcopal service follows essentially the same routine no matter which church you attend, we were able to find the rhythm quickly. I admit I took some pleasure in being able to recite a lot more from memory than at that first service at Ascension. I still stumbled, here and there, during the Confession of Sin. Soon after, I looked up to where the priest stood at the table. He had just poured the wine and broken the bread. He faced us and lifted the wine and wafers above his head.

He said, "The gifts of God for the people of God."

And then, just like at the Church of Ascension, I felt my legs go loose and I knew, once again, that Emily and I had done the right thing by coming to service that day. This moment, when the priest calls the congregation to partake in the body and blood of Jesus Christ, is the closest the church service comes to time travel. That's often how it feels for me. While the rest of the rituals—the prayers and the songs—are all about what happened after Jesus died, this is a reenactment of his life. This moment, its repetition across millennia, is as simple as a myth. That's why it lasts. Before being executed, Jesus shared a meal with his friends. The meal only matters because of the great mystery, the great misery, that came for Jesus soon after.

After the ceremony the priest, Father Jim, greeted us with a smile. He was in his sixties, tall and slim, and he wore glasses and a hearing aid. Later we learned he had a purple belt in Brazilian jiujitsu, and every summer he and his wife served in a ministry in El Salvador. Father Jim quickly herded us over to the coffee and snacks set up at the back of Holyrood. We met Velva and George, Jacqui and Shoji, Felix and Erma, Ed Vargas. We met Loraine, the organist, and Eleanor and Frank, members of the vestry. To a person they were sweet and welcoming and idiosyncratic. Emily and I knew, before we'd even left the building, that this would be the church where we were married.

3

We were married at Holyrood that August. Our son, Geronimo, was born the next May and we had him baptized there. After he came we stayed away for a while. His morning naps fell right during service and even the Lord himself wasn't going to interrupt that. When we finally got our routines down and showed up on a Sunday morning, Geronimo proceeded to coo, babble, and cry the whole time. We were embarrassed and tried to sneak out, but Father Jim stopped the service to call us back. Most of the congregation were in their fifties, sixties, and seventies. One of them, Felix, pulled me close when we returned to the front.

"It does us good to hear a baby in here," he said, waving to the high ceilings. "You let him cry if he's got to cry. We love the sound."

Emily and I looked to the others and, to a person, they nodded or smiled. Of course there are a thousand churches where we would've been booted out on our asses for the same thing, or at least glowered at the whole time. A thousand bookstores, too. We took this as one more piece of evidence that we'd chosen the right church for us. We brought Geronimo with us each week, and when our daughter, Delilah, was born a year and a half later, she joined the crew. Got baptized there, too. Now, when the congregation breaks to share the Peace of the Lord, the kids get picked up, hugged, and kissed by nearly everyone while Emily and I are almost totally ignored. At those times Holyrood's service feels like a big family picnic.

Since I'm a writer and roll in a generally liberal, hyper-educated crowd, few aspects of my life cause greater confusion than my regular church attendance. It either baffles some friends or even, somehow, offends them. Mostly I just don't bring it up. The reasons I returned to my church, and some sense of faith, are so personal it seems impossible to explain quickly in a social setting. At least not without sounding like I'm proselytizing, and I've got no interest in that. But since you've read along with me this far, maybe this is a fine place to try.

As I think back on it now, I like my mother's understanding of God very much. The idea of a distant father, or mother if you like, seems strikingly honest, ruthlessly clear. I think it took a lot of courage for my mother to believe in an absentee deity. "God has decided he can't be reached." My mother used to say that all the time. "So I've stopped trying to reach him." It's worth noting that she didn't mean she'd stopped believing, only that she'd long given up on the idea that a response was soon to come. This is a more sophisticated take on faith than I gave her credit for as a child.

"Do you really believe in God?" one old friend asked me outright one night at Flannery's Bar. I could see he had a series of arguments all ready to lob at me. I guessed he'd been reading Richard Dawkins and Christopher Hitchens. But his question misunderstood the point of why I returned to church. Why I'm so glad my wife and kids regularly attend with me.

Right now Christopher Hitchens has discovered, undoubtedly, whether God is real. Either he's feeling shocked and humbled or he's feeling nothing at all. I'm willing to guess that either outcome would satisfy the man. But Richard Dawkins doesn't know and neither do all the true believers of whichever faith you like, and neither do I. It's the absence of this last answer that compels me. There's an emptiness at the center of existence that will never be filled for as long as you're alive. You will never genuinely know until you're forced to know. This is terrifying and thrilling. There's a hole in exactly the place where all our eyes are drawn. It's the ultimate unknowable.

Maybe this is why I love the moment when we reenact the Last Supper so much. I don't know if I believe in Jesus the historical figure or Jesus the Son of God. But when my congregation shares in the bread and the wine, the body and the blood, I believe we stand together, making a kind of circle around that depthless emptiness in the center of life. I prefer to share the camaraderie and the tenderness and the fear. This is the thing I now understand my mother missed when she opted out of going to church with me. God wasn't going to answer her, so she thought there was no reason for the service. But if I'm honest, I'm not trying to reach God when I attend—just my wife and my children and my friends. Every week I find them. Every week they find me.

If the 1 Percent Stifles New York's Creative Talent, I'm Out of Here

DAVID BYRNE

I'm writing this in Venice, Italy. This city is a pleasantly confusing maze: once an island of fortresses, now a city of tourists, culture (*biennales* galore), and crumbling relics. Venice used to be the most powerful city in Europe—a military, mercantile, and cultural leader. Sort of like New York.

Venice is now a case study in the complete transformation of a city (there's public transportation, but no cars). Is it a living city? Is it a fossil? The mayor of Venice recently wrote a letter to the *New York Review of Books*, arguing that his city is, indeed, a place to live, not simply a theme park for tourists (he would like very much if the big cruise ships steered clear). I guess it's a living place if you count tourism as an industry, which I suppose it is. New York has its share of tourists, too. I wave to the double-decker buses from my bike, but the passengers never wave back. Why? Am I not an attraction?

New York was recently voted the world's favorite city—but when you break down the survey's results, the city comes in at number one for business and only number five for living. Fifth place isn't completely embarrassing, but what are the criteria? What is it that attracts people to this or any city? Forget the business part. I've been in Hong Kong, and unless one already has the means to live luxuriously, business hubs aren't necessarily good places for living. Cities may have mercantile exchange as one of their reasons for being, but once people are lured to a place for work, they need more than offices, gyms, and strip clubs to really live.

Work aside, we come to New York for the possibility of interaction and inspiration. Sometimes, that possibility of serendipitous encounters—and I don't mean in the meat market—is the principal lure. If one were to vote based on criteria like comfort or economic security, then one wonders why anyone would ever vote for New York at all over Copenhagen, Stockholm, or some other less antagonistic city that offers practical amenities like affordable healthcare, free universities, free museums, common spaces, and, yes, bike lanes. But why can't one have both—the invigorating energy and the civic, intelligent humanism?

Maybe those Scandinavian cities do, in fact, have both, but New York has something else to offer, thanks to successive waves of immigrants that have shaped the city. Arriving from overseas, one is immediately struck by the multiethnic makeup of New York. Other cities might be cleaner, more efficient, or more comfortable, but New York is funky, in the original sense of the word—New York smells like sex.

Immigrants to New York have contributed to the city's vibrancy decade after decade. In some cities around the world, immigrants are relegated to being a worker class, or a guest worker class; they're not invited to the civic table. New York has generally been more welcoming, though people of color have never been invited to the table to the same extent as European immigrants.

I moved to New York in the mid-1970s because it was a center of cultural ferment—especially in the visual arts (my dream trajectory, until I made a detour), though there was a musical draw, too, even before the downtown scene exploded. New York was legendary. It was where things happened, on the East Coast, anyway. One knew in advance that life in New York would not be easy, but there were cheap rents in cold-water lofts without heat, and the excitement of being here made up for those hardships. I didn't move to New York to make a fortune. Survival, at that time, and at my age then, was enough. Hardship was the price one paid for being in the thick of it.

As one gets a little older, those hardships aren't so romantic—they're just hard. The trade-off begins to look like a real pain in the ass if one has been here for years and years and is barely eking out a living. The idea of making an ongoing creative life—whether as a writer, an artist, a filmmaker, or a musician—is difficult unless one gets a foothold on the ladder, as I was lucky enough to do. I say *lucky* because I have no illusions that talent is enough; there are plenty of talented folks out there who never get the break they deserve.

Some people believe that hardship breeds artistic creativity. I don't buy it. One can put up with poverty for a while when one is young, but it will inevitably wear a person down. I don't romanticize the bad old days. I find the drop in crime over the last couple of decades refreshing. Manhattan and Brooklyn, those vibrant playgrounds, are way less scary than they were when I moved here. I have no illusions that there was a connection between that city on its knees and a flourishing of creativity; I don't believe that crime, danger, and poverty make for good art. That's bullshit. But I also don't believe that the drop in crime means the city has to be more exclusively for those who have money. Increases in the quality of life should be for all, not just a few.

The city is a body and a mind—a physical structure as well as a repository of ideas and information. Knowledge and creativity are resources. If the physical (and financial) parts are functional, then the flow of ideas, creativity, and information are facilitated. The city is a fountain that never stops: it generates its energy from the human interactions that take place in it. Unfortunately, we're getting to a point where many of New York's citizens have been excluded from this equation for too long. The physical part of our city—the body—has been improved immeasurably. I'm a huge supporter of the bike lanes and the bikeshare program, the new public plazas, the waterfront parks, and the functional public transportation system. But the cultural part of the city—the mind—has been usurped by the top 1 percent.

What, then, is the future of New York, or really of any number of big urban centers, in this new Gilded Age? Does culture have a role to play? If we look at the city as it is now, then we would have to say that it looks a lot like the divided city that presumptive mayor Bill de Blasio has been harping on about: most of Manhattan and many parts of Brooklyn are virtual walled communities, pleasure domes for the rich (which, full disclosure, includes me), and aside from those of us who managed years ago to find our niche and some means of income, there is no room for fresh creative types. Middle-class people can barely afford to live here anymore, so forget about emerging artists, musicians, actors, dancers, writers, journalists, and small business people. Bit by bit, the resources that keep the city vibrant are being eliminated.

This city doesn't make things anymore. Creativity, of all kinds, is the resource we have to draw on as a city and a country in order to survive. In the recent past, before the 2008 crash, the best and the brightest were lured into the world of finance. Many a bright kid graduating from university knew that they could become fairly wealthy almost instantly if they found employment at a hedge fund or some similar institution. But before the financial sector came to dominate the world, they might have made things: in publishing, manufacturing, television, fashion, you name it. As in many other countries, the lure of easy bucks hoovered this talent and intelligence up—and made it difficult for those other kinds of businesses to attract any of the top talent.

A culture of arrogance, hubris, and winner-takes-all was established. It wasn't cool to be poor or struggling. The bully was celebrated and cheered. The talent pool became a limited resource for any industry, except Wall Street. I'm not talking about artists, writers, filmmakers, and musicians—they weren't exactly on a trajectory toward Wall Street anyway—but any businesses that might have employed creative individuals were having difficulties surviving, and naturally, the arty types had a hard time finding employment, too.

Unlike Iceland, where the government let misbehaving banks fail and talented kids became less interested in leaping into the cesspool of finance, in New York there has been no public rejection of the culture that led to the financial crisis. Instead, there has been tacit encouragement of the banking industry's actions from figures like Mayor Bloomberg. The nation's largest financial institutions are almost all still around, still "too big to fail," and as powerful as ever. One might hope that enlightened bankers would emulate the Medicis and fund culture-makers—both emerging artists and those still in school—as a way of ensuring a continued talent pool that would invent stuff and fill the world with ideas and inspiration, but other than buying blue-chip art for their walls and donating what is (for them) small change to some institutions, they don't seem to be very much interested in replenishing the talent pool.

One would expect that the 1 percent would have a vested interest in keeping the civic body healthy—at least, that they'd want green parks, museums, and symphony halls for themselves and their friends, if not everyone. Those, indeed, are institutions to which they habitually contribute. But it's like funding your own clubhouse. It doesn't exactly do much for the rest of us or for the general health of the city. At least, we might sigh, they do that, as they don't pay taxes—that we know.

Many of the wealthy don't even live here. In the neighborhood where I live (near the art galleries in Chelsea), I can see three large condos from my window that are pretty much empty all the time. What the fuck!? Apparently, rich folks buy the apartments, but might only stay in them a few weeks out of a year. So why should they have an incentive to maintain or improve the general health of the city? They're never here.

This real estate situation—a topic New Yorkers love to complain about over dinner—doesn't help the future health of the city. If young, emerging talent of all types can't find a foothold in this city, then it will be a city closer to Hong Kong or Abu Dhabi than to the rich fertile place it has historically been. Those places might have museums, but they don't have culture. Ugh. If New York goes there—more than it already has— I'm leaving.

But where will I go? Join the expat hipsters upstate in Hudson?

Can New York change its trajectory a little bit, become more inclusive and financially egalitarian? Is that possible? I think it is. It's still the most stimulating and exciting place in the world to live and work, but it's in danger of walking away from its greatest strengths. The physical improvements are happening—though much of the crumbling infrastructure still needs fixing. If the social and economic situation can be addressed, we're halfway there. It really could be a model of how to make a large, economically sustainable, and creatively energetic city. I want to live in that city.

Traveling from Brooklyn

LYDIA DAVIS

I recently started thinking about travel, and I thought about it for several days. Then, while I was thinking about it, I was one day actually doing some traveling of a modest kind when an incident occurred that taught me something about my limitations where travel was concerned, and where danger was concerned, and really about my limitations in general.

The kind of travel I dream about doesn't make any sense for me, since I'm a middle-aged woman without much money and with a family that keeps me more or less tied to one place unless I take all or part of the family with me, and I don't really have enough money to do that and still maintain the home where we live.

I dream of setting off on foot across the country with a simple backpack, a little money in my pocket, and a rough plan. In an early version of this dream I was dressed in jeans and boots, I was so thin that my jeans were loose around my legs and hips, and I didn't wear glasses. As I dreamed about this, I didn't ask the question of how I could be so thin if I was not thin, how I could wear no glasses if I wore glasses, and so on. In the latest version, since I'm older now, I see myself in tailored pants and walking shoes, thick-waisted, and wearing the glasses that I actually wear. I still have no very precise plan in this dream, however, and when I run out of money I still find work as a waitress in any town I come to, and move on when I have some money. I visit the South, at last, and then I head west, though I don't try to go all the way to the Pacific coast. It used to be that I would try to end up somewhere in Montana or Wyoming, the emptiest of the states, and get work on a ranch. Now the emptiness of those states frightens me, and I prefer the deserts of the Southwest, which I have actually visited twice already. In the earliest version of my dream, there was the possibility that a cowboy would fall in love with me. In a later version, it had to be one of the older cowboys. Now I find some sort of companionship, but I don't specify what sort. I also don't address the question of what will become of the rest of my extremely dependent family while I am gone, a family that has grown steadily larger since I first had this dream.

The kind of traveling I do most, these days, is on the subway, going no farther than from Brooklyn to Manhattan, or, even worse, from one part of Brooklyn to another. From Atlantic Avenue I might go to Borough Hall, from Court Street back to Pacific Street, from Borough Hall out of Brooklyn to Canal Street, from Grand Street back down to Atlantic Avenue, and so on. Sometimes the subway car is so full that I have no room even to open a book, and sometimes so empty that I look up at each station to see whether a dangerous person might be entering the car or a safe person leaving it. Usually the ride gives me a chance to rest: I read, look at the people around me, and recover from whatever it was, at home or away, that I just went through. I may also try to prepare for whatever I may be about to go through, at home or away, but it is always easier to work out what has just happened than what might happen, so when I try to prepare for what is coming, my mind tends to wander, and then I daydream, sometimes about what great or small things I may do at home, and sometimes about leaving home.

Once, however, when I was on the B train traveling from Pacific Street in Brooklyn to 14th Street in Manhattan, something happened that stopped me from daydreaming or reading. I was waiting for the train at the Pacific Street station. When the train drew in, a crowd of teenagers burst out of the train shouting, screaming, and pushing, which is the way teenagers often behave in the neighborhood of Pacific Street and only seems violent to me because I'm not one of them. They were so jammed together I could hardly make my way among them. After I got onto the train and sat down, and while the train was still in the station with its doors open, a few girls poked their heads back into the car to continue making fun of an odd-looking woman sitting across from me, a very thin creature all in black, eyes clotted with thickly blackened eyelashes under a high black hairdo, dressed in a black suit with black net stockings. I had seen her before on this subway line. Her bearing was always arrogant, but today she seemed frightened as well. All she did, though, was look straight ahead of her, which meant she was looking almost straight at me.

The doors closed, the train left the station, and I took out of my purse an essay on free will that had come to me in the mail that day from a friend. If you sit on the north side of the B train while you are going into Manhattan over the Manhattan Bridge, you can see the Brooklyn Bridge move slowly against the buildings of Lower Manhattan. Especially when the sun is shining on one face of the stone bridge and the brick, glass, stone, or cement buildings and the other faces are in shadow, but also at night, and in rain and fog, the sight is arresting enough so that a few passengers always stand up and move to a position where they can watch it without looking past the heads and hats and shoulders of the other passengers. Because I take so many different subway lines from Brooklyn to Manhattan I tend to forget that this particular train will come out onto the bridge, and so I am often surprised by the sudden daylight and then the slowly passing rooftops in the foreground below and then the dramatic view ahead. This was a day, however, when the view soon seemed to represent a difficulty and a danger more than anything else.

At the next station, DeKalb Avenue, which was the last station in Brooklyn, the woman in black got off. The train started up again and moved on toward the bridge. Before it went above ground, I looked up from my essay because four teenage boys came through the car walking toward the front of the train in single file cursing loudly. This in itself, though it made me nervous, was not very unusual. Then, as my eyes dropped to my page again, there was a sound of something heavy being slammed against the glass section of one of the doors. I looked up. I did not see that any of the boys was holding anything, so I did not know what had slammed against the glass. The glass had not broken. The passengers just sat still, though they were all watching. When the boys returned a little later, striding with long steps in the other direction, still cursing loudly and banging the doors as they came to them, I kept my feet in close under my knees and my eyes down on my reading, afraid of provoking them.

I went back to my reading, though I was on the alert, and for a minute or two everything was quiet. As the train moved above ground, however, the door to my right, toward the back of the train, slammed open and ten or twelve people came lurching through it in a tight bunch looking scared. I immediately stood up.

Someone shouted, "Get the baby out of here," and people made way for a young woman pushing a stroller down the car toward the front of the train as other passengers hurried in front of her and behind her. I hurried along with them without waiting for an explanation. Some of the people who had run in from the car behind stayed where they were, and some of the people from this car joined the people hurrying into the next car. I stopped in the middle of the next car, holding on to a pole and looking back into the car behind, but as soon as a fresh wave of people came hurrying into that car from the car behind, looking scared, I ran on into the next car forward.

No one knew exactly what was happening, though I heard the word "knife." Somewhere near the back of the train, I thought, those boys had to be doing something awful, but how many people they were hurting, I didn't know. I knew only that a lot of people were scared, and running, and I imagined that the boys were coming forward from car to car. As more people hurried forward into each car, I kept running and stopping until I reached the very front of the train, right next to the motorman's compartment, where I suddenly saw that by doing this I had possibly put myself into a trap. Through the open door of the compartment, I watched the conductor and the motorman muttering to each other, the conductor bending over the motorman and the motorman looking straight ahead at the tracks.

The train was now creeping out onto the bridge. Close to the people bunched together in the very front, an older woman stood by herself blinking and blurting out fearful remarks in German. A small Hispanic woman cried into her boyfriend's arms. I was shaking. I felt sick.

The conductor and the motorman took turns speaking into a short wave radio, saying over and over again, "Command center come in," but no sound came back from the apparatus. At last the motorman stopped the train at the approach of another train coming in the opposite direction on the next track, and the two men signaled through the window. They then shouted to the driver to try and get through on his radio and tell the command center they had an emergency and needed the police and the E.M.S. to meet them at Grand Street. That was the next station, on the far side of the river. They went on trying to make contact themselves, and then they seemed to reach the command center but could not make themselves understood, yelling into the radio that one car was covered in blood. The more often they said the words "police," "emergency," "assault," and "stabbing," the more restless the passengers around them became.

The train was moving very slowly over the bridge and then stopping above the water. It stood still more than it moved. The bunch of passengers up in the front of the train alternately kept quiet and broke out in questions and complaints. As the motorman continued to move the train forward, a few feet at a time, the conductor, a large, red-headed man not in uniform, stood next to the motorman's compartment with its open door, patiently answering some of the passengers' questions. Then, like a priest, he laid his broad hand for a moment on the head of the German woman and then on the head of the Hispanic woman and then on mine.

Word came that the police were on their way, and the train started forward again, this time without stopping. It crossed the bridge and went underground. When it came within sight of the Grand Street station platform, it stopped in the tunnel and waited again until some policemen appeared under the bright lights ahead.

The train drew up only as far as the catwalk at the mouth of the tunnel. The conductor lifted a seat next to the first door and turned a switch that opened just that one door. He explained that none of us could leave. We all argued. The platform was right there and we could be out of the train so easily, and up out of the station too.

Six policemen climbed in over the railing that ran alongside the catwalk, and after them a heavyset emergency medical service orderly in a short-sleeved white shirt and black pants, carrying a doctor's bag and a stretcher. The policemen and the orderly disappeared into the next car, walking back toward the rear of the train. At the sight of the policemen my fear had begun to go away, but it went away completely, though I still felt sick, only once the policemen were actually between me and whatever had happened in the back of the train.

I did not have to wait long before the four boys were brought handcuffed into the car. I watched as they were searched. Near them, a tensely grinning boy was examined by the orderly, who pushed up each of his eyelids with a fat thumb and shone his flashlight against the pupils of his eyes. When the four boys and the victim had been taken out onto the platform, the conductor closed the door and the train pulled all the way into the station. Now the passengers were asked to leave the train immediately.

Instead of waiting for another train, at this point, I went upstairs to the street, where the sun was shining, the air was fresh and cold, snow was piled up against the curbs, and police cars and an ambulance were clustered around, parked at odd angles to the subway entrance.

The four boys were there too, being searched again by the police. Both the policemen and the boys seemed tranquil, but the policemen were cheerful whereas the boys were glum. The policemen were handling the boys gently: out here in the strong sunlight, each officer carefully removed a hat from a boy, softly and slowly felt it all over—the folds of it, the brim, and the crown—and then carefully, almost affectionately, replaced it on the boy's head, straightened it, and settled it more firmly.

A policeman sitting inside a squad car told people through a loudspeaker to move on, and although I felt I had a right to stay and watch, I moved on.

Later, I tried to tell a few different people about this incident. But it was a hard story to try to tell: nothing much had actually happened. Worse things than that happen all the time. Everyone I told it to seemed to want the story to end in a death, or a bad injury, or some other catastrophe.

What I discovered, though, during this afternoon, was that I did not have the physical courage I thought I had, and was in fact foolishly excitable, among the first to panic and run for safety toward someone in authority, like that tall conductor. I was disappointed in myself. Yet, I thought, perhaps if the danger had been just a little different, I would have been brave.

The incident did not completely eliminate my dream of traveling across the country alone. But though my dream continues to recur regularly, it assumes a more and more abbreviated and perfunctory form, as though weakening, gradually, in the face of its own unlikelihood.

Walt Whitman on Further Lane

MARK DOTY

In 2009 I bought a house in The Springs, on the far-east end of Long Island. (Locals disagree over whether to call the place Springs, or the Springs, or The Springs; that this is talked about at all may begin to give you some sense of the character of the place.) It seems odd to say "*I* bought a house," since I was married at the time; my ex and I first saw the house together that summer, when our spirited and so-thoroughly-not-what-you'd-expect realtor Rebekah drove us to the place, and led us around the small gray-shingled cottage and into the back garden. Up the slope—the gentle tail end of the Ronkonkoma moraine, the last glacier's line of sand and stones that's trailed here ten thousand years down toward Accabonac Harbor—were three tiny cottages. This was a small town for sale, my own MacDowell! Between us and them, a dazzle of flowers and a small pond fed by a thunderous artificial waterfall. Privet hedges, an expanse of grass veined with the shadows of big maple limbs. We were a ten-minute walk from the bay, a mile from Frank O'Hara's grave, a bit farther to the market where Jackson Pollock traded a painting for groceries in the austere winter of 1948. I could see little distance between this and perfection, though the waterfall would have to go.

From the very beginning, I had the sense this was *my* house. Had I been open to such indications, this might have predicted the looming end of the sixteen-year marriage that was already dwindling toward its quiet close. I planted boxwood and built stone walls, remaking the garden, as every gardener must do, to bring it closer to my own image of Eden, and the new perennials surged with ardor. Under the new fig, which reached to an unexpected height, box turtles waited in the August shade with their beaks open for windfall fruit. There were screech owls that cried like strangled altos. The fish pond birthed whole societies of frogs, harrowed by big steel-blue dragonflies, and tiny ones of an intense orange.

Money was tight—I'd cashed in some retirement funds and scraped every spare coin to buy the place—but I couldn't bring myself to deny that garden much of anything. A potted English rose, a stainless steel pitchfork, the allium bulbs with blooms like orbs of silvered violet? Of course. No surprise, given my sense of ownership, that Paul never seemed to quite inhabit the place; he kept his socks and underwear in plastic bags on the closet floor, as if he were at any hour ready to take flight. In a while we agreed we'd be happier without each other. But that's another story.

When people ask where my place in the country is, I tell them "out on the East End" or "Amagansett," and in fact the property sits right on the dividing line between towns; the deed says the house is in the village of Amagansett, while the mailbox is located in the town of East Hampton. I use the name "East Hampton" more than I used to, but I never use the phrase "The Hamptons." Like "Hollywood," it's a name that evokes mythic dimensions that have nothing to do with geography. I find myself saying things like "It's not fancy," or "It's just a little place." Then inevitably I feel I'm protesting too much. I don't want to impress anybody with my privileged life, nor do I want to seem to be doing so, nor do I want to apologetically explain that my land's unrelated to any glossy accounts of the lives of the rich. My neighborhood—patches of woods and fields, salt marsh and high bluffs over the water—is composed largely of the self-employed who can manage this far from the city: writers, psychologists, and the retired, plus some ex- and current fishermen and construction workers born and raised here. There aren't any mansions, and my nearest famous neighbor is Laurie Anderson, who posted in our general store a lovely thank-you to the community after the death of her dear husband, the late Lou Reed. Alex and I—Alex is the man I live with now—would see them on our local bit of beach in summer, as white as you might imagine in their black bathing suits, and do our bit to honor their privacy. And past her house is the home of Judith Lieber, the designer of the most splendid minaudières, beaded clutch purses to carry to galas, in witty designs: a Buddha, a watermelon, a spectacular silvery fish whose belly pops open to hold lipstick, keys, and cab fare. She has a private museum too, open on summer weekends, to display her craft and her husband's paintings, and I'm sorry to say I have never been.

Class anxieties are not easily dismissed, perhaps especially for Americans, who don't talk about them all that much. My father's father, a carpenter, lost whatever he had in the Depression, and shot squirrels in the Tennessee hills to feed his family; my mother's people were millet farmers nearby in Sweetwater. When my mother, who loved to draw, received the gift of a pad of drawing paper for Christmas, she covered every inch of both sides of the pages. Her younger sister fell to some childhood illness and my mother watched her mother cut up her one fine possession, a red velvet opera cape, to sew it into a shroud. My father, the first in his family to go to college, joined the Corps of Engineers. I have done better than my parents, as their generation wanted their children to do—and as we're told will no longer be among the master narratives of American lives, in a new and unstable era.

But no one seems to have told East Hampton this news, at least not the East Hampton that dwells, a part of each year, in the lush green realm south of the highway. Maybe I feel a little nervous about my status as an historical anomaly, a middle-class poet with tenure, an apartment in Chelsea, and a cottage out east, but there is nothing like the South Fork of Long Island to remind one that privilege is dazzlingly relative.

Case in point: late this spring, a hedge fund manager bought some land on Further Lane, an understated, paradisial road that runs through bosky dells (the soft-edged green somehow invites a pastoral diction). There is a fairly recent modern house on the property, and a rare pair of eighteenth-century structures, once the workshops of a family of clock and furniture makers, smooshed into one in the 1940s. But what the buyer wanted was the land, sixteen acres that stretched from Further Lane to the Atlantic's wave-beaten edge. Wanted it enough to pay $147 million for it, making it the most expensive residential property in the United States.

How large a pile of twenties or hundreds would that be; what might one do with such a sum? Since $147 million means nothing to me, I'm perfectly willing to say the land between Further Lane and the sea is worth it. (Could it be that the sum is unimaginable to the hedge fund princes, too, and thus they're free to dream with money on such a gargantuan scale?) There are great open meadows, perhaps potato fields once, or pasture land. On some of these shining greens a few horses still graze, nearly always accompanied by companion deer; at twilight the elegant does graze in seemingly every field. From the distance of the road it's easy to imagine that in that green tranquility they have at last set down the eternal vigilance of their species and are for once at ease. There are groves of sparsely branched oak, thicker maples, and beautiful exclamations of sassafras and shadblow and the occasional holly. Geometric lines of privet hedge veil some distances and frame others, the subtle curves of shallows and rises lend the land character, and the dark and silken soil welcomes every shade of green. These fields and woods, ponds and dunes seem to partake of the endless in a way that many landscapes do not; perhaps so much loveliness seems to promise not limit but more and more, that Further Lane will go on unfolding. It's often misty near dawn and at twilight, and on days when the Atlantic fog never burns away, the visible world's entirely about the veil and the promise of the concealed.

When I want to describe this landscape, I think of the opening stanza of Walt Whitman's "Out of the Cradle Endlessly Rocking," a lush and dreamy description of a nocturnal walk to the beach, somewhere on the Long Island shore. It's a single sentence, as many of Whitman's stanzas are, one constructed to place and disorient us at once—that is, to lead us forward through a boy's remembered night walk, and to set us, like that boy, unmoored in the wild night of this place, under the spell of a singing bird who will give the poet the marvelous, ambiguous gift of his vocation. The mockingbird's song and the ceaselessly sounding September sea call a boy toward the beach at night, just as they are calling down the years to the adult poet's memory, bringing him to a place of origin, to the desolate ground where, he will learn, all songs begin.

> Out of the cradle endlessly rocking,
> Out of the mocking-bird's throat, the musical shuttle,
> Out of the Ninth-month midnight,
> Over the sterile sands and the fields beyond, where the child
>   leaving his bed wander'd alone, bareheaded, barefoot,
> Down from the shower'd halo,
> Up from the mystic play of shadows twining and twisting as
>   if they were alive,
> Out from the patches of briers and blackberries,
> From the memories of the bird that chanted to me,
> From your memories sad brother, from the fitful risings and fall-
>   ings I heard,

From under that yellow half-moon late-risen and swollen as if with
    tears,
From those beginning notes of yearning and love there in the mist,
From the thousand responses of my heart never to cease,
From the myriad thence-arous'd words,
From the word stronger and more delicious than any,
From such as now they start the scene revisiting,
As a flock, twittering, rising, or overhead passing,
Borne hither, ere all eludes me, hurriedly,
A man, yet by these tears a little boy again,
Throwing myself on the sand, confronting the waves,
I, chanter of pains and joys, uniter of here and hereafter,
Taking all hints to use them, but swiftly leaping beyond them,
A reminiscence sing.

This is a physical world inextricable from one lit up by the movements
of the spirit. "Down from the shower'd halo,/Up from the mystic play
of shadows twining and twisting as if they were alive" suggests a mist-
ringed moon and a walk through a fantastic leaf-shadow realm, but it
also evokes a soul coming into being, that which has come from above
and that which has arisen, in the meeting-ground between worlds which
is the self.

Whitman's power here lies in the remarkable force of his syntax,
which creates a complex, fractured motion, as if we view this scene
through a crystal of memory, one that breaks time into planes of light and
of action. He starts with three lines beginning with *out*, telling us this
meditation comes from the sound of waves, from the music of a mockingbird, and from a September midnight. The next four lines commence
with *over*, *down*, *up*, and *out*, sending us through the scene in scrambling
motion. Then come eight lines beginning with *from*, a list of origins
of this particular reminiscence that swiftly turns into an exploration of
the sources of this poem, and of poetry, which is made of "the thousand
responses of my heart never to cease." This poem will tie the past to the
present, bringing the boy and the man together, a man who's in a hurry
"ere all alludes" him. He must sing while he has time to do so, but there
is in that song also a promise, that through it he may also unite the present to the future, by singing this song "here and hereafter," projecting
himself into the ongoing present.

Whitman desired—with a passion seemingly as strong as any in his life—to be read, in his own time and ours. In fact, in all of his huge body of work I can find mention of only two things he wishes to possess: the love of a comrade and the attention of the reader. This latter desire is not bound in time; no poet seems to speak to the audiences of the future with such uncanny certainty; "I thought long and hard of you," he writes in "Crossing Brooklyn Ferry," "before you were ever born." His greatest treasure, clearly, is company; what good is the song of myself without you to hear it, or to join in?

It's perfectly possible that Walt Whitman walked the land near Further Lane, a remote agricultural and fishing region in the 1850s, inhabited by the resourceful baymen the poet admired. He summered several times with his sister in Greenport on the North Fork, taught school in a number of Long Island villages, and wrote enthusiastically of his boating and walking trips along the shore. What would he have made of the astonishing price tag paid for land he would have held it an illusion to "own"?

He makes clear, in a famous passage of advice from the prose preface to the first edition of *Leaves of Grass*, what he thinks of wealth:

> This is what you shall do: Love the earth and sun and the animals, despise riches, give alms to every one that asks, stand up for the stupid and crazy, devote your income and labour to others, hate tyrants, argue not concerning God, have patience and indulgence toward the people, take off your hat to nothing known or unknown, or to any man or number of men, go freely with powerful uneducated persons, and with the young, and with the mothers of families, read these leaves in the open air every season of every year of your life, re-examine all you have been told at school, or church, or in any book, dismiss whatever insults your own soul; and your very flesh shall be a great poem, and have the richest fluency . . .

"Riches" and "richest" invite attention: the former is an accumulation of wealth that deserves our contempt, the second a condition of the body when the soul is nourished. I love the way Whitman counters his own arrogance in this passage: yes, we should read his book in the open air, four times a year, and yes, we should re-examine what we have been told in any book, including his. *Do I contradict myself? Very well then, I contradict myself.*

The compassionate stance suggested by Whitman's advice is borne out in the poems. In those sweeping catalogs of citizenry with whom he—identifies? merges? is of a piece?—there is no noticeable judgment of privilege; his characters "tend inward to me, and I tend outward to them." When he records that "on the piazza walk three matrons stately and friendly with twined arms," I assume that their leisure, their location, and their bearing identify them as persons of privilege, yet he meets them with the same equanimity brought to all. If he places himself on the side of the poor or the socially rejected, it's not because they are necessarily more worthy, but because they are undervalued, their worth mostly unnoticed. The prostitute with her "tipsy and pimpled neck" and "the venerealee," characters whose depiction made early Victorian audiences uncomfortable, are welcomed into Whitman's big human parade—as though the speaker were, indeed, giving alms to anyone who asked. No one and no thing is unworthy of his attention, and he's keen to admit into his universe the presence of strangers. "Do I not often meet strangers in the streets and love them?" he writes in a remarkable poem in the first edition of his book, a piece that underwent many revisions and wound up less remarkable, with the clunky title "Song of Occupations." Indeed, his generation must have been particularly struck by the great influx of population into American cities—young men, especially, migrating to urban centers to work as an agrarian economy began a great shifting. Did it seem a novelty, to be awash in Manhattan's streets full of strangers? In the eighteenth poem in his 1860 "Calamus" sequence, later racily titled "City of Orgies," Whitman describes the joy of street cruising:

> …O Manhattan, your frequent and swift flash of eyes offering
> me love,
>> Offering response to my own—these repay me,
>> Lovers, continual lovers, only repay me.

Again, it's company that Whitman wants, and in this context it's intriguing to note the economic metaphor. He paid attention, and when the gaze of the stranger is returned, he is repaid, in a metaphoric construction he'll use in a number of poems. It's astonishing to discover how much pleasure Whitman takes in urban company, when we're used to Romantic poets decrying the city's degraded, unnatural conditions. Whitman loves New York in part because of the way the permissive anonymity of the city opens realms of sexual possibility, and of every other sort of rubbing up against strangers, too. A poem of praise called "Mannahatta" ends, in an 1860 version later redacted: "The city of such young men, I swear I cannot live happy without I often go talk, walk, eat, drink, sleep, with them!" There is a minor army of biographers and scholars out there who want to tell you that "sleep, with them" did not mean in 1860 what it means now. I don't know what other nineteenth-century poet has so energetically splashed his queerness across the page, and what other has been so thoroughly explained away. Reductive categories of uncertainty abound: Passionate friendship? Omnisexual desire? Mere auto-erotic fantasy? These dismissals bring my inner drag queen to the fore, she who just wants to roll her eyes and say, *Whatevah.*

It's remarkable that this good-natured lustiness is so imbued with tenderness; what makes these poems so irresistible is the deep affection they beam toward anyone, toward whatever person—particularly a "low or despised one"—and how they "stand up" for such souls:

> Why, what have you thought of yourself?
> Is it you then that thought yourself less?
> Is it you that thought the President greater than you? Or the rich
>   better off than you? or the educated wiser than you?
>
> Because you are greasy or pimpled—or that you were once drunk,
>   or a thief, or diseased, or rheumatic, or a prostitute—
>   or are so now—or from frivolity or impotence—or that you
>   are no scholar, and never saw your name in print . . . .
>   do you give in that you are any less immortal?

The generosity of this passage might remind a reader that to "despise riches" is not necessarily to loathe the rich. Whitman makes it clear elsewhere that's he's quite happy to accept alms, in the form of financial support for his work, from any rich person who'd care to contribute. What would he say to the purchaser of a $147 million bit of gorgeous acreage? Something like this, perhaps, a bit from one of his notebooks:

What is it to own anything?—It is to incorporate it into yourself as the primal god swallowed the five immortal offspring of Rhea and accumulated to his life and knowledge and strength all that would have grown in them.

That, I would think, is as much a challenge to me, on my third of an acre on the wrong side of the highway, as it is to the billionaire with his forest and fields hurrying down to the wild Paumonok shore. And equally difficult for the one who legally owns no land at all; to accumulate into oneself the life and knowledge and strength of what one "owns." I look at my garden, this July ablaze with new color and the wind-shifted pattern of so many leaf shapes, and find that this interior accumulation is exactly what I want to do, perhaps the same internalizing Rilke suggests in the *Duino Elegies*, when he says the earth wants "an invisible re-arising in us." If Walt Whitman could visit me in East Hampton now, we could talk about this, and about the deep inequities which make such interiority difficult—perhaps for the rich as well as for the poor—and about that astonishing price tag on Further Lane, which I think he would find equally vexing and hilarious.

Contributors

A cofounder of the musical group Talking Heads, **David Byrne** has also released many solo albums in addition to collaborating with such noted artists as Twyla Tharp, Robert Wilson, and Brian Eno. His art includes photography and installation works and has been published in five books. He lives in New York and he recently added some new bike racks of his own design around town.

Garnette Cadogan writes about arts and culture for various publications. He is coeditor of the forthcoming OXFORD HANDBOOK OF THE HARLEM RENAISSANCE and is at work on a book on rock-reggae superstar Bob Marley.

Bill Cheng is the author of SOUTHERN CROSS THE DOG. He received his MFA from Hunter College in New York. He lives in Brooklyn with his wife.

Teju Cole writer and photographer, was born in the U.S. in 1975 and raised in Nigeria. He is the author of two books: a novella, EVERY DAY IS FOR THE THIEF, which was a *New York Times* Editors' Pick and a Telegraph Book of the Year; and a novel, OPEN CITY, which won the PEN/Hemingway Award, the Internationaler Literaturpreis, and the New York City Book Award, and was nominated for the National Book Critics Circle Award. He teaches at Bard College.

Molly Crabapple is an artist and writer in New York. Called "An emblem of the way art can break out of the gilded gallery" by the *New Republic*, she has drawn in Guantanamo Bay, Abu Dhabi's migrant labor camps, and with rebels in Syria. Crabapple is a columnist for VICE, and has written for publications including the *New York Times*, *Paris Review*, and *Vanity Fair*. She was shortlisted for a Frontline Print Journalism Award in 2013, and received a Gold Rush Award from RUSH Philanthropic Arts in 2014. Molly's illustrated memoir, *Drawing Blood*, will be published by Harper Collins in 2015. Her work is in the permanent collection of the Museum of Modern Art.

Lydia Davis is the author, most recently, of CAN'T AND WON'T (Farrar, Straus & Giroux, 2014), THE COLLECTED STORIES OF LYDIA DAVIS (FSG, 2009), a new translation of Flaubert's MADAME BOVARY (Viking / Penguin, 2010), a chapbook entitled THE COWS (Sarabande Press, 2011), and a long narrative poem entitled "Our Village" in TWO AMERICAN SCENES (New Directions, 2013). In 2013, she was awarded the Man Booker International Prize for her fiction.

Jonathan Dee is the author of six novels, including A THOUSAND PARDONS and THE PRIVILEGES, which won the St. Francis College Literary Prize and the Prix Fitzgerald and was a finalist for the Pulitzer Prize. A frequent reviewer for *Harper's*, a Contributing Writer for the *New York Times Magazine*, and a former Senior Editor of *The Paris Review*, he has received fellowships from the National Endowment for the Arts and the Guggenheim Foundation.

Junot Díaz was born in the Dominican Republic and raised in New Jersey. He is the author of the critically acclaimed DROWN; THE BRIEF WONDROUS LIFE OF OSCAR WAO, which won the 2008 Pulitzer Prize and the National Book Critics Circle Award; and THIS IS HOW YOU LOSE HER, a *New York Times* best-seller and National Book Award finalist. He is the recipient of a MacArthur "Genius" Fellowship, PEN/Malamud Award, Dayton Literary Peace Prize, Guggenheim Fellowship, and PEN/O. Henry Award. A graduate of Rutgers College, Díaz is currently the fiction editor at *Boston Review* and the Rudge and Nancy Allen Professor of Writing at the Massachusetts Institute of Technology.

Mark Doty's FIRE TO FIRE: NEW AND SELECTED POEMS won the National Book Award for Poetry in 2008. A new collection of poems,

DEEP LANE, will be published by W. W. Norton in 2015. He is at work on a prose book about Walt Whitman, desire, ecstasy, and limit. He teaches at Rutgers University.

Dave Eggers is the author of many books, and is the cofounder of 826 National, a network of nonprofit writing and tutoring centers around the country.

Jonathan Safran Foer is the author of the award-winning and best-selling novels EVERYTHING IS ILLUMINATED and EXTREMELY LOUD AND INCREDIBLY CLOSE (both Houghton Mifflin) as well as two works of nonfiction: EATING ANIMALS and THE NEW AMERICAN HAGGADAH (both Little, Brown). He was included in *Granta*'s "Best of Young American Novelists" issue; in *The New Yorker*'s "20 under 40" list of the best young writers in the U.S.; and his books are published in over thirty languages. He is now working on a novel (forthcoming 2015).

John Freeman is the author of THE TYRANNY OF E-MAIL and HOW TO READ A NOVELIST. The former editor of *Granta*, he lives in New York and teaches at the New School and Columbia. He is the founder of the literary journal FREEMAN'S, which will launch in the fall of 2015. He served on the board of Housing Works from 1999 to 2008.

Tim Freeman was born on Long Island, New York and grew up in Sacramento, California. He attended Del Campo High School and holds a bachelor's degree in English from Utica College of Syracuse University. He has previously written essays, poems, Q&As, book reviews, and talking point pieces for online journals, alternative newsweeklies and community newspapers. Tim currently lives in Richardson, Texas.

DW Gibson is the author of NOT WORKING: PEOPLE TALK ABOUT LOSING A JOB AND FINDING THEIR WAY IN TODAY'S CHANGING ECONOMY. His work has appeared in publications such as the *New York Times*, the *Washington Post*, the Daily Beast, the *Village Voice*, and *The Caravan*. He has been a contributor to NPR's *All Things Considered* and is the director of the documentary *Not Working*.

Gibson is currently working on an oral history of gentrification which will be published in April 2015. He serves as director of Writers Omi at Ledig House in Ghent, New York, which is part of the Omi International Arts Center. He is also the cofounder and codirector of Sangam House, a writers' residency in India.

Chaasadahyah Jackson is fifteen years old and attends the High School of Fashion Industries. Chaasadahyah enjoys writing very much and has been a student at 826NYC for five years, where she has been published in a number of chapbooks. In her free time, Chaasadahyah enjoys learning new things, hanging out with friends, and playing tennis.

Sarah Jaffe is a journalist covering labor, economic justice, social movements, politics, gender, and pop culture. She is the cohost, with Michelle Chen, of *Dissent Magazine*'s *Belabored* podcast, as well as an editorial board member at *Dissent* and a columnist at *New Labor Forum*. She is at work on a book about social movements in America after the 2008 financial crisis.

Lawrence Joseph's most recent books of poems are INTO IT and CODES, PRECEPTS, BIASES, AND TABOOS: POEMS 1973–1993, published by Farrar, Straus & Giroux. He teaches law at St. John's University School of Law and lives in New York City.

Victor LaValle is the author of one story collection and three novels. His most recent novel is THE DEVIL IN SILVER. He has been the recipient of numerous awards including a Guggenheim Fellowship, an American Book Award, and the Key to Southeast Queens. He teaches creative writing in Columbia University's MFA program.

Valeria Luiselli was born in Mexico City and grew up in South Africa. She is the author of the book of essays SIDEWALKS and the internationally acclaimed novel FACES IN THE CROWD, both translated into multiple languages and published in the U.S. by Coffee House Press. Among her recent projects are a libretto for the NYC Ballet and THE STORY OF MY TEETH, a novella written in installments for workers in a juice factory. Her short fiction and non-fiction in English have appeared in the *New York Times*, *Granta*, *Brick*, and *McSweeney's*. She lives in Harlem.

Colum McCann was born in Dublin, Ireland. He is the author of six novels and two collections of stories. He has won several major international awards, including the National Book Award, the International IMPAC Dublin Literary Award, and a Guggenheim Fellowship. In 2005 he was nominated for an Academy Award. His work has been published in more than thirty-five languages. His novel LET THE GREAT WORLD SPIN was a best-seller on four continents. He is Distinguished Professor of Creative Writing at Hunter College in New York, where he lives with his wife and three children. For more information, go to colummccann.com.

Dinaw Mengestu a recipient of the 2012 MacArthur Foundation Genius Award, was born in Ethiopia and raised in Illinois. His fiction and journalism have been published in the *New Yorker*, *Granta*, *Harper's*, *Rolling Stone*, and the *Wall Street Journal*, and he is the author of three novels, most recently ALL OUR NAMES. He lives in New York with his wife and two sons.

Téa Obreht's debut novel, THE TIGER'S WIFE, won the 2011 Orange Prize for Fiction and was a 2011 National Book Award Finalist. Her writing has been published in the *New Yorker*, the *Atlantic*, *Harper's*, *Vogue*, *Esquire*, and the *Guardian*, and she has been named by the *New Yorker* as one of the twenty best American fiction writers under forty. She was a 2013–2014 fellow at the Cullman Center for Scholars and Writers, and is currently working on her second novel.

Patrick Ryan is the author of the short story collection SEND ME and the novels SAINTS OF AUGUSTINE, IN MIKE WE TRUST, and GEMINI BITES. His new collection of short stories will be published by Random House in 2015. He lives in New York City.

Michael Salu is a creative director, artist, and writer. His fiction, non-fiction, and art have appeared in a range of publications including *The Short Anthology*, *Grey Magazine*, *Under the Influence Magazine*, and *Granta*. He also runs a multidisciplinary creative agency: http://salu.io.

Rosie Schaap writes the Drink column for the *New York Times Magazine*, and is the author of DRINKING WITH MEN: A MEMOIR. She has also been a bartender, a fortune-teller, a librarian at a paranormal society, an English teacher, an editor, a preacher, a community organizer, and a manager of homeless shelters. She was born in New York City and still lives there.

Taiye Selasi is an author, photographer, and screenwriter. Born in London and raised in Boston, she holds a BA from Yale and an MPhil from Oxford. Her debut novel, GHANA MUST GO, published in eighteen countries, was selected as one of the 10 Best Books of 2013 by the *Wall Street Journal* and the *Economist*. In 2013 she was named one of *Granta*'s Best of Young British novelists. She lives in Rome.

Akhil Sharma was born in Delhi, India, in 1971. He immigrated to America as an eight-year-old. The author of two novels, AN OBEDIENT FATHER and FAMILY LIFE, he has been published numerous times in the *New Yorker* and the *Atlantic Monthly*. He lives in New York City and teaches at Rutgers, Newark.

Zadie Smith was born in northwest London in 1975 and divides her time between London and New York. Her first novel, WHITE TEETH, was the winner of The Whitbread First Novel Award, the *Guardian* First Book Award, The James Tait Black Memorial Prize for Fiction, and The Commonwealth Writers' First Book Award. Her second novel, THE AUTOGRAPH MAN, won The Jewish Quarterly Wingate Literary Prize. Her third novel, ON BEAUTY, was shortlisted for the Man Booker Prize, won The Commonwealth Writers' Best Book Award (Eurasia Section), and the Orange Prize for Fiction. Her most recent novel, NW, was published in 2012 and has been shortlisted for the Royal Society of Literature Ondaatje Prize and the Women's Prize for Fiction.

Hannah Tinti's story collection, ANIMAL CRACKERS, has sold in sixteen countries and was a runner-up for the PEN/Hemingway award. Her best-selling novel, THE GOOD THIEF, was a *New York Times* Notable Book of the Year, recipient of the American Library Association's Alex Award, winner of The Center for Fiction's First

Novel Prize, and winner of the Quality Paperback Book Club's New Voices Award. In 2002 she cofounded the award-winning magazine *One Story* and for the past twelve years has been its editor in chief. In 2009 she was awarded the PEN/Nora Magid award for excellence in editing. She teaches creative writing at Columbia University's MFA program and at the American Museum of Natural History in New York City.

Jeanne Thornton is the author of THE DREAM OF DOCTOR BANTAM (a Lambda Literary Award finalist in 2012) and THE BLACK EMERALD. She is the copublisher of *Rocksalt Magazine* and Instar Books, as well as the creator of webcomics *Bad Mother* and *The Man Who Hates Fun*. She is an undying fan of the Beach Boys and is writing her next novel about them. For now, she lives in Austin, Texas.

Maria Venegas was born in Mexico and immigrated to the United States when she was four years old. She's the author of BULLETPROOF VEST, which was published by Farrar, Straus & Giroux in June of 2014. Venegas's short stories have appeared in *Granta* and *Ploughshares*. She has taught creative writing at Hunter College and currently works as a mentor at Still Waters in a Storm, a reading and writing sanctuary for children in Bushwick. She lives in New York City.

Edmund White has written twenty-five books, including a biography of Jean Genet, for which he won the National Book Critics Circle Award. He is also the author of a trilogy of autobiographical novels—A BOY'S OWN STORY, THE BEAUTIFUL ROOM IS EMPTY, and THE FAREWELL SYMPHONY. He has written brief lives of Marcel Proust and Arthur Rimbaud and a book about unconventional Paris called THE FLANEUR. His most recent published work of fiction is JACK HOLMES AND HIS FRIEND. His memoir, INSIDE A PEARL: MY YEARS IN PARIS, came out in 2014. He is a member of the American Academy of Arts and Letters, an officer in the French Order of Arts and Letters, and a winner of the France-Amériques award. He teaches writing at Princeton and lives in New York City.

Acknowledgments

Junot Diaz's "The Money" was first published in *The New Yorker* June 13, 2001. © Junot Díaz, 2014. Reprinted by arrangement with the author.

David Byrne's "If the 1% Percent Stifles Creativity, I'm out of Here" was first published in *The Guardian* October 13, 2013. Reprinted by arrangement with the author.

Jonathan Safran Foer's "The Sixth Borough" was first published in *The New York Times*, September 17, 2004. © Jonathan Safran Foer, 2014 Reprinted by arrangement with the author.

Lawrence Joseph's "So Where Are We?" was first published in *Granta* 116: Ten Years Later, Summer 2011. Reprinted by arrangement with the author.

Zadie Smith's "Miss Adele Amidst the Corsets" was first published in *The Paris Review* in the Spring 2014 issue. Reprinted by arrangement with the author.

A portion of the proceeds from sales of this book will go to Housing Works.

Housing Works is a healing community of people living with and affected by HIV/AIDS. Our mission is to end the dual crises of homelessness and AIDS through relentless advocacy, the provision of lifesaving services, and entrepreneurial businesses that sustain our efforts.